JUDGE DREDD
YEAR ONE
OMNIBUS

MICHAEL CARROLL // AL EWING // MATT SMITH

WWW.ABADDONBOOKS.COM

An Abadden Books™ Publication
www.abaddonbooks.com
abaddon@rebellion.co.uk

This omnibus first published in 2014 by Abaddon Books™,
Rebellion Intellectual Property Limited,
Riverside House, Osney Mead, Oxford, OX2 0ES, UK.

Second Printing: July 2016

10 9 8 7 6 5 4 3 2

Editor-in Chief: Jonathan Oliver
Commissioning Editor: David Moore
Design: Sam Gretton & Oz Osborne
Marketing and PR: Rob Power
Head of Books & Comics Publishing: Ben Smith
Creative Director and CEO: Jason Kingsley
Chief Technical Officer: Chris Kingsley

Judge Dredd created by
John Wagner and Carlos Ezquerra.

ISBN: 978-1-78108-274-4

Printed in the US

Introduction

Borag Thungg, Earhlets!

Every character has their early years: James Bond, Sherlock Holmes, Indiana Jones... even a cloned future cop like Judge Joe Dredd. We've seen the young cadet that would become Ol' Stoney-Face in John Wagner and Carlos Ezquerra's flashback epic *Origins*, and we picked up the Judge's career around 2100 AD when the strip first started way back in Prog 2, but anything in between—from graduation in 2079 through to becoming a fully fledged street Judge—has been pieced together from fleeting references in various stories. His relationship with his corrupt clone-brother Rico, his contemporaries from the Class of '79—all played their part in forming the man who would be Dredd, but it's an era of his life that's been rarely seen.

So what was Dredd like in 2080, his first year on the streets of the Big Meg? Fresh out of the Academy of Law, he was arguably a bigger stickler for the rulebook than the old man we know today—rather than the nervous bumbling of other fictional noobs, Dredd, Jr. has fifteen years of training in the hardest school on Earth behind him. He has no doubts, no qualms in what he does—enforcing the Law is what he's been created for. But what's interesting is looking at the character with the benefit of hindsight, an aspect that the three writers in this zarjaz collection take full advantage of.

Two of the novellas here—*City Fathers* by Matthew Smith and *The Cold Light of Day* by Michael Carroll—were originally published as e-books but are making their print debut alongside a scrotnig all-new story, *Wear Iron*, by Al Ewing. All three reference Mega-City history and Dredd's place within it, sometimes seizing on a piece of continuity (the Mega-City 5000 race, for example, first mentioned in Prog 40) and spinning a new tale from it. Not unexpectedly, Rico features heavily—these stories taking place between the brothers' competitive time at the Academy and Rico's fall from grace—and the interesting dynamic between the two allows for some candid insights into Dredd's inner character, and perhaps the humanity that he tries so hard to suppress in a bid to be the Judge he feels he should be, and to honour the legacy of his clone-father, Eustace Fargo.

Enjoy, Terrans, these snapshots from the beginning of the legend that would be Mega-City One's greatest lawman.

SPLUNDIG VUR THRIGG!

THARG THE MIGHTY

CITY FATHERS

MATTHEW SMITH

MEGA-CITY ONE
2080 A.D.

One

"I THINK WE can rule out suicide."

"How so?"

"You're standing on his pancreas."

Dredd glanced down at his feet and the sticky brown-red smear beneath his boot. He grunted an apology and stepped back, closer to the door. Part of the organ came with him, leaving a thin trail across the carpet. He felt awkward and impatient at a crime scene—surplus to requirements, perhaps. After the initial adrenaline rush of discovering the body, there was little he could do but wait for the med and tek teams to finish their work, and he was finding it difficult knowing where to place himself. He slid to one side as a pair of auxiliaries squeezed through with a stretcher.

It was doubly hard with the room sprayed as it was with viscera. There seemingly wasn't a surface or item of furniture that hadn't been spattered by the contents of the victim's gut, his torso sliced open from gullet to navel. He was sitting back in his chair by the window, waxy and stiff like a hollowed-out anatomist's model, the gore fanning around him. It had dried dark and textured on the walls and ceiling, seeped into the floor. The stench was ripe.

"He couldn't have ingested a micro-explosive?" Dredd asked, watching as McCready trod delicately around the corpse, shining a torch into its face and stomach cavity, poking matter with the end of his pen. "Unlikely, I know, but I've heard of it being used before as a means to an end."

"No," McCready replied, shaking his head as he continued his inspection. "No scorch marks, no residue to suggest that. He wasn't blown open from the inside, he was stabbed, repeatedly. The cuts suggest a bladed weapon—kind of a frenzy killing, to have caused these kinds of wounds and this amount of trauma." He straightened up. "I'd say you were looking at either a maniac or a creep making a point. And then," he added, nodding at the far wall, "there's that."

Dredd followed his gaze to the symbol painted in blood. It had been slapped on hurriedly, with little finesse, and much had dribbled down onto the sofa beneath it so its intended design was not easy to discern. The letters ICU had been blobbily added underneath.

"A gang tag?" McCready offered.

"Intensive Care Unit," Dredd murmured. "Local punks, morons for the most part. Spend much of their time fighting amongst themselves. Something like this seems out of character." But that didn't discount the possibility that this was a revenge slaying for some slight or betrayal: he had to admit, it had the ritualistic air of a gang snuff, the gruesome showiness of it a warning to others. He'd get units to round the ICU up, see what they had to say within the unforgiving walls of an interrogation cube.

Only problem was, the vic had no history of ever running or dealing with one of the many street gangs that operated in the sector; that, and the fact that at the time of his death he was working for Justice Department.

"Eye See You," McCready intoned. "Could that be relevant, given the vic's occupation?"

Dredd grunted in thought. "Maybe."

He had caught the call a couple of hours earlier whilst on routine patrol: neighbours at Robert Shaw block had been making complaints about the smell emanating from one of the apartments. Eliciting no response, the Judge had overridden the lock and entered, discovering the source of the problem slumped in a chair beside a large picture window and a powerful telescope. He must've been dead for at least three days.

Control identified him as Jacob Croons, a twenty-three-year-old with peeping busts stretching back to his juve days. He had serious voyeurism issues—had even sought out counselling after doing his first month in the cubes—and was a persistent offender, totalling over twenty counts within the past six years. The last arresting officer had wisely decided enough was enough, and offered him an ultimatum: utilise your talents in a positive fashion and peep for the city, or enjoy a spell in a psych-ward. Croons had unsurprisingly opted for the former, and so was set up as a Justice Central-sanctioned peeper; one of the Judges' many eyes in the metropolis, a linked network of spies reporting all suspicious activity and criminal movements to their masters. It was an arrangement that had brought decent results—peepers were nothing if not diligent—and according to his records, Croons had a higher-than-average hit rate. He was a man who clearly loved his work; passionately, some might say.

Integral to that job—and also for the peeper's own safety—was secrecy. He would've been instructed to tell no one about what he did, and to keep all monitoring of suspects utterly discreet. Looking around the deceased's apartment, Dredd surmised that Croons had little trouble with that side of things: the man had basically been a shut-in. His kitchen cupboards stocked with multiple tinned foodstuffs, the single sets of plates and cutlery, and the minimal clothing all painted the picture of a man who entertained alone. All he'd lived for was his obsession, to watch and record, to catch sight of the forbidden, and if his home was austere and functional everywhere else, his viewing equipment was state of the art, and spotlessly maintained. The huge digital telescope dominated the living space, connected to a humming, blinking black monolith of a computer. Everyone he'd seen, everyone who'd passed under his gaze, was captured, filed and stored in Croons' beloved machinery.

The downside of such a reclusive existence was that none of the citizens who lived around him could shed much light on his murder. Dredd had cursorily canvassed Croons' neighbours while he'd waited for the med and tek teams to arrive, and they'd told him nothing. Few could remember even seeing him leave his apartment, and, of course, no one had heard anything out of the ordinary, or witnessed visitors entering (security cameras in a rundown block like this were predictably absent, either stolen or sabotaged). Not for the first time, he felt that engaging the cits to aid him in his investigation was a waste of time; they saw nothing beyond their tri-d sets, showed no interest in the comings and goings of their fellow blockers. Each habitat was a world unto itself, sealed off from the others. Everyone minded their own business. He endured their customary remarks about his age with the grace he thought they deserved, and they quickly shut up when they realised that their quips were being greeted with a stony silence. He handed out a couple of fines while he was there—overdue pet licences, and one count of noise pollution—promising to be back with a 59c if they weren't paid promptly. They started showing some respect, then.

Croons' body was being bagged and placed on the stretcher. McCready nodded for it to be removed.

"Any DNA lifted off the corpse?" Dredd asked.

"No, none that I could find. No fingerprints either, on the stiff, the window, the telescope or the computer, which suggests to me the murder was premeditated. Creeps came with the express purpose of killing him and leaving no identifying traces behind. Gloved, unquestionably; maybe even with a change of clothes, given the amount of blood that would've been shed."

"You're thinking more than one perp?"

"I'd say so. Bruising around the shoulders indicates another pair of hands holding down the vic from behind as he was stabbed in the chair."

"But why go to the trouble of leaving no identifying

traces, and then painting *that* on the wall?" Dredd muttered to himself. "Why draw attention to themselves?"

McCready shrugged. "Beats me. The blood on the wall's the victim's own, you won't be surprised to hear. Smeared on with the knife, I expect, which they took with them."

Dredd looked back towards the apartment's front door. "No sign of forced entry..."

"Nope. Croons must've not only opened the door for them but also invited them in. Clearly he wasn't expecting what they had planned for him."

"So he knew them, he recognised them..." Dredd's gaze circled the room before fixing on the telescope. "What have we got on that?" he asked, nodding towards it. "Who was the last subject that Croons was monitoring?"

"We've got some idea," one of the teks replied, raising his grey-haired head from behind the computer. "The perps have hacked into this, deleted the majority of the files. Or it's possible they forced the vic at knifepoint to call them up and got him to bin them. Either way, the records for the past eight months are gone. We—"

"Check with Croons' liaison at the local sector house," Dredd interrupted. "He would've passed on any pertinent information."

"Yeah, thanks for that, son. We've already checked. Cases up to the beginning of the month had been brought to a conclusion. Anything the deceased was working on in the last couple of weeks he had yet to pass the info on."

Dredd walked to the window, the city spread before him. It was an extraordinary view; Croons had had at least four blocks within his scope, and the dozens of pedways between each of them. He would've had all manner of illegalities parading before him, any number of zziz deals, muggings, gang rumbles... a multitude of suspects. "When did the liaison last speak to him?"

"About a month ago, when the last case was actioned. Said Croons had given no indication of being scared of anything, or thinking his life might be in danger."

"Terrific." Dredd watched a hovercab attempt an unlawful U-turn, forcing a flock of batgliders to quickly disperse, and made a mental note of the licence number.

"However," the Tek-Judge continued, "as I was saying, we have got something. They tried to destroy the telescope too, but didn't do a very good job. These things are tougher than they look. We've managed to reconstruct one of the recordings, and it shows that the day he died, the telescope was pointed at an apartment in William Holden, just over there." He nodded at the block directly opposite the one in which they were standing.

"Which apartment?"

"774/F," the tek answered, glancing at a pad in his hand. "Registered to one Travest Vassell. Served a five-term in 2066 for Stookie smuggling; a known dealer, manufacturer and distributor of narcotics. Linked to a couple of unsolved drugs murders too."

"Good," Dredd said, turning away from the window. "Forward me a copy of the recording. I'll follow up the Vassell lead." He marched towards the door, adding as he left: "And watch the attitude. Don't ever call me 'son' again."

McCready and the tek exchanged looks. "That's you told," McCready said, slapping his colleague on the back.

DREDD TOOK THE el to Vassell's apartment while Control filled him in on the dealer's history. He'd been selling narcotics since he was a teen, always an independent trader, never part of a cartel. He'd moved around the sector some in the past two decades, had a handful of aliases that he hid behind, but Vassell was his parents' name—used to live in Chuck Jones, over in Sector 80, now deceased—and seemingly the moniker he adopted the most. He was a regular user: his first bust was for Umpty possession when he was sixteen, did a month in the juve cubes. Since then he'd always been on Justice Department's radar; his MO was all over an abandoned zziz factory that was raided three years ago, and his name would perennially circulate intercepted shipments of contraband out of Banana City. The fact that he was still walking the streets was testament to a sound business head—he never dealt with the flakes that were going to get stoned, incompetently try to rob a bank and then sell their supplier down the river for a reduced sentence—and a slippery ability to either evade the law altogether or not be caught holding.

The drug snuffs his name was linked to were tangential at best, and frankly it was unlikely he was involved: a couple of slab-rats gunned down outside the southside stackers and a suspected mule minus a head found stuffed in the trunk of a mo-pad didn't sound like Vassell's handiwork. He was far too savvy to get his hands dirty. In fact, the more Dredd heard about him, the more he begrudgingly began to believe that the dealer was an unlikely fit for the Croons killing; it was difficult to imagine him putting his revenue at risk in such a way. He certainly wouldn't have anything to do with a band of idiots like the ICU.

Dredd gave a nominal rap on the door before putting his boot through it. The instinctual warning was leaving his throat as he passed over the threshold and swung his Lawgiver to bear on the apartment, but it instantly died in his mouth as he realised that the bird had flown. The place was empty, cleared out. He relaxed, holstered his gun, and cast an eye about the living space: this hadn't been a hurried evacuation, with clothes and detritus still strewn over the furniture. Possessions had been packed up and removed—what little, he guessed, there had been. This smelled of a short-term let. It was clean, Spartan, the closet containing minimal appliances; Vassell must've rented it just as a base. Dredd would call in forensics as a matter of course, but he doubted they would find anything that would give them a clue as to where the dealer had gone, or much of what had transpired within these walls. Similarly, the vendor would tell him that the rent was paid in cash, nothing to lead back to the creep.

Standing before the living-room window, Dredd looked back at Shaw, and wondered if it was possible that Vassell could've known he was being watched by Croons. Surely there was no way to discern the peeper's telescope at this distance? And was Vassell really capable of butchering the Justice Department operative, if he thought a deal had been compromised? He had no previous record for violent crime. So if Vassell wasn't in the frame, could those he was dealing with be responsible? Perps he hadn't encountered before: vicious, brutal, ruthless, a new gang moving into the sector...

Dredd paced, imagining Wallace, one of his old Academy tutors, murmuring in his ear: *extrapolate, extrapolate...*

Creeps that could be aware that they were being monitored from a block away. Creeps that could gut a man, and let those that found the remains be aware of who had done it with a symbol painted in blood. Creeps that could've quite possibly scared Vassell enough to have vacated these premises. The more Dredd ran with the idea, the more he felt that the dealer had got himself entangled in a transaction that was out of his league. In the Judge's mind, all the signs pointed to non-humans. An alien outfit, looking to stamp their mark on the underworld; only they could have the sensory or psychic perception to pick up on Croons watching them from another building.

Eye See You... Perhaps McCready hadn't been far off the mark.

He had to check out Croons' last peep that the teks had managed to reconstruct. He left the apartment at speed, and tore back down to his Lawmaster parked outside.

Dredd accessed the bike computer and called up the file: it was shot at night, so the visuals were crackly and indistinct, and while the equipment had tried to enhance the picture through heat signatures, penetrating Vassell's closed blinds, it hadn't achieved much more than capturing five humanoid shapes standing in a loose circle. There was nothing in their manner to suggest that four of them were off-worlders, but there was also the possibility that they could be shapeshifters; after all, Croons had opened his door to them, he hadn't been intimidated by their presence.

The telescope had a sonic magnifier, pushed to the max for such a distant eavesdrop, hence the audio was muffled. Dredd strained his ears, trying to pick sense out of the white noise.

"...want to try it... drokk..."

"...it'll be incredible..."

"...buyers... going to... hit people..."

"...demand... wait till you get... gonna be payday, my man..."

"When can... I'm all over..."

It faded to a hiss as the silhouettes moved further into the apartment. The accents and vernacular had all been Mega-City; no one sounded like a visitor to the area, though such things could be imitated by someone seeking to infiltrate the populace, of course. Vassell appeared relaxed in their company and excited by what was being discussed; clearly, he was impressed by whatever narcotic he was planning on distributing for them. There had been no indication that they knew they were being monitored, and were going to take Croons out before he could relay any information he'd gleaned to the authorities.

Dredd gunned the Lawmaster's engine and peeled onto the sked. First things first: to put out an APB on Travest Vassell, and pull the dealer in for questioning. He was convinced the creep was not guilty of murder, but he was partnered up with some newcomers on the scene, and Dredd wanted to know who they were and what they were bringing into his city. Aerial units could be fed Vassell's mugshot, see if they couldn't capture him at one of his regular haunts, and Dredd thought he could also swing by the new Psi-Division, ask one of their remote viewers to cast out a line, pick out his face in a crowd. Strange methods, he had to admit, but you couldn't argue with the results the fledgling department had so far attained.

Meanwhile, Dredd had an appointment with one of the dealer's known associates, who he anticipated was going to relish helping the Law with its inquiries. He twisted the throttle and weaved in amongst the traffic, heading downtown.

Two

His head felt scratchy.

Jack Calafaree sat at his desk, unable to concentrate on the words glowing on the VDU before him. His forehead prickled with sweat, yet his eyes were dry. He swiped his brow, slicked his fingers through his hair, and blinked, trying to force some moisture into them, but they remained stubbornly sensitive, as if they'd been forced open under a hot light. He rubbed his temples and looked down at his keyboard, taking deep breaths, then glanced up at the screen: text swam, floaters peeling apart the letters, obscuring them. Nausea began to stir in his belly, his skull starting to chime like a bell.

Jack swore under his breath, and spun in his chair, away from the computer, digging the heels of his hands into his eyes until stars burst behind them. It didn't ease the throbbing. One drokker of a migraine was coming down the pike, he thought, but he knew this was different: he felt ill, hot, sweaty, viral. These were the signs that his body was going to begin failing him soon, a machine whose warning bulbs were now flickering.

He stood and walked a circuit of his office, hoping that he could distract himself from the pain, but the sensations came with him; each footstep seemed to make the top of his head vibrate. He wondered what it could be: a germ he'd picked up on the zoom train that morning? Food poisoning? The latter didn't seem likely considering how fastidious he was about his diet, and the fact that he ate in some of the sector's most expensive restaurants several evenings a week. Since he didn't even drink as a rule, he'd never suffered the debilitating effects of a hangover, which this was what he'd always assumed they would feel like. He ran every morning, used the block gym at weekends; he felt sicknesses like this were a betrayal of his body, an indicator that it wasn't as honed as he'd like. What was the point of arming your system's defences against such infections when it fell prey to them as easily as sitting next to some malodorous vagrant coughing out bacteria across a crowded carriage?

He staggered back to his desk and yanked open a drawer, rooting amongst the contents for the vial of uppers he knew was in there. That, he had to admit to himself, was his one vice: drugs. They were, in his line of work, a necessity, like a window cleaner's cable harness or a Judge's daystick; he couldn't safely operate without them. No amount of detoxes, low-rad meals or limb-punishing exercise could allow him to do his job as well as several species of stimulant coursing through his bloodstream, whether it be sugar, a rarefied caffeine substitute, or a small quantity of prime zziz. They activated his brain, fired his imagination, enabled him with the confidence and bulletproof self-belief to tackle the city's money markets. He didn't consider himself a criminal anymore than the umpteen bozos out there medicating themselves into a stupor to escape the misery of their existence—it was simply what got him through the day. He was addicted, true, but he was also addicted to generating vast sums of creds for his bosses, and no one would ever claim that was unhealthy.

Jack popped the cap on the container and dry-swallowed half a dozen pills, hoping that once they got his pulse racing it would take his mind off his crunching headache. He was not one for stewing on illness, to stumble back to bed to whine and feel sorry for himself; that was for the weak, for those with a weedy constitution. Better, he thought, to work your way through it, ignore the frailties that your below-par body was susceptible to and prove you were stronger in spirit. You could overcome such trials if you put your mind to it. Or that was the theory, anyway.

Unfortunately, the fact of the matter was—today, at least—that in practice it was proving a lot more difficult. Nothing was shifting the pain that was crawling around his brain, and if anything it was steadily increasing in magnitude, like a vice tightening its grip. He stared down at his hands holding the pill container and they were shaking, trembling uncontrollably. He'd never had symptoms like these before, of any malady he'd succumbed to in the past. He was starting to feel scared that he was losing possession of his faculties: light was bleeding in from the edges of his vision, giving him the impression that his fingers were lengthening. White spirals, like tiny curlicues of electrical energy, leaped from the tips.

Jack inhaled sharply, his heart pounding faster, and he dropped the tablets, scattering them over the office carpet. He had to get out of here, hail a cab to take him home. Screw stoicism: he was having a panic attack, or some kind of bad trip. Reaching for his jacket, slung over the back of his chair, he lurched as if the entire building had tilted, his legs jellifying beneath him, and only by propping himself up on the desk did he stop falling on his face. The room expanded, way beyond its possible dimensions, the door telescoping back like it was on rails.

The door, he thought. His secretary was on the other side of it. She could help him, if he could just get word to her. She'd clearly see that he was having an episode.

He reached across and jabbed the intercom. "Shareen?" he whispered, his voice croaky. He coughed, cleared his throat. "Shareen, can you come... come in here?"

"Why, Mr Calafaree, are you all right?" The reply emanating from the speaker sounded somehow mocking to his ears. He shook his head. His senses were shot, he realised, and nothing he saw or heard could be trusted.

"Please, I'm not... not well. Hurry."

He slumped back into his chair just as he heard the door bang open, somehow at the end of a bright tunnel. Footsteps clattered towards him—how could they be so loud on carpet, he dimly wondered—and the next second he felt hands upon him, moving him. There were too many for one person, Jack knew, and they were coalescing into thicker limbs, like tentacles, wrapping tight around his midriff, squeezing the breath from his lungs. He yelled, struggled to free himself, and lashed out, feeling his fist connect with flesh. The contact galvanised him. He swung again, enjoying allowing his anger free rein, even though he was blind by now, a pale mist shrouding his sight. He wanted to hurt because it grounded him, gave him something on which to focus. All sense of what he was, all spatial awareness, was vanishing, reality trickling down a plughole. If he could concentrate his rage, channel his instinct for destruction, he wouldn't disappear altogether.

He heard glass shatter, and screams penetrated the fug. Coolness washed over his skin, and for one brief moment lucidity returned as he found himself gazing at the city spread before him. Then he was flying, wind whipping pieces of Jack away like he was ash, until nothing was left.

CHIEF AMONG THE subjects that cadets were taught at the Academy, Dredd remembered, perhaps more important than firearm accuracy, bike handling or applied violence, was how to hold yourself as a Judge. Your bearing is instilled into you from day one until the moment you graduate, and it will separate you from the general populace to a far greater degree than the uniform and the badge. Technical skills can be practised beyond the day you step out into the crowd for the first time, knowledge of the Law can be revised and built upon over the years, but unless the rookie can face the city and project the correct air of intimidation and vigilance, then the criminal element will stomp them back into the 'crete. Perps smell fear like sandsharks sense blood, and have the uncanny ability to zero in on an officer even the slightest bit unsure of himself, using that to their advantage. Let the creeps know right from the off that you're on their case, and you will save a hell of a lot of time and unnecessary aggravation: a good Judge doesn't even have to unholster his gun or draw his daystick, in some cases, to get results. Of course, the wiseguys will always need the message reinforced, but most lowlifes buckle under a solid glare and a downturned mouth.

The tutors insisted that age should make no difference; that the way a Judge carries himself when he's twenty will be much the same as he does five decades down the line. Experience was without doubt invaluable, but a citizen should respond to a badge equally, no matter how many years were behind it. It was essential this relationship between the people and their guardians was enforced from the start, and the ex-cadet with the newly awarded full eagle would do well to make damn sure that they're taken seriously the instant they strap on the boots and don the helmet.

Dredd had a full twelve months on the streets, with nothing to prove, and yet found himself heedful of these lessons as he approached Erikson's club on Monmouth. He supposed that, in the fullness of time, heading into dangerous territory such as this would become second nature and he wouldn't think twice about bearding known felons in their lair any more than he would about interrogating a witness or storming a block in the midst of a war. It was his duty to uphold the Law: he would go wherever his presence was required, and where order needed to be maintained. That was his job, his life, what he'd been bred for, and what fifteen years in the Academy had honed him into. There was no question of a faltering of his belief, or a lack of confidence in his abilities: it was merely the unavoidable awareness of his youth that made him double-check his stance and procedure. It was a weakness that he knew he'd have to iron out; as soon as you became self-conscious, it meant your concentration was lapsed elsewhere. A Judge should act without consideration of himself: he was, after all, simply a weapon of justice.

Stanton Erikson was one of Vassell's known associates from his YP days, a fellow neighbourhood drinking buddy and habitual user who'd expanded into extortion, gambling and racketeering. He'd pulled mealy-mouth time on possession charges when he was younger, but now carved a—notionally, at least—legitimate career as a businessman and property owner. While publicly he wouldn't have anything to do with a dealer in narcotics like his old friend, it was understood amongst the clientele that he turned a blind eye to the sale of select merchandise in his club, and Dredd suspected that Vassell wasn't averse to using it as a safe haven for certain transactions.

At this hour of the day, the bar was empty besides the twenty-four-hour deadbeats and cardboard city refugees nursing cold cups of synthi-caff and killing time. Dredd could've pulled any one of them up and shook them down to see what fell out, but now was not the time. In any case, they knew well enough that he knew their guilt: he could see it in their eyes as they watched him pass, furtive glances up beneath furrowed brows, and the hurried manner of their leaving. He gave each of them a measured stare, something to take with them, letting them be aware that no secrets escaped him.

"Erikson here?" he asked the serving droid stacking crates, who jerked its thumb wordlessly towards the office door situated at the far end of the bar. A pair of goons peeled themselves from a shadowy alcove and intercepted him before he could reach it; one slipped inside, knocking quietly as he did so, while the other—a mohawked lunk with embossed kneepads and an unmistakable bulge under his left armpit—stood before the Judge, eyebrow raised.

"Help you, officer?" The creep had the overly polite demeanour of a career criminal that betrayed both an outright lack of respect and invariably something to hide.

Dredd didn't answer at first and was instead cocking an ear over the meathead's shoulder, where he could hear murmured voices emerging from the office. Sounded like Erikson was being prepped. He turned his attention back to Mohawk. "I'm here for your boss. You want to continue interfering with my duty, I can take you in too."

"Heeeeyyy," the goon answered, mock hurt, bravado and idiocy an unhealthy mixture. "Mr Erikson's a busy man. Ain't right that he's hassled like this. Listen"—he reached into his back pocket and produced a wallet—"how about we settle this nice and discreet, like?"

He'd barely finished speaking before he was swung and slammed against the bar, the hand holding the wallet yanked up behind his back until he dropped it. He hissed in pain. "What the drokk...? It was just a suggestion."

"It was an attempted bribe," Dredd replied in the creep's ear as he kept him pinned over the countertop.

"Never stopped any of you jay-boys before."

"Then I guess you picked the wrong Judge. Perverting the course of justice carries a statutory six months' encubement." He reached into the perp's jacket and pulled free the hand cannon nestled there, smacking it down next to Mohawk's head. "I trust your licence for this is up to date too?"

"Cut me a break—"

"I'll cut you nothing, meathead." Dredd produced a pair of cuffs and fastened them round the clown's wrists, wrenching him upright and forcing him into a nearby chair. "Stay there until I'm finished. I'd advise you not to do anything stupid unless you want the two-year sentence you're currently looking at increased."

"I apologise, Judge," a voice offered to his left, and Dredd turned to see Erikson emerging from his office, the other gorilla in tow. "My employee was not acting on my orders, I assure you."

"Seems to me that if the first thing a creep does is reach for the creds, he's used to making pay-offs. Just how many are in your pocket, Erikson—council members, tax officials?"

Erikson shook his head and made an empty-handed gesture. "As I say, that is not a business practice I associate myself with."

"No, you're a regular Mr Clean these days, aren't you, citizen?"

"Was there a reason for this visit, Judge Dredd?" The club owner was implacable. "I believe we were raided only last month—where nothing incriminating was found, I might add—so surely we can't have come to Justice Department's attention again already?"

"A name from your past—Travest Vassell. He still frequents this dive, I take it?"

Erikson shrugged. "A lot of people come and go, Judge. I don't see—"

"Stow the act." Dredd took a step closer to the other man, aware that the muscle hovering at Erikson's shoulder was bristling. "You're fooling no one. You want to protest your innocence, you can explain down at the nearest Sector House why two of your men are carrying unregistered firearms." He locked stares for a second with the other bodyguard, noting a thin sheen of sweat coating his brow—he'd surmised correctly, it seemed. "Or shall we take it in there?" Dredd continued, nodding towards the office. "Go through some paperwork—I'll call down O'Brian in Accounts Division, set him on your files."

"Enough, enough," Erikson replied testily, closing his eyes in a long, languid blink. "Vassell—yes, he still comes by of an evening. Or he did; I haven't seen him for a week or so."

"What does he deal when he's here, do you know?"

"I couldn't tell you, Judge, and you can lie-detector me on that. If we see each other, we shoot the breeze for five minutes, reminisce, then I'm circulating, playing the good host. Anything Travest gets up to on these premises, I'm not privy to—and frankly, I don't wish to know."

Dredd sensed he was speaking the truth. "Bearing in mind that you are the property owner, and anything that goes on within these walls is your responsibility, that's a rather lax attitude to take."

"I have my staff to oversee security and criminal matters. If anything escapes their routine surveillance, well... nobody's perfect, are they?"

"You say you haven't seen Vassell for a week," Dredd said, changing tack before he lost his temper. "What do you remember of your last meeting?"

Erikson pursed his lips and thought for a second. "Nothing out of the ordinary," he answered. "Travest was in fine form, happy. Said he was working on a deal that was going to make him rich."

"He didn't elaborate?"

"No, just that he was acquiring a bulk stock of merchandise. To be honest, he's been saying that he's going to be a millionaire for years. That fabled golden deal that was always just around the corner."

"Is it unusual that you haven't seen him for this amount of time?"

"Maybe. He usually puts in an appearance most weekends; I can't think of a time when he hasn't... He's missing, I take it? I'm presuming that's what this little chat has been about."

"Vassell's wanted in connection with a murder case, but has seemingly gone to ground. He comes by here, it would be in your best interests to let us know."

"Now who's offering incentives?" Erikson murmured, smiling at the cuffed Mohawk sitting glumly to Dredd's right.

"Not so much an incentive, more a stark choice," Dredd said, dragging the bodyguard to his feet. "I find out that you've been harbouring Vassell or impeding the investigation, I will come down here and have this place torn apart brick by brick, and you will never see daylight again." He turned and marched towards the door, pulling Mohawk behind him.

"You play hardball for someone so young, Judge," Erikson called out, laughing, as Dredd stepped back onto the street.

He snapped Mohawk to a holding post and called it in for pick-up, taking the opportunity to see whether there had been any confirmed sightings of Vassell; Control responded in the negative. The operator added that several members of the ICU had been arrested and were in the process of being questioned. Dredd asked to be kept informed of any developments.

Glancing back at the club, he spotted the other goon leaving surreptitiously by a side door, carrying a powerboard under his arm. He climbed aboard, kicked it into life and zipped away in an easterly direction. Intrigued, Dredd swung onto his Lawmaster and shot off in pursuit.

Three

DREDD RADIOED IN to the nearest H-Wagon patrolling overhead. "Got a skysurfer, green underjak, orange plasteek backpack, heading east through Sector 30, currently in the vicinity of the Nolan tangle, running parallel with Overman zoom line. Can you confirm you have visual?"

"Sighting confirmed. Do you want us to engage?"

"Negative. Monitor direction and keep me informed. I want to see where this creep is going."

Dredd expertly wrestled the Lawmaster through traffic, holding off letting loose with the siren lest it alert the goon that he was being followed. He wouldn't be suspicious of the Justice Department craft—they were a common enough sight amidst the choked skies above the city, and it could follow at a considerable distance—but he would probably hear a Judge's bike screaming along the sked. Dredd slalomed between the articulated juggernauts and mo-pads, keeping an eye above on the skysurfer. Occasionally, he'd disappear from view, swooping between the gleaming steel and glass canyons, but by sticking close to the zoom line he didn't stray far and Dredd was able to catch sight of him again before long.

Was it a betrayal of the badge and the life to which he was dedicated to take pleasure at moments like this, he wondered. At the Academy they'd done everything they could to burn out every emotion, turn the cadets from flawed human beings into dispassionate, fully functional machines, capable of dispensing objective summary justice as befits the Law, not swayed by their own feelings. The capability of love was rigorously removed; enjoyment of leisure activities forbidden to the point where anything outside the enforcement of justice was eroded away, leaving only the Judges' own monk-like existence. To exercise, they sparred, brushed up on their daystick-handling, used weights. To relax, they grabbed a handful of minutes in a sleep machine. There was no recreation, no chance to spend quality time with friends or family—such ties were abandoned the instant they began their training. All they had were their lives as Judges, and it was a serious, one-track route where there were no opportunities for distraction.

That was the plan, the grand scheme, at least: to manufacture each year lawmen and women as judicial automatons for which their only interest was keeping a lid on anarchy and punishing the guilty, the pinnacle of fifteen years of study and survival in the toughest school on Earth. He more than most—cloned in a laboratory with his brother from the genetic stock of the Father of Justice, created for one role and one role only, with no childhood to speak of outside a

Justice Department facility, no dreams or desires before he became devoted to the Law—should find the frivolities of personal satisfaction needless. Yet he was ashamed to admit he felt a surge of adrenaline as he sped through the city streets, bending with the momentum as the growling Lawmaster engine powered him forwards, the fat tyres chewing up the rockcrete. How could he—how could anyone—not respond favourably to being in the grip of such control? It was when he was weaving like this at such velocity that he felt most connected to the metropolis, that it was there to be disciplined at his hand. It was impossible to escape the endorphin rush, yet at the same time, at the back of his mind—the anchor that weighted him—was the knowledge that he was equally a servant of the city. He knew he must never forget that: it was the core truth that some Judges found themselves released from, and consequently spun off into their own dark gratifications. It had happened to... someone close to him, and Dredd had witnessed at first hand the corruption that came with it. Seeing base urges being indulged like that made him appreciate the attempts by the Academy to strengthen resolve and hammer out an iron will, forge a pure force for justice that wouldn't succumb to pleasure or be diverted by everyday considerations; to be beyond temptation. The authority that a Judge wielded was too important, too open to abuse, for it to lie in the hands of the weak and easily coerced. It was essential there was strength of purpose—and why there had to be such strict penalties for those Judges that failed in their duty. The standard sentence of twenty years on the mining colony of Titan, the inmates surgically altered to adapt to its harsh environment, demonstrated that Justice Central had to be above reproach, that nothing was harder on the Law than the Law itself.

So ought he feel ashamed of his own fleeting flashes of humanity, that he experienced spikes of excitement like this? He didn't think so. If they'd wanted robots they would've rolled urban pacification units off the production line years ago and saved themselves all the trouble and expense of teaching people how to be Judges. Nobody wanted to be policed by meks—few trusted droids, even now. You had to be able to make judgement calls, come to snap decisions when the situation required it. It made them better Judges not to see everything in black and white.

He roared on, leaning into the curves of the megaway, down through Naomi Watts underpass, engine booming within the confined space, fluorescents flickering across his visor, before barrelling back out into the light again, sliding between lanes. A Fintan Neebo minivan pootling way too slowly in a four hundred kph zone got short shrift as he passed it, Dredd softening on the accelerator just enough to thrust a fine through the driver's window. He barely heard their protestations before he had peeled away, full throttle.

Dredd's helmet radio barked: "Your suspect is descending, heading for an industrial area on Banks."

"Wilco. I see him."

"You still need us for surveillance?"

"No, stand off, aerial. I'll take it from here."

He watched as the meathead swept in to land, kicking up a flurry of dust as he touched down beside a chainlink fence. The area was a reclamation quadrant, part of the old city awaiting bulldozing; there were a few spots like this all over MC-1, dating back pre-Atomic Wars and scarring the landscape like old sores that refuse to heal. It was a bustle of abandoned warehouses and container depots, the 'crete cracked and festooned with weeds, some rusty trailers still lying slumped where they'd been left decades ago. The buildings appeared little more than shells, windows smashed, the roof of one structure half collapsed.

Dredd glided to a standstill a block away from where Erikson's minder had propped his powerboard up against a wall and was screeching open a gate that had once been padlocked; he didn't need to be that close to it to see that the lock and chain had been snapped in two with boltcutters some time previously. The creep squeezed his way into a gap in the gate when it swung open only by a few centimetres, his backpack snagging on the wire; he tugged at it and tumbled through. Picking himself up, he trotted off towards the nearest of the warehouses, casting a suspicious eye over his shoulder as he went.

The setting smelled of narcotics factory, Dredd thought. These were the kind of grounds drugs manufacturers favoured: disused, out of the way ruins. Plenty of privacy, a slim chance of being disturbed. He swung himself off his Lawmaster and edged towards the gate, keeping an eye out for cameras or trip-alarms; he couldn't see any, but if this was an operation of any kind of size, they would have some semblance of security. There wouldn't be much chance of approaching from the front without being detected, he presumed. He could, of course, call the H-wagon back and request a laser strike, but that felt like using a sledgehammer to crack a nut; and he wanted to know what Erikson's man was doing here, and any answers could end up being incinerated in a fireball. No, better to draw them out, see what sort of opposition he was facing.

He jogged back to his bike and squatted beside it. "Computer, I want you to proceed forward and not stop unless you hear my command, understood?"

"That's a rog."

Dredd stood up and allowed the Lawmaster past as it rolled ahead towards the gate, then backed up against the wall to watch. It hit the fence, which showed a modicum of resistance before it bowed and a section collapsed, and the vehicle trundled on into the forecourt of the industrial complex. It had gone barely ten metres when it was met by a rattle of automatic weapons fire; ricochets pinged off the chassis and bodywork, but didn't slow its advance. It crawled on, bullets pocking the ground around it, until Dredd murmured into his helmet mike and ordered it to stop. It halted instantly, and a few seconds later so did the guns.

Voices drifted through the smoke and dust; Dredd unholstered his Lawgiver and crouched low, tracking the movements of the silhouettes emerging from the warehouse, assault rifles slung at their hips. He counted six of them coming out to investigate. He was about to issue a warning when something caught his eye to his right: it was the meathead's powerboard, propped up. He glanced back at the approaching perps, an idea forming.

"Judge's bike," he heard one of the men say.

"No stomm, Harlen, how did you tell?" another replied.

"What I mean is, where's its owner? It didn't just arrive here by itself."

"Onboard comp on these things has got a bigger brain than you, pal. You'd be surprised at what it can do."

"Could be a malfunction," a third offered. "A rogue machine. The way it trundled in here, it ain't as if it meant business."

"Maybe. But radio back to Parker, get him to start clearing out. We can't take the risk that there isn't a jay out there looking for his ride. Let's go—we'll stick an RPG under this; probably the only way to take it out, short of a nuke."

"Shame. Nice wheels," the first man started to say, but broke off as he and others looked up. They had a split second to register the object tumbling towards them before it hit the earth and exploded, a cloud of noxious gas blossoming in all directions. They shouted and scattered but the vapour had already enveloped them and snuck down their throats; they coughed, staggering, a couple dropping to their knees, eyes streaming.

"S-Stumm..." one choked, holding a hand over his mouth, using the other to try to waft away the gas, but by now a greasy billowing fog was surrounding them. Three of the perps were unconscious, one was vomiting into the dirt; none of them paid any heed to the figure on the powerboard who'd dropped the grenade on their heads and swept past in the confusion.

"Bike, proceed forward, maximum speed," Dredd ordered, glancing back at the six prone figures in his wake. Stumm was designed for interior use—it worked best in confined spaces—but even in the open like this its effects were instantaneous. It would dissipate quickly but its job had been done. His Lawmaster shot forward, accelerating rapidly.

Dredd turned his attention back to the warehouse he was approaching. He guessed he was about twenty metres from the entrance. Cadets received basic tuition in all modes of transport, and while he was no expert in handling a board like this, he knew enough to be capable. He peered beneath him—the bike was matching his velocity, so he leaned forward and descended, flattening the board a few centimetres from the saddle. Ten metres now. It occurred to him that while he'd been graded on high-speed powerboard pursuit, receiving passable marks for his balance, control and skill, the Academy had never actually tested him on this particular manoeuvre: leaping from a board onto a moving Lawmaster. Eight metres. They'd probably consider it a flourish too far, a needless stunt. Six metres. Either that, or no one has attempted it before. Four. But he had to hit the factory at speed to gain the advantage. Three.

He jumped.

The moment his rear foot left the accelerator pad, the board halted immediately, reverting to hovering stationary a metre off the ground. He slammed into the bike's seat and jerked forward, his gauntleted fists finding the handlebars and twisting savagely on the throttle. The machine growled and rose up briefly on its back wheel, power surging through it. Two metres.

"Full manual control," Dredd growled.

"Wilco."

One.

He flicked a switch and engaged the bike cannons, the twin barrels spewing forth a terrifying barrage of rapid-fire ammo, bullets chewing up the wooden door like it was paper. He crashed through it moments later in an explosion of splinters, the Lawmaster shrugging off the collision with barely a tremor. The noise was immense, a cacophonic din like something had erupted beneath the ground.

He didn't slow, didn't allow himself pause to assimilate his surroundings, but processed as he worked. The interior of the building was a factory production line, much as he'd anticipated: boxes piled up against a far wall, bench surfaces covered in the detritus of drug manufacture—test tubes, scales, needles, pipettes. The air reeked of sweetness, and he flipped down his helmet respirator, conscious of the swirling powder.

Several of those perps within that had a moment earlier been weighing, chopping and bagging were blown off their feet by Dredd's entrance, a handful cut down by the bike's guns. The rest leapt to cover, using the tables for protection, and returned fire. Dredd drew his Lawgiver and selected his targets, placing a few well-aimed ricochets off the piping to catch the creeps cowering there, before skidding the Lawmaster to a halt and dialling up the amplification on his mike.

"Weapons on the floor now!" he ordered. "You're all under arrest!" His voice, distorted by the respirator, echoed off the high ceiling like Grud's own judgement bestowed upon the guilty.

The demand was ignored, his words met by a further hail of bullets, and he rolled off the bike, seeking safety behind it. He estimated there was perhaps a dozen meatheads still out there, and none of them were likely to surrender; they'd gone beyond the point where talking their way out of this mess was a viable option. Given the choice between death or twenty years in an iso-cube, they were very clearly opting for the former. He wasn't going to disappoint them, but nor was he going to allow them all to find escape via a Standard Execution through the skull. He wanted answers first.

But he needed to thin the numbers. He caught sight of the crumbling brickwork up by the skylight windows and fired off a high-explosive round, the wall exploding in a flash of orange and brown, the 'crete crumbling in heavy, metre-long chunks. Debris rained down and the perps sheltering beneath it scrambled to their feet to escape, leaping into Dredd's view: he pumped the Lawgiver's trigger as they appeared, bullets thunking into torso and heads, five of them hitting the floor as quickly as they'd come. A crack sheared through the plaster, and the roof groaned; he instinctively looked up, noting the dust sprinkling from the iron beams. The old pre-war building couldn't sustain this kind of damage; it was only a matter of time before a supporting wall collapsed. He needed to move fast. He hadn't seen Erikson's man amongst the drugs soldiers, and there was no reason for him to risk his life if he wasn't in their employ. Unless there was a back way out he hadn't noticed, the creep still had to be on the property.

"Control—Dredd. I need back-up, the old industrial estate on Banks," he muttered into his mike. "Drugs factory, six or seven perps still on scene. Need about same number of helmets to surround and contain."

"That's logged, Dredd. Units on their way."

There was a metal staircase leading to a gallery that ran the perimeter of the warehouse, and from what he could ascertain, an office housed up there.

He ran for it, guns snapping at his heels, taking the steps two at a time. A round snicked his right arm and he grimaced, glancing at it, relieved to see it had sliced the flesh but gone no deeper. He reached the top and booted through the office door, walking in on a fat man brandishing a machine-gun. Dredd ducked and fired, putting three SE rounds in a neat group in his chest. Fatboy flew back and landed face-up on a mildewy desk, scattering creds in all directions. Dredd quickly scanned the office for any other threats before his eyes rested upon the pair of legs jutting out from beneath the workstation that the dead perp was now cooling upon. He kicked one of the exposed ankles and told their owner to slide out slowly. Erikson's goon emerged, hands raised, smeared with dirt and sweat, casting a terrified eye over the corpse. For hired muscle, he'd clearly never been near a firefight before.

"That the man you came to see?" the Judge asked, nodding towards the stiff. "Who was he?"

"P-Parker. Local supplier."

Dredd spotted the open rucksack and the piles of creds spilling from it. "You here as a bagman, I take it? With Vassell missing, Erikson's having to buy in his merchandise from another source."

"Mr Erikson knows nothing about this. I'm here for myself."

"Hmph. I'll bet." He unhooked a pair of cuffs and locked them around the creep's wrists. "Still, this is becoming something of a habit for Erikson's employees." He forced the guy into a chair. "It seems desperate, too—like you were prepared to take a risk to come here. What were you after? Can't be just zziz, you could pick that up on any street corner."

"What can I say, I got a problem."

"It was Vassell's drug you were after, wasn't it? This... alien compound."

The man's brow furrowed. "Don't know nothing about no aliens."

"He's partnered with off-worlders. That's where he's getting it from, right?"

The man shook his head, bemused. In the distance, Dredd heard sirens as his back-up arrived, and he yanked the perp to his feet. "We'll see how helpful you'll be down at the sector house. Move." He pushed him towards the door.

But he had the nagging suspicion that the creep's confusion was genuine. Which begged the question—if Vassell hadn't gone into business with out-of-towners, who had he done a deal with, and where was he getting the drug from? Dredd had a resigned feeling he was going to have to talk to one man in particular to find out the word from the underground.

Four

THE SHADOWS WERE closing in, she was sure of it.

She watched them crawl across the walls, ooze along the floor, fill the corners and crevices of the room with their inky darkness, and she was convinced that with each movement they were edging towards her, stealing the light as they crept nearer. She was conscious of how insane this sounded even as she thought it, how irrational. It was her five-year-old self's imagination running wild, awake and scared in her gloomy bedroom in the early hours of the morning, half asleep and petrified, trying to fathom what she was seeing and her dreamstate filling in the blanks where she lacked an answer. But she was twenty-three, and surely past these kinds of nightmares—so why was she curled up on the mattress, trying to tell herself that the room wasn't alive?

She screwed shut her eyes, then opened them: the blackness seemed deeper than ever before, the lamp on the floor by her pillow weak and faltering. She wanted to reach out and pick it up, check it was working properly, but that juvenile fear of drawing the monsters' attention by moving was abroad in her head; she had to stay still, enveloped in her blanket, hands and feet under the covers, her breathing quiet and steady. To break the status quo was to invite catastrophe.

Judi had never felt lonely in this apartment before; in fact, she'd cherished the solitude. The Gloria Vanderbilt block was a slum, and most of the habs were deserted; silent, empty absences dotted throughout the building. In fact, she believed she was the only resident on her floor. She knew there were others, like her, using the block as a squat: she intermittently heard her neighbours rather than saw them, distant shouts and screams, laughter, the occasional dull thud of an explosion or accompanying rattle of gunfire. She rarely ventured beyond the apartment's threshold unless it was a drugs run, or to steal supplies from the local hypermart, and even then it was a straight return trip to the street and back. She had no desire to explore any of the floors either above or below her, or meet the owners of those voices that punctuated the night, as much for her personal safety as anything. But when you had an all-consuming narcotics habit, it was not necessary to seek out company. Friendships were not required. It was just her and her addiction, and the dark, abandoned corridors and stairwells had always suited her just fine, an extension of the vast, echoing chamber within her that she needed to chemically fill on a daily basis in an attempt to feel... something.

She'd spent more than a few years sleeping rough before she'd found this place. Cast adrift by gunrunner parents—whose bodies would eventually be discovered in a rad-pit, a bullet in each heart courtesy of the Cuidad Barranquilla buyers they'd try to sell faulty stub cannons to—Judi was living in cardboard city by the time she hit her mid-teens, picking up a not inconsiderable zziz habit along the way. She thieved, walked the slab, did a handful of months in the juve cubes, but always came back to where she started, her body and mind craving stimulants to escape the here and now. She lost several teeth to her sugar fix, blew her sleep cycle on caffeine, rotted her liver on the home-brewed synthi-vodka that got passed around the braziers, and yet still she wanted more. She was set on a path of self-destruction that she couldn't get off, each drug numbing her even as her veins coursed with intoxicants, each trip taking her further into a cold, remote state of being. She relied on them to feel human, and they were slowly but surely killing her.

This hab had been the acquisition of a fellow user she'd hooked up with a couple of years ago, and they'd burrowed themselves away in here, lost in their own drugs intake, ninety per cent of their interaction when they weren't blissed out of their minds revolving around where they were going to grab their next score. Theirs was a strange relationship to the outsider, but it had a junkie's sense of rhythm—she thought they were almost like an old married couple, so little interest they had in the other's feelings and so concerned they were with their own selfish needs. She had to admit that, when he went out one night on a foraging mission and never returned, she felt no great sense of loss; indeed, she didn't even notice for a day or so. She hadn't conventionally cared for him and didn't miss his presence. The apartment just appeared a little bigger, that was all.

So she'd lived here, content for the most part with her own company, her home never giving her cause for concern before. But now, as the shadows swirled over the ceiling and the light dimmed further, she felt under assault, besieged by her surroundings. Judi wondered if she could last out the night, simply lie still and wait for morning, but panic was bubbling up inside her, a claustrophobic anxiety that was urging her to get up and get out. Something was whispering in her ear that once the darkness had consumed the room entirely, then she would vanish too, piece by piece. She could feel sweat trickling down her brow, nausea lodged in her chest—if she was to go, she had to go now before she threw up or fainted.

Judi steeled herself, then flung off the blanket and staggered to her feet, her head feeling heavy and swollen. Shapes flew in the gloom—long, thin worm-like entities that circled and snapped—and the bedroom door looked like it was merging into the wall, sealing her in. She ran for it, her legs wobbly, and managed several steps before she pitched forward, smacking her temple on the bare floorboards, leaving a smear of blood like a spatter of ink. She crawled, refusing to glance behind or above her, just wanting to escape, yet it was like wading through tar. She had the sudden fear that she was drowning, that she was going to sink into the blackness, and she screamed for help, for someone to come and take her hand and pull her free of this quagmire.

She thrashed violently, kicking her feet, reaching out for something to hang on to, and her fingers closed around a sharp cylindrical object: she brought it closer to her face and realised it was a discarded hyperdermic needle. She rolled onto her back and swung it before her like a weapon, trying to fend off the creatures that lived in the dark, but the shadows swarmed over her arms and legs, gripped her ankles, pinned her shoulders. Judi stabbed at them, wanting to hack her way free.

Once they covered her face and poured down her throat, the last of the light winked out entirely.

Did Dredd feel intimidated as he dismounted his Lawmaster and looked up at the apartment complex before him? He told himself he wasn't, but the slight pause before entering belied his hesitancy. He admonished himself and strode purposefully into the building: there was no reason for such behaviour, though he knew plenty of others who were nervous around Rico, both perps and Justice Department personnel alike.

Unquestionably, his clone-brother was a forceful presence—some might say a dangerous man; an unpredictable and venal one, certainly—but Dredd would do well to treat him as an equal, not to display any sign of being cowed in his company. One had never overshadowed the other since their days at the Academy: they'd always been bonded by blood, two halves of the same gene-stock, proud to be part of a prestigious lineage that was woven into every blood cell and hair fibre. They were embodiments of everything Eustace Fargo had stood for, had wanted the Judges to be, and from the moment they were removed from the birthing tanks they were inseparable siblings, each prepared to take a bullet for the other.

At least, that was how they were at the beginning—on the gun range, in the classroom, on the streets, the pair of them united in their abilities as lawmen, the best of the badge. But upon graduation, something happened to Rico and their paths diverged. It was a permanent split, it seemed, and one from which there was no chance—or desire, on his brother's part—of return. Dredd felt no small sense of regret at this: it was, after all, like watching a part of yourself turn its back on everything you were created for and believed in. But mostly it was distaste that he felt when he heard the name Rico Dredd, and despair at the level of corruption to which the man had sunk. That Fargo's precious DNA had become twisted in such a way was appalling; even more so when you considered that the Father of Justice's progeny still wore the uniform and was to all intents and purposes still an officer of the Law.

The block that Rico called home was symptomatic of his decadence—a ritzy building in Oldtown housing a number of suspect businessmen and councillors, it reeked of ill-gotten creds and aloofness. Although there were some at the Grand Hall who believed allowing Judges to have their own apartments was too much of a distraction, the current regime encouraged living amongst the citizens to foster good relations. Indeed, Dredd had not long moved into a sparse hab in Rowdy Yates, his colleagues recommending he employ a cleaning lady (an Italian woman was coming to be interviewed next week). However, Rico was entrenched amongst the elite, subsumed in a culture of self-gratification, and the fact that he was still here was indicative of how lax things had become.

To say that the brothers had seen increasingly little of each other since they gained the full eagle was an understatement; there was no love lost between them. Once they'd been close, had seen through their graduate years together, but now they were kin in name only. What had happened to Rico, what made him drift away from devout adherence to law and order, was unknown; why, when they shared so much in biological terms, should one twin be the opposite of the other was a mystery. There had been no turning point, no epiphany, just a slow descent into violence and an increasing body count. Perhaps there was something locked in Fargo's genetic code that Dredd had managed to avoid, but was hidden there all the same. It was unthinkable to consider the suggestion that the bloodline was tainted, but the nugget of concern remained lodged at the back of Dredd's mind: Rico's fall had to have been precipitated by something in his nature. Yet, despite this, he had no sympathy for the man; he was everything a Judge was meant to be ingrained against becoming.

Rico, unsurprisingly, saw Joseph as a joke, a stickler locked into an archaic system of self-denial and obsession, trying to stem the tide of lawlessness in a city that was forever teetering on the edge of anarchy. In his eyes, it was a fight none of them could win. Rico saw his response as the only sane choice; to do otherwise, to battle and break heads without reward, was lunacy.

Dredd travelled to Rico's floor and rapped on the door to his lux-apt. It had been several months since they'd last spoken; while the brothers had nothing in common anymore, Rico had an ear to the criminal underworld that made him a useful contact and sounding board for information when it came to the latest developments amidst the upper echelons of the Mega-Mob.

A woman answered his knock—a different one, Dredd noted, from when he was last here. Blonde, elegant, bedecked in jewellery, she looked at him with a disdain he wasn't accustomed to seeing in those that found him standing on their doorstep; then, when her gaze travelled to his badge, she emitted a small sigh, nodded, and motioned for him to enter. She gestured towards the living room with a hand clutching a cocktail, the slightly lethargy of her movements revealing how many she'd had prior to that.

Rico was reclining in a lounger with his back to Dredd as he walked in, an identical drink cradled in his hand, the Tri-D tuned to a shuggy game. "Hey, Joe," he exhaled wearily before his brother had even rounded the chair and into his field of vision. He shifted himself in his seat to study his visitor. "Long time."

Rico was wearing sunglasses indoors for some reason, an unbuttoned garish shirt over a bare chest, and shorts. He looked a mess: unshaven, pale and blotchy, his eyes—when they peered over the tops of the glasses—bloodshot, his hair like straw. He stank, too, of sweat and sourness. Dredd's lip curled in repulsion despite trying not to react, and Rico caught it, smiling broadly. "Yeah, good to see you too. Offer you a refreshment?" He dangled the cocktail before him.

Dredd declined with a curt shake of the head.

"Wise. Very wise," Rico said, draining the glass. He pushed the shades up onto his brow and swung his legs off the chair, getting unsteadily to his feet. Standing before him, Dredd could see that height was about all they had physically in common; his brother had put on weight, his belly protruding, his jowls puffy. He couldn't imagine him passing a fitness report in this state. It was an indictment of the administration at the Grand Hall that he was allowed to keep his badge at all. Their leniency was an outrage.

Rico stumbled over to a drinks cabinet and started to fix himself another. "So what can I do for you, Little Joe? I take it this isn't a social call." He squinted at an empty bottle. "Darlene, do we have any more shampagne?"

"That was the last of it," the woman answered, slinking into the room and seating herself on a couch, curling her feet up under her.

"Gruddammit," Rico muttered under his breath, rattling through the contents of the cabinet.

"Rico, don't you think you've had enough?" Dredd said, casting an eye around the apartment. It was opulent but frayed; gone to seed, like its owner.

"Don't judge me, brother. You're not talking to some panhandling jughead you've collared on the street. Since when have you cared about my personal business, anyway?"

"It's my concern when I see you destroying yourself. You're an embarrassment to the uniform."

"Please," Rico said, rolling his eyes, "spare me your pity."

"I have no pity for you. What I see is contempt for the bloodline, and revulsion at what you've become."

"What *I've* become?" Rico slammed down his glass on the countertop. "Look at *yourself*, you sanctimonious drokker. If you didn't have your daystick rammed so far up your backside, you might relax enough to have some sense of self-awareness. You're a company man, Joe—you go where they point you, you swallow the party line. You're what they made you to be, nothing more."

"You were once the same."

"Yeah, but I shrugged off the DNA straitjacket, didn't I? I refused to be Fargo's ghost, a splice off the old man. Your life was mapped for you the moment a cell was first grown in a Petri dish, and you never questioned it, never saw there was anything beyond that. I decided that yes, there was."

"No, Rico, all you've done has been to fill it with distractions. All the potential is still there, and it's just fallen into neglect. You squandered it."

Rico bowed his head, sighed theatrically, then looked up. "Why. Are. You. Here?"

"Your criminal connections. I know you have contacts in the underworld. Have you heard anything about an off-world gang moving in on the dealers in the sector?"

Rico laughed, a rasping, barking sound. Out the corner of his eye, Dredd saw his brother's squeeze jump at the sudden noise; she'd been drifting off into a stoned reverie. "You're some piece of work, you know that, Joe?" he said. "You take the moral high ground, look down your nose at me, yet think you can tap me up for info when you need to. What makes you think you can come in here, lay down the law, and expect me to help you?"

"Because that's all you're good for now. You're a disgrace as a Judge."

"And this is meant to convince me how, exactly?"

"For all your failings, that badge that you carry should still mean something."

Rico shook his head. "Joseph, we exist in different worlds. I have no loyalty, no commitment. I stand with no one but myself."

"That's patently clear. But once, as cadets, you stood with me. 'Like clones,' remember?"

"Get over yourself," Rico muttered darkly. "It means everything to you, our bloodline, doesn't it? Fargo's heritage... Let me tell you, it's not easy to live up to, is it? You coming here, looking for help, investigation stalled—have you realised that you have to *work* at being a Judge, little brother? That's it not all in the genes?"

Dredd turned to leave. "This was a mistake. I shouldn't have come here."

He'd taken no more than three steps when Rico called out: "Joe." Dredd stopped, half turned. "Indulge my curiosity: what's the case?"

"Drugs snuff," he replied, his back still to his brother. "I think it's connected to new merchandise that's hitting the streets. And I think alien creeps are bringing it in."

"You know what this narcotic is?"

"No, but its reputation seems to be preceding it. Every joker wants a piece."

Rico grunted, then Dredd heard ice cubes filling a glass followed by the splash of liquid. He took another step towards the door. "You're wrong about the off-worlders," Rico said between sips, causing Dredd to pause again. "If a foreign element had muscled into the sector, I would've heard about it. There's nothing out there to suggest that."

"You come across any drugs talk, any mention of new product?"

"Some; fortunes to be made, that kind of

thing. Nothing by name. But whatever it is, it's homegrown."

"A tag for the ICU was painted at the crime scene. I don't make them for this." Control had told him that the gangbangers had been released, their testimony standing up to lie detection.

Rico laughed. "You'd be right. Those clowns aren't killers."

Dredd nodded and looked over his shoulder at his brother standing behind the cabinet, one hand on the countertop to steady himself, the other swirling his drink. The woman was snoring quietly as she dozed. "I'll see you around, Rico."

The other man raised his glass in salute, and slipped the shades back into place, watching as Dredd exited the apartment.

Five

ANGER AND FRUSTRATION gnawed at him throughout the day, the case feeling as if it was slipping through his fingers. Rico's words jabbed at him like a splinter under the skin, and he had considered whether his brother was in fact being entirely honest with him; it was well within his character to send Dredd down the wrong path, muddy the waters, obfuscate the investigation. The possibility had even occurred to him that Rico himself could be involved in the drugs operation—either by backing it financially or aiding the import of the narcotics—and he was deliberately feeding Dredd the wrong information. His clone sibling had fingers in all manner of illegal endeavours, and if there was money to be made he would not hesitate to protect his investment.

But Dredd had doublechecked with Wally Squad officers embedded within the sector's criminal fraternity and they too reported that they had no evidence that an alien element was at large. They had seen no newcomers inveigle their way onto the scene, heard no gossip of off-worlders. Whispers of Vassell's wonder drug had reached them and the talk spoke of amazing highs and relentless demand and the creds that were there for the taking, but none of them had seen or spoken to the dealer himself, and the scuttlebutt was that he was preparing to launch it onto the market. Dredd gave the undercover operatives strict instructions to contact him the instant that Vassell surfaced and to keep the elusive creep under constant surveillance.

It was clear that the alien assumption he'd made was incorrect, and he was back to square one with regards to finding the peeper's killers. He remained convinced that the murder was connected to this fabled drug that had got the local perps so excited, but was no closer to ascertaining who was cooking it up and supplying it. Failure was a sensation he was unfamiliar with since the Academy; he'd always pursued every case with a dogged tenacity and a determination to bring those responsible to account. It was in the blood, he didn't know any other way. So Rico's barbed comments that the legacy the two of them represented wasn't always easy to live up to cut deeply, as they'd no doubt been intended to. It was an enormous honour—vast, the highest imaginable—to carry Fargo's DNA in his genes and to continue his work; it was equally a part of him, right down to the cellular level, that he didn't want to disappoint his clone-father. He supposed that was what drove him to some extent, that sense he'd be found wanting by comparison. He was the son of the man, there was no question of that. It was what made it doubly strange that, while Dredd distilled the essence of Fargo, Rico, from identical tissue stock, should exhibit tendencies that were an anathema to everything that the bloodline stood for. That Rico had failed to live up to the legacy was plain to see; but Dredd would be nothing like him, and was as committed to justice as Fargo had been. The awareness of Dredd's own fallibility, though, hadn't entered into the equation, and it was this—perhaps the side of his nature that most would call human—that infuriated him. He was young still, he knew that, but he was at the same time impatient. He had standards to maintain, and anything less was doing a disservice to a memory and an ideal.

The call came through at the peak of his bad mood, and it suited him fine: Ollie North lux-apts had erupted again, waging war on neighbouring Len Ganley block, and all units in the vicinity were required to assist. The workout would be just what he needed, he mused, to dispel the black cloud that had settled upon him, and indeed he found his spirits rising as he joined his fellow Judges on the perimeter of the buildings. The two starscrapers were both partially on fire, entire floors swallowed by gouts of orange flame and roiling smoke, and yet still the residents fought on, bright bursts of gunfire crackling from roof to mezzanine. Emergency H-vehicles orbited on the periphery, trying to stem the spread of the inferno with water cannon or offer a lifeline to those attempting to escape, but the ferocity of the violence was forcing them back.

Dredd turned to the helmet nearest to him—Halliwell, a forty-year man. "What's the plan?"

"Operation Command wants the blocks pacified floor by floor. Citi-Def in North are holed up from two-twenty to two-forty; they need to be taken out so we can get the med-services in."

"How'd it start?"

The other Judge shrugged. "Grud knows. Some imagined slight or petty grievance. It never takes much to send these meatheads buggo." He unholstered his Lawgiver and checked the magazines, slamming them back into place. "Must be the time of year. Or there's something in the water."

"What do you mean?"

"You get that feeling..." Halliwell murmured, looking up at the embattled buildings. "You can sense when the cits are on the verge of tipping over into outright mania. It's like a tension in the air." He glanced at Dredd. "You done a graveyard shift yet?"

"Sure."

"Then you know what I'm talking about. That feeling when things are coming to a head, that the pressure's about to blow. Nothing unusual about that amongst the spugs—but recently even the respectable creeps are losing it. You catch what happened to that investment banker yesterday?"

Dredd shook his head.

"High-flying corporate suit, executive vice president, worked for Dillman Nash over on Goodman, went futsie. Ranted and raved, attacked his secretary, then threw himself out the hundred-and-sixth-storey window. Took two droids and a hose to scrape him off the slab. Work colleagues say he was fine right up until five minutes before he took the dive. Completely lost his mind."

"And it's not an isolated incident?"

"No, there's been others, if you track back the last three days. We're not talking mass suicides here, but still there's been an anomalous rise in the number of unlikely cases of FS syndrome."

"What did the autopsy reports say?"

"You'll have to talk to the case Judge about that. Like I say, maybe it's the time of the year, or the weather, or their favourite Tri-D show was cancelled. There's always some cretin taking a leap out of his apartment window 'cause he can't take it anymore. Seems to me that the only time they stop trying to kill each other is when they're killing themselves."

"Huh." Dredd watched a senior Judge near the entrance to the blocks coordinating the uniforms for the assault on North. "Or maybe it's something else."

"Like what?"

"You said it yourself: something in the water."

"No, too localised for a contaminant," Halliwell replied. "These are individuals going nuts, not whole swathes of cits. This"—he nodded towards the chaos tumbling around them—"is everyday Mega-City mania. I see this pretty much every rotation. If they were babbling to themselves and cutting their own throats, then I'd say we had a problem." He swung himself off his Lawmaster and unhooked his daystick from his belt. "They're gonna use sonic cannons before we go in—make sure your helmet's audio dampners are on."

Dredd nodded.

"See you on the other side," he said, stomping off to join the massed ranks of Judges swelling in the shadow of Ollie North. Dredd could see the sonics being wheeled into position; radar-shaped devices that emitted a targeted stream of high-frequency noise that was designed to confuse and debilitate. With any luck, they'd knock much of the fight out of the rioters before the Justice Department personnel went in to mop up.

Dredd checked his own weapon, ensuring he was well equipped with ammunition, and pondered on what the other Judge had told him. It kept coming back to drugs, he thought. That was the common element, and his Academy instinct told him it was too much of a coincidence not to be linked to what was going on amongst the crims in the narcotics trade. It stood to reason that if there was a noticeable trend—that individual cits (an investment banker, no less) were bugging out—then there had to be a root cause. Their foodstuffs or air supply couldn't be spiked without it affecting others, so it had to be something personal to them. Could they have been slipped a hallucinogen? And to what end—what did the perpetrator gain from sending the victims fatally insane? Just some random malicious mischief-makers, juves out to cause trouble and not caring who they hurt? It could be there was a link between the vics that might point towards someone with a grudge, that they might share some previously uncovered history. He would have to dig deeper, and the first port of call was finding out who the case Judge was and snagging a look at the toxicology reports on the bodies.

But right now there was some Law to administer.

The sonic cannons had done their job, and as Dredd stormed the first block corridors, a few of the North residents were still reeling from the effects, clutching their ears, noses bleeding, several with vomit caked down their fronts. They put up little resistance, barely able to hold a gun, much less aim and fire it. Dredd herded them towards the exits, instructing them to surrender to the officers waiting outside with the catch-wagons. They trooped obediently and resignedly to their fate, each looking at three to five years minimum. He figured they should feel lucky they were still alive—any insurrection like this was always met with a brutal and sustained show of force. The audio disruption had, in fact, saved many of them from a Standard Execution bullet between the eyes.

He wondered if some of them even knew why they were fighting their neighbours, or if they had simply followed suit, driven by that pack mentality and mass psychosis that typified any block war. Overcrowding and tribal rivalries, simmering discontent and boredom were the usual ingredients for an uprising, and it just needed a trigger to spark the flame of anarchy—something as innocuous as an unreturned greeting, a rumour of an insult, or the resurgence of a decade-old argument was all it took to turn regular (if easily led) citizens into armed maniacs fighting for their building's cause. Any unspoken resentments flourished, jealousy turning to murder, reason abandoned in the rush to pour blame on the target of their frustrations. To make matters worse, as Halliwell had commented, these sudden outbursts were not rare occurrences but part of life in the Big Meg, the result of living on top of a giant, industrialised tinderbox. Employment was virtually non-existent, lives were deemed utterly pointless, insignificant within the vast Judicial system; this had to find a vent somewhere. It was, unfortunately, human nature, and it was Justice Department's job to keep a lid on it when it periodically erupted.

It was also human nature to rally around a figure, for there to be a focal point driving the rage and fanning the flames of hatred, and more often than not it was a Citi-Def captain—a borderline psycho with a uniform and a troubling arsenal. Citi-Def—armed civilian defence squads, initially created to be called upon in times of need, and for the citizens to staff their own citywide militia—caused more headaches than they helped, and many at the Grand Hall questioned how long they would be allowed to operate before Justice Central stepped in and stripped them of their powers. As far as Dredd understood it, it was a right-to-bear-arms deal that successive Chief Judges had been reluctant to revoke, knowing how strident those that stood behind that particular piece of legislation were. The fact that each block had a cadre of these creeps ostensibly to protect the thousands within each building from foreign invasion or catastrophe, but who instead were more prone to flipping out and encouraging conflict at every turn, was one of the many factors behind why the metropolis was this perpetual boiling cauldron of madness. Thus, the presumption was that the engineers of Ollie North's attack on Ganley were the block's Citi-Def unit, which was why the Judges were moving in to eliminate that threat and cut the heart out of the riot.

Dredd mounted the stairs to the next level, the crackle of gunfire above him. He hit the corridor shooting, downing a nutbag with a pair of automatics. A door to his left opened a crack and an elderly face peered out, plainly petrified; he snapped at it to stay inside and it promptly vanished from view. There was a return of fire from the far end of the corridor from at least two gunmen, shot peppering the plaster on the wall ten centimetres from Dredd's head; he swore and ducked, swiftly flicking the setting on his Lawgiver to Heatseeker in one fluid motion and then responding with a couple of homing shells. He didn't have time to confirm they'd hit their intended targets—though the muffled cries that followed seconds after he'd pulled the trigger spoke volumes—but continued his rapid ascent, issuing warnings and taking out meatheads in equal measure.

Given how much he'd been trained in this kind of urban warfare environment, it was almost a performance, a note-perfect display. When his Academy schooling kicked in, he had to admit he felt in the moment: his balance poised, his senses heightened, fifteen years' worth of knowledge fuelling every step and action. He'd been right to believe that this would bolster his confidence as a Judge. This was where he felt at home; any concept of what he could or couldn't aspire to be, any legacy locked up in his genes that may seem as much an obstacle as it was a point of pride, faded into the background, drowned out by the roar of his gun, the crunch of lawbreaker jaws dissolving beneath his fist, the immediacy of bringing order where there was chaos.

The tide was turning, he could see it in the faces of the perps, their lack of surety. Shots were going wild, panic was setting in, the Judicial onslaught swamping their initial rush towards lawlessness. He surprised a gang of juves coming out of an apartment, evidently having looted it—their fearless loyalty towards their block clearly only went so far if they could steal off their neighbours while they were otherwise distracted—and they bolted once they realised he was there, dropping the tri-d set two of them were carrying between them and leaking purloined jewellery in their wake. Dredd quickened his pace, conscious of not appearing to give chase but followed in a steady, implacable pursuit with the purpose of instilling in the crims a sense that they could not escape, that fleeing was futile. He watched them scramble into a nearby domicile, slamming the door behind them, but it was a pointless gesture; even they must've known it, Dredd thought. Nowhere for them to go, in a block surrounded by Judges—what did they think they were going to do? Hide under the bed? There was never any accounting for the brightness of your average cit, but the temptation of illegalities made everyone's IQ drop a few points.

He booted in the door, instantly facing down a trembling teen with a homemade stuttergun. Dredd, framed in the doorway, was an easy target, and he heard the urgent insistences of the kid's friends backed up against the far wall to fire, but he did not move; instead, he holstered his Lawgiver and folded his arms, filling the threshold with his presence. The juve—whom Dredd realised was only a little younger than he was—redoubled his grip on the weapon he clutched desperately, its wavering barrel aimed at Dredd's chest, but he looked terrified. A weird calm descended—for brief moments, the fire and fury around them diminished, as if he'd turned up his helmet's audio dampeners to maximum, and even the spugs shut up.

"Hard, isn't it?" Dredd said finally.

The kid didn't answer. He was sweating profusely, his breath coming in short gasps.

"Feels heavy in your hand, I bet," Dredd continued.

"That dead weight making your arm shake. Muscles straining, heart hammering. You know why? Because that's not plas-steel you're holding—it's your life, your future. Your choice."

The juve brought his other hand up to steady his aim. He was trying to appear resolute.

"He's just a drokkin' baby Judge, Skeet," one of the gang hissed. "Blow him away."

"Yeah, take a shot, Skeet," Dredd said, opening his arms. "Can't miss at that distance."

Skeet's eyes widened, his complexion paling. From the cast of his expression, suddenly offered the opportunity, it was clearly seeming less and less like a good idea as the seconds ticked by. Dredd decided to end this now, and reached forward and snatched the stuttergun from the juve's grip; he let it go without much resistance.

"You think I'm some green rookie straight out of the Academy dorm? You think you're the first creeps to pull a blaster on me?" Dredd asked, turning the weapon over in his hands. "You don't think I deal with idiots like you every day? You threaten a Judge, you shove a gun in my face, you better be prepared to know how to use it—and you, kid, were never going to squeeze that trigger."

With that, he grabbed Skeet by the scruff of his shirt and threw him back into the block corridor, and motioned with his head for the others to follow. The scurried to join their friend without a word, unable to meet Dredd's gaze. "Five years apiece," he called after them. "Move!"

He was back in charge. Drokk you, Rico.

★ ★ ★

Co-ordinating with the other lawmen blitzing Ollie North, they pushed upwards to where the Citi-Def bozos were hunkered down, aided by an H-wagon circling the building and firing Stumm gas canisters into areas still controlled by the cits. With their respirators down, the Judges waded through levels where visibility was virtually nil and relied on their helmets' infra-red vision to pick their paths, choking residents materialising out of the thick fog and stumbling past them in a frantic bid to find fresh air. Many had already collapsed, unconscious bodies slumped in doorways.

They reached a barricaded section out of which the defence nuts were still conducting their war on Ganley, and bypassed it with a few well-placed high-explosive shells. The creeps on the other side didn't seem massively surprised to see them and turned their fire on the Judges without a second thought, evidently believing the jays were in collusion with the Ganley blockers. There was no question the North Citi-Def had lost it: one look in their bloodshot eyes told Dredd that they'd gone over the edge and they weren't coming back.

The Judges executed them all without mercy.

Six

THE DIVE WAS jumping tonight, there was no question of that.

Klein glanced around her and had to admit she'd never seen the bar packed like this before; they'd surely have to start turning people away at the door, and it was barely eleven pm. Quite why there was such a show of force on this wet Tuesday evening—Weather Control having programmed in a solid six hours of light drizzle—she didn't know, but they were all here: the bikers, the gangbangers, the weirdies, the norms, the spugs and the dopehounds, all rubbing shoulders, all crammed within the four sweaty walls of this down-at-heel stommheap. There were better drinking establishments metres away, so it wasn't like everyone was frequenting this place because it was a happening venue, somewhere to be seen; indeed, your decision to come through that entrance said more about your lack of taste and discretion than it did of your fashionableness.

From her position at a corner table—she'd been here since late afternoon and was grateful she'd managed to secure such a decent vantage point when it'd been half empty—it was a sea of faces and voices, a heaving throng that she did her best to surreptitiously scan without dwelling too long on a given figure, lest she draw suspicion. Between studying the crowd, she took sips from her glass, a synthi-vodka she'd been nursing for a couple of hours; partly because she didn't want to battle through the masses to buy a replacement, and partly because she didn't want to get drunk. She gave the impression she was mildly inebriated—slurring her words as she sung quietly to herself at random intervals, enough to discourage any unwanted male attention, even if they weren't put off by her appearance—but she was secretly sober. She couldn't afford for the alcohol to dull her awareness.

Malone's was routinely on Justice Department's radar as a known perp hangout, although the proprietor himself was smart enough to keep his nose clean and his books in order, despite repeated raids and spot checks. There was never any hard evidence to sanction closing the place down—it wasn't exactly salubrious, and Klein wouldn't want to eat anything that came out its kitchen, but it stayed just the right side of legal—although in all likelihood the creeps would simply move on to the next watering hole if they did manage to condemn it. It had never been established how it became an underworld meeting place, or why especially; these things often had a way of accruing traditions. But for the last few years the Judges kept a constant eye on who was frequenting the bar through spy-cams and infiltration, gleaning information from audio surveillance. It had become a regular haunt of Klein's for the past six months or so, to the point where she was now a familiar face amongst Malone's patrons; one more barfly sliding into unconsciousness in the corner, an alcoholic who stumbled out of the stackers each morning to seek oblivion in a bottle. The crims that gathered in the back rooms looked through her now, used to her presence and disdainful of her tatty rags, her greasy hair and the wild cast to her eyes. She was just another sap off the streets, who'd inevitably be found frozen solid inside a dumpster one morning and lamented by no one. She wasn't anybody that mattered.

What she was, unbeknownst to them, however, was an undercover Judge.

Klein had been operating in the area plainclothes for over a year, long separated from the local sector house and a life in uniform, abandoning her previous identity to embed herself amongst those that walked the slab: the homeless, the drunks, the junkies, the lost. It was the ideal social group in terms of visibility; these were the ignored and forgotten, perpetually existing in the background but transparent to the regular cit. It meant she could drift between the creeps, eyes and ears open, listening, collating and reporting back, with little fear of detection. There was a small circle of other Wally Squad Judges within the sector that kept in contact, and they met and compared notes on what they'd been observing at bi-monthly intervals in case there was some crossover of information, but for ninety per cent of her time, Klein acted alone, playing a part that consumed her entirely. It was a role that she had to enact convincingly if she wasn't going to blow the whole network of undercover officers, so she would often find herself rooting through trash for her next meal, sleeping in hostels and begging for chump change. She'd been attacked by crazies on three occasions—kicked their asses every time; so resoundingly, in fact, that she'd gained something of a reputation as a pugilist and not to be messed with—and contracted a stomach infection at least once from a diet of foodstuffs stolen from the backs of hypermarts, but this kind of thing, she reasoned, came with the job.

There were a lot of familiar faces amongst those that were packing out Malone's tonight, which she'd come to know and recognise in her months staking it out: a few pimps and their girls; an ex-con with an ARV rap sheet as long as your arm; a contingent of democrat troublemakers. The biker crews were the most dangerous—zziz freaks to a man, and with a pathological hatred for the jays, they were hopped up on any amphetamine they could lay their hands on and indulged their appetites for destruction on a nightly basis. If they ever rumbled her cover, she would not live to see another morning. They were notorious dope pushers too, flooding the central sectors with particularly dirty narcotics, cut with all manner of poisons.

Drugs changed hands as a matter of course on a night like tonight, and she could see the bundles and wraps being passed back and forth without a huge amount of discretion. Klein sensed a certain urgency amongst the buyers, though, as if they were expecting something else, and more than a few pairs of eyes turned towards the door every time it opened to admit the latest arrival. It looked like some were waiting for a delivery, and were growing impatient. Her interest piqued, she kept half her attention on the entrance too.

When, at 23:14, she saw who it was they were waiting for, she realised she had to get to a phone.

DREDD PULLED UP alongside White on a viewing post overlooking the Kate Moss zipway. Beneath them a fast-flowing river of traffic streamed along the sked, the roar of engines and tyres screaming on rockcrete rolling up to meet them. It was a thunderous backdrop of sound that enveloped the two Judges, a constant drone interspersed by strident horn beeps or the squeal of a Lawmaster peeling across lanes in pursuit of a miscreant.

"White." Dredd acknowledged his colleague with a nod. The other man—only five years older than Dredd but with acid burns from a tanker crash ravaging his left cheek and jaw so he appeared twice that age—returned the gesture. "Thanks for meeting with me."

"It's fine. You said you were interested in the Calafaree suicide?"

"Is that what it's being labelled as?"

"Death by misadventure, really. He clearly took something that sent him over the edge, but it's impossible to ascertain if he knew his own mind when he went out the window."

"Witnesses say he was raving."

"Yeah, he attacked his secretary, put her in hospital—broke her nose, fractured her cheekbone. By the time others in the building made it into his office they say he'd lost it, had to be pulled off the woman, and was ranting as if he was terrified of something. They tried to restrain him but he broke free, and climbed up onto the ledge."

"Terrified... You think he was hallucinating?"

"Without doubt. Vic was a walking drugstore—I checked his desk drawers and pulled his home apart, and he had stashed every kind of pill imaginable, both legal and illegal. He was a serious doper; I mean, we're talking industrial-level quantities of drugs here."

"You find anything you didn't recognise?"

White shook his head. "No, it was all fairly standard stuff. But a bad batch of FX could've possibly brought on that kind of anxiety, driven him to take his own life."

"Maybe. What did the post-mortem say?"

"Inconclusive. Creep was slab-meat when he was delivered to the meds, but they couldn't find any trace in the blood samples of an unknown element. Plenty of sugar and caffeine, but nothing unusual."

"Damn." Dredd looked out across the city, lost in thought for a few brief moments. "What about these other cases with a similar CoD?"

White half-laughed, half-sighed with exasperation. "Yeah, well, that's where it gets interesting. Calafaree's death was high-profile, got a lot of media coverage—rich-boy banker, stoked on illicit pharmaceuticals, takes the plunge, you know the kind of thing—and the details flagged on five other suspicious stiffs over the past week. At the time they were passed off as futsies, but background, character, it just seemed unlikely."

"You got the details?"

"Yeah, I'll punch it up." He entered the info into his bike computer. "OK, here we go, in chronological DoD order," he said, running an eye over the text scrolling before him. "Sura Blanchard, twenty-six, wife of the property tycoon Marvin Blanchard, carves up their apartment with a las-knife before slitting her own throat; Les Bumpf, forty-three, head of accounts at MekTek, hangs himself; Austin Jillagon, nineteen-year-old politics student at MegaU, beats his lecturer unconscious in front of the rest of his class and then runs headfirst into a plate-glasseen window; Bodley Hume, thirty, unemployed droid engineer, climbs feet first into the public garbage grinder in the Jeff Bridges block recreation park; and Angie Fluck, fifty-seven, housewife, sets her neighbours on fire—the Patersons in Geoffrey Howe—then jumps into the flames herself. They average out about one a day, though Hume and Fluck died within twelve hours of each other."

Dredd's mind raced, trying to find connections. The Blanchards lived in a mansion on Treddick, six blocks away from William Holden; Bridges and Howe were even closer, just round the corner, effectively. MegaU was in Central but the campus accommodation stretched this way. MekTek was out near the east wall, though.

"What was Bumpf's address?" he asked.

"Uh... 48/C Margaret Atwood. Left behind a wife and four juves."

Atwood was on the other side of Shaw.

White could see the other man ruminating. "It mean something?"

"The five of them all lived within a two-mile square of William Holden block. Drug dealer I'm chasing operated out of there, name of Travest Vassell. Wait, where was Calafaree living?"

"He had a place on the Epstein estate—"

"Two minutes from Treddick. He was practically on the Blanchards' doorstep."

"Swanky area like that, I'd be surprised if they didn't know each other."

"You said the futsie angle seemed unlikely?"

White scratched his scars. "Yeah, psychologically they were sound. No previous mental-health issues. But apart from Blanchard and Calafaree, all had priors for drug possession and abuse; all had done cube time for it. The rich creeps just hid it better."

"So they'd know where to go to get some if they wanted to."

"This Vassell meathead."

Dredd nodded. "Right. The word on the slab is that he's acquired this new merchandise that he reckons is going to make him rich. So far no one's seen anything of it—but what if he soft-launched it amongst a few of his regulars, tried it out on them. The stuff's being trailed as having this incredible high, so they wouldn't take much convincing."

"That's always assuming the drug has anything to do with their freakouts. They were passed off as futsies because the medical reports couldn't find any trace in the vics' remains of an irregular outside contaminant."

"Then it must be undetectable, disperse in the body's system. Or the meds don't know what to look for. It seems too much of a coincidence otherwise—new narcotic surfaces on the market, cits start dying."

"I agree, it's suspicious. But without any hard evidence linking the two, it's still just circumstantial.

If we knew for definite that Vassell was supplying Calafaree, then we could probably connect him to the other vics. But drug dealers don't leave business cards."

"Too many bodies piling up around this creep for him not to be involved. I've got a dead peeper, murdered because he witnessed something that went down in Vassell's hab."

"If it is the case, then the drug's lethal in the extreme. I mean, does Vassell even *know* what the hell he's giving to people, what he's going to be distributing throughout the sector? What the drokk is in it?"

"Your guess is as good as mine. The priority is finding him and stopping him before more get their hands on it. I've had an APB out on him for the past twenty-four hours, but he's gone to ground. Meanwhile, six users have ended up in Resyk, in all probability because of something they'd taken."

"Possibly seven. I hadn't linked a stiff that was discovered last night because she didn't fit on a social level with the other vics—thought she'd just overdosed. Units pursuing an organ-legging gang followed them into Vanderbilt, that slum block over on the west side. It's a notorious hideout for junkies and creeps on the run; place needs demolishing. Anyway, in the course of their sweep, they found a dead female, early twenties, hypodermic embedded in her carotid artery, obviously self inflicted. But from the expression on her face, they said, it was like she'd been scared to death."

"Was she ID'd?"

"DNA records named her as Judi Jones, but that just yelled alias..."

"You're right. She's—*was* really Abigail Snood. Sometime dealer and slabwalker, bigtime user."

"You knew her?"

"Only by association. She used to be Vassell's girlfriend."

Dredd's helmet radio crackled, silencing him before he could say anymore. "Dredd, just received a call from a Wally Squad operative stationed on Bevel Street, insisted the info be relayed to you immediately. She said, 'He's here.'"

DREDD TORE ALONG the sked, issuing orders via Control as he went: he wanted any undercover units in the area to keep Malone's surrounded and exits covered, but from a discreet distance. Too many uniforms would spook Vassell. They were to stand off and eyeball him only, wait until Dredd got to the scene; a lone Judge cruising past was not going to set off any criminal antennae unnecessarily.

Bevel Street was in the low-rent end of the sector, colloquially known as 'Puke Alley' by the locals because of the number of cheap bars that were stationed along its length. It was popular with vagrants and junkies, taking advantage of both the cut-price alcohol and the minimal camera presence—it remained something of a blind spot in Justice Department's surveillance network, which was why they had so many of Wally Squad on the ground—and as such organised crime chose it as regular meeting place, using the surrounding dregs for cover. It was the kind of place he should've guessed Vassell would be hiding out in; with petty lawlessness and public disorder offences rife, it was easy to maintain a low profile and slip through the cracks.

Dredd decelerated as he approached Bevel, the

crowd thickening with late-night revellers, and he had to pick his way through the throng, the Lawmaster's engine rumbling as it crawled along the thoroughfare. He was conscious of attracting more than a handful of hard stares from those he passed, groups of drunks instantly sobering as they were caught in the beam of the bike's headlamps and parting like waves before his advance; he made sure he gave them all the impression he was taking note of every one of them. He even threw a few backward glances to hammer the point home, a silent order to behave.

He saw Malone's—a gaudy, neon-festooned wreck with what looked like fire-damaged walls and more than couple of bullet holes pockmarking its frontage—appear to his left, and he slowed as he gave it the once-over, noise spilling out from within. He continued to the next corner, spying the slump of a human figure curled up amongst rubbish sacks in the mouth of a narrow passage, and stopped next to it.

"Got reports of a beggar making a nuisance of themselves," he said.

"Dunno anythin' 'bout that," the figure slurred in reply.

"Come on, on your feet," he ordered, swinging himself off his bike and then lifting away several of the trash bags with the end of his daystick. The figure grumbled but moved finally when Dredd gave it a gentle kick to the feet. He hauled it up the rest of the way, an actual face of a recognisable gender emerging from the layers of grimy clothes and blankets, and told her to stand by the wall.

"Well?" Dredd asked as he gave the pretence of patting her down.

"He went into one of the back rooms, creeps

have been going in and out," Klein answered, whispering. "I think he was expected; there was a lot of anticipation prior to his arrival. The place is packed: word must've got out that he was coming here tonight."

"How long has he been on the premises now?"

"About ten to fifteen minutes."

"He come with anyone?"

"Nope."

"OK. Keep your people monitoring the bar in case he makes a break for it. I've asked uniforms to stay back so there won't be much in the way of assistance, should you need it."

"Understood."

Dredd stepped away from Klein, and gave her the briefest of nods. Then he strode back up the street towards Malone's, daystick still in his hand, his grip on it tightening as he reached the entrance.

Seven

It was as if the entire bar held its breath.

Dredd paused in the doorway and faced a hostile crowd, dozens of sullen eyes fixed in his direction. Klein hadn't been exaggerating; the place was heaving, standing room only. Prior to striding inside—he'd ordered the two robo-doormen stood sentinel at the entrance not to allow anyone else in after him, under pain of deactivation—Malone's had been raucous, a jumble of laughter, shouts, and beery conversation. Once the clientele were aware of his presence, though, the noise dribbled to a halt, heads turning to investigate the spreading silence and gazes coming to rest on the uniformed figure motionless by the door, clutching his daystick in one gauntleted hand and tapping it lightly into the other. No one said a word; some looked nervous, guilty consciences rushing to the surface at the merest sight of a Judge badge, but most studied him with hatred.

He walked down the short three steps to the

main floor and proceeded towards the bar, bodies reluctantly parting to allow him past. He was aware that the path behind him was being blocked, that they were sealing him in even as they shuffled out of his way, but he did not glance back. They would be dealt with soon enough, if need be. He rapped on the countertop and beckoned the barman over with a crooked finger.

"Travest Vassell on the premises?"

"Who?" the guy serving replied dismissively; unusually for a pit like this, he was human and not a mek. In his forties and with a face blunted by violence, he had previous cube time written all over him; literally, it seemed. The tatts carved into his forearms were undoubtedly Iso-block originated.

"Lie to me and it'll cost you a year."

The bartender went to answer when a reedy voice piped up to his left: "Ain't you a bit young to drink in here, Judgey?" Several drunken sniggers followed. "Think you'll find the candy store's down the street."

Dredd turned slowly, zeroing in on the mouth; a long-haired biker musclehead running to fat, propped up on one meaty elbow. Half his jaw had been replaced with a razor-toothed metal plate. His heavily lidded eyes bloodshot, he was clearly floating on more than just alcohol fumes. A pair of his cronies basking in the creep's bravado instantly lost their stomm-eating grins under Dredd's gaze, but his seemed oblivious to the trouble he was bringing on himself, swaying a little, breathing hard. He smiled and added: "Buy you a soda, if you want one, juvie."

"I'll give you ten seconds to rein that mouth of yours in," Dredd warned slowly, "before I book you for insolence."

"*Whoooaaaa,*" came the inevitable slurred response. "You're gonna take me in, kid? What you gonna do, strap me to the back of your hover-scooter?" He took a step forward, his pint sloshing over his hand. The smile disappeared from his face as he drew closer. "Seriously, little Judge. What you gonna do?"

Dredd slammed his daystick into the creep's groin with such force he was sure he heard it connect with his pelvis. Air exploded out of the meathead in a high-pitched shriek and he dropped, but before he touched the sticky, beer-soaked floor, Dredd caught him by the ponytail and yanked him upwards, wrapping an arm around his throat. "I'm through being polite with you punks," he growled in the guy's ear, though he was speaking as much to the audience watching in stunned fascination. "You will show me, and you will show the Law, some respect." He bounced the drunk's head off the edge of the countertop—his metal jaw making a dull clunking noise as it rebounded—and let him fall, then in one movement reached across and grabbed the bartender's shirt and all but pulled him over the bar. Glasses went skittering in every direction.

"Now: Vassell. I know he came in here. Where is he?" Dredd could feel himself losing his temper, the events of the past twenty-four hours taking their toll. His Academy tutors had warned him about keeping it in check, but some days he could feel his patience dissipate like moisture on a hotplate. His judgement was under threat of being impaired, he knew; he hoped it was something he could improve his control over as he got older. He'd heard of too many other Judicial careers run aground by twenty-year men finally snapping and doling out what they thought were well-deserved beatings.

"I... I swear, Judge..." the creep stammered. "Never heard of him..."

You could see why the perps congregated in a place like this, Dredd thought, if this was the kind of loyalty shown by the staff. He moved his visored face closer to the other man's. "Is that so? How about we take you down to the Sector House, have the Psis root around in your brain, expose what you really know. Or maybe we'll go the chemical route, flood your bloodstream with truth drugs until all the dirty little secrets coming spilling out."

"No..."

"You know what an interrogation cube is like, I bet. Not somewhere you want to visit twice, is it?"

"Look, m-maybe we can do a deal here..."

His helmet radio cut the guy off. "He's rabbiting, Dredd. Figure identified as Vassell was seen climbing down the fire escape to the rear of the bar. You want units to intercept?"

"No, he's mine. I want this place taken apart, everyone inside pulled in for questioning, as many helmets as can be mustered. Blood samples taken, without exception."

"Wilco."

Dredd released the bartender, who slumped back against the optics, and he turned to face the crowd again, sheathing his daystick. "This establishment is under arrest. You will remain here until officers arrive to remove you to the nearest sector house."

A mixture of a groan and an angry shout of defiance rippled through the throng. A couple of more foolhardy individuals swore furiously and took a step towards him. Dredd drew his Lawgiver, and they instantly backed off. "Out of my way," he growled. "Now." A channel opened between the bar's patrons as they shrank back, and Dredd shouldered his way to the door, tearing it open just as a pat-wagon pulled up outside with half a dozen uniforms aboard. He nodded and jerked a thumb behind him. "Round them up."

The maze of alleys Malone's backed on to was too awkward for a Lawmaster to negotiate, so he took off on foot, ears and eyes keen. Still, he reasoned, it didn't hurt to have a little aerial assistance. "Control," he murmured into his helmet mike, "do we have spy-in-the-sky, vicinity Bevel Street?"

"Affirmative."

"Redirect to Sheedy Walk, keep me posted on Vassell's position."

"That's a rog, just give us a second. Wait... We're picking up a moving target, just coming out of Sheedy and heading for Clay Plaza. Estimate he's maybe two minutes ahead of you."

"Understood. Keep your eye on him."

Dredd picked up the pace, sprinting through the litter-strewn passages, the amber glow of the streetlamps casting a doleful light. He leapt over numerous bodies sleeping rough and automatically listed the violations in his head, but had no time to stop. Those that saw him—this faceless apparition charging past, uniform blending with the night, boots slapping down on the slab—cowered behind their blankets, taking an extra-long swig of hooch, and wondered if it was a nightmare made flesh, especially as those hidden eyes seemed to penetrate their very souls as it turned its head to briefly study them.

He at last caught sight of Vassell, scrambling up another fire escape affixed to the side of a fleapit hotel. He appeared to be having trouble pulling himself up the ladder, and so Dredd closed the distance between them in a matter of seconds. "Vassell!" he roared, Lawgiver raised. "You're under arrest! Stop or I will fire!"

The perp looked back, one hand clinging from a rung, his eyes widening as he saw Dredd. He yelled in fright and redoubled his efforts, swinging his legs up and hooking his ankles around the nearest rail, trying to ascend even faster, but his limbs seemed uncoordinated, heavy. Dredd fired a warning shot that ricocheted off the metalwork by Vassell's midriff; he yelped but didn't stop.

"Vassell! This is your last warning!" Dredd wanted answers still, he didn't want to drop him permanently. But the creep wasn't slowing and showed no signs of offering surrender. He aimed carefully and put an SE round through the man's upper arm, ensuring he lost his grip, and he tumbled a few metres to the ground, hitting the 'crete with a thud. He lay on his side, unmoving.

Dredd strode over to the prone figure, holstering his gun. He'd intentionally shot Vassell in the meat of his bicep, bypassing bone and artery, just enough to knock the wind out of his sails. He needed him alive, but the fall might've stunned him. As Dredd reached the drug dealer, expecting him to be barely conscious, Vassell rolled to his feet and, leading with his injured arm, barrelled into the Judge, evidently unconcerned by his wound, driving his shoulder into Dredd's sternum. The man was stronger than he'd anticipated and Dredd stumbled backwards, slipping and landing on his back. Vassell tried to get his hands around the Judge's throat, but Dredd twisted and headbutted him, his helmet shattering the perp's nose. There was enough respite for the lawman to roll Vassell off, but the creep kept coming, blood smeared over his face. He looked bestial, but in his eyes there was fear, as if he felt he was fighting for his life and it was pure adrenaline that was fuelling him.

No. There was something else, now that he could see the creep up close. The dilated pupils, the sweats, the pale skin, no sense of his own physical trauma—Vassell was tripping on something, and Dredd was fairly sure he knew what. The meathead had got high off his own supply. But the Judge had only one comedown available in his arsenal: he powered his fist into the perp's face, bursting his lip and splintering teeth. The shock and pain were enough to put him on his ass once more, and Dredd was going to make sure he stayed there. He stomped a boot on Vassell's chest, holding him down long enough to cuff one wrist then dragged him over to the fire escape and snapped the other bracelet around the lowest rung of the ladder. He stepped back to catch his breath and for a moment watched the drug dealer as he whined through a ravaged mouth and tugged at his binds like an uncomprehending animal.

"Vassell," Dredd said, trying to get the man to focus on him. "The drug. What is it? Where did it come from?"

The creep rolled his eyes in a bovine manner, seemingly petrified. He scooted back away from the Judge, as far as the cuff would allow; clearly he was seeing something far worse in his mind, conjured by the narcotic. Dredd reached forward and grabbed his chin, wrenching his head to one side, studying him, then gave the perp a slap; Vassell's eyes briefly flickered back to the here and now, slowing their relentless shimmer.

"Vassell," Dredd tried again. "Can you understand me?"

"Help me..." he whispered, shivering, constantly glancing over his shoulder.

"You're safe. But I need you to help me. Tell me what it is, what you've taken."

"The dust... it gives you... gives you dreams..."

"Who are you working for? Who's supplying you?"

"Gift, they said it was. Once... once the eye was closed, our minds would open..."

"'Eye'? Vassell"—Dredd crouched close to the perp—"look at me. What do you mean? What eye?"

"The eye in the sky, it had to be closed. It would see too much."

"You mean cameras, watching you?"

"They knew the eye was there, they knew it had to be closed." The dealer swallowed, his face glimmering as a film of perspiration coated it. "They wouldn't... wouldn't give the dreams before the eye was closed..."

The peeper, Dredd realised. Croons. That's the 'eye' he was talking about. Croons wasn't murdered because of what he'd seen—he was killed *before* the merchandise was handed over. The perps had known Croons was there, living in that apartment, knew he was a peeper for Justice Department, and butchered him before he could record their faces.

Dredd stood up, furious with himself. He'd played this investigation wrong, approached it from the wrong angle—Croons wasn't just an unlucky witness snuffed because he saw something he wasn't supposed to; he was *known* to the killers. The ICU gang tag was a red herring, designed to throw them off the scent. He should've looked into Croons' past, his associates, because somewhere there lay a clue as to why this lethal 'dust' was being circulated on the streets, and who was responsible.

Vassell had started to scream and pound his unchained fist against his forehead. He was no longer intelligible, merely burbling. Dredd radioed in for a med-wagon and a straitjacket—the dealer was heading for a kook-cube, and the Judge wanted to tag along to see what the psychs had to say.

To ENTER THE psych-block was to enter a nightmare. Desperate cries and moans echoed down the sterile corridors, those imprisoned within the padded cells trapped inside their own private hells. Many—the dangerously insane, those whose minds had been irretrievably broken by life in the city—would never leave the facility without radical treatment, their frontal lobes burnt away. Hundreds were housed here, and in thousands of blocks like it dotted all over the metropolis, guarded and maintained by a contingent of med-Judges. They were dark, bleak places, with a constant backdrop of human suffering—no surprise, then, that those that visited if only for a brief time wanted to leave as soon as possible lest they succumb to, or were infected by, the madness that pervaded the building.

Dredd looking through the viewing window at Vassell, bound and whimpering in the corner of his cube, slowly tapping his head against the wall. He had made no further sense, and retreated into his hallucinations, trying violently to escape whatever visions were hounding him.

"I have no doubt," Kendricks, one of the psychs on duty that had examined him, said, "that if he wasn't restrained he would attempt to take his own life. He's exhausted now; the delusions must be burning up his energy. But there seems no respite from them."

Units had scoured the flophouse Vassell had been heading for, and found several bags of suspicious-looking powder hidden beneath the floorboards of his room. There was a substantial amount of creds too, suggesting that the dealer had already started selling it on the streets. Dredd glanced at his colleague standing behind him. "What do you make of it?"

Kendricks shook his head. "We've found nothing untoward in his bloodstream. It's unusual but not without precedent for a substance to disperse in the system and leave no trace behind. Evidently, whatever he's taken is extremely powerful, and even the tiniest amount can cause this complete psychological breakdown. Having done a preliminary analysis of the samples we've retrieved, I'd be surprised if it had been created in the city."

"Brought in from overseas, you think?"

"More likely off-planet. I've never seen symptoms so severe, long-lasting and ultimately fatal, and the chemical make-up is unusual. It's a compound we've never encountered before."

"He called it 'dust'..."

"Inhaled, most probably. Delivered straight to the brain." The medic jerked a thumb at Vassell through the door. "You say he was dealing this stuff? Why take it himself? That seems to be breaking a cardinal rule amongst drug traffickers."

"Yeah, I've been wondering that myself. From what I've pieced together from witness reports from the bar, I think he was under pressure to prove that it was safe, and that it delivered the hit that he'd promised. He'd been heavily hyping it as an amazing high, and obviously tonight he'd announced that he was going to start distributing it at Malone's. That accounts for the turnout—everyone wanted a piece."

Kendricks nodded. "Well, we'll continue our tests on it, see if we can learn more about it. Vassell's no use to us now; I doubt we'll get an intelligible word from him again."

Dredd slammed home the shutter on the viewing window. The uniforms that had rounded up the clientele at the bar reported that half a dozen creeps started exhibiting the telltale freak-outs in the back of the catch-wagon, and by the time they'd been processed at the nearest iso-block were fully blown frantic: aggressive, terrified, jabbering. They'd been transferred here, and were ensconced somewhere in the bowels of the facility, on another corridor exactly like this one, climbing the walls of their respective cells. Little could be gleaned from the bar patrons that were still capable of making sense—a few had heard on the underworld grapevine that Vassell was packing merch like no other and was looking to sell, and others had seen him talk to the barman and then disappear into a back room, with a few wiseguys following and returning moments later out of their gourds. A witness said that one had told him everything looked and felt sharper, brighter, like the contrast on the world had been adjusted. If that was so, the initial euphoria upon taking the drug must last no more than fifteen minutes or so before the bad trip set in.

Who had supplied this drug to Vassell in the first place? The dealer was just a conduit, a way to disseminate the stuff onto the streets; persons unknown had brought it to him, sold it to him, and if Kendricks' theory was right then it had been imported from another planet. Did they know that the drug triggered such a violent reaction—indeed, were they deliberately poisoning the well? Using Vassell as a patsy to distribute a lethal narcotic that fractured the minds of all who took it?

And they knew Croons, knew what he did and where he lived. Dredd had called up the peeper's file, trying to find clues in his past where he would have come into contact with drug manufacturers and smugglers, but the man had been a lonely case, subsumed by his abiding voyeuristic desires, not one with criminal affiliations. Judge Henry Novak was recorded as being the last arresting officer at the time, who'd put him forward as a peeping operative, offering the man the choice between heavy cube time or working for the city. Dredd wondered if Croons had disclosed anything pertinent to him.

"Control—Dredd," he murmured into his helmet mike, raising a hand in farewell to Kendricks as he marched towards the welcome sight of the psych-building's exit. "Can you forward a message to Judge Novak to get in contact with me when his rotation finishes? When's he due off the street?"

"Uh, Novak was transferred from Street Division six months ago. If you want, I can check to see if he's at his station right now."

"Oh?" Dredd answered, walking out into the breaking dawn. "Where was he transferred to?"

"Port authority. He's in Customs at Atlantic Hoverport."

Dredd stopped. "Say again?"

"Atlantic Hoverport. Records say Novak was busted down to Customs due to irregularities in his arrests. Reading between the lines, it looks like he was a bit too happy with the daystick."

Wheels turned in Dredd's mind. *Extrapolate, extrapolate...* "Control, can you put out a call to bring Novak in to the nearest Sector House, but don't tell him the request came from me. Say he may have been assigned faulty Lawgiver ammo and the armoury is calling it in for replacement. I don't want him spooked.

"Then," he added grimly, "prep Burlough at the SJS."

Eight

"FROM THE BEGINNING."

"This is ridiculous! I'm not being interrogated by a drokkin' *boy*—"

"From the beginning."

"No, I refuse to participate in this farce. Under whose authorisation have you dragged me in here?"

Dredd didn't reply, but instead wordlessly stepped aside. Burlough slid out of the shadows, her helmet tucked under her arm, the interrogation cube's spotlights gleaming on her onyx-black skull earrings. She was an imposing sight—nearly two metres tall, with her raven hair pulled into a severe bun, accentuating the angular cast of a narrow, sharp-featured face—and Dredd wondered if Judges of a particular physical build or temperament were hand-picked for the SJS, or they just naturally drifted towards it. Justice Department's internal affairs section, tasked with investigating and rooting out corruption and wrong-doing amongst the ranks, was only for the committed, for those who were prepared to accept a life of being feared and grudgingly respected not just by the city's populace but also by their own colleagues. The Special Judicial Squad was a byword for dogmatic adherence to the letter of the Law, with a strict, zero-tolerance policy on those that fell outside it; spot checks, strip searches and random appraisals were a regular occurrence for those in uniform, conducted by SJS officers with all the tact and diplomacy you'd expect of a department whose chilling reputation preceded them like an acrid stench that signalled trouble was on its way.

Burlough placed her helmet gently on the table beside the chair in which Novak was strapped, the syringes and other instruments also lying there clinking against it, and stood before him. Her every movement was measured, fastidious. She put a hand on either chair-arm, and leaned close. Novak's piss-and-vinegar attitude vaporised almost instantaneously under the laser-bore of her cool blue eyes, emanating not an iota of human warmth or sympathy. He was in his fifties and had seen his share of action, was a commended officer, and yet he paled in the presence of the SJS, his mind undoubtedly churning with the possibilities of what was to come. Sweat gleamed on his skin, and he swallowed as if his throat was constricted. Dredd hung back, watching Burlough work, intrigued by Internal Affairs' methodology and quietly impressed with its effectiveness.

"Judge Dredd contacted my office," she said finally, "believing that a member of Justice Department personnel was involved in criminal activities; to wit, that he was using his position as an Atlantic Hoverport customs official to aid the import of smuggled illegal narcotics from an off-world source. Reviewing the evidence, I concurred that the case warranted further investigation from my perspective. That, Judge Novak, is the authority under which you find yourself held today, pending charges that will almost certainly have a twenty-year Titan sentence attached.

"Now," she added, straightening and folding her arms, gazing down at Novak imperiously, who was all but shaking, "how you want this conversation to continue will influence your eventual outcome. Play ball and you'll find me most accommodating; prove useful and you might not have to leave Earth at all. Perhaps a nominal five to eight in a Cursed Earth workfarm, and then bumped down to Traffic on your return, who knows? But start talking."

She glanced over her shoulder at Dredd, who joined her in regarding the weary-looking Judge in the chair. "From the beginning," he repeated.

It started when Deek Carver and his family moved into Ronald Neame in 2077.

Deek had been mobile infantry—119th armoured division, operating out of the Sirius Cluster—and was invalided back to Mega-City with a paper lung and half a kilo of shrapnel in his thigh when an ammo dump went hot. Coby Carver and fifteen-year-old Maggie had seen it as a silver lining kind of deal; they'd been trying to persuade Deek not to sign on for another tour of duty for months prior to the accident, reasoning that the situation in the quadrant was only going to get worse, and they felt so very far from home, barracked with the other army spouses and kids on the personnel freighters. They missed the sky, and air that wasn't recycled. Most of all, they wanted to feel secure that their husband and father was always going to be there, that they wouldn't have to spend every minute of every day dreading receiving the news they always feared. After he spent six weeks in a military hospital, robo-docs grafting synthiskin onto his arms and chest, he was in no position to argue, and was given an honourable discharge.

Deek had been on active service for so long, life in the Big Meg took some getting used to. Crowds put the zap on him, and he found he was short of both patience and temper. Their apartment in Neame was tiny, far smaller than the cabins the army had given them, and he felt claustrophobic, like he was constantly tripping over Coby and Maggie. He snapped at them, a pent-up anger spilling out from he didn't know where. He thought life away from the military would be freer, less restrictive, but if anything he felt more hemmed in, too many people at every turn. He became short of breath, and experienced flashbacks; the block meds diagnosed them as panic attacks, and proscribed him some pills to chill him out.

But the truth was, he hated it here. He hated the gangs of spugs loitering in the corridors, casting an eye over your every move, sizing you up, waiting for the chance to follow you into a darkened stairwell. He hated the Judges, who made their presence felt in every aspect of the metropolis and whose overbearing dominance instilled a constant sense of guilt into a cowed populace. He hated the size of the place and its complexity, like a knot he couldn't unpick; he missed the austere simplicity of his bunk and the regimented rhythms of life within the battalion. He felt he didn't belong here, like he was a foreign body that hadn't been properly assimilated into the social system. When he walked the slab—which he did often, to exercise his leg, it becoming painful if he remained cooped up indoors for too long—he was an outsider, peering in at an environment he didn't understand and couldn't warm to.

He talked with his childhood friend, another ex-army grunt, who lived with his wife and their odd, loner son over in Shaw, when he could, but Marv Croons offered little in the way of answers. He considered Deek institutionalised, incapable of existing outside of the military, and suggested he try attending a veterans' group, meet others who might also be struggling on civvy street. He went along to a few meetings, but the others seemed mentally scarred to Deek, genuinely shellshocked, barely aware of the here and now. He found their company distressing. He wasn't the same as them, was he? Had he really left part of his sanity back on the operating table?

He grew morose and taciturn, withdrawing into himself, and it cost him dear. Twelve months into their relocation to Mega-City One, his marriage to Coby was in name only; they hardly said a word to each other, two ghosts haunting the same hab, drifting past with little acknowledgement. Maggie unsurprisingly spent as much time as she could away from the site of her parents' disintegrating relationship and began to hang with a group of juves a couple of floors down. She became sweet on a kid about her age, Hartley, and they spent almost every waking moment together.

His wife, meanwhile, commenced an affair with a guy who worked behind the counter at a nearby hottie house, and they eventually fled up north somewhere to a commune.

If Deek had had an inkling then of what was to come, he would've made more of an effort to save what was left of his family, of course he would've. He would've sharpened up, got his act together, intervened on the path that his daughter was intent on taking. As it was, he barely noticed Maggie's absence in the apartment, much less the creds that were vanishing from his wallet or her irregular nocturnal habits. He was aware of a surly juve—Hartley, he presumed; they were never formally introduced—hanging around the place whenever she breezed through, whose half-closed eyes and louche manner suggested that his mind was clouded with more than just teenage disaffection, and something stirred in him, some parental alarm was triggered, that was warning him he should really be protecting her, shielding her from meatheads like this, who he had come to recognise as the worst the city had to offer. It was little drokkers like this that represented everything he despised about living here—inured to violence and its consequences (the kid fiddled with a las-knife he kept in his overjak pocket when he was waiting for Maggie), addled by addictions, apathetic to a future for which there were no prospects of any kind—and Deek was losing his only child to their legions. But his depression seemingly blocked his attempts to take action as lethargy constantly swamped him, and when he did summon the energy to challenge the kid, he was sneered at and dismissed with nothing more than a snort of derision. He got a similar response from Maggie herself. He was just as much a loser in their eyes, a semi-crippled dult who couldn't keep his marriage together and now struggled to get out of bed in the morning.

So he failed her and paid the price. He was roused late one night by an incessant hammering on the apartment's front door, and when he opened it was confronted with the sight of his daughter bleeding to death in the corridor, bullet holes in her chest and belly. Judging by the crimson trail that was left in her wake, she'd had to crawl home clutching her wounds. She was crying and asking for him and her mother, and she died minutes later in his arms, her final moments witnessed by several curious neighbours peering out from around their own doors.

The Judges told him that their investigations led them to believe that Maggie had been murdered by drug dealers she was involved with and had possibly ripped off—Hartley's remains were dredged out of a rad-pit in the next sector—and the autopsy revealed that she was a heavy zziz user, as well as showing numerous other illegal substances in her body. When they searched her bedroom, they discovered over thirty thousand creds hidden in her wardrobe. Deek was recommended that he find somewhere else to live in case those responsible came looking for their missing money, and he numbly agreed. He never did discover if anyone had been arrested or charged with Maggie's death; he got the impression the Judges saw killings such as these as the inevitable outcome for idiots who played with fire.

With the help of Marv, he moved to William Holden—close enough to his friend's family for support, should he need it—and was assigned a grief counsellor, who spent most of the ten minutes she allotted him passing on the details of other organisations that could help. There was one that caught his eye—a bereaved fathers circle—and though reluctant, he reasoned that if he'd stuck with the veterans' group it might've aided him psychologically and as a consequence he might've done more to save Maggie's life from descending into criminality. He had to talk to someone—Coby was impossible to contact, in all likelihood still unaware that her daughter was dead—if only to assuage for a few hours the alternately suicidal and homicidal thoughts that rampaged around his brain.

He knew as soon as he met the other dads that it had been the right thing to do: they were all like him, all victims of the amoral scum the city spat out, and all had similar stories, speaking of the rage they felt towards those that had taken their children's lives, their own powerlessness, their distrust of the Judges. There was an enormous sense of relief at unloading the bile that had built up in him since Maggie's funeral, and to be in company that understood what he was going through. For the first time since he'd arrived in the metropolis, he felt he was somewhere he belonged. Deek found himself particularly allying with three other men—Bud Tronjer, Dane Novak and Biv Hubbly—who'd lost their offspring in gang rumbles and petty juve rivalries, and they began to meet outside of the group evenings, drinking until closing time several nights a week. Both Deek and Bud no longer had any immediate family, so the former often crashed the night, when too drunk too stagger home, on the latter's Mo-pad. Tronjer worked as a security guard at Atlantic Hoverport, overseeing those that disembarked from the cruise ships that docked almost daily; he helped get Deek a job as a steward, and with it a sense of stability.

But the desire for vengeance still simmered. Whenever the four of them met up, they discussed at length what they would do if they could take control from Justice Department, how they would bring retribution down on the mobsters and the pushers, the gangbangers and psychopaths, who helped foment the culture of violence in which the whole city stewed, and for which innocents suffered. The entire criminal underworld needed to be destroyed from within—the Judges were proving just too ineffective—if they were to stop more lives being lost. Despite the rhetoric, however, they admitted quietly to themselves that it was mostly the alcohol talking, and it would've remained nothing more than a pipe dream if it wasn't for the convergence of events that followed.

Firstly, Deek's friend Marv and his wife were carjacked one night and both thrown to their deaths from the megway. Their senseless, random murder underscored everything the four men had been talking about, and Deek—already in a fragile state of mind—felt the centre of his world drop away from him, a cold, hard knot of fury lodging in his chest. The Croons' son Jacob seemingly dealt with the loss of his parents by becoming even more obsessed with watching from their apartment window—trying to catch sight of who was responsible, perhaps, or just jealously studying those countless other lives beyond the glass that had yet to be touched by the city's malign influence. Either way, he became a hermit, unwilling to venture beyond the hab's threshold unless he had to.

Secondly, Bud confiscated a suspicious substance

from a pair of stoned tourists returning from a round trip to the Speelor moons. He'd caught passengers using drugs before, but this was something he'd never seen before—a mauve powder with a coppery smell. They claimed a guide had sold it to them, told them it was crushed babooba root, a powerful hallucinogenic favoured by the native shamans. Just one grain dissolved in a solution could send the user on a two-hour trip. Bud chose not to throw the wrap into the incinerator, as per company policy, but hung on to it, intrigued, and found a mention of it in a guidebook. He was surprised to learn that star pilots occasionally took fractional doses to leaven the psychological effects of light-speed, which, though highly risky, they managed to get through the med-tests because it left no trace in the bloodstream. The book cautioned that babooba root taken in any quantity larger than singular grains was highly dangerous.

Thirdly, by a complete coincidence, the Croons boy was busted for peeping by Dane's Judge brother Henry, setting him up to work for Justice Department. An officer who believed vigilance and harsh penalties were essential if crime was to be combated, and the guilty punished, Novak Senior encouraged Jacob to keep his fellow citizens under constant surveillance. When he was investigated himself for his somewhat flexible approach to the Law—the report citing the disproportionate number of juves on his patrol vector with broken limbs and fractured skulls—he was demoted from Street to Customs. Becoming acquainted with Deek and Bud through his sibling, Novak would casually mention the multitude of illegalities that were still taking place out on the slab, right under the Judges' noses, that nobody was doing anything to stop. Lives were still being ruined, the perpetrators still escaped justice.

A plan was formed.

"YOU AND CARVER and the rest brutally murdered his best friend's son?"

"I wasn't there," Novak protested. "I'd told them about Croons, knew he was keeping an eye on Vassell. They'd decided they were going to take the peeper out, make sure he didn't see them selling on the drug to the dealer. But I didn't know what they had planned, how far they'd go—"

"They redecorated the apartment with him," Dredd snapped.

"They were trying to divert attention away from themselves, make it look like a gang revenge killing, bring down the helmets on the street scum. I think it was Tronjer who came up with the idea of painting the symbol on the wall, like the perpetrators were marking their territory. It was all a ruse to give a false impression of who was responsible."

"They told you this."

"Afterwards. Croons was dead and Vassell had the dust, there was nothing I could've done."

"Do you know how many man-hours have been wasted chasing false leads? And in the meantime, the narcotic was being distributed, lives were being lost."

"I... I was compromised, Dredd," Novak murmured, looking down. "I was involved. I'd helped them get the drug into the city. To have cubed them would've meant the end for me too."

"And it's worked out so well for you otherwise, hasn't it?" Burlough said, snorting.

"Why Vassell? Why choose him to distribute it?"

"Deek had seen him around William Holden, seen a regular flow of customers coming through. He seemed a good fit."

"These creeps, Carver and the other three," Dredd growled, leaning in closer to the other Judge. "How crazy *are* they?"

"They're obsessed. They want to destroy the criminals, wipe out the users and the pushers indiscriminately, get retribution on the kind that they lost their children to. They've released this dust into the underworld so the perps kill themselves, go out of their minds through their own appetites." Novak held Dredd's gaze. "They're doing our job for us. They're targeting the creeps far more effectively than we ever can. These aren't innocents that are dying here. Their methods may be different, but what are they doing that's any different from our own sanctioned crime prevention—"

"Never mind the fact that you're complicit in murder and drug smuggling, Novak; you're truly no longer fit to wear that badge if you honestly believe that," Dredd replied, turning to leave. "There's a poison circulating out there, and this sector's about to descend into chaos. What you've helped unleash is going to cause untold damage."

"This sector?" Novak said and chuckled.

Dredd stopped in the doorway and turned his head. "What?"

"Carver and his friends have ambitions greater than that. You think Vassell was the only dealer they contacted? Why stop there? They've got the supplies to see their plan roll out across half the city."

Nine

"THEY'RE DOING OUR *job for us.*"

Novak's words rang through Dredd's mind as he burned rubber towards Atlantic Hoverport. Carver and the rest of the creeps truly thought they were on the side of the angels, taking a retaliatory strike against the perps that had destroyed lives, and doing so not criminal-by-criminal like everyday vigilantes—stalking their prey in shadowy alleys, putting a bullet in each pusher and maniac's head—but by poisoning the source of the problem and letting the addicted do the holy work to themselves. It didn't matter that anyone that came into contact with the drug was at risk—whether it be a one-time user, a juve experimenting, or a hopeless junkie—because all were guilty in their eyes; all were responsible for feeding the monster that caused so much pain, who had wrenched their children from them. Organised crime was funded by narcotics money, bystanders were murdered in gang conflicts sparked by territorial disputes, decent cits robbed or killed for a few creds to pay for the next fix, babies born with the same chemical dependencies as their parents, tragic lives mapped out already; at every level, its presence caused harm, like background radiation. Carver and co. were intent on wiping them all out, cauterising the infection, purifying the city.

But it was retribution that was colouring their motives, not the Law. Novak had said that the grieving fathers were obsessed, and Dredd hadn't been slow to pick up the inference in what the Judge had told him: that their fanaticism was only of a slightly different stripe to his own devotion to duty. His mission was to judge and to punish, to administer justice, to enforce control—what were they doing but culling the crims in one fell swoop? Did it matter if a few sleazebags and dopeheads ended up in Resyk? Wouldn't *he* end up putting them there himself if they crossed his path, with zziz in their pockets and a las-knife tucked into their belts? Novak had been the kind of officer that couldn't discern the difference, that Carver's crew had simply been the guys with the *cojones* and sense of moral conviction to see it through. When it came down to it, taking the creeps out like this was just one step further from breaking a punk's arm as you slammed him up against a wall for a shakedown. The scumballs had it coming. Drokk it, he could hear Novak arguing, they were fighting a war here.

Dredd refused to brook the notion. The fathers had long lost any sense of rationality—they'd brutally murdered Croons with cold, premeditated determination, even taking the time to divert the blame, cloaking their activities in the M.O. of one of the very gangs they despised, and were contaminating an entire sector, not caring who was driven insane. Their actions, their all-consuming hunger for revenge, proved they were unhinged, and what they wanted to achieve could never be condoned. He would come down hard on anyone who behaved as self-appointed guardians, slaughtering in the name of their own private vendetta; he felt it was an obligation to reassert the authority of the badge, demonstrate where the seat of power lay. No one outside of the uniform could kill with impunity, no matter who was the target.

Dredd had radioed ahead and checked with Atlantic once he'd left Novak in the hands of Burlough and the SJS: Carver and Tronjer were logged on as having arrived for work at the port. He'd requested that all flights out be temporarily grounded, in case the pair were planning on skipping city, country or even planet, and that a security alert be declared as the reason—nothing to make the perps suspicious. There was no reason to believe that they knew the Judges were on to them, or that their scheme had been broken wide open, and he wanted it kept that way until they were in custody. Helmets were to be mobilised at all exits under the same emergency pretext.

He called up Dane Novak and Biv Hubbly's addresses—the former was a spivot technician registered as living in Bill Kerr block, the latter rented a bed in John Russo stackers, a kind of halfway house for those of no fixed abode. Hubbly was alcoholic, unemployed and flagged as having been in psychiatric care, diagnosed with acute paranoia and suicidal tendencies ever since his son had been caught in the crossfire of a surf-by gang shooting. Judging by the desperate state of his medical reports, there was no way he would've been able to organise something like this without the others' commitment, and according to the docs his mental condition apparently left him highly suggestible. Dredd mused that he wouldn't be surprised if it was Hubbly that had wielded the knife in the Croons snuff, being the only one of the four with an arrest record for violent conduct after he'd assaulted a nurse. It would account for the frenzied manner of the vic's death: a blade placed in Hubbly's hand, and then the others goading and cajoling him into performing the deed while at least one of them held Croons down. All of them were unstable, but Hubbly was particularly on a hair-trigger. Dredd instructed nearby units to attend both home addresses and apprehend the suspects if they were there, adding that care was to be taken when handling Hubbly.

He heard the screaming crowd a fraction of a second before he saw the reason for it: the cits congregating on Hudson plaza were fleeing a scrawny-looking dult in a blue towelling bathrobe flapping around his bony frame, who was advancing on anyone within swinging distance of the cooking laser he gripped in his right hand. Dredd decelerated and swung off the sked, shouting a warning to the creep to drop the weapon, but once he drew close enough he could see that the man was beyond coherent thought. Eyes rolling, sheathed in sweat, he instantly reminded Dredd of the babbling wreck Vassell had become, and the Judge realised he was another of the poisoned users. He seemed barely conscious of the fact that Dredd was approaching, peering around with jerky bird-like movements as if surrounded by phantoms, and jabbing the laser to protect himself. Dredd yanked hard on the Lawmaster's handlebars and skidded the rear wheel round in a half-circle, slamming into the perp and knocking him off his feet. He flew several yards before hitting the ground in a heap, but was clearly crazed enough not to stay down; he clambered to one knee, trying to find the energy to pull himself up, hand reaching out for the dropped laser. Dredd didn't have time for this. He put a bullet through the meathead's shoulder, spinning him onto his back, where he lay groaning, and then patched through a call for a med-wagon.

"Gonna be at least six minutes until support can be with you, Dredd," Control informed him. "Getting reports from all over the sector. Futsies are coming out of the woodwork."

"Not futsies," Dredd grunted, grabbing a handful of towelling robe and dragging the drooling nutjob towards the nearest holding post on the far side of the square, a thin streak of blood left in their wake. "They're dust-smokers. They've inhaled tainted narcotics. Warn all units that they can't be reasoned with, and should be treated with utmost caution. They're violent, hallucinating, and incapable of acting rationally. Terminate with extreme prejudice if necessary, but otherwise incapacitate and deliver to a med facility. They're straitjacket jobs—they'll try to take their own lives if we haven't done it for them already." He hitched the man up so he was sitting with his back to the post and cuffed him to it, looked around and beckoned to a young woman amongst the crowd of rubberneckers.

"How many cases?" he asked Control.

"Twenty-seven reported so far. No pattern to them, just random crazies popping up all over. Five have already jumped from their apartment windows... Wait, incident register has just leapt to thirty-two."

Drokk, Dredd thought, how were they ever going to contain this thing? He had to find out who the other dealers were that Carver and co. had supplied, cut off the distribution. He wouldn't save everyone, he knew that—already percentage numbers were dancing through his head of those affected and those potentially who could be spared the same fate—and it was now a damage limitation exercise. Could they do more to head off a brewing disaster without causing mass panic? An idea popped into his head.

"Control, put an order through to the broadcast division, my authorisation, instruct them to put together a citizen information 'vert, to be released immediately. No specifics, just that a bad batch circulating on the streets is highly dangerous, and anything bought within the last forty-eight hours is to be destroyed. Have them put it out on all channels, repeating every half hour, including public billboards."

The girl he'd picked out sidled up to him and he impatiently motioned for her to crouch next to him.

"That's going to need the Chief Judge's approval, that level of exposure," the voice in his ear told him.

"Fine, get it," Dredd snapped. "But move, quickly." He turned to the woman. "I want you to apply pressure to this man's wound, keep it there until the med-wagon arrives. Shouldn't be more than a few minutes." He stood, adding: "Ignore anything he says, he's deranged."

"Er, I'm not sure..." she replied, running her gaze up and down the robed creature rambling and bleeding at her feet.

"Don't worry, he's no threat now. Your assistance is greatly appreciated, citizen." He jogged back to his bike before she could protest any further.

WHEN HE REACHED Atlantic Hoverport, he had to pick his way through a Judicial perimeter, helmets turning away traffic, bundling angry cits into the back of catch-wagons if they chose not to comply immediately. A vast electronic bulletin board on the side of the terminal stated that all flights were suspended following the discovery of a suspect package. While half the units were keeping travellers from entering, the other half were denying those that were seeking to leave, claiming no one could be released until camera footage had been studied. Unruly crowds formed on either side of the blockade, but the Judges kept them in order, individuals occasionally pulled out and made an example of. A few swift blows with a daystick and the loudest voices fell silent.

Dredd pushed his way into the building, surveying the scene. Dejected-looking passengers sat in departure lounges staring glumly at the information displays, while the droids behind the check-in desks patiently dealt with enquiries. Juves ran riot as their parents argued. It was chaos, but it was contained. The place was locked down and no one was going anywhere, much to their obvious chagrin. Now it was a matter of finding the creeps he was looking for.

"Dredd, it's Mansell, over at Russo stackers," his radio barked. "Hubbly's dead. We found him in a PF cubicle with his wrists cut."

Dredd didn't pause but continued to cut through the throng, heading for the security offices. Bud

Tronjer worked as a guard at the facility; that would be his first port of call. "How long?"

"Meds reckon he's been dead between six to twelve hours. Thing is, they're not convinced it's suicide. Bruising on the arms suggests he was held and there's a suspicion from the angle of the wounds that a third party may have held the knife."

Dredd quickened his pace. Could Carver and Tronjer have realised that Justice Department was on their case, and started cleaning house? Hubbly was potentially the weak link, the psychologically unstable of the four, and the one most likely to crack under interrogation. Then again, maybe Hubbly had been showing signs of guilt and remorse, making noises about confessing, and his friends acted to shut him up before he ruined their plan. He didn't doubt for one second it was them that had performed the deed; the faked suicide was their M.O. all over. No one was safe, it seemed, from their psychotic ruthlessness.

"Control, who's been dispatched over to Bill Kerr?"

"That'd be Neary and Phelps."

"Patch me through." There was a brief second of dead air. "Neary—Dredd. Any sign of Novak?"

"Negative. His wife's here—says he didn't come home last night, hasn't been seen since yesterday. We're pulling her in, see what she can tell us, but my instinct is she knows nothing."

"Get forensics to tear that apartment apart. He may have something incriminating hidden from her."

"Wilco."

Dredd wrenched open the door to the sec-office, several startled faces glancing up from the CCTV monitors to greet the new arrival. "Tronjer—where is he?"

"Bud?" the nearest uniformed man replied, scratching his beard. "He's, uh, working the crowd at gate six. That right, Phil?" He cocked his head over his shoulder.

"Yeah, rota says that where he should be," another said.

"Show me," Dredd demanded, indicating the screens. The guards parted to allow him access to the bank of monitors, one of them pointing at the stocky, burly figure casting an intimidating eye over a clearly restless mob of frustrated holidaymakers. He was holding a finger up to his ear, his mouth moving, evidently having a conversation as he studied the comings and goings before him. "You all have comms, I take it?"

"Yeah," the one known as Phil answered, a little bemused, "though if he was talking to one of us, we'd be picking up the chatter. He must be using another channel."

"Speaking to someone at the hoverport still?"

"Oh, yeah, they don't have that much range. Listen, why do you want Bud anyway?"

"He's got information pertinent to a case of mine." Dredd spun on his heel and made for the door.

"Hey, Judge," one of the sec-men called after him, "what's the deal with this supposed suspect package? We're all in the dark here; no one's telling us anything."

"Just keep the cits under control," Dredd muttered without looking back. "It'll be over soon. But until then, the situation should be considered dangerous."

He slalomed through the people, resisting the urge to unholster his Lawgiver as a means to get them out of his way; he couldn't risk a stampede if they anticipated a bullet festival. He saw the signage for gate six and made a beeline for it, catching a glimpse of Tronjer still talking animatedly into his mike as he paced. Dredd slowed and tried to ease his way amongst the crowd as he got closer, but the guard changed direction unexpectedly, turned his head and fixed the lawman directly in his sights. For a long, frozen moment, they stared at each other, both caught by surprise, each instantly and simultaneously knowing that the game was up.

"Get out! Get out now!" Tronjer yelled into his headpiece and drew an electroshock weapon from his hip without hesitation. The cits around them jumped at the creep's sudden exclamation and panicked, shoving their way to escape, pushing Dredd aside as he drew his Lawgiver. He fired, but the aim was compromised, his SE round shattering the stun-gun a millisecond before the stun-pulse hit him full in the chest with the force of a construction-mek's wrecking ball. He was knocked onto his back, his ribs feeling as if they'd been crushed, his heart and lungs constricted. A couple of other cits collapsed too, bowled over on the periphery of the blast, and fell either side of him. He struggled to breathe, skull pounding, vision hazy; as if underwater, he was aware of screams echoing, and hundreds of pairs of legs scissoring past. He grasped his Lawgiver firmly and pulled himself to a sitting position, swinging the gun to bear on where Tronjer had been a fraction earlier.

But the man was gone.

Ten

No, not gone. *There.*

Dredd saw Tronjer pushing through the crowd, the congestion slowing him as he fled back into the main body of the hoverport, angry shouts from those that were being unceremoniously barged to one side punctuating his escape, and the Judge hauled himself to his feet, head swimming as he stood. The effects of the stun-pulse lingered, his eyesight blurry, a tightness still wrapped around his chest, making breathing painful. He took a step forward and the strength briefly left his leg, the muscles protesting; he wobbled for a second, feeling disarmingly vulnerable. He counted himself lucky that he'd managed to shoot the creep's weapon the moment it had discharged, knocking it fractionally off-target: if he'd taken the hit as was intended, he'd be unconscious for at least several hours, with possible lasting nerve damage. The reduced charge was not unlike being smacked in the face with a daystick without the benefit of a visor, an experience he was unfortunately acquainted with during his many hand-to-hand training sessions at the Academy. Then, his ears would ring for days after a blow to the head; now, his skull felt as if it was swaddled in cotton wool, an ache combined with a seeping numbness.

Dredd instinctively raised his Lawgiver in Tronjer's direction, but knew he couldn't fire; his vision was too unreliable. He lowered it with a grunt, knelt to check the pulses of the two cits that were lying pole-axed nearby, then straightened and started to limp in pursuit.

"Are... are you all right, Judge?" an eldster to his left nervously asked.

Dredd glanced at her, aware of the perspiration dripping from his nose and chin, conscious of what he represented, of what must not be diminished or seen to be broken. "I'll live," he replied through gritted teeth, and set off at a steadily increasing pace.

Tronjer couldn't escape, couldn't make it through the cordon, and all flights were grounded, but clearly Carver was also somewhere in the complex, and together they must have a plan for getting past the barricades. Dredd staggered on, following the pointed fingers of aggrieved bystanders, and caught sight of the security guard running towards the baggage-handling area. He spurred himself to double his efforts. He knew he could—standard procedure was probably *should*—call in back-up to assist, cut down the ground that needed covering, but pride stayed his hand from radioing in the request; pride and more than a little determination. This was *his* case—he would see it through to completion. What message did it send if they mobilised the heavy mob to bring a pair of lawbreakers to book? If there was to be respect in the Law, it had to be seen to be delivered robustly by the badge, that a couple of meatheads like this were no match for a Mega-City Judge. Perhaps it was a stubborn streak, a leftover from his clone-father; a desire to do things his way, a tenacity for passing judgement by his own hand.

It was almost an entirely droid workforce sorting the luggage, and they paid Dredd little heed as he entered. He swiftly scanned the space, ducking low to try to glimpse his quarry between the conveyor belts and stacked grav-lifts, but there was too much confusion, too much movement to gain a fix. He felt a figure looming behind him, and swung his Lawgiver automatically, finger poised on the trigger, but it was a loading-bot attempting to turn around, warning beacon flashing. Dredd shook his head, breathed out, but didn't relax his grip on his gun. He could do with some assistance to peel apart the layers of noise and distraction: he switched the helmet-view to infra-red, blanking out the machinery, zeroing in on any red spots of warmth.

There. A human silhouette was tiptoeing between the containers, back against the wall, head swivelling left and right. Dredd didn't hesitate: he crouched and ran, using a transporter trundling past as cover, grimacing as his muscles groaned. The figure appeared none the wiser, peering round boxes in the other direction. Dredd stood, flipping off the infra-red, and brought his gun to bear as he sidestepped into the aisle that the perp was hiding in.

"On the floor! Now!" the Judge roared. "This will be your only warning!"

The man's arms shot up as he turned to face Dredd, panic etched on his features. It wasn't Tronjer. It was Carver. Dredd recognised him from the cit ID files that he'd downloaded to his Lawmaster. He looked terrified.

"I said, on the floor," the lawman repeated. Carver duly dropped to his knees, hands still in the air. Dredd kept his gun trained on him as he edged forward. "Where's your accomplice, Deek? Where's Tronjer?"

"L-listen, Judge, I... I never wanted to..."

"Answer the question."

Carver licked his lips, visibly shaking, his eyes screwed shut. "I never m-meant to..."

"Too late for regrets," Dredd snarled, now standing over the creep. "You knew the damage you were doing; you knew the lives that would be lost."

"You misunderstand," a voice said behind him. "Deek means that he never wanted a Judge to die. That was never the plan. But you've made it unavoidable."

Dredd turned, just as a wrench was brought down hard and heavy on the side of his head. His helmet cushioned some of the blow, but the force of it still knocked him to one side, careening him off a crate and onto his hands and knees. His Lawgiver went skittering across the floor.

He looked up, a coppery tang in his mouth as blood trickled from his nose, and saw Tronjer kick his gun under a pallet as Carver joined him, pulling a snubnose from his waistband, and levelling at Dredd. He appeared significantly less scared now, though not entirely happy about the situation. Dredd concurred; his skull was pounding. But he was determined not to display any signs of weakness to these punks.

"I guess you baby Judges are still a little raw," Tronjer said. "Still a little green. That's the second time I've knocked you flat on your back in as many minutes."

"Maybe it's experience telling me to shoot first in future," Dredd growled, wiping blood from his face with the back of a gauntlet.

"That's if you *have* a future." Tronjer held out a hand. "Your boot knife too, please."

Dredd reached forward and eased the blade from its holster, tossing it at the two men's feet. "There's no way out for you," he said. "Hoverport's sealed off."

"We know. But we're getting out of the city nevertheless. Smuggling ourselves out"—Tronjer indicated the storage containers around them—"with the help of a few friends we have amongst the flight crew."

"You're leaving? What about your work to rid the city of the criminal element? You're going to leave that unfinished?"

"Regrettably so. We would've liked to have rolled it out further, but I suppose it was only a matter of time, once the scum started dropping, before the jays would take an interest. Still, enough of the dust was disseminated to prove a point."

"And get your revenge."

"No," Carver replied, his voice catching in his throat. "There can never be enough for that."

"You think this was justice?" Dredd said quietly. "It was obsession, madness. You murdered to further your plan, became as ruthless as those you professed to despise and wanted to eliminate, even as far as disposing of Hubbly. What about Novak? Has he been dealt with too?"

Carver and Tronjer exchanged a glance, telling Dredd all he needed to know.

"Guessed as much. Threatening to bail on you, was he?"

"Dane got scared, same way Biv did," Tronjer answered. "They both became risks, problems we couldn't afford not to tackle. They knew from the beginning the stakes, how committed we had to be for this to work."

"Committed? It's insanity."

"What do you know, Judge?" Carver yelled suddenly, lashing out at Dredd with a boot to the head. "You don't know what it's like, to lose your child to the drokkers that prey on this city. You're meant to protect us, but you weren't there for my little girl, none of you were. You'd failed, and we had the strength of purpose to do what we had to do."

"Easy, Deek," Tronjer soothed, casting a wary eye over his shoulder.

"No one said life would be easy," Dredd said, turning away to spit a globule of blood on the floor. "You think yours is the only sob story? Suck it up, pal. But don't commit mass murder and call it judgement."

"It was payback—"

"It was four psychos who took the Law into their own hands, nothing more. Adding to the body count was never going to bring your kid back."

Carver was trembling, and Tronjer looked at him, concerned. "Stay cool, Deek. We need to do this smart and clean. You want to give me the gun?"

"No," Carver rasped and crouched, jamming his

blaster under Dredd's chin, pushing his head back. "You'd rather the filth lived, huh, Judge? That Maggie died for nothing?"

"Way I heard it, if her old man hadn't been such a loser, who knows how things might've turned out differently."

Carver wailed like a wounded animal and tensed his grip on the gun, his breaths coming in short bursts.

"Thing is," Dredd continued, "I don't think you can pull that trigger, 'cos it's not me you want dead. You've got no beef with the Judges. You want to see the guilty one, the one that deserves punishment, look a little closer to home."

Carver froze, staring at Dredd—or maybe he was studying his reflection in the visor. But the hesitation was enough: the Judge powered his fist into the man's face, demolishing his nose and driving him to the ground. He snatched the gun from Carver with his other hand and in one swift movement aimed and fired it at Tronjer, who had barely time to back away before three slugs hit him in the belly and chest. He pirouetted on the spot, leaving behind a crimson smear across the side of a container, then crumpled in a heap.

Dredd turned his attention to Carver, who was slowly picking himself up. "You can choose how this ends, citizen."

The man stood motionless, head lowered, his features a mask of blood. "It ended a long time ago," he murmured.

"Save it for the psych-wardens. Let's go, creep." Dredd motioned with the blaster. "The sentence is life."

"Always was," Carver replied, raising his eyes and fixing them on the snubnose. Then he charged, waiting for the final bullet to bring it all to a close.

Dredd obliged without further deliberation.

"I UNDERSTAND OUR cases intersected."

Dredd turned from his surveying of the clean-up at Atlantic and saw White approaching through the cordon. He nodded in acknowledgement.

"You've been brought up to speed, presumably."

"Yeah. I saw the public health warning you ordered broadcast. Apparently it was partly successful—sector houses noted an increase in narcotics being flushed. Must've saved a few lives."

"Only partly, though?"

"Well, something on this scale was never going to be stopped entirely. You cut off the source, and the distribution of babooba dust will slow to a trickle, but more cits are going to die before that happens. Too many out there for it to vanish overnight."

Dredd had to concede the point. Once the drug had been released, it was impossible to control or eradicate it fully until it played itself out. Even then, some enterprising creep would probably try to synthesise their own variant. He felt unsatisfied: he wouldn't be able to guarantee the cits' protection, not from themselves.

"Don't beat yourself up about it," White said. "Nothing more you could've done."

"I made mistakes. Things I missed."

"Hey, we're only human."

Dredd wanted to answer that that wasn't enough, but couldn't formulate the words to express what he meant by it. This is what he was engineered for; he had to have high expectations for himself, and for every officer in uniform, for if they failed, then the badge, Fargo's legacy, meant nothing.

"I better go," Dredd said. "Meds want to book me into the speed-heal. They think I got a fractured cheekbone, some muscle damage."

"Meatheads went to work on you."

"I'm sure I'll have worse," Dredd replied as he strode back towards the street.

About the Author

Matthew Smith was employed as a desk editor for Pan Macmillan book publishers for three years before joining *2000 AD* as assistant editor in July 2000 to work on a comic he had read religiously since 1985. He became editor of the Galaxy's Greatest in December 2001, and then editor-in-chief of the *2000 AD* titles in January 2006. He lives in Oxford.

THE COLD LIGHT OF DAY

MICHAEL CARROLL

MEGA-CITY ONE
2080 A.D.

One

DREDD DISMOUNTED HIS Lawmaster and switched his helmet's speakers to noise-cancellation mode, to muffle the roar of the crowd. It made a difference, but not as much as he'd have liked.

Though the streets were teeming, a wide clearing had automatically formed around him—it happened any time he stood still for more than a few minutes, as though the crowd was a living organism that regarded a Judge as an unwelcome infection. He turned slowly, watching the citizens at the edge of the clearing.

Every citizen had something to hide, something they felt guilty about. Something that made them sweat when a Judge was nearby.

Once, a few days after they graduated from the Academy of Law, Judge Gibson had said to him, "Joe, I'm starting to think that the whole *city* stinks of sweat. You get that? You walk up to a citizen and, bam, he's got pit-stains. Happened to me a dozen times already."

"Cite them for public hygiene violations," Dredd had suggested.

"Sure. Give them *another* reason to be scared of us. That'll help."

Now, nearly a year into the job, Dredd had seen his share of terrified citizens. Even today, with all the excitement building for the annual Mega-City 5000 race, the citizens grew quiet as the Judges moved among them, bubbles of silent panic filtering through the throng.

A man waving a large "Spacers Suck!" flag saw Dredd, quickly looked away, and was now standing very still, the crowd's chant of *"Mutants Forever!"* dying in his throat on the first syllable.

The short, bald man next to him said, "'Moo'? Whaddaya mean, 'Moo'? That some kinda *insult*? You sayin' the Muties are cows? 'Cos if you *are*, pal, you an' Freddie Fist here are gonna be gettin' to know each other real drokkin' intimate!"

Dredd placed his hand on the bald man's shoulder. "Maybe Freddie Fist would like a date with Debbie Daystick."

The bald man swallowed audibly. Under his breath he muttered, "Oh, sweet Jovus!" Then, louder, "No, Judge. Just makin' banter, that's all."

"Banter, huh?" Dredd hauled the man out of the crowd. "Name and address."

The man's eyes were wide, his head already studded with beads of perspiration. "Ted-Teddy LeFevre. Apartment fifty-four, Winker Watson Block. I swear, I didn't mean anything! I'm not the violent type."

"How many warnings have you got, LeFevre?"

"None, Judge. I promise."

"You've got one now. Threatening behaviour."

He grabbed LeFevre by the collar, pulled him closer. "We're watching you. Understood? Might find myself dropping by Winker Watson Block tomorrow. How's that sound to you? What are you hiding, LeFevre?"

"Nothing! I swear! I *super*-swear! I've never been in trouble with the law!"

"Until now. You're on the watch-list, citizen." He let go and shoved the man back into the crowd, then continued on his way.

Almost every Judge in the city was on the streets today, patrolling the crowd. Arrests and spot fines were already up two hundred per cent on the average day, and it wasn't yet eight o'clock in the morning.

Dredd spotted a familiar glint of light off to his left—the tell-tale reflection of sunlight on a Judge's helmet—and strode in that direction. The crowd parted around him: a Judge rarely had to ask a citizen to move out of the way.

The other Judge was female, tall and slender, maybe ten years older than Dredd. She nodded at him as he approached, and glanced at the name on his badge. "Dredd. Don't know you, do I?"

Dredd returned the nod. "Judge Safford. No, we've never met. Crowd behaving themselves?"

"Been on the clock three hours now. Sixteen arrests. You?"

"Just came on." They stood side-by-side and looked toward the cordoned-off street. The crowd was packed twenty-deep on this side of the street, probably twice that on the other side.

"This your first one?" Safford asked.

"Yeah. Word is it gets pretty intense."

"*Intense* doesn't cover it. It's a foregone conclusion that either the Spacers or the Muties will win, so most of the cits don't care about who hits the finishing post first. They just want to see some carnage. Word of advice: once the bikers reach this point, watch for dunks and taps. The crowd gets so wild you could probably barbecue a baby and they wouldn't notice."

"Dunks and taps," Dredd said. "Got it."

"How long have you been on the streets, Dredd?"

"Almost twelve months."

"Class of '79. Good year, I heard. You're one of the *twins*, right? Heard you both scored top marks pretty much all the way through the academy."

"That's right."

"Then tell me what laws are being broken right here, in front of you."

"None," Dredd replied. "But there's potential."

"There always is. Specifically?"

Dredd nodded toward a middle-aged man holding a mini-cam. "Illegal recording of a sponsored event. Can't arrest him until the race actually starts." To their left, a hottie-vendor who was far-too-casually wheeling her cart away. "Probably unlicensed trader. Possession of a hottie-cart isn't illegal. We'd need to witness her exchanging goods for creds before we can arrest her. Same with the two juves behind us. Both wearing new, identical, home-made Spacers t-shirts, both carrying full backpacks. Bootleggers."

Safford turned to look. "Huh. Missed that myself. Not bad." She turned back and nodded toward a man wearing a long coat. "And *you* missed that guy. Bulge in his coat. Possible concealed weapon."

"I saw him," Dredd said. "Mid-fifties, pasty skin, sallow eyes, slight tremor in his hands, rash of small blisters on the side of his neck, trouble keeping his head raised. He's in the advanced stages of a flesh-wasting disease, probably Lundsgaard Syndrome. The bulge under his coat isn't a gun. It's his med-pack. Sufferers of Lundsgaard Syndrome can't process certain proteins—the med-pack does it for him."

"Impressive," Safford said.

"Not really. He was in your line of sight—you couldn't have missed him. Figured you'd already checked him out. The fact that he's not in cuffs, and that he hasn't moved away from us, tells me he's not breaking the law."

"I mean, impressive that you correctly diagnosed his condition. You training for med?"

"No. But I read the textbooks, pay attention to the lessons."

Judge Safford smiled. "You *can* relax a little now and then, Dredd. You're not in the Academy any more. No need to keep hitting the books. You're not a Judge twenty-four-seven."

"Can't say I agree with that, Safford," Dredd said. "A Judge is always on duty."

Another smile. "You'll learn soon enough. Can't keep your shoulder to the grindstone all the time. All work and no play makes Dredd a dull boy."

"Disagree with that, too. The grindstone is what keeps a Judge *sharp*." He stepped away. "Be seeing you, Safford."

As he moved on through the crowd, he could sense Judge Safford watching him. She was like a lot of the older Judges he'd met. They thought of him as naive, idealistic. Green around the edges.

Didn't bother him, as long as it didn't stop them doing their job.

He spotted a dunk sidling toward a young couple—the man's wallet was clearly visible in the back pocket of his trows—before the dunk just as smoothly shifted direction and sidled off. Dredd turned around and spotted a man of a similar age hurriedly looking away; the look-out, who'd warned his pal there was a Judge present.

Already, the look-out was slipping through the crowd, heading in the opposite direction from the pick-pocket.

Can't catch both, not in this crowd... Dredd took a deep breath, and bellowed, "Halt!"

The look-out skidded to a stop, as did every citizen in earshot.

Dredd pointed to the look-out. "You. Stay put! Got that?"

The man nodded feebly, and Dredd turned and ran in the other direction.

He'd only had a few seconds to glimpse the pickpocket, mostly from behind, but that was all he needed to recognise him again.

In the Academy, the cadets were trained to recognise people not just by their faces, but by their clothing, their footwear, their gait, the way their hair was parted, cut or shaved at the back of their head.

He quickly spotted the dunk again. The man was now running flat-out along the outer edge of the crowd, deftly weaving around the other citizens.

Dredd pounded after him, the soles of his department-issue boots slamming heavily onto the rockcrete, making that distinctive sound that informed the innocent that a Judge was approaching and they'd better get out of the way.

The dunk vaulted over a rail onto a quiet street—Dredd added jaywalking to the man's growing list of crimes—and darted across to the opposite sidewalk, where he collided with a burly woman, knocking her into a store's doorway.

As Dredd leapt over the rail, he pulled out his lawgiver and roared, "Heat-seeker!"

Immediately, the fleeing man threw himself face-down on the ground.

Well, that *worked*, Dredd said to himself. It was something Rico had suggested back when they were cadets: "We spread the rumour that a heat-seeker can't hit you if you're lying flat on the ground—the perps'll hit the deck if they think one's coming."

Dredd crossed the road and reached down to grab the would-be pickpocket by the arm, hauled him to his feet. The man was trembling, slick with sweat, the lower half of his face smeared with his own blood where his nose had scraped along the rockcrete.

"I didn't do nothin'! Don't shoot me!"

"Consider yourself lucky the heat-seeker missed," Dredd said. "Instead of execution, you're getting six years in the cubes. Two months for jaywalking, twenty months for assaulting that pedestrian, same again for fleeing, two years for intent to commit."

"That..." The man looked up into Dredd's visor. "But that's only, uh, five years and six months! What about the other six months?"

Dredd pointed down at the man's blood on the ground. "Littering. Six months."

He cuffed the perp and dragged him to the nearest holding-post, then called it in to Control.

In the store's doorway, he checked on the burly woman. "Are you hurt, citizen?"

She looks past Dredd toward the holding post. "Damn fool near kilt me! He oughta be locked up!"

"He will be. And I'll remind you that interfering with a criminal awaiting pick-up will get you a mandatory five years." He jerked his thumb over his shoulder. "On your way."

He crossed the street once more and returned to the look-out, who was standing exactly where Dredd had left him, trembling.

"I'm sorry, Judge! I swear. I'll never do it again!"

"I believe you," Dredd said.

"Then... Then I can go?"

"No. Intent to aid a perp in the commission of a crime. Two years. Plus another year for endangering the safety of a Mega-City One Judge." Dredd spun the man about, grabbed his arms and slapped cuffs onto his wrists.

"*Endangering...?*" The perp craned his head to peer over his shoulder at Dredd. "This is bogus! How did I endanger you?"

"You informed a known criminal of my whereabouts."

"But... But... No. No, that doesn't make sense! You didn't *know* he was a criminal then!"

"But *you* did. Want me to add failure to inform on a known criminal? That's another two years."

The man started to cry. "I'm sorry. Really, I'm sorry!"

"I know," Dredd said. "I understand. You've learned your lesson?"

Still sobbing, the man nodded. "Yeah." He sniffed. "So you're not *really* arresting me?"

Dredd pushed the perp ahead of him. "What makes you think that? I just asked if you've learned your lesson."

The speaker in Dredd's helmet beeped: "Control to Dredd. Multiple homicide, two Judges dead. Funex Eaterie, Bevis Wetzel Plaza, sector sixty-three."

"Sector sixty-three's a thirty-minute ride from here, Control," Dredd replied. "Maybe twice that with the crowds and the road-closures."

"Your presence has been requested, Dredd. Immediately."

Two

In Sector 276, possibly the northernmost sector of Mega-City One—the claim was also made by the inhabitants of Sector 275, and was a constant source of tension between the neighbouring regions—Chief Judge Clarence Goodman mounted the steps leading to the podium suspended over the race's start line.

Goodman was a large, barrel-chested man with a deeply-lined face and, in private, an often gruff, stern manner. In public he liked to present himself as "everyone's favourite older uncle," a term created by spin-doctors employed by Hollins Solomon, his predecessor. It hadn't worked for Solomon, but then Solomon had been "a cold-hearted, weasel-faced, self-serving scumbag," in the words of his own predecessor Eustace Fargo.

Now, as Goodman strode along the walkway toward the podium, he took his time. Off to one side, he saw himself on the fifty-metre-high holographic image projected onto the side of Ridley Scott Block.

A hundred news cameras were focussed on him; every move he made would be analysed at length over the coming days. "Goodman's looking a little old" would be the most common observation. "See how he has to hold onto the rail? Seems unsure of himself." There would, of course, be counter-views from his unflinching supporters: "The Chief Judge looked noble and resplendent in his garb of office as he surveyed the cheering crowd below, his ever-present smile the surest indicator of his love for this magnificent city and its loyal citizens."

In truth, Goodman felt neither particularly unsure nor very noble. Announcing the start of the race was a job, same as any other. And the race itself was a distraction. Whether he liked it or not, he was patron to almost eight hundred million citizens, most of them unemployed and hungry for anything that might give meaning to their lives. The Mega-City 5000 would keep them occupied for a few days. With a bit of luck, someone new might win this year—that *would* give them something to talk about.

The race was open to anyone, as long as they got their applications in early and didn't have a criminal record. It had grown from the MegNorth Sector Run, established in 2068. Back then, it had simply been a race from the west side of Sector 276 to the eastern border of Sector 275.

Twenty metres below the gantry, the bikers and their mechanics were dashing to and fro, conducting last-minute checks on their machines. This year, over a hundred of them had passed the tryouts. Today, eight unevenly-balanced teams and a handful of independents would race from north to south in a wide zig-zagging route chosen so as to cover as much of the city as possible—if only the more camera-friendly parts.

A new twist this year was a split in the route in Sector 235: the two branches of the fork were the same length—six-hundred and sixty-seven kilometres—but the right branch looped wildly and skirted close to some of the nicer-looking city-blocks in the hopes that potential overseas tourists might be tempted to change their opinions of the city, and the left branch traversed a string of elevated highways, rising and falling in what the organisers promised would be a majestic fashion.

The contenders were free to choose whichever route they preferred, and already this was the subject of much speculation among the commentators—and, Goodman was certain, the bookies.

Gambling on the Mega-City 5000 was illegal, of course, and as such was a great source of revenue for the Justice Department. Goodman's accountants had run the figures. If betting on the race were legal, the Department could expect to recover slightly over a billion credits in taxes. But by prohibiting gambling, the Department could keep any and all funds seized by the Judges from back-room bookies. Already, over a hundred bookies had been marked for later investigation. The accountants estimated a haul of somewhere north of two and a half billion.

Below, the mechanics and support staff had vacated the starting grid, and now one hundred and eight bikers were mounted on their machines, engines humming, eager for the green light. The favourites were at the rear of the cluster, and by tradition they would take the first few hundred kilometres at an easy pace to give the newbies a chance. Not that it would make much difference in the long run: everyone knew that the winner would be either a Spacer or a Mutie. They had the best bikes and the most experience.

A voice in Goodman's earpiece said, "Sir? Ready when you are."

"Got it, thanks."

He stepped up to the podium and put on his best "I'm-a-nice-guy-and-you-can't-help-liking-me" smile. "Citizens of Mega-City One..." A deliberate four-second pause. "Welcome..." A two-second pause, then, louder, "To the Mega-City 5000!"

The roar of the crowd was almost deafening, and Goodman took a small step back, hamming up his reaction.

"We've got some fine racing ahead of us today, folks!" Goodman continued. "So enjoy the show, cheer for your favourites, and... *let the race begin!*"

Green lights flashed, a siren blared, and the air was filled with the screech of tyres and the cloying stink of burning synthetic rubber.

Goodman peered over the edge of the platform in time to see the participants slowly wending their way along the street, skirting around some poor unfortunate whose UniMagno's only tyre chose the exact wrong moment to develop a puncture.

Fifteen hours to the finishing post, Goodman said to himself. He knew that some of the Judges had their own wagers—cash free, he hoped—on the outcome. Not on the race itself, but on the number of citizens who'd die today. There was always at least one spugwit dumb enough to be dared by his pals to scale the barriers and dart across the track. Or a skysurfer trying to make a name for himself by buzzing the bikers. Or someone wearing a bat-glider who was under the impression that the minimum height restrictions only applied to *other* people. Or an idiot in a city-block who'd lean too far over the balcony rail to get a better view.

As he descended the steps, he reminded himself that people are, individually, fairly smart. Collectively, however, people are morons. *What was that equation again?* He asked himself. *The collective IQ of a crowd is the average IQ divided by the number of people present. Sounds about right.*

Yes, some people would die directly because of the race, but on the other hand, the city was home to close to eight hundred million people... On the average day, three citizens would choke to death on the plastic toy in their morning cereal. It didn't make one damn bit of difference *how* big the manufacturers made the animated "Choking Hazard!" warning on the box. There was always someone too utterly stupid to notice that their spoonful of small, light-brown Synthi-Flakes also contained a large pink plastic turtle.

In his years as a Judge, Goodman had seen some spectacularly stupid deaths, like the woman who starved to death after she locked herself inside her open-topped sports car, or the guy who was convinced that the "throwing the kids into the deep end of the pool in order to teach them to swim" method might just work for human flight.

As Goodman strode toward the waiting Justice Department H-wagon, a young reporter broke free of the press enclosure and darted toward him, recorder extended. "Chief Judge, Chief Judge! Dan

Dandahn, Screaming Tweenie Weekly, Channel Minus-One—Do you have a few words for our viewers?"

Goodman stopped, and turned toward the camera floating a few centimetres above the reporter's shoulder. "I do."

"Great!" The reporter tapped the camera. Beneath its lens a small display showed the InstaFeedback approval rating: the number was climbing up from forty-one per cent. "Kids, I'm with Chief Judge Clarence Goodman! Chief Judge, what would you like to say to our viewers?"

The Chief Judge glowered into the camera's lens. "Listen carefully, kids... We're watching you. Break the law, and we'll know about it even before you do." He leaned closer and the reporter took a step back. "If you're ever unsure whether what you're about to do is illegal, ask yourself this: would I do it if there was a Judge standing next to me? If the answer is no, then *don't do it.*"

The camera's screen showed an approval rating of sixty-two per cent. *Not too shabby*, Goodman thought.

The reporter muttered, "Uh, thanks... Can I ask you what you think of the latest trends in—"

Goodman grinned at the camera. "Hey, kids. Here's something else for you. I've not made an arrest since I became Chief Judge. You want to see me take down a perp?"

The approval rating shot up to eighty-four.

"Fantastic!" the reporter said, quickly looking around. "Who's the lucky perp?"

Goodman grabbed the man's shoulder. "You are. You climbed a Justice Department barrier when you left the press area. Barriers are there for a *reason*, creep. Five months in the cubes." Goodman signalled to a street Judge, who rushed over, grabbed the reporter by the arm and started hauling him away.

"Incredible!" The reporter shouted. "Kids, this is Dan Dandahn reporting to you live from his own arrest by the Chief Judge himself! I can't begin to tell you what an honour this is!"

Goodman took a last look at the camera before he boarded the H-wagon. The approval rating was now ninety-eight per cent. *I can live with that*, Goodman said to himself.

Three

Seamus "Shock" O'Shaughnessy allowed most of the other bikers to pull ahead of him. Some of the first-timers shot out in a mad dash to take the early lead, but the seasoned riders held back. The Mega-City 5000 wasn't about who'd started well, but who crossed the finish-line first.

Shock was leader of the Spacers, and it had been three years since a Spacer had won the race. Last year and the year before, the Mutants had taken first place. Shock was determined that was not going to happen again.

To his left, riding parallel and noticeably not paying him any attention, was his counterpart in the Mutants, Napoleon Neapolitan, last year's winner. For months the media had been whipping up a storm about the rivalry between Shock and Napoleon, chiefly fuelled by the teams' own publicity departments.

Now it all came down to today. Napoleon was by far the bookies' favourite at three-to-one-on:

a citizen putting down three credits would win one. Shock was at five-to-two-on, slightly more attractive odds for the punters. The big money was on the independent riders. Gavin Sable was the public's golden child, known to be a dependable but inexperienced rider. Most of the bookies were offering twenty-to-one-against on Sable. Shock had heard of a man in MegWest who'd sold his apartment and almost all of his belongings to raise one hundred thousand credits. He'd put it all on Gavin Sable in the hope of winning two million.

By the end of the race, that man was going to disappointed as well as broke and homeless. The winner of this year's Mega-City 5000 would be either a Mutant or a Spacer. They had the numbers, and they had the skill.

The Spacers and the Mutants had been rival gangs since before the atomic wars, their history predating Mega-City One by decades. Initially, there had also been another two major biker gangs vying for control of the east coast of America, but the Angels had been hunted down and wiped out by the Highwaymen after a long and particularly bloody feud, and then in turn they'd been destroyed by the Mutants and the Spacers working together.

But that alliance had been tenuous at best, and had only lasted a few years. No one remembered what had sparked the current animosity—the original antagonists had been killed long ago—but they all understood that the gangs were enemies.

Since the rise of the Judges, all of the city's biker gangs had drastically curtailed their activities. The Spacers and the Mutants had, separately, officially "gone legit." They hired publicity agents and lawyers, marketing people and managers. They presented themselves as family-friendly clubs and associations—the Mutants once successfully sued a news channel that had referred to them as a gang—and they held membership drives and charity runs. They turned up to protest the closing of hospitals, and to support liberal politicians. They made a lot of noise about unfair treatment whenever one of their members was arrested, unless there was no doubt the member was guilty, in which case they publicly thanked the Judges for rooting out the "undesirable elements that give the rest of us a bad name."

But in the shadows, the gangs were as vicious and territorial as ever. They used knives to settle scores, because bullets made too much noise and were too easy to trace. They dealt drugs and weapons, they carried out hits for hire, they ran protection rackets and gambling dens, kidnapped children of wealthy families, organised riots at public gatherings, fenced stolen goods, grabbed citizens off the streets and smuggled them out of the city and sold them into slavery.

The general public knew little of that. Most of the citizens of Mega-City One regarded the Muties and the Spacers in the same way they regarded enthusiasts of other hobbies, like the Judge-spotters and the sky-surfers, the fatties and the hair-collectors and the cereal-commercial re-enactors.

DREDD'S LAWMASTER PURRED to a stop outside the Funex Eaterie in Bevis Wetzel Plaza. Already, ten Lawmasters were present, and as Dredd climbed down from his bike, a med-wagon rose swiftly into the air, the flashing red and blue lights competing with the glow from the neon sign above the diner's door.

The three Judges standing outside the diner glanced at him as he approached, then turned back to resume their conversation.

Dredd didn't care for that. Two Judges had been murdered: these men should be on full alert, not squandering their time in pointless speculation. He strode up to them. "What's the situation?"

Judge Perry—an older man, somewhere in his late thirties, with grey stubble on his chin—looked him up and down, sizing him up. Dredd liked that even less. "Dredd. Sector Chief wants you. Inside."

The diner's doors opened as Dredd stepped up to them, and a med-Judge pushing a laden body-slab ushered him inside. "Took your time. Mendillo's in the kitchen." The corpse on the slab was draped in a standard-issue body-sheet—red, so that the blood didn't show if it seeped through—but it was clear from the outline that much of its head was missing.

The inside of the diner was a slaughterhouse. Blood dripped from the ceiling fixtures, covered the walls and windows in intricate arcs, was smeared across the tiled floor and the plastichrome furniture, and ran in thick rivulets down the glass display stands. To Dredd's right, three teams of med-Judges were frantically working to save bullet-riddled citizens, while around them forensic teams photographed and scanned every square centimetre. Dredd quickly counted the bodies and the gaps in the blood-pools: at least fifteen citizens dead. Possibly more: one corner booth was splattered with a collection of body parts that could have been three or four people.

A Judge noticed him looking toward the corner and said, "Concussion grenade, probably. Very little shrapnel, just hyper-compressed air. The grenade explodes in front of the target and directs the blast back. Anyone in the line of fire within about four metres is shredded." The Judge shook her head. "We've retrieved five thumbs from the mess already, so that's at least three victims with that one shot."

"Where would a citizen get hold of a shell like that?"

The Judge shrugged. "Beats the hell out of me. They haven't been manufactured since the war, and they're pretty unstable. That's why no one makes them any more: they have a tendency to spontaneously explode all on their own. I remember back in '71, when I was assigned to Texas City. A guy found a dozen of them and thought they'd make nice paperweights. He gave them out to his friends. Man, *that* was messy. Four of them exploded on the same day. We thought it was a terrorist attack. Took us ages to track down the rest of them."

In the diner's kitchen, Sector Chief Daniel Mendillo looked on as another Judge was interviewing a young woman. She trembled as Dredd entered, and tugged tighter on the blanket around her shoulders.

"He came in shootin'," the witness said. "I never bin so scared in my life!"

"Can you describe him?" the Judge asked.

Dredd said, "She can't. She's lying. Opportunist, hoping for air-time on the networks or compensation from the diner."

Mendillo—a short, stocky man with grey hair and heavy bags under his eyes—turned to face Dredd. "What?"

"Perp didn't come in shooting," Dredd said. "Positions of the bodies, fallen shell-casings and bullet-holes in the walls show that he was already inside before he opened fire. He shot his way *out* of the diner, not in. Suggest you book her for obstruction and order a psych-eval."

The interviewing Judge took a deep breath and let it out slowly. "Listen, kid, don't tell me my job, okay? I've been doing this since before you were born. Witnesses often confuse the order of events. She—"

"You seen the room out there?" Dredd asked. "Perp had two weapons besides the grenade. One with large calibre rounds, explosive tips. Probably a point-seven-six recoilless. Standard mag contains ten rounds. Used that first, took head-shots. When he ran dry, he switched to a high-velocity handgun. Gut-shots, chest-shots."

"I don't see what *any* of that's got to do with the veracity of the witness's statement."

"There's no blood on her," Dredd said.

Mendillo sighed through gritted teeth. "Stomm. He's right. Get her out of here, Carney. Just... Just throw her out. There's more than enough to worry about without having to book her too."

Judge Carney took the woman by the arm and wouldn't look Dredd in the eye as he manoeuvred her around Dredd toward the doorway.

Mendillo began, "Dredd, this concerns you because—"

Dredd interrupted. "Hold it." He turned and called after Judge Carney. "The *other* way, Carney. Take her out through the back. Don't contaminate the crime scene any further. And if you want my advice"—this was directed to Mendillo as much as Carney—

"if you're not going to charge her, you'll put her somewhere secure until the scene has been released. The networks pay well for early inside scoops."

"Do it," Mendillo said. "Thirty-six hours at least."

Wordlessly, Carney led the woman out through the back door. Dredd and Mendillo watched them go, then Mendillo said, "Just want to check. You're Joe, not Rico?"

Dredd nodded.

"Good. I called in Judge Amber Ruiz to head up this investigation—she's on the way—and she requested you. You answer to her. Understood?"

"Yes, sir."

Mendillo took another deep breath, then exhaled quickly. "All right. Here's the situation. Judges Collins and Pendleton were on patrol nearby, responded to the shooting. Perp took them both out. They were good Judges. Knew them personally: Pendleton and I were in the Academy together. So I want this drokker found. I don't care what it takes. Got that?"

"Understood."

"Ruiz will fill in the blanks. Until she gets here, touch nothing and keep your mouth shut." He moved toward the door, then stopped and looked back. "And stay clear of the other Judges. Don't do to them what you just did to Carney. They're pissed enough with you as it is without you showing them up and making it worse."

Dredd stiffened at that. "Sir?"

Mendillo ran his hands through his greying hair. "Ruiz will explain... Look, I'm not blaming you. I've been a Judge long enough to know how things sometimes go down. But we lost two of our own today. That generates its own special kind of anger, and angry Judges make mistakes."

From the doorway of the diner's kitchen, Dredd watched as the forensic team and med-Judges went about their work. Occasionally, dark glances were thrown in his direction, but he refused to let that bother him. Instead, he concentrated on their work and resisted the urge to point out errors.

One of his classmates at the Academy, Judge Hunt, had for a year or so enjoyed a lame running joke: "Joe's the only cadet who'd report himself for infractions." That came to an abrupt end when Dredd reported another cadet for fooling around with a Lawgiver: the cadet had pulled his gun on Hunt, pretending to arrest him for "being a total dweebo." Their tutor had reprimanded the cadet, taken the Lawgiver from him, and subsequently found that the cadet had forgotten to remove the live ammunition from the gun after target practice. One accidental squeeze on the trigger, and Hunt would have been on his way to Resyk. That had been in year three at the Academy, when the cadets were eight years old.

Now, Dredd counted three minor errors by the Judges investigating the crime scene. They were mistakes that, in all likelihood, wouldn't make any difference to the case, but it was all Dredd could do not to point them out. One tech-Judge was so focussed on his work that he didn't notice he was standing on a fragment of shell-casing. In the doorway, a street Judge was looking into the diner, watching the proceedings, instead of keeping an eye on the street, and just outside, Judge Perry—the older man who'd confronted Dredd on his way in—was unconsciously opening and closing one of his belt-pouches as he talked to his colleagues, an indication of agitation and nerves. Judges were trained not to display such signs: perps could pick up on them.

As he watched, another Lawmaster pulled up, stopping the required distance from the doors. Judge Ruiz dismounted and greeted Perry and the others with a nod. She removed her helmet as she strode through the doorway.

Dredd was pleased to see Ruiz take a moment to examine the scene before she entered fully—even looking up, as Dredd had done, to check the ceiling—then she carefully stepped around the gore as she made her way toward him. Ruiz was thirty-four, average height with a strong build. She kept her head shaved and her face clear—some other female Judges looked like fashion models from the neck up: trendy hair-styles, make-up, even ear- or nose-rings

"Joe Dredd. It's been a few years. I heard you got the full eagle. Never doubted it. How have you been?"

Dredd wasn't quite sure how he was supposed to answer that. "I've been a Judge" didn't feel like the right response, but nothing else came to mind. He resorted to, "A little confused as to why *I've* been called here, and why some of the Judges seem to think I've done something wrong."

"Mendillo didn't tell you?" Ruiz asked. "No, of course he didn't. Never was comfortable with confronting other Judges with bad news." She smiled at that. "You mightn't think it to look at him, but when he was on the streets, he was one of the toughest Judges in the city."

"What is this about?"

"Down to business. Of course. You haven't changed much, have you?" She stepped past him into the diner's kitchen. "Close the door behind you... All right. Joe, the perp has been identified as Percival Chalk. That name mean anything to you?"

"I remember him."

"Good. Then you'll remember how long his sentence was."

"Five years. Some thought it a little harsh at the time, but as I recall you backed me up on that."

Ruiz set her helmet down on a chair, then crossed her arms and leaned back against a work-counter. She stared at him. "I did. So you remember how long ago that was?"

"Five years and two months. So Chalk served his time and now he's turned to murder?"

"Right. But we don't yet know *why*. That's what you and I have to find out."

Dredd nodded slowly. "And Sector Chief Mendillo wants you to take the lead because you were the only Judge present when he was first arrested. Where do we start?"

"We start by getting something straight. What happened five years ago... Well, someone screwed up, and scuttlebutt is blaming you. Word is spreading that Chalk is a Judge-killer and that's down to your mistake."

Dredd considered that. "I'm not aware of making any mistakes."

"They're saying that your judgement was flawed." Ruiz kept her eyes fixed on him, not blinking. "Do you understand what that means, Joe?"

"I understand. And I deny the accusation. My judgement was sound."

"That's what I thought then," Ruiz said. "Now, I'm not so sure."

THE CURSED EARTH
2075 A.D.

Four

"HOT-DOG RUN" WAS the informal name given to out-of-city excursions by cadet Judges. They were intended to get them used to working as a team, handling their Lawmasters over difficult terrain, and dispensing instant justice: aspects of judging that they were taught at the Academy, but lessons were no substitute for actual experience.

The year-eleven cadets, under the supervision of Judge Amber Ruiz, undertook a gruelling two-day ride—seventeen hours each day on the bikes—deep into the Cursed Earth south-west of Mega-City One.

Night had fallen by the time they reached their destination: the outskirts of Eminence, one of the many ruined-and-rebuilt pre-war towns that still blighted the landscape of what was once North America. Judge Ruiz ordered a dismount. "Town centre's ten kilometres west. We camp here for the night. You know what to do."

The sixteen-year-old cadets arranged their Lawmasters in a circle, facing out: the bikes' sensors would alert them of the approach of anything larger than a rad-rat.

Cadets Hunt, Wagner and Gibson were assigned to prepare the rations, while Joe and Rico Dredd took first patrol on the perimeter.

Once they were out of sight of the others, Rico said, "Hold up a sec, Joe." He turned his back on his brother, unzipped the fly on his uniform and emptied his bladder into the darkness. "Ahh... *Man*, that feels good! Nothing better than peeing in the open air, right?"

"Sure," Joe said.

"What about you? You've got to be bursting."

"I'll wait until you're done. Can't both be distracted at the same time."

When Rico was finished, Dredd took his turn at relieving himself.

"So what's this about, you reckon?" Rico asked as they resumed patrol. "We here at random, or has Ruiz got something planned?"

"Guess we'll find out soon enough."

"Yeah." Rico stopped, and put his hand on Joe's arm. "Smell that? Woodsmoke. Not more than a day old. We're not alone out here."

"I know. Saw fresh tracks in the dust a few kilometres before we stopped. Three vehicles. Thread impressions were deep, the edges clean. That means—"

Rico finished for him: "New tyres. Which tells us they're probably not muties. Muties never have anything new. The vehicles are from the city." He walked on. "Guess we could always *ask* Ruiz what's happening."

Joe followed after his brother. "She won't tell us until she thinks we need to know."

"True." Rico turned around to face Joe, walking backward ahead of him. "How do you think we're doing? Overall, I mean. Not just here."

"Okay, I figure." Joe shrugged. "We're still top of the class."

"Guess we have Daddy to thank for that. Good genetic material." Rico slowed to let Joe catch up with him, and they continued walking side-by-side. After a few minutes, Rico said, "Ever wonder why they made *two* of us? I'm thinking it was one of those eggs-in-one-basket things. Better to have two of us in case one dies."

Joe said, "I don't think about it much. We are who we are. Although..." He paused.

"Although what?"

"I sometimes wonder if maybe we're not the *only* two. If they could make two, why not four? Or eight? *Any* number?"

"Maybe they did, and we're the only two who survived."

"Or maybe there's others and they just haven't told us about them," Joe said.

"Could be," Rico said, then shrugged. "I'll tell you *this*, bro... I am not going to be a carbon copy of anyone else. I'm going to be my own man. Way I see it, Fargo's DNA is a foundation, not a blueprint. You get me?"

"Sure, yeah," Joe said, though he didn't have much enthusiasm for the subject. Sometimes, yes, but not now. Not when they were on duty. He stopped walking and pointed to the ground, almost invisible in the darkness. "Feel that?"

"Asphalt under the sand," Rico said. "Cracked and melted. So what?"

"So the sand is thinner here. Something's displaced it." He stopped, unclipped the flashlight from his belt, and crouched down. "Get down here, in front of me. Shield the light in case anyone's watching."

When Rico hunkered down, Joe switched on the flashlight. "More tyre-tracks. Very fresh. Deep, too. Wide wheel-base... Wide enough for a '71 or '72 Chameleon. Vehicle of choice for heavy-duty work in the Cursed Earth. Unladen weight is, what, about two thousand kilograms, right?" Joe turned and looked at his own footprints behind him, then ran some quick mental calculations. "Depth of the impressions suggest it's carrying at least another two thousand kilos. That's twenty-six, maybe thirty people... But you wouldn't easily get thirty people onto the back of a Chameleon. Whatever their cargo is, it's heavy."

"Hmph," Rico said. "You actually worked that out in your head? Joe, you've *got* to get a life."

Joe switched off the flashlight and stood up. "Heading *out* of town. So... new tyres, vehicle's four years old at most, heavily laden. Scavengers."

"You reckon?"

"Best guess."

"Makes sense," Rico said. "These old towns hold a lot of treasure, if you know where to look."

"We should mention this to Judge Ruiz."

"Figure she already knows."

AT DAWN, THE cadets woke. Joe and Rico had had four hours' sleep—more than enough to keep them going for the rest of the day.

As they were consuming their morning rations, Ruiz said, "Pudney and Slate, you stick with the bikes. Run a full diagnostic on every one of them. And do them consecutively—couple of years back a bunch of cadets in your position decided to run all the diagnostics at once, to save time." She paused. "The good news is that one of them actually *survived* the attack that they didn't see coming.

"Gibson and the Dredds, you're with me, and we're on foot. Hunt and Wagner, you're joining McManus and Ellard on perimeter. Comms are patchy out here, and we don't know who's listening in—only use the radios if you have no other choice."

Cadet Gibson said, "Sir, if someone's listening, they won't be able to unscramble the signals. We use a 9-7-5 encryption matrix protocol. It's impossible to crack that without the keycodes."

Ruiz gave him a withering glance. "Anyone?"

Hunt said, "If someone *is* listening, doesn't matter whether they can understand what we're saying. They'll know that we're here."

"Exactly," Ruiz said. She looked around at the cadets. "Eminence is home to at least three hundred muties. They'll mostly steer clear of us if they know we're coming, so we leave them alone unless they present an immediate danger, and that's highly unlikely. The danger we *are* facing is a band of gun-runners. Our sources tell us they've been stockpiling weapons in preparation for smuggling them into Mega-City One."

"How many perps?" Joe asked.

"Exact number is unknown, but we can expect at least ten perps present, possibly a lot more. Any more questions?"

Everyone looked at Joe. He didn't disappoint them. "What's the source of the intel?"

"Local informant," Ruiz said. "The gun-runners have been making their exchanges in Eminence for the past three years. They assemble here every few months, and when their deals are done they celebrate. They run riot through the town. The inhabitants are sick of it—life out here is hard enough as it is."

Rico said, "Figure our best approach is to wait until the deal is done. Easier to pick them off when they're drunk or stoned."

"Disagree," Joe said. "Gun-deals on this scale will have the weapons crated until the money changes hands. We stop them *before* the deal. Afterwards, we'll be facing perps who are drunk and *armed*."

"Joe's right," Ruiz said. "Anything else? No? Good. Hunt, go find McManus and Ellard, brief them. The rest of you, stay alert. You are not in the Academy now. There are people—and things—out here that can and will kill you without hesitation. You kill them first."

2080 A.D.

Five

DREDD AND RUIZ stood on either side of the door to Percival Chalk's apartment. It was an old building, constructed in the late twentieth century, one of the few of its era still standing in the city. A crumbling, damp relic of the days of plasterboard and timber, of breezeblocks and mortar.

Ruiz raised her Lawgiver and quietly said to Dredd, "If he's here, perp's likely to be wearing armour. Set to AP."

Dredd shook his head. "Disagree. Walls are thin—armour-piercing rounds would pass straight through."

Ruiz considered that. "Good thinking. Standard Execution rounds." She rapped on the old wooden door with the butt of her gun. "Judges! Open up! You've got ten seconds!" She waited a cursory two seconds before nodding to Dredd. "Do it."

The left side of the door showed half a dozen locks: Dredd took a step back and lashed out at the right side of the door with his boot, putting all of his weight into the kick. As he'd figured, the door's heavy locks held, but the hinges—just steel plates screwed into the wooden doorframe—gave. The door crashed inward.

Even before the splintered door crashed onto the thin, faded carpet inside, Dredd launched himself forward, spun in the air and landed on his back in the centre of the room, Lawgiver clenched in his right hand.

"Empty," Ruiz said from the doorway. "Figured as much." She looked down at Dredd as she stepped over the fragments of the door. "What sort of a move is that?"

Dredd rolled onto his side and pushed himself to his feet. "Situation like this, perps don't expect to have to shoot *down* at a Judge."

He looked around the small apartment. The room was no more than five metres square, and contained nothing but a narrow, unadorned bed, an old sinkstove and, against one wall, a rack of empty cupboards with the doors long since removed.

"Doesn't even look lived in," Ruiz said. "We're not going to find much. What do you think? The parole board secured this place for Chalk upon his release, and it's the address he used when registering for welfare. He probably never showed up."

"He was here." Dredd sniffed the air. "Cheap deodorant." He leaned over the bed's bare mattress and inhaled. "Reasonably fresh—didn't sleep here recently."

"So he was staying with a friend. Unlikely he could have afforded a hotel or flophouse." Ruiz looked around once more. "OK. Call it in."

Dredd activated his helmet's radio. "Dredd to Control."

"Control. Go ahead."

"Send a forensic crew to my location. I want a deep clean, full DNA sweep." He turned in a slow circle as he talked, taking in the entire apartment. "I want the IDs of everyone who's been in this apartment in the past two months."

"Wilco, Dredd. Despatching a team to you now. Be advised that traffic restrictions will delay their arrival."

Ruiz asked, "So what's your reading on this, Dredd?"

"Used the place for mail and storage, maybe," Dredd said. "He carried two guns at the diner. The handgun could be concealed anywhere, but the point-seven-six recoilless is a lot harder to hide."

A voice from the hallway shouted, "Hey! The drokk's going on here?"

Dredd turned to see a well-dressed, middle-aged man come to a halt as he stepped through the doorway.

"Oh." The man's face drained of colour. "Great. Judges. What's... What's the problem?"

"Identify yourself," Dredd said.

"I'm Zeddy. Zederick D'Annunzio. I own the building. I live in the penthouse. I heard the noise and..." The man looked down at the door. "Who's gonna pay for *that*?"

"What's your relationship with the tenant of this apartment?" Ruiz asked.

"Who, Chalk?" D'Annunzio shrugged. "Just business. I've never met the guy. He was an ex-con, like about half my tenants. The deal was set up by the parole board. He leaves the rent money in an envelope under my door, first of every month. Always on time, too, unlike most of the spugwits in this place." He smirked. "Heh, got a funny story about that, actually. This one time—"

"You know where Chalk is now?" Dredd asked.

"Uh, no." The man shrugged again. "Like I said, never met him. It's like that a lot around here. Like, the guy directly upstairs? Been here gettin' on for three years, only met him twice. They keep to themselves. Lotsa ex-cons are like that, y'know? A few years in the cubes screws them up so much they just kinda shut down when they get out. Like, they become institutionalised, is that the word?"

Ruiz said, "Just answer the questions, citizen. Do you know whether Percival Chalk had any contact with the other tenants?"

"Couldn't tell you, Judge." D'Annunzio took a step back and narrowed his eyes. "Wait... What, is he *dead* or something?"

"Not yet," Dredd said.

Ruiz said, "You're about to be audited, citizen. We'll need to see all of your rentbooks and tax receipts."

The man's face sagged. "Right. That'll be tricky. See, you know how it is. There's taxes and there's *taxes*, right? I mean, I'm no shirker—I pay my way. But sometimes when it comes to people like this guy, who pay in cash, sometimes I kinda..." He stopped, took a deep breath and let it out slowly. "How much trouble am I in?"

"More than enough. Your tenant Percival Chalk is wanted for multiple homicides, including the murder of two street Judges." Ruiz moved closer toward the owner, passing in front of the window. "Any information you can give that might aid in the apprehension of—"

Judge Ruiz was falling forward even as Dredd reacted to the slight *crack* from the glass in the window.

He grabbed her arm and jerked her toward him, dropping at the same time. "Sniper! Down!"

Zederick D'Annunzio said, "What?" and there was a second *crack* from the window, and a crimson bloom appeared in D'Annunzio's thigh. He dropped to the floor, screaming.

Dredd flipped Ruiz over, checked the wound. The bullet had pierced the Judge's back, just below her right shoulder-blade. "Straight through." He activated his helmet radio. "Dredd to control. Judge down, my location. Immediate assistance required. Sniper, most likely on the roof or upper floors of the building opposite. Get spy-cams on that location. Am about to engage pursuit." He reached out and grabbed hold of D'Annunzio's collar, dragged him over to Ruiz. "Citizen on site will administer first aid to Judge Ruiz."

Trembling, D'Annunzio stared at Dredd. "What?"

Dredd was already getting to his feet. "Seal her wounds until the medics get here. She dies, that audit is definitely going to happen."

"But I don't know how to—"

"Just don't let her bleed out. Stick your fingers in the bullet holes if you have to."

D'Annunzio shouted something else, but Dredd didn't hear it: he was already out of the apartment and pounding down the hallway.

Dredd didn't have time to wait for the elevator: he raced down the narrow stairway, taking the steps four at a time. "What do you have for me, Control?"

"Med-team's on the way. ETA six minutes. Spy-cams deployed. Back-up's converging on your location, four helmets. All we can spare."

Dredd vaulted over a rail and landed on the level below. "Not good enough, Control!"

"Best we can do right now, Dredd."

On the ground floor, Dredd raced toward the main door. It was one of the building's newer features. Heavy, bullet-proof security glass. Opening the door would mean slowing down, and every second lost greatly reduced his chance of catching the sniper.

Without breaking stride, he thumbed his Lawgiver to Hi-Ex and fired in one swift motion. The intact door was blasted from its frame by the high-explosive shell. It soared across the quiet street and crashed heavily into the wall of the building opposite.

Dredd raced through the still-burning doorframe and out into the street.

The building across the street was a newer block, ten storeys high, a high-rent block of the sort that attracted wealthy senior citizens: heavy security, fully-automated systems.

"Control—Dredd. Immediately lock every door in Ralph Bellamy Block, freeze the elevators. Track my position—unlock and open each door as I approach, close and lock after me."

"Acknowledged. Alerting block's manager and owner."

The main door opened in front of Dredd and he raced through, his heavy footfalls immediately muffled by the thick carpeting. As he pounded up the stairs, he figured this would be a fruitless chase: the sniper would be long gone by the time he reached the roof. A block like this, the sniper would have bribed or threatened the manager or one of the tenants to gain access. The doors and windows were totally—

He abruptly stopped on the stairs between the eighth and ninth floors, turned and raced back down, feeling like a year-three cadet. "Control—release the block. Perp's not here."

"Wilco, Dredd. Do you require a forensic sweep?"

"Unnecessary, Control. He was never here."

Dredd reached the street just as two Lawmasters screeched to a stop outside Percival Chalk's building. The Judges were Hayden and Oakes, each at least twice Dredd's age.

"After me," Dredd shouted as he passed them, running back into the dilapidated block. As he raced up the stairs he called over his shoulder, "Fifth floor, apartment 20. Judge wounded, citizen attending. Medics en route."

He barely had time to hear, "Who the drokk does *he* think he—?" from Hayden before his own thundering footsteps drowned out the Judge's voice.

He heard movement above him, and unclipped a set of cuffs from his belt as he ran. He passed a young woman on the stairs, slapping the cuffs on her without slowing down or explaining what he was doing: the odds were good that she wasn't the sniper, but he wasn't about to take that risk.

Another three flights, then he was shouldering his way through a thin wooden door and out onto the building's roof.

Nothing.

A collection of rusting old lawn furniture, power and TV cables snaking from one side of the roof to another, half a dozen skylights spattered with bird-droppings, and a small plastic cage holding a pet rat—but no sniper.

Dredd quickly circumnavigated the roof, and counted four places where the sniper could have climbed down onto the neighbouring buildings. Then he crossed back to the front edge of the roof, and found the spot where the sniper had lain in wait.

He got as close to the spot as he could without disturbing any evidence the sniper might have left behind, then peered down across the street to the windows of Ralph Bellamy Block. The glass was bullet-proof, and as reflective as a mirror. With the right ammunition, any decent sniper could have made the shot: the glass opposite would reflect the window of Chalk's apartment, and all the sniper had to do was lie in wait for someone in the apartment to get close enough to the window.

Dredd knew that if he examined the correct window opposite, there would be a tell-tale mark on the glass.

He returned to Chalk's apartment to see the owner, Zederick D'Annunzio, sitting on the bed—his arms and hands covered in blood—as Judge Oakes crouched over Ruiz, pressing a medi-patch to the wound on her back.

D'Annunzio looked up at him, his face drained of all colour except for fresh bruising around his left eye. He said nothing.

"What's her status?" Dredd asked Oakes.

"She's holding on." The Judge turned around to look at Dredd. "You. *That* figures. This creep says you told him to stick his fingers in the wounds."

"He's right. I did."

"Huh." Oakes glanced at D'Annunzio. "My apologies, citizen. Didn't *look* like you were helping her."

"Pulled me offa her and the other one kicked me in the *face*," D'Annunzio said.

"Where *is* the other one?" Dredd asked.

"Hayden's checking the block opposite. You called in a sniper, right? Block opposite's the only place where he could get a shot at this sort of angle."

A med-team arrived as Dredd was explaining how the sniper had made the shot. The three-man team assessed Ruiz's wounds. "Reckon she'll make it. Bullet was through-and-through. Not much damage—must have been low velocity. What about the cit?"

"Patch him up here," Dredd said. "I'm not done with him."

Six

Seamus "Shock" O'Shaughnessy pulled back on the throttle of his Blenderbike and risked a quick glance behind him. Vavavoom Grupp, lead rider of the Bearangel Clan, was still right on his tail, breathing his exhaust fumes, just as she had been for the past eighty kilometres.

The screen mounted between the handlebars of Shock's bike told him that he was in twenty-first place, right where his race-planner told him he should to be at this stage. In sixteen kilometres he'd move to overtake Arthur Dekko—a Mutie, but not a serious challenge—in twentieth, then sit on that position for another hour or so.

This was Shock's fourth time running the 5000. And he was determined that this time he was going to finish better than second place.

Last year had been so close—two seconds between him and that drokker Napoleon Neapolitan, and less than a minute from the finish-line Neapolitan's bike sputtered and wavered, slowed down enough for Shock to narrow the gap.

And then, just as the front edge of Shock's lead spoiler came into line with Neapolitan's, the drokker had laughed and surged forward. After a thirty-nine-hundred-kilometre race, he beat Shock by four metres.

For Shock—and for most of the racers—it wasn't just the adoration of countless fans, or the sense of glory that came with being the winner of the Mega-City 5000: It was the money. Napoleon Neapolitan had signed fifteen sponsorship deals before he'd even walked to the podium to collect his trophy.

The only sponsor who'd approached Shock was for a company that specialised in certain medical treatments for men and whose motto was "Sometimes, being in second place is *important*!" Shock had signed the deal anyway—money is money, and twenty thousand credits was significantly more money than he felt his pride was worth, even after the city took its sixty per cent tax—but if he'd been *first*... Rumour had it that Neapolitan had earned over two million creds in the past year.

Right now, Neapolitan was in sixtieth place, hanging back with the core of the Muties' team. Shock's own crew, the Spacers, were scattered from fifth position—Jaunty Monty, Shock's number-two rider—all the way back to last place. That was Rennie The Wrench, the team's on-road mechanic. Rennie's oversized bike didn't have a hope in hell of winning, but he was a mechanical genius and his bike carried emergency repair equipment that might just help a stranded Spacer get over the line.

A kilometre ahead of Shock, a cluster of five riders slowed as they approached Carlo Imperato Block. They veered to the left edge of the cordoned-off road, almost close enough to brush against the straining fingertips of the thousands of cheering on-lookers crammed up against the temporary barriers.

Shock eased off a little on the throttle, dropping his speed down to two-fifty. He'd studied the route—he knew what was coming next.

Arthur Dekko either hadn't studied, or he'd forgotten, or he just plain didn't comprehend what he was riding into.

Shock's screen showed the Mutie zooming to the right, overtaking the slowing five-man cluster, and Shock could picture him grinning at them, maybe even giving them the finger as he passed.

Shock dropped his speed a little more. If Dekko had been paying attention at all, he'd have noticed that the crowd lining the street ahead was denser. He'd have spotted the dozen TV cameras hovering over the track. He'd have realised that the wise rider slows way the drokk down if the audience looks a little too eager for a wipe-out.

Brown Clancy, three positions behind Shock, contacted him over the radio: "You seein' this, Shock?"

"Yeah, I see it."

"Should we warn him?"

Shock suppressed a laugh. "Hell, no."

It was too late anyway: Arthur Dekko's powerful Yomama 500 roared past the slowing riders, arcing around them at almost three hundred kilometres an hour.

It was a little after ten in the morning, and Weather Control promised a clear, bright day. The morning sun reflected off the curved roof of the Drunkatorium, and Dekko emerged from the shadow of Carlo Imperato block and rode straight into the glare.

Shock had ridden this sector many times, and more than once he'd been dazzled by the sudden blinding reflection. At the right time of the day, the building's curved, mirror-like roof channelled the sunlight into a narrow beam.

Arthur Dekko screamed. His bike wavered. The hovering TV cameras crowded closer, jostled one another for the best angle. A hush of anticipation fell over the crowd.

Throughout the city, two hundred million people edged closer to their TV and Tri-D screens to get a better look at Dekko's bike as it careened back toward the right side of the street.

Many of those who watched later argued strongly that it was the Crash of the Race, and even the usually distracted and rambling pundits in Channel Epsilon's commentary box had nothing but praise for the spectacular manner in which Arthur Dekko's life came to an end.

Shock switched his bike's screen to a TV channel. He couldn't do anything to circumvent Dekko's fate, so he figured he might as well enjoy the show.

The bike scraped along the barrier for a few seconds, with the wildly blinking and still screaming rider desperately clinging on. His protective suit almost instantly lost the battle of friction with the rough, pitted surface of the barrier. From his right calf, Dekko lost a good deal of skin and muscle tissue—which, naturally, later became the focus of a lawsuit between two overeager souvenir hunters—then he was momentarily able to regain control and steer the Yomama away from the barrier.

And that was when he passed through the blinding beam of reflected light for a second time.

The powerful bike slammed against the barrier on the road's left side and ricocheted back into the centre of the road, leaving Dekko's left arm behind, torn off at the elbow.

Half-blinded, with only one arm, Dekko completely lost control and the bike tumbled to its side and into a long, slowly-spinning skid that ground the rest of Arthur's body into a smeared red paste.

Long before the remains of the bike had scraped to a stop, Shock and a dozen other riders had passed it, the wheels of their own machines painting crimson trails of blood and gore for another kilometre.

The screen on Shock's bike showed a close-up of Dekko's still-twitching left hand, and one of Channel Epsilon's commentators observed, "Oh, now that's a *bad* crash."

His fellow commentator agreed: "Indeed it is, Peter, and, you know, it puts me in mind of Griswold Glennon's little tumble two years ago. Happened much in the same manner, though that one was considerably less fatal."

"Oh, that's right, I remember that, Ted. How *is* old Griswold doing these days?"

"Still can't cough without wetting himself, Peter."

THE CURSED EARTH
2075 A.D.

Seven

JUDGE AMBER RUIZ listened to the cadets converse as she led them into the small town. How they interacted with each other—especially in situations like this, where they were in an unfamiliar and possibly hostile environment—was a good indicator of how they would measure up as Judges.

"I really don't like the way these freaks are looking at us," Cadet Gibson said as they walked along the centre of Eminence's main street.

To Ruiz's left, a woman with what looked to be a record-breaking case of acne stood with her mouth agape as they passed. She was shirtless, wearing only a ragged pair of old y-fronts, and every visible centimetre of her skin was covered in swollen red and yellow pustules. As Ruiz glanced in her direction, a thumb-sized blister on the side of the woman's nose split, leaking its viscous contents past her blood-encrusted chapped lips and into her open mouth.

"Jovus..." Rico muttered. "You see that?"

Still with her attention on the Judge and the Cadets, the woman noisily cleared her throat, then leaned over and spat a globule of thick green phlegm and custard-yellow pus into the dirt.

Grud, that's *one that's going to stay with me*, Ruiz thought. Aloud, she said, "Eyes *front*, Cadets. No ogling the women. Judges are meant to be celibate."

"That wouldn't be much of a hardship out here," Rico said.

Ruiz glanced back to see him nudge Gibson with his elbow. "Scale of one to ten, how desperate would you have to be to—?"

Gibson shuddered. "Look at them, living in their own filth and grubbing around in the dirt for food. Seriously, why do we even allow these ugly drokkers to breed?"

"Allow?" Ruiz asked. "Cadet, they're *people*, not animals. They deserve our sympathy, not contempt."

Gibson scoffed. "Well, if they're people, why aren't they allowed in Mega-City One or Mega-City Two?"

Rico said, "Because the normal cits don't want to have to look at them. The muties'd end up in ghettoes and that would cause more problems than just keeping them out. They're better off out here."

Ruiz sighed. "Joe?"

Joe nodded. "Rico's right. But that's not the whole story. The law banning them from the cities was originally passed to keep out anyone who'd contracted radiation poisoning during the war. If they'd been allowed to mingle with the non-contaminated citizens, the fear was that millions would have been infected."

"Correct," Ruiz said. "Ionising radiation generates free radicals—unpaired particles that can warp the structure of DNA and break down cells. That can cause the body to decay, or tumours to form. There's evidence to suggest that, prior to the war, President Booth's geneticists developed a virus that could boost human resistance to radiation. The stories say that virus worked, after a fashion. Fewer of the infected died, but it screwed up the survivors' DNA so much that they... Well, you can see for yourself. What's important to remember, Gibson, is that these people didn't choose to live like this. They just chose to *live*." Ruiz suppressed a smile: on her last hot-dog run into the Cursed Earth, she'd said pretty much the same thing.

Those cadets had been impressed. *These* three didn't seem to have even noticed. Rico and Gibson were still glancing sidelong at the bare-chested woman, and Joe... Well, you could never tell what was going on there. Some of Joe's instructors had once unofficially voted him "Most likely to crack under pressure and kill the rest of us as we sleep." Others felt that he would certainly graduate the Academy—his and Rico's test scores were exemplary—but that he'd never be able to cut it as a street Judge. He didn't seem to have much in the way of empathy. As far as Joe was concerned, the Law was everything.

Part of Ruiz's mission on this run was to assess Joe and determine whether it would be better to steer him into one of the more technical departments. Forensics, maybe. He certainly had a good eye for detail, and his encyclopaedic memory would make him a great boon to that department.

Halfway along the street, a tall, slim man strode out to meet them. He wore an old-fashioned undertaker's coat—complete with tails—over a gaudy knitted sweater, and a leather flying cap with goggles that were now resting on his forehead.

"Got to be the Mayor," Ruiz said.

The man seemed perfectly normal at first glance, but as they neared him his stance looked awkward, and it took Ruiz a moment to realise that he had two knees on each leg.

She stopped two metres away from the Mayor, and nodded a greeting.

"We don't get many Judges around here. Welcome to Eminence, folks. Name's Genesis Faulder. Guess you could say I lead these people."

He extended his hand, and Ruiz shook it without hesitation.

"Judge Ruiz, Mega-City One. Heard you've been having some trouble. What can we do to help?"

Faulder peered past Ruiz. "These your boys? Fine looking lads." He pointed toward Joe. "How much do you want for that one? My eldest is about his age, and if all his parts are in working order, then—"

"They're not for sale," Ruiz said. "And they're not my sons. They're cadets." She smiled. "But you know that, don't you? This is all part of your small-town charm."

Mayor Faulder returned the grin. "It always helps to be underestimated by strangers, Judge." He tilted his head toward a large, store-fronted warehouse. "We can talk in my office. Your boys mind waiting out here?"

Judge Ruiz turned to the cadets. "Don't stray too far. Keep your eyes open. Try to avoid engaging the locals." She looked at Joe as she spoke, though he was the least likely to get into trouble.

She followed the Mayor into the store. It was packed with racks of canned goods, most of the cans having long since lost their labels.

"I'm the chief supplies officer as well as the Mayor," Faulder said. "And the banker. And I run the mail service." He stopped, and turned back to face her. "Hell, I'm the town doctor too, when I need to be. You can't survive out here without picking up a few skills." He jerked his thumb over his shoulder, toward the back of the store. "Office is back there. Come on through."

THE CADETS HAD been alone for less than five minutes when Gibson turned to Rico. "Want to check this place out? Joe'll stay here and keep watch, right?"

"We have *orders*," Joe said.

"Vague instructions, at best," Rico replied. "C'mon, a bit of freak-spotting won't hurt anyone." To Gibson, he said, "You see that guy on the way in who didn't have a head? Now, *that's* a mutation."

As they walked away, Joe heard Gibson say, "I once heard about a mutie woman who had two breasts."

"Two? So what's so odd about that?"

"One hanging out of each side of her neck, that's what."

Joe kept his expression neutral as he watched them leave. He wanted to argue with them that they should stay put, but it wouldn't do for cadets to be seen squabbling, even out here. Besides, they weren't technically breaking any rules.

He heard the sound of something scuffing on the ground behind him, and turned to see a small mutant boy lying face-down on an old skateboard as he pulled himself out of the mayor's store. The boy's legs trailed out behind him, boneless lumps of scabbed, filthy flesh that were barely recognisable as limbs. The door slammed shut behind the boy as he asked, "You a Judge?"

"Not yet," Joe replied. "I'm training to be one." He wasn't entirely sure where to look.

"I could be a Judge," the boy said. "Doesn't look hard, just tellin' people what to do all day."

"And making sure that they do it," Joe said. "Enforcing the law is considerably more work than just declaring it."

The boy nodded for a moment, then asked, "What?"

Before Joe could answer, the boy propped himself up on one elbow and with his free hand reached out towards Joe's boot. "How much for the boots? Them're good boots. I'll give you... six credits. I got the money back in the house. C'mon an' I'll—"

"The boots aren't for sale."

The boy looked up at Joe again. "Hey, wanna see sumpthin'? Sumpthin' *cool*?"

"No."

"All right, I'll *tell* you. It's a dead dog-vulture, down by the river." The boy scooted backwards a little. "No one else knows about it an' I was thinkin' we could go poke it with a *stick*."

"Not interested."

The boy hesitated for a moment, then said, "You'll *like* it. It's on the way ta where that old Judge's body is up on the cross. Yeah, some old fella came in a few months back an' he was tryna arrest Stumpy Nigel fer sumpthin', an' Stumpy's missus put a bullet in the Judge's back. They stringed him up an' left him ta die."

Joe stared down at him. "You telling the truth?"

"Sure, yeah. That's why I hadda ask if you was a Judge, on accounta you gotta different costume."

"It's a uniform, not a costume." Joe glanced at the door of the mayor's store, then said, "All right. Show me."

The boy grinned and began to propel himself down the street on his skateboard. Joe fell into step next to him.

"You're from the Meg, right? What's yer name?"

"Joe Dredd."

"I'm Lamb."

"That's... An unusual name."

"Yeah. When I was bornd the mayor ast my maw, 'Whatcha wanna call 'im?' and she said, 'Name him after his father,' an' then she passed out an' the mayor ast around who my paw was, an' someone teld him my paw was on the lam."

Lamb talked constantly as they made their way through the small town, but the further they travelled from the mayor's store, the quieter the boy became. They reached a crossroads, and Lamb inclined his head to the right. "We gotta go down this way to th' river. I'll hafta climb over the fence, so that's gonna be tricky an' you'll hafta help me."

Lamb scooted around the corner. "Normally, see, when I get to the fence I tie a rope around the board an' then I hafta drag it over when I get to the other side, unless I wanna crawl all the way to the gate, but that takes even longer. You can just throw it over for me. That'll save time." He grinned up at Joe. "An' you won't just keep the board or throw it away or anythin' like that, right? We're friends now, right?"

"Don't you have any other friends?" Joe asked.

"Sure, yeah. There's my *maw*, an'... an' my gramma, an' there's my half-sister Emily, but she's only three. Mosta the other kids in town don't liketa play with me 'cos I can't run." He stopped, and pointed ahead. "All right, there's the fence. We're nearly there."

The crude wooden fence was less than a metre high.

Joe crouched down next to the boy, grabbed him around the chest and lifted him over the fence, then scooped up the skateboard and climbed over.

Lamb laughed as he slithered back onto the board. "That was great! No one's ever lifted me before!" He began to propel himself down the gently-sloping riverbank. "Come on, I'll show you where the dog-vulture is. There's all, like, maggots an' beetles all over it. Crawlin' in its eyes and outta its mouth—it's really cool."

"I'd rather see the body of the Judge."

"Yeah, okay... Only, it's pretty *far* an' I'm not sposta go there an' I'm not even sposta *know* about it, I think, an'..."

"You're lying," Joe said. "Is there a dead Judge or not?"

Lamb looked down at the ground. "They tole me to get ridda you. They got *guns*." He looked up at Joe. "They beat up the lady Judge an' said they'd kill my maw if I didn't distrack you but *you* can stop them, can't you? You're nearly a *Judge*."

Joe felt the skin crawl on the back of his neck. "They're already here."

MEGA-CITY ONE
2080 A.D.

Eight

Zederick Marybeth D'Annunzio winced as the med-Judge poked a long, thin probe into the wound on his thigh.

"Through and through," the med-Judge said to Dredd. "No fragments, missed the bone. Some minor vessel damage... Should heal nicely."

They were in D'Annunzio's apartment, with the landlord stretched out on a long canvas-covered sofa. Dredd had insisted that D'Annunzio be removed from Chalk's apartment—"he's already contaminated the scene; let's not make it worse"—and D'Annunzio had complained and moaned as he dragged himself up the stairs.

Dredd was sure D'Annunzio was hamming it up, but right now wasn't the time to cite the citizen for slowing the progress of an investigation.

The med-Judge finished cleaning and sealing the wound. "That'll do it. Keep off the leg for the next forty-eight hours, citizen." He turned to Dredd.

"Heard about Pendleton and Collins. They were good Judges. That's on you."

Dredd ignored that. "Check on Ruiz. Any change in her condition, let me know immediately."

"I'm just saying that—"

Dredd nodded toward the door. "You're done here. Out."

The med-Judge hesitated for a second, then gathered his equipment and left the apartment.

"D'Annunzio, you lucid?"

"What? No! I never touch the stuff!"

"I mean, are you clear-headed right now?"

"Oh. Yeah." The man looked down at his leg. The med-Judge had sliced through his brand-new FantyPance to get access to the wound. "Feels a bit numb, but kinda nice, y'know? Whatever was in that hypo is doing the trick. So how much am I gonna get?"

"Get?"

"You know. Compo. I got shot 'cos of you, and now I've gotta repair a window and two doors, plus these pants ain't cheap. So what's the deal?"

"The deal is that you tell me everything you know about Percival Chalk and I don't haul you in on any of the dozen violations I can see right now without turning my head. Drag your heels and I'll order a full investigation on this rat-hole. Everything you've *ever* done will be brought to light. You understand me?"

"Look, I don't know what you want! I already told you I didn't know Chalk. Never even *saw* the guy!"

"That door in the lobby. Security glass, bullet-proof. Expensive. Why'd you have that installed?"

D'Annunzio shuffled himself into a sitting position. "We had some trouble a couple of years back. Guy came here after a ten-stretch... Roman Chantell, his name was. In for assault. Some creeps came lookin' for him. They shot the place up. What's that got to do with anything?"

"That model door is fitted with an intercom and camera."

"Yeah, but they weren't wired up. It would have cost me an extra five grand, and the sort of tenants we have here don't get many visitors, so I didn't bother."

Dredd pulled out his radio-mike. "Dredd to control... Send the tech-team out to retrieve the door—they'll know which one—and extract the inbuilt camera. I want names and details of every face captured in the past two months."

"On the way, Dredd."

D'Annunzio asked, "What for? I told you the camera wasn't wired up."

"We might get lucky," Dredd replied. "Repair team will be here in a day or two, citizen. Until then, stay put."

"But I was gonna go watch the race!"

"Not my problem."

Dredd left the man complaining and groping around on the sofa for the TV's remote, then made his way back down to Chalk's apartment.

A Judge met him in the doorway. She was in her mid-twenties and barely came up to Dredd's shoulder. "Brenna, forensics. We've scanned the place upside-down and inside-out. Chalk definitely spent some time here, but not much, judging by the amount of DNA evidence. We've got eight other traces.

We're running them now against the database, but nothing's flagged on the perp list."

"The roof?"

"Minute particles of metal lubricant at the spot you figure he shot from. It's WD-400, common stuff. Very simple ingredients, so there's no way to tie the sample into a specific batch. Not that that would help much. You can get the stuff at any hardware store in the city. We also got some boot prints in the dust, pretty fresh, too. Weather control ordered a downpour last week to wash the road surfaces for the race—guess they wanted to make the city look clean for the foreign viewers, too—so we know the prints aren't more than five days old."

"But you can't say whether the prints belong to the shooter."

"No way to be sure," Judge Brenna said. "For all we know, the shooter came in on a skysurf board. That'd explain how he got away, too. I've taken the liberty of polling the spy-cams, but I don't expect much—almost every cam has been on the race's route since early this morning." She took a small step back, and peered at Dredd for a moment. "You look like him. Not identical, but there's definitely a resemblance. Fargo, I mean. I met him once."

"I ordered a check on the building's security door."

She smiled at him. "Not one for chit-chat. Got it. Yeah, I heard about the door. But I don't get the point. The camera wasn't linked up."

"That model is fitted with a Pentakon PerfekteAugen. Reliable camera, decent resolution, minimal circuitry. Powered by solar energy absorbed by its own lens. Its memory can store about a year's worth of footage."

"So...?"

"So the PerfekteAugen is *always* on, Brenna. It's got built-in motion and proximity detectors. It's easier and cheaper for the door's manufacturers to build the one model and just not connect the camera's output if the buyer doesn't want it. So the camera's always recording, even if it's not connected to anything. Get that footage analysed. We're looking for anyone who might have come looking for Percival Chalk."

The young Judge nodded. "Okay... How do you *know* all that?"

Dredd stepped past her into the apartment. "I read."

Inside, another Judge was examining the bullet-holes in the window, but otherwise the apartment was bare, its few contents having already been removed for closer inspection.

Behind him, Brenna said, "I heard what everyone is saying about you, Dredd. For what it's *worth*..."

He turned to face her. "It's not worth anything. My judgement was sound back then. I bear no responsibility for Chalk's subsequent actions."

"Sometimes we make decisions—*judgements*—that feel right in the heat of the moment, but later, in the cold light of day..." She shrugged. "You've only been on the streets a year. You'll learn."

THE CURSED EARTH
2075 A.D.

Nine

JUDGE RUIZ LAY on the rough ground, breathing slowly and steadily as she tried to build a mental picture of her location. Her captors had stripped her of weapons, tied her wrists and ankles, and pulled a mouldy canvas sack over her head.

Now, the voice of Mayor Genesis Faulder came from somewhere close behind her. "Tomorrow. You were told that Ynex would be here tomorrow! Why in the seventeen hells did you have to come here *today*?"

Ruiz said nothing. She hadn't spoken since her capture, and had no intentions of breaking that streak now. There were at least five of them, she knew, though two of them would never harm anyone again. One had had his throat torn out when they'd grabbed her, and the other was now missing his eyes.

But another of her captors had proved to be considerably stronger than he looked: the mutant was short and thin, but his muscles were like steel cables. He had grabbed her from behind, one arm around her neck, crushing her throat, and a filthy, bony hand pressed hard against her mouth. She had been within seconds of passing out when something slammed hard into the backs of her knees. Ruiz had collapsed, the fall dislodging the man who'd been choking her but allowing several more to move in on her with heavy boots and hard-edged rifle butts.

Several ribs had been fractured, and her face was a mess of cuts and bruises, but they hadn't killed her yet. That, at least, was a positive sign. Though a sign of *what*, she wasn't yet sure.

Ruiz had already been scheduled for the hot-dog run when word reached Mega-City One that Ynex was using the town of Eminence as one of his trading points. The man—it was assumed Ynex was male, since most of the nomadic mutant tribes were led by men—scoured the Cursed Earth for caches of pre-war weapons, and somehow those weapons found their way into the hands of perps inside the city.

An automated message pod had been despatched to Eminence, informing the mayor that help was on the way. Though the Judges officially only ruled within the city limits, it wasn't uncommon for them to extend their reach into the Cursed Earth, especially when doing so would be to the city's benefit.

Now, Mayor Faulder crouched close to Ruiz and hissed, "You screwed up the *plan*! When we learned you were coming, we were going to turn a bunch of low-life nomad scum loose on you. You'd shoot them down and you'd go away happy thinking that you'd stopped Ynex. Grud-*damnit*!"

A second man's voice said, "Keep your stomm together, Faulder. Man, you are one major drokkin' idiot! You should have done nothing—be a damn sight easier to deal with her and the cadets if you'd left it to us."

"So now what do we do?" a third man asked. "We kill them, the Jays'll swarm on us like bees after an open sugar-truck. We *don't* kill them, same thing'll happen."

The second man replied, "And we've still got these here drokkin' *scavengers* to deal with."

So that's *how they're getting hold of the weapons*, Ruiz said to herself. *They ambush the teams of scavengers. Makes sense—get someone else to do the digging and excavating for you.*

Then Faulder said, "They never arrived here. That's how we play this. In a week, maybe two, more Judges'll come looking for them. We make damn sure that everyone in the town knows the story. They never showed up. 'Fact, when their back-up does arrive, we make like it's them we're expecting. We'll be all, 'You Judges were supposed to be here *ages* ago, what kept you?'"

The third man said, "Yeah. Yeah, that could work. But it won't be just the four of them—there'll be others, camped outside of town. Probably all cadets, but we can't underestimate them. These kids are, what, fifteen or sixteen? That means they've got a decade of training behind them. They're kids, but they're not *children*, if you get me."

"Think you mean that the other way around," the second man muttered. Then, louder, he added, "All right. The three in town, we get them back here. Deal with them before we go after the rest of their party. Faulder, that crippled kid you sent out to distract the cadet who was waiting outside... Send someone out to find him. Be easier if we lead them in one at a time."

★ ★ ★

Joe found Gibson and Rico poking around a store that sold unfathomable objects made out of baked clay.

"What the hell *is* that?" Rico asked the store's owner, a misshapen man with an abundance of extra fingers. He lifted up what looked like a beverage mug with an irregular row of holes in the base. "Hey, Joe, what do you make of this?"

"Outside."

Gibson put down an object that could have been a water bottle, had it not been solid. "We're just having a look around."

Joe threw a glance at the store's owner, then grabbed Rico's arm. "Let's go."

Gibson followed them out. "Come on, Joe. It's not like—"

"Ynex is here."

"You sure?" Rico asked.

Joe nodded. "The mayor's working for him. Apparently we got here a day earlier than they'd expected. There's a dozen, maybe more—kid who told me can't count past twelve."

Gibson stepped back from the others and glanced along the main street. "Damn... Wondered why everyone seemed a little uneasy. Thought they were just intimidated by us."

"All right," Rico said. "We have to assume that Judge Ruiz has already been taken. We can't do this alone. Gibson, get back to the camp, bring the others. On foot. Set the bikes on full auto, send them around to approach the town from the west. That should create a big enough distraction for us to get inside the mayor's store and extract Ruiz."

Joe saw movement reflected in the store window. "Behind me… Someone's coming, heading right for us," Joe muttered. "Gibson, get moving. And take it slow and casual—we can't let them see that we're suspicious."

The cadet began to move away, but it was too late. The approaching stranger called out, "Fellas? Hey, fellas! The Judge sent me out to find you!"

Joe turned and saw an unshaven, barrel-chested man grinning at them.

"If you're not busy sight-seeing, that is," the man added with a light chuckle. He inclined his head back toward the mayor's store, and the cadets fell into step beside him. "I'm Hieronymus Planter. I keep the local inn. Say, if you guys want to stay in town tonight, I'll give you a good price. I'm sure we've got enough space. How many are in your party?"

Gibson said, "Forty, including us."

Damn it, Joe thought. *That's the wrong approach! You don't tell the perps that there's more of us in order to scare them off—you tell them there's fewer so they'll be unprepared!*

"Forty, huh?" the innkeeper said. "Jeez, that's more folks than we have rooms. Some of you'll have to double-up. You be OK with that? It'd still be more comfortable than sleeping outdoors." He turned to Joe. "Young Lamb's not with you? Thought I saw him talking to you earlier."

"He wanted to play," Joe said, keeping his attention on the street, wondering how many eyes were on them right now. "I'm a cadet. We don't play." After Lamb had told Joe that Ynex's men had captured Judge Ruiz, Joe had told him to find his mother and take her as far out of the town as possible.

"You guys go ahead," Gibson said. "I should get back to the others." To the innkeeper, he added, "I'm tending the heavy weapons. Manseeker missiles, mortars, the chain-guns..."

"I'm sure that can wait," Planter said. "She told me to bring all three of you. She insisted."

Joe saw Rico glancing at him, and knew what his brother was thinking: one of them should hang back a little to get a better handle on the situation. Without turning to Rico, he gave a slight nod.

The innkeeper stopped outside the store and gestured that they should enter ahead of him. "Go through to the warehouse out back. That's the mayor's office."

Gibson pushed open the door and Joe followed him, but Rico stopped in the doorway. "Say, you get a lot of visitors to Eminence, Mister Planter? Can't be too easy keeping an inn going around here."

"The river brings some custom," Hieronymus Planter said. "Hunters and prospectors, mostly, during the rainy season. Go on in. What Mayor Faulder has to say isn't for *my* ears." He gave a small laugh. "I'm just the dogsbody."

"Sure, yeah," Rico said. "Right behind you, guys."

Joe looked back to see Rico leaning against the doorjamb as he pulled off one of his boots.

"Damn sand gets everywhere," Rico muttered.

Rico couldn't delay for more than about twenty seconds without drawing suspicion. Joe hoped that would be enough, because in about thirty seconds he and Gibson were going to draw their weapons, no matter what was happening.

MEGA-CITY ONE
2080 A.D.

Ten

SHOCK EASED OFF the throttle as he neared Treat Williams underpass, the twenty-four-kilometre-long tunnel that marked the quarter-point of the race. Ahead of him, the first-placer Desmond Redmond—one of the few freelancers in this year's race—was keeping up the speed, a brave strategy. Three years ago an enthusiastic juve had been turned into flesh-jam when, to win a bet, he'd suspended himself from the tunnel's ceiling armed with a spray-paint can. Tagging a rider would have given him ultimate bragging rights; instead, the juve's ropes had slipped and he'd managed to get his head squashed by the front wheel of Natalie Harbinger's souped-up Steamrover.

The Steamrover had spun out of control following the collision, and, in a blind panic, Harbinger had hit her vehicle's "Eject" button. *Not the wisest move when you're in a tunnel*, Shock thought. Harbinger's widow was now one of the race's most vocal opponents, a bitter woman who still wore black and cringed every time the spectacular accident was shown on TV. Which, around the time of the race, was about every ten minutes.

Shock pulled wide as he approached the tunnel's entrance, and the proximity warning on his bike's screen started flashing—someone was coming up fast behind him.

Shock swore under his breath as the rider's name appeared: Napoleon Neapolitan.

Neapolitan was riding a custom-built two-wheeler, a precarious-looking vehicle that on its unveiling the previous week had had all the bookies in a panic. His machine didn't look stable, but then this was Napoleon Neapolitan, judged by many to be the greatest biker the city had ever seen. If anyone could ride the contraption to victory, it was him.

Almost any wheeled vehicle was permitted in the race. The only checks the officials made were to ensure that no one was hiding an anti-grav motor somewhere inside their machine. Not that they didn't try to smuggle them on board, or disguise them as something else. Only a few minutes before today's race started, two riders were disqualified for using tiny AG motors pulled out of skysurf boards.

Napoleon Neapolitan's new ride was definitely wheel-based, but its twin two-metre-diameter wheels were side by side instead of in sequence. Each wheel had its own engine, with Neapolitan's seat suspended between the two.

Shock's screen blipped again: a call from Neapolitan.

Great, Shock thought. *He's going to try to psych me out.* Neapolitan would record the call and endlessly play it back later on the chat-show circuit, as he had done for previous races. Still, however bad Neapolitan made him look, at least it was publicity. Better to be laughed at than ignored.

He muttered, "Accept," and Neapolitan's grinning face appeared on the screen, flickering light and dark as he passed under the tunnel's lights.

"Hey, Shock."

"Napoleon. That's a nice little toy you've got there. What's the power?"

"About ten per cent more than yours. Listen, how about you quit now and save yourself the embarrassment? Just pull over to the side and let the big boys play. You can spend the day doing something productive, maybe. Or, here's an idea, you could go to a bar and watch TV. I hear there's a great race on at the moment. You might enjoy that—there's a rumour that you're interested in racing."

Shock ignored him and drew close to the next rider in front, a member of the three-man Chief Cog team, a group of popular TV-show presenters who always participated for laughs. This one was The Ferret, the smallest and cheekiest of the three, a chirpy daredevil who—along with his pedantic teammate Sergeant Dawdle—was forever failing to crawl out of the shadow of their leader, the brash, craggy-faced know-it-all Jeremiah Kentson.

"What do you say, Shock?" Neapolitan asked. "I'll give you fifty credits if you quit. That's more money than you'll make coming in last."

Ahead, The Ferret was weaving from one side of the tunnel to the other, and Shock could see the top of his helmet bobbing about, a sure sign that the man was recording a commentary. The Ferret was riding a reconditioned Shuddermeister, painted in pink with yellow dots, its colour-scheme no doubt the result of some hilarious prank by his teammates.

Shock increased his speed and came up alongside the Shuddermeister, took a moment to glance at the smiling man inside the bike's bubble canopy, then pulled ahead. He debated for a moment whether to remain in that position, in full view of the cameras bolted onto the front of The Ferret's bike. It might mean more screen-time when the next special episode of *Chief Cog* was shown.

But Neapolitan was still on his tail, still goading him. Shock continued to accelerate, and behind him Neapolitan pulled up next to The Ferret and gave him a friendly salute.

Damn, Shock thought. *I should have done that—that's a couple of seconds of air-time for sure, even if he doesn't win.*

But Shock was determined that this time Napoleon Neapolitan was not going to have much in the way of bragging rights. Spacer pride was at stake. The Mega-City 5000 was a dangerous race, and accidents happened. One way or another, Napoleon was not going to cross the finish-line.

THE PERFEKTEAUGEN CAMERA built into the door of Zederick D'Annunzio's building had proximity sensors that turned the camera on when a person approached. It had recorded a little over four exabytes of footage in the past year.

Facial recognition software discarded ninety-seven per cent of the footage, flagging one hundred and fifty-five citizens who'd visited the building in that time. Most were eliminated immediately—known relatives and friends of D'Annunzio or his tenants, delivery people, maintenance workers—leaving four names for Dredd to check.

The entire process took less than fifteen minutes, most of that time due to delays on the Justice Department networks caused by the extra surveillance on the Mega-City 5000.

Dredd sat on his Lawmaster outside D'Annunzio's building as he ran checks on each of the four citizens. Three of them had visited the building several times before Chalk's release from the iso-cubes. That left one name: Riley Moeller. Moeller had been suspected—but not charged—of trading illegal weapons back in 2075. Around the time of Chalk's arrest.

"Control—Dredd. I need the current location of one Riley Moeller, Jeffrey Abrams Block."

"Stand by. System's a little overloaded right now. I've added Moeller's name to the queue."

Dredd fired up the Lawmaster and peeled away from the side of the road. "En route to Jeffrey Abrams Block. You find Moeller elsewhere, point the nearest Judge at him. I want him conscious and unharmed."

Dredd roared along 4007th Avenue, weaving in and out of the slow-moving traffic. Ahead, the lights at the junction with Alston Buck Road turned red. Dredd hit the traffic override controls on his Lawmaster and the light switched back to green.

Jeffrey Abrams was one of the city's newer blocks, a two-hundred-storey-tall cylinder that towered over the rest of its sector. Dredd had visited the block before, investigating a domestic disturbance; its interior didn't live up to the promise of its gleaming glass-and-metal shell.

Inside, the walls were unfinished, the electrics and plumbing exposed. Uncovered light fittings cast sharp-edged shadows across the bare floors, and the poor sound-proofing allowed the slightest noise to travel from one side of the block to the other. The Mega-City One housing authority had basic standards for what were considered to be habitable conditions, and Jeffrey Abrams Block only passed inspection because its aggregate score was boosted by its high resistance to fire—and that was because there was little in the block that could burn.

Dredd pulled onto the slip-road leading off 4007th Avenue and checked his screen for Riley Moeller's apartment number. "Dredd to Control."

"Go ahead."

"Approaching Jeffrey Abrams Block, ramp entrance. Send an elevator to the thirtieth floor, locked for my use only."

"Uh, Dredd, that procedure's only for *priority* cases. If—"

"This *is* a priority, Control. Just do it."

After a tiny, almost imperceptible pause, Control replied, "Acknowledged. Elevator will be waiting for you."

Dredd grunted a reply and shut off the comm-link. Justice Department Control was manned chiefly by cadets, invalided Judges and tech support staff, and usually they gave him anything he requested, but today some of them seemed slow in responding. He didn't know whether that was because of the increased workload due to the race, or because many of the senior Judges blamed him for the deaths of Collins and Pendleton.

It shouldn't be like this, Dredd told himself. *Judges are expected to be impartial when dealing with the citizens; we should be the same with each other.*

It was a leftover from the days of Chief Judge Solomon. Before Goodman was appointed, corruption among the Judges had been rife. Or if not out-and-out corruption, at least incompetence, which was just as bad.

Though Clarence Goodman's administration, working with the Special Judicial Squad, had done great work in straightening out and clarifying the role of the Judges, some of the old squabbles and grievances had yet to be eliminated.

Many of the older Judges resented Dredd and Rico, solely because of their link to Solomon's predecessor, Eustace Fargo. Fargo had been a hard-lined, no-nonsense Judge who had always made it clear that the Judges existed to serve the citizens, not the other way around. "We're not their rulers," Fargo had once told a gathering of senior Judges. "We're their caretakers, if anything."

Dredd had always held true to that belief. Some Judges had friends among the civilian population. A few even had lovers, though that was strictly against the rules. They saw judging as a career, not as a life.

And Dredd knew that many Judges thought of him as "Junior Fargo." He didn't have friends outside of his own class at the Academy, and even then he didn't socialise with his former classmates. They were just Judges he knew better than other Judges, that was all. Rico, on the other hand, did sometimes socialise. Though they were genetically identical, their personalities were quite different.

Joe Dredd had often wondered why that was so.

He and Rico had had the same experiences when they were cadets. Neither had been shown favour by their tutors—most of the time the tutors couldn't tell them apart—and all of their test scores matched almost perfectly. But still, somehow, they had ended up as two very different Judges.

Judge Morphy, one of Dredd's mentors during his time at the academy, once asked them—separately—what they'd intended to achieve when they graduated. Rico had told Morphy that he wanted to be the best possible Judge. He'd keep the citizens in line. He'd be firm with them, but compassionate. "I'll uphold the law," Rico had said.

Joe's response to the same question had been briefer, and very different: "Justice."

"Meaning?" Morphy had asked.

"Sometimes the law will be wrong," Joe had replied in a matter-of-fact manner. "In those cases, we *change* the law so that it serves justice. That's what's important. That's why we do this."

Even now, many years later, Dredd had not changed his opinion. The law was the law, but wasn't eternal. It wasn't immutable. Like Judges, it existed to serve the people, not censure them.

The situation with Chalk only strengthened his resolve. Dredd knew that what had happened five years earlier in Eminence could have been played differently, but he still believed that he had made the correct decision then—despite the outcome—and he had no regrets.

THE CURSED EARTH
2075 A.D.

Eleven

THE WEAK LIGHT from the grimy windows faded further still as Joe followed Cadet Gibson through the labyrinthine racks toward a door set into the back wall of the store.

Under his breath, Gibson muttered, "What do you think? Ambush?"

"Could be," Joe said. "Could be nothing, though. Stay alert."

"Good idea. Never would have thought of that."

Joe took another glance back, and spotted his brother entering the store, followed by the innkeeper. "Rico's in."

Gibson reached out to grab the door handle with his right hand, allowing his left to casually drop closer to the gun on his hip. "I'll take point—hang back a second or two, Joe."

Joe nodded. A couple of seconds could make all the difference if someone was waiting for them on the other side of the door. With Rico taking up the rear, they stood a good chance of at least one of them making it out alive.

Gibson pushed open the door and strode through into the large warehouse.

There was no immediate sign of danger, so Joe followed him. The warehouse was dark and damp, and this side of it was almost empty. Heavy wooden beams—some way down the road to rot—supported a patchwork roof of rusting corrugated iron strips, peeling plywood sheets, and the hoods of old pre-war cars, bolted together. The floor was nothing but packed dirt, stained with oil and engine grease.

"Over here, boys!" Mayor Faulder's voice called from the far side of the warehouse, where a flickering electric light in one corner showed tall stacks of wooden and plastic crates.

"Damn," Gibson muttered. "This does *not* look good."

A voice off to the left said, "Drop your weapons, baby Judges!"

Joe threw himself forward, spinning to land on his right side, Lawgiver already drawn, aimed and fired while he was in the air. His shot streaked past the back of Gibson's head—the cadet was crouching, in the process of drawing his own weapon—and buried itself in the shoulder of a shotgun-wielding man.

Joe rolled to his feet—a *thud* from the doorway behind him told him that Rico was already dealing with Hieronymus Planter—and spun as a mutant dropped from the rafters. The mutant was tall and lithe, naked except for a loin-cloth, thick boots and gloves, and swinging a heavy circular saw blade fixed to the end of a chain.

As Joe was taking aim at him, another mutant, almost identical but considerably shorter, rushed at him from the shadows to his right, spinning twin swords so fast that Joe could barely see them in the weak light.

The taller mutant's blade-on-a-chain was also a blur: it whipped out at Gibson's left arm, knocking the Lawgiver from his grip.

Joe fired a shot at the sword-swinging mutant—the bullet struck home, right in the centre of the mutant's bare chest, but barely slowed him.

The mutant grinned. "Me an' me brother got *bullet-proof skin*, Judgey! What do you say to *that*, eh? You—"

Joe shot him in the mouth. The bullet transported a good chunk of the back of the mutant's head into the shadows.

From the far side of the warehouse, behind the wooden and plastic crates, Judge Ruiz's voice called out, "Aim high!"

She's on the ground, Joe told himself.

He was about to launch a volley of shots through the crates when another voice called out, "No! Hostages here!"

At the doorway, Rico was standing over Hieronymus Planter's twitching body. Nearby, Gibson had taken down the other bullet-proof mutant by kicking him in the groin—the mutant was on his side now, groaning and clutching at himself.

Rico was looking back out through the doorway. "More coming... *Lots* more. Me and Gibson will hold them off. Go find the boss, Joe!"

Joe nodded and kept to the side as he approached the crates. There was no telling who or what else might be lurking. He guessed that Ruiz couldn't see where she was—if she could, she'd have warned him about the other hostages.

As he passed the nearest of the crates it erupted in a shower of wooden splinters and metal fragments. Joe threw himself to the side, automatically putting his arms up to shield his face. He hit the ground, rolled and landed in a half-crouch, to see Mayor Genesis Faulder aiming a shotgun at Judge Ruiz's head.

Ruiz was lying on her side, wrists and ankles tied, stripped of most of her uniform, a cloth sack over her head. Nearby, sitting up against the wall, was a chained man wearing the familiar coveralls of a Mega-City One scavenger. Beyond him, four other scavengers—two women, two men—were huddled together, being watched by three more mutants, all carrying automatic rifles.

"I'll puree her head and my men'll kill the others if you take *one more step*, boy!" Faulder said. "Grud-*damn*, but you city-folk are a lot harder to kill than you look."

From the far side of the warehouse came the sound of heavy gunfire.

"Tell your friends to stand down," Faulder said. "Right *now*!"

Joe lowered his weapon, but held onto it. "You haven't shot Judge Ruiz yet. That tells me you need her alive for something..."

Faulder viciously jabbed the muzzle of his shotgun into the side of Ruiz's head. "Just drop your drokkin' weapon!" He kept glancing past Joe toward the front of the warehouse. "And order your men to stand down!"

"You don't know where the rest of the squad are camped," Joe said. "You can't take the chance that there's not a hundred of us."

"Gun on the floor, boy! Right *now* or—"

Joe flipped his wrist and fired three shots. The first ripped through Mayor Faulder's gun-hand, the others took out his lower knees.

Faulder collapsed, screaming, on top of Judge Ruiz, and the remaining three mutants whirled around, swinging their guns in Joe's direction.

He put a bullet through the nearest one's eye, another through the second one's throat. The third, partly shielded behind the second, threw his gun aside. "I surrender!"

Joe knew it was a feint—even before his rifle hit the ground, the mutant was reaching for the sidearm on his hip. Two shots through his chest, less than a centimetre apart, assured that the mutant's pistol didn't clear its holster.

The man in the scavenger's overalls sagged, visibly relieved. "Thank *Grud*! They ambushed us and—"

"Shut up and stay put," Joe said. He crossed over to Ruiz, grabbed Faulder by the arm and hauled him off the Judge. He slapped a set of cuffs on Faulder's wrists, then crouched next to Judge Ruiz and pulled the sack from her head.

She blinked up at him through swollen eyes. "Good save, cadet."

"How many others?" Joe pulled out his boot knife and began to saw through the ropes around her wrists.

Ruiz shook her head. "I'm not sure. Three, at least. One of them had a grip like *steel*—It was like being strangled by a robot. Small guy, mutant. Smells like warm garbage."

"Think I got him," Joe said. With Ruiz's wrists free, he flipped over the knife and handed it to her, hilt-first. "You're injured. Stay down—I'll see if the others require back-up."

He turned as he straightened up, and on the edge of his vision he saw the scavenger grabbing Faulder's shotgun.

Still sitting, the scavenger was aiming the shotgun at the Mayor. "He damn near *killed* me! I ought to—"

"Drop it!" Judge Ruiz said.

"I heard them talking... The guy you came here to stop—that's him! Genesis Faulder *is* Ynex!"

"*Drop the gun!*" Joe roared, his Lawgiver aimed at the scavenger's grip.

Faulder suddenly spasmed. Joe spun around to check—and at that moment the scavenger fired.

The shotgun blast tore Mayor Faulder's head from his neck.

Joe snatched the shotgun from the scavenger's grip and drove his boot into the side of the man's head. He tossed the weapon on the ground next to Ruiz. "Watch him. He moves, shoot him."

As he ran back to join Gibson and Rico, the thought briefly crossed Joe's mind that he'd just issued orders to a street Judge. He didn't think that Ruiz would make anything of it, but it wasn't generally considered proper conduct for a cadet.

WITHIN AN HOUR, the body count was in double figures and the town of Eminence was in need of a new mayor.

Out on the street, Joe told Gibson to return to the camp: "Send McManus and Ellard back toward the city—they're to ride without stopping until they can get a clear signal through. We need a med-team and transport for thirty prisoners and hostages. And bring the rest of the cadets back here."

He turned back to see the hostages emerging from the store, two of them half-carrying Judge Ruiz. In full daylight, the extent of her injuries became clear: her left ankle was broken or fractured, unable to support her weight. Her right shoulder looked to be dislocated—her arm dangled uselessly by her side—and her limbs and torso had been slashed dozens of times.

Joe and Rico rushed over to them and grabbed the Judge, gently lowered her to the ground.

"Damn... they *tortured* her," Rico said. He looked up at the hostages. "If you're not hurt... Go inside, find a medical kit, blankets, clean water. Rip the place apart if you have to."

As the hostages ran back into the store, Ruiz coughed, then winced at the pain. Her eyes fluttered open. "Status?"

"You're the only one of us injured," Joe said. "I've sent Gibson for help."

She nodded slightly. "Good work. You get them all?"

"Reckon we did," Rico said.

Joe straightened up and looked around. More of the townspeople had emerged from their homes and stores, and now there was a semi-circle of nervous on-lookers. Joe strode toward the man who appeared to be the oldest. "What happened here?"

"'Twas the mayor," the old man said, leaning a little to peer past Joe. "Him and the others useta send out raiding parties to plunder the other towns. Then they got wind of the scavengers an' they figured it'd be easier just to take the stuff offa them."

"But the mayor's the one who called the city for help."

A woman nearby said, "No, that was me." She looked normal, except that she had a second set of small ears in front of the usual two, and beneath the fresh bruises on her face Joe could see a family resemblance with the boy, Lamb. "I work for him. *Worked*. I sent the message in his name. When he found out, he..." She faltered. "Thank you for coming."

"More help is on the way," Joe said. "But it could be a day or two before it gets here." He heard footsteps behind him and turned to see the first hostage—the one who'd shot the mayor—approaching.

"I'm sorry," the man said. He was still trembling, clutching the side of his face where Joe had kicked him. "They ambushed us. Wasn't the first time we came under attack, but usually the raiders just take whatever we'd managed to find and let us go."

Joe nodded. "Makes sense, from their point of view. You can only steal from a dead man once." He turned back to the townspeople. "Show's over. Disperse."

A man in the crowd said, "You can't tell us what to do! This is *our* town—you have no jurisdiction..." The man faltered as Joe stared at him, then fell silent.

"Disperse," Joe repeated.

In a few seconds, Joe and the scavenger were alone on the street. As they returned to Judge Ruiz, Joe asked, "Name?"

"Chalk. Percival Chalk. I'm sorry," the scavenger said. "I wasn't going to really shoot him, but then he moved and I thought he was getting up and so I just pulled the trigger."

The other hostages had found blankets, a very basic first-aid kit and even a pillow, and were now tending to Judge Ruiz.

Rico stood next to Joe. "The crates in there? They're full of guns. Old stuff, mostly, but a few newer weapons too. They look like they've been wiped clean, serial numbers burned off. In a few days those guns would have been in the hands of Mega-City One's perps."

One of the other hostages—a stocky blonde woman—said, "*We* found them; most of them, anyway. About forty kilometres north of here there's an old farmhouse. I figure it belonged to a survivalist—the cellar was packed with guns and ammunition."

Chalk nodded. "That's why they send us out here," he said to Joe. "Properly oiled and wrapped, a good-quality sidearm can still be functional after a century. Same with the ammo, if it's kept dry." He looked pleased with himself. "Yeah, that cache is one of our biggest hauls yet. We get a bonus for each functioning gun we recover."

On the ground nearby, Judge Ruiz called out, "You..." She was looking at Chalk. "You're lucky Dredd didn't just shoot you the second you picked up the gun. He was well within the law to do so."

"That's true," Rico said, "*I* wouldn't have hesitated."

"I didn't hesitate," Joe said. "I assessed." He turned to the scavenger. "Percival Chalk, you're a citizen of Mega-City One and subject to the city's laws. You were ordered by a Judge to drop the gun. Your failure to do so resulted in the death of a suspect."

The man stepped back, eyes wide. "What? That's insane—I was defending myself!"

"You grabbed the gun *before* Faulder moved. Five years in the cubes."

"No! No, you're just a *cadet*—you can't issue sentences!"

Judge Ruiz said, "He can, in this circumstance. I was out of commission—the cadet took over. I stand by Cadet Dredd's judgement."

MEGA-CITY ONE
2080 A.D.

Twelve

DREDD POUNDED ON the apartment door with his fist, loud enough to be heard over the noise of the TV inside. "Judge. Open up."

The TV was muted, and the door slid open a few centimetres. Scarred, meaty-looking fingers grabbed the edge and pulled it open the rest of the way.

Riley Moeller was a big man. As tall as Dredd, but broader across the shoulders. His pale-skinned face and dark-rimmed eyes told Dredd that he didn't get out much. "What? I've done nothing wrong."

Dredd moved closer and Moeller stepped aside. The apartment was small, but relatively neat. A main room that served as kitchen, dining room and lounge, with two interior doors, one leading to a bedroom, the other to a bathroom. Against one wall was a narrow floor-to-ceiling bookcase, its shelves packed with old books. "You got receipts for all those books, citizen?"

"What? No, not all of them. Most of them are fifty, sixty years old. That's what I do—I trade old stuff with other collectors. I do sell *some* stuff, but I have invoices for everything I sell or buy. You can check with revenue. I don't deal in stolen goods, if that's what you're thinking. Look, what's this about?" He gestured toward the TV set. "I'm watching the *race*."

In the corner of the main room, the TV was tuned to Channel Epsilon. On screen, a long vehicle—riding on six wheels, one after the other—was accelerating past a century-old refurbished Dune buggy.

"I want Percival Chalk. You're going to tell me how to find him."

Moeller frowned. "Chalk? I barely know the guy, these days. What do you want him for?"

Dredd stepped further into the apartment and closed the door behind him. "You visited Chalk's block four weeks ago. Why?"

"I heard he got out. Just wanted to check on him. We used to work together. He was a scavenger, I was an assessor. They'd bring in stuff they found out in the Cursed Earth or the undercity, and we'd figure out whether it was junk or something useful. That's where I got interested in old stuff. The scavengers would sometimes bring in books or old videodiscs." Moeller sat down on the edge of an armchair. "Look, man, I don't know what you want Chalk for, but I'm telling you it's got nothing to do with me."

Dredd crossed over to the dusty bookcase. Here and there, spacing the books out, were small ornaments and old toys. There was a gap between a fraying, hardcover volume of *Princess Pony Tales for Boys* and an eight-centimetre-thick paperback called *Flail and Crown Volume Four: Lore of the Marauder's Maul,*

Part 2. In the gap was a clear circular impression in the dust. "What was here?"

"A coffee mug. Traded it at a collectors' fair a few weeks ago."

Dredd turned back to Moeller. "Coffee's illegal, citizen."

"I know that. But mugs aren't. You'd have liked that one. It said, 'World's Best Judge.' It was made back in the twentieth, for a high-court judge."

"What did you and Chalk talk about?"

"Just, you know, stuff. The old days. He'd had some interest in collecting back then. That's why he got into scavenging. He was always hoping to get a big score. They were allowed to keep anything they found, as long as it wasn't illegal."

Dredd stared unmoving at Moeller for a few seconds. He knew how imposing the uniform could be, especially the dark visor that hid the Judge's eyes. Hardened perps had been known to crack under nothing more than a Judge's stare.

It wasn't working on Moeller. Dredd decided to take a more direct approach. "This morning Percival Chalk entered the Funex Eaterie on Bevis Wetzel Plaza, sector sixty-three. He shot dead seventeen citizens and two Judges. You are the only link to him that we have."

Moeller shook his head. "No. No way! I had nothing to do with that!"

"Five years ago you were suspected of being involved with an illegal weapons deal."

"Yeah. And I was *innocent*. Check the reports. An undercover Judge heard I collected antiques and he got the wrong idea and thought I was a weapons dealer. He interrogated me for six *hours* before he realised he was wrong. That's all that happened. But because I was a suspect, I lost my *job*. I..." He stared at the Judge's badge. "Dredd. That was *you*, wasn't it? Chalk told me. A cadet called Joe Dredd sentenced him to five years just for trying to save his own life!" He looked away, disgusted. "So now what? You're going to lock me up just for *knowing* Chalk? Yeah, that figures." He looked back at the TV. "If you're going to arrest me on a made-up charge, at least wait until the drokkin' race is over."

Dredd reached out and grabbed Moeller's arm, hauled him to his feet. "You're hiding something."

"I'm not, I swear!"

Still holding onto Moeller's arm, Dredd kicked out at the man's leg and forced him face-down to the floor. He planted a knee on the small of Moeller's back and quickly cuffed his wrists behind his back. "Riley Moeller, on the charge of failure to report a potential crime, I sentence you to two years in the iso-cubes."

Moeller tried to squirm free. "No! You can't do that!"

"Struggling. That's the same as resisting. *Three* years."

"Damn you, Dredd—you're a fascist! *All* you drokkin' judges are fascists!"

"Sedition. *Ten* years." Dredd grabbed hold of the man's hair, and pulled up his head. He leaned closer. "Want to go for twenty?"

"I don't know anything!"

"Why'd you go see Chalk?"

"Because I used to know him, that's all! I heard he was out and I just thought it'd be the right thing to do, to check on him!"

"I'm not buying that, Moeller. No one else from Chalk's old life came to visit him. Why you? You make it a habit of visiting ex-cons?" Dredd stood, and took a step back.

Moeller rolled onto his side, stared up at the Judge. "Look, I promise you I had no idea *what* he was planning!"

"But you knew he was planning *something*."

"No, I thought he was just venting. I mean, yeah, he *said* that he was going to make amends, but people always say stuff like that when they think they've been wronged. They never *do* it."

Dredd said, "Amends... Then his attack on the diner wasn't random. He was targeting someone." He activated his helmet radio. "Control—run a check on the victims of the Funex Eaterie shooting. Flag anyone who had a past association with Percival Chalk."

"Sector Chief Mendillo has already ordered that, Dredd. No known connections. Though forensics are still trying to identify some of the bodies."

"The victims of the concussion grenade?" Dredd asked.

"Right. They're filtering the remains for teeth, came up with four upper-left canines so far. So that's four victims at least. Still waiting on the DNA results."

If Chalk was targeting someone, Dredd said to himself, *it seems likely he'd use the grenade to make sure of the kill.* "Acknowledged, Control. Send a H-wagon to my location. We're taking in Riley Moeller for a complete particle-scan and interrogation. He knows something, but he's not talking."

Dredd crouched next to Moeller. "You know what a particle-scan is, creep? You won't enjoy it. Every square millimetre of your skin is probed right down to the subcutaneous tissue. Your blood is extracted, and while it's being filtered, nanobots will crawl through your capillaries. Don't worry—we have ways of keeping you alive while that happens. Your fingernails and toenails will be removed, every hair plucked at the root. Different nanobots will be injected into your lungs to scour the alveoli. And it's all done without any anaesthetic that might interfere with the readings. The whole process takes *hours*, and they don't stop looking when they find something. It doesn't end until every foreign particle larger than an atom has been removed from your body."

"You can't do that to someone—that's torture!"

"No, it's investigation. And it's the easy part. The hard part comes when you have to explain the purpose of every suspicious particle. Now, that can take *weeks*. We'll do the same to your apartment, of course. Most of your possessions won't survive the process. All those precious books will end up as nothing but powder. The good news is, if we don't find anything suspicious we'll let you *keep* the powder."

Even as he was speaking, Dredd realised what it was that he'd missed. The gap in the bookshelves; the circular impression in the dust. It *could* have been made by a mug, as Moeller claimed. But it could have been something else, too.

He hauled Moeller to his feet, dragged him over to the bookcase, pushed his face close to the gap. "Explain!"

"I don't under—"

"You're going to tell me how Chalk got his hands on a concussion grenade!"

"How would *I* know?"

"Chalk contacted you when he got out. He wanted weapons. You're the right man for that because you were one of his liaisons back when he was a scavenger!" He forced Moeller's arms higher behind his back, and the man yelped in pain. "That void in the dust is the right size for a grenade. You sold it to Chalk—that makes you an accessory to murder."

"You can't prove that!"

"I'm a Judge. I don't have to prove it. Suspicion is enough." He pulled Moeller back from the bookcase and spun him around so that they were face-to-visor. "Weapons trading is a class-one felony, Moeller," Dredd spat. "That means life without parole. And not in a cushy iso-cube. You're looking at hard labour. The Cursed Earth, or a trawler in the Black Atlantic. Or maybe mining the asteroid belt. You're strong, fit... You might even last a couple of years."

Moeller's face sagged. "I..." He dry-swallowed. "Promise to reduce my sentence and I'll talk. I'll tell you everything."

"No promises. No deals. Your sentence doesn't mean you get to skip the particle-scan... After a few minutes of that you'll be telling us everything anyway."

"Chalk contacted me, when he got out. Tracked me down through a friend of a friend. He told me... Look, what happened five years ago in that town, well, it didn't go down the way you thought it did. I don't know *all* the details..."

"Tell me what you do know."

"Chalk wasn't just a scavenger. He was a gun-runner. His team smuggled old weapons into the city. You swear to me I won't get the Black Atlantic and I'll tell you the names of the assessors who helped them."

"I told you," Dredd said. "No deals." He paused for a second, then added, "But it can't hurt your case to cooperate."

Moeller nodded. "All right. In that town—whatever it was called—Chalk was working with the mayor. Chalk always knew where the other teams of scavengers were. He'd tell the mayor and they'd send out raiders, take any guns the scavengers had found. Then every few months Chalk's people would go to the town and load the haul of weapons onto their trucks, take them back to the city. But... I don't know what happened exactly, but they had a falling out. Maybe the mayor wanted a bigger cut, or something. Either way, when you and the other cadets and that Judge went to the town, the mayor thought that Chalk had sold them out."

Behind Dredd, the door to the apartment was pushed open and two Judges entered. "Dredd. You called for a H-wagon."

"We're not done here yet," Dredd said. "Talk faster, Moeller."

"Chalk killed the mayor with his own gun, right? You were there, you saw that. But what you didn't see was that just before you got there, the mayor was about to kill Chalk. And that gun was part of Chalk's weapons shipment. All the weapons were always cleaned, but Chalk had taken that one out of the crate to show the mayor. That was the real reason he grabbed it—because he knew that you'd be checking all the weapons for prints and DNA."

"And Chalk didn't want us to know that the reason his DNA was on the gun was because he'd *already* handled it."

"Right," Moeller said, nodding. "The others with Chalk... They were part of his crew. They'd sided with the mayor. They wanted Chalk out of the picture as much as the mayor did. But when you rescued them, none of scavengers could say anything about the others without implicating themselves. If you hadn't arrested Chalk, he'd have taken his revenge on them a long time ago."

"So that's who he's targeting. His former colleagues."

Moeller was staring at the floor. "He asked me for weapons. The grenade was the only thing I had. I don't deal weapons, never did. I had the grenade because, well, in good condition they're worth about seventeen thousand credits to a collector."

"I want the names and locations of the people Chalk is targeting."

"And you'll reduce my sentence?"

"No. But delay any longer and I'll *increase* it. Only offer you're going to get, Moeller. Start talking."

Thirteen

In his office in the Grand Hall of Justice, Chief Judge Clarence Goodman had one of his desk's monitors tuned to the race—with the sound muted—while through the others he conducted the afternoon situation reports.

Standing on the other side of the desk, Goodman's assistant Judge Brannigan read stats from a datapad. "Reported crimes are down on the average day, sir. Down quite a *lot*, actually."

"A quarter of the population is on the streets watching the race," Goodman said. "Same thing happened the last couple of years. When they get home and discover that their pockets have been picked or their homes have been burgled, we can expect a massive surge in reports. Instruct the call centres to double-up on staff for the next twenty-four." Goodman turned to the screen showing Sector Chief Daniel Mendillo. "Where are we on the sector sixty-three diner shootings?"

"Judges Amber Ruiz and Joseph Dredd were investigating," Mendillo said. "Ruiz has been injured, shot by an unknown sniper. Likely the same perp from the diner, but that's not been established yet. She's alive, but her condition's still critical. Dredd's carrying the investigation alone. He's established that the killer's targeting former colleagues. Right now he's en route to the closest."

Goodman sat back. "Dredd... Good Judge. What sort of back-up are you giving him?"

"Tech support, forensics... Nothing on the streets, if that's what you mean. We just don't have the helmets."

Goodman glanced at the monitor displaying the race. "The killer picked the right day for it. Which makes me think that it's not a coincidence."

"Yes, sir. Dredd suggested the same thing."

Goodman leaned closer to the screen showing Mendillo. "I'm the Chief Judge. Eight hundred million people rely on me to make good decisions. Do you comprehend that?"

"Sir?"

"You think this office is so far above the streets that I can't still have my finger on the pulse? I know what's going on. I'm not a drokkin' *idiot*, Mendillo. I see the reports before you do, and I know how to interpret them. A lot of other Judges are blaming Dredd for this. They think that Pendleton and Collins would still be alive if Dredd had executed Chalk five years ago."

Mendillo hesitated. "He *did* have that option, sir. It was his decision not to exercise it. Any fallout from that is—"

Goodman thumped his fist on the desk. "Enough!

I've looked at that case. Dredd's judgement was sound then. Ruiz stood by him, and so do I. If a Judge can disarm and disable a perp without killing him, then that is the Judge's first obligation. Joseph Dredd is no more responsible for Chalk's actions than I am. I'm aware that our resources are stretched thinner than usual today, but you will make damn sure that Dredd receives all the support he needs. Even if that means we have to pull Judges out of crowd control and replace them with Sector Chiefs. Understood?"

"Yes, sir."

"Any Judge who knowingly hampers Dredd's investigation will find themselves being interviewed by the SJS. *Any* Judge, Mendillo."

Mendillo nodded. "Understood, sir. I'll see to it personally."

"Do that," Goodman said. "Or *I'll* see to it personally."

SEAMUS "SHOCK" O'SHAUGHNESSY felt his pulse quicken as he pushed harder on the accelerator. His Blenderbike curved slowly but smoothly past Aposcar Kresky's brand-new Honda-Davidson XM940 and slipped into tenth place.

Coming up was a section of the route that the riders had nicknamed The Crowbar. The name was coined by racing pundit Murray Strider, who—when pressed for an explanation--said, "this is the one that separates the men from the boys." Strider's comment had him immediately blacklisted by the Mega-City One Association For Wimmin And Grrlz Who Ride Bikes, but that had only served to boost his profile, which was why he'd said it.

The Crowbar was a thirty-kilometre stretch that wove through the blocks of sector 192, a zig-zagging mess of short runs connected by right-angled turns. Recommended maximum speed through The Crowbar was one hundred KPH, though most riders were expected to take it at less than half that speed.

This was where Shock intended to take the lead. Right now, Napoleon Neapolitan was eight positions behind him, and his custom-built two-wheeler was untested on such a tricky route. It certainly didn't look like it could corner worth a damn: its wheels were too large and its centre of gravity too high. With a little luck, Napoleon would take a turn too fast and end up with his skull driven into his chest cavity.

Shock's comm-link buzzed into life, and his race-planner Amanda Quisling asked, "You read me, Shock?"

"Loud and clear, boss."

"Just heard that De Oro is going to try to take The Crowbar at full speed. He reckons his machine is up to it." Jules Castel De Oro was in fourth position, riding a tank-tracked Vista Tachyon. "So, you know, watch out for flying debris and body parts."

"Gotcha. How are the rest of the team doing?"

"They should be on your screen, Shock."

"That just tells me where they *are*. What's the mood like back there?"

"Gardiner and Clayton are going to pull in front of Sharry Bean in about four minutes. They'll slow her down—that should give McHattie a clear run past her. He can open the throttle then and should be able to move into fifteenth."

"Cool. What about Jaunty Monty? He disappeared off the list a few minutes back—haven't had time to check."

Quisling paused. "Jaunty's gone, Shock. Mutie clipped him as he was taking Hangman's Turn."

"Damn... He's dead?"

"Yeah. Sorry. I know you were friends. He left instructions... His winnings are to be divided up among the survivors on the team. That's twenty grand apiece, right now. Small consolation, I know."

Shock spotted an oil slick far ahead and eased to the left to avoid it. "What do you mean, winnings?"

"Jaunty bet against himself. He always did. He put fifty grand down that he'd not make it to the half-way point. Got four-to-one from The Smilin' Aztec."

"Why the hell would he—"

"Because if he wins the race, he doesn't care about losing the stake, and if he loses the race, he wins the bet."

Shock laughed. "Damn. That's smarter than I ever gave him credit for. No wonder the drokker was always happy. Should have done the same thing myself."

Quisling said, "Shock, you'll hit The Crowbar in ninety seconds. Come out of it in one piece."

"That's the plan." Shock shut off the comm-link and focussed his attention on the road ahead.

Here, as he approached The Crowbar, temporary seating had been erected on either side of the road, packed with thousands of cheering fans, each of whom had paid at least two hundred credits for the privilege. When it came to the Mega-City 5000, the citizens weren't afraid to spend good money in the hope of seeing their favourite biker, even if it was only for a second or two as he or she zoomed past.

Directly ahead of Shock, the independent rider in ninth position—Gavin Sable—slowed way down. Shock cruised past him, then nudged his bike to the right and drew parallel with Tiana Valdivia in eighth, just as Valdivia had been edging to the right side of the track in order to take the first corner of The Crowbar.

This forced Valdivia to slow down and draw back. On Shock's monitor, Valdivia fell into position right behind him, and Shock pulled his first dirty trick of the race. It wasn't technically against the rules, but it was the sort of thing that very much divided the fans. He flipped a switch on his controls and his Blenderbike's rear brake light came on.

Valdivia, thinking that Shock was slowing down, reacted by hitting her own brakes. It was a simple idea and Shock grinned to himself as he saw the gap between them immediately widen.

That should have been the extent of it, but Valdivia had been taken completely by surprise. She'd hit the brakes too hard, and her bike wobbled, and wavered. Its front wheel suddenly flipped to the left and then Valdivia was in the air, tumbling, her bike shedding jagged metal fragments as it spun and crashed along behind her.

Valdivia came down head-first with a noise loud enough to be heard even over the gasps of the crowd.

Shock didn't directly see what happened next—he was already past the next corner and gaining on the rider in seventh place—but the TV cameras caught every moment of it, and relayed it to his bike's screen.

Gavin Sable was moving too fast to safely avoid the debris from Valdivia's bike. His front wheel collided with the fuel tank, crushing it, spraying the road with the high-octane compound.

Aw crap, Shock thought. *Just one spark and—*

A shard of Sable's bike, later determined to be a drive-shaft, crashed down onto the road's surface. The fuel erupted, a massive ball of white-hot flame that turned the rest of the bike—and much of Sable's body—into burning shrapnel.

It was the biggest single-crash accident in the race's history: ten riders killed within seconds, six of them muties.

Shock forced himself to keep calm, telling himself over and over that it wasn't his fault. Valdivia had been too close, she'd over-reacted to the brake-light trick. *She should have been a better biker,* Shock told himself. *Who the hell allowed her to participate, anyway? There ought to be laws about that sort of thing. If you're not up to standard, you shouldn't be permitted to enter the race.*

As Shock neared the end of The Crowbar, his screen showed him that Napoleon Neapolitan had come through the crash unharmed, his bike's oversized wheels allowing him to ride over most of the debris with little damage.

Shock's screen flickered and Napoleon's face was glaring out at him. "*You* did that, Shock. That's six of my men wiped out. Screw the rules. Screw the *race*. You're a dead man riding."

Fourteen

RILEY MOELLER HAD given Dredd a list of five names, all former scavengers. Dredd recognised the names of all except one, Winston Fierro. Five years ago, when everything fell apart for Chalk in Eminence, Fierro had been temporarily seconded to a team combing the undercity, the ruins on top of which Mega-City One had been constructed.

Of the five, only Dean James Squire and Rhea Kinsley were still operating as scavengers. They had both applied for and been granted leave to return to the city and watch the race.

Fierro and the others were now unemployed, their contracts terminated one by one as the constant scouring of the Cursed Earth had picked the wastelands clean of useful materials. "All three of them are still in the city," Control told Dredd.

The closest to Moeller's apartment was Marshall Rose, resident of James Blocker Block. Control confirmed to Dredd that Rose was at home: thirty minutes ago he'd gone online to order a Mega-City 5000 souvenir thermal underwear set during one of the race's many commercial breaks.

Dredd was minutes away from the block when his radio buzzed. "Dredd? This is Judge Franklyn, at Blocker... It's not good news. Rose is dead. So's his partner and three friends who were with them watching the race. Not more than a few minutes, I'd say—blood's still dripping down the walls. Perp came in through the door, shooting. Took Rose down with a large calibre. Likely the same point-seven-six recoilless from the diner. We're pulling the block's security cams and I've called for back-up to run a door-to-door on the block, but I wouldn't hold out any hope."

Dredd was already veering off into a cross-street. "Acknowledged, Franklyn. Stay on the scene until forensics can identify the friends."

Dredd checked his bike's screen. The next closest potential target was Avril-Jane Morante. He called up her citizen's ID card, showing a stocky woman with blonde hair: Dredd recognised her as one of the other hostages from the mayor's warehouse in Eminence.

Should have been a full investigation, Dredd said to himself. There had been no reason to suspect Percival Chalk of anything beyond the killing of Mayor Genesis Faulder, but as the only Judge present, Ruiz should have ordered a complete background check on the other hostages. *Sloppy work. Even if Ruiz* had *been beaten and tortured, she should have known better than to believe their side of the story without checking it out.*

Avril-Jane Morante's block was on the west side of Sector 179, and right now Dredd was sixty-four kilometres away in Sector 55. On a normal day, it would take him twenty minutes to cover that distance. Today, traffic was a lot lighter because everyone was watching the race... But Sector 179 was cut right down the middle by the fastest stretch of the Mega-City 5000.

"Dredd to Control. I require an air-lift. Get a H-wagon to my location ASAP."

"Nearest available H-Wagon is in Sector 40, Dredd. ETA fifteen minutes."

"Not good enough. Find the closest *un*available one and *make* it available."

"You're still looking at twelve minutes minimum, Dredd. What's your destination?"

"Joanne Vanderbilt Block, Sector 179." Already, Dredd could hear the roar of the crowd gathered around the race's route.

"Understood. I'll—" The voice of Control was cut off, and another voice said, "Dredd—this is supervisor Walton. Word from Judge Meacham at Vanderbilt. Citizen Morante is dead. Meacham is in pursuit of two male suspects, one matching the description of your perp. They're still in the block. I've ordered it to be sealed but current response times are slow."

"Drokk..." Dredd focussed on the road ahead. To get from his current location to Joanne Vanderbilt Block, he'd have to cross the race line at some point. There were underpasses and flyovers, but nothing that wouldn't take him too far out of the way. The fastest route was straight through. "Walton, I'm westbound on Avenue Double-A, four minutes ten away from the track."

"I see you, Dredd. But—"

"Order the crowd-marshals to clear me a path through to the track, and shift the barriers wide enough for me to pass through. Two metres should be enough. Same on the other side. I'm cutting across the track."

"Recommend against that action, Dredd. The race leaders have just emerged from The Crowbar, and right now they're going hell-for-leather to establish their positions. That's a four-hundred kilometre stretch... By the time they reach your position they'll be touching five hundred KPH. Cutting across them would be—"

"You'd better be getting it done while you're talking to me, Walton," Dredd snarled. "Three minutes fifty."

Walton muttered, "Grud-damn it..." and began shouting orders. "It's in progress, Dredd. No guarantees. You hit the barriers at the speed you're going and there'll be another Judge for us to bury, if we can find all the pieces."

Ahead of Dredd, Avenue Double-A straightened out, giving him a clear run to the race's route.

As he peeled out of the last curve on The Crowbar, Shock slammed on his Blenderbike's accelerator and afterburners at the same time. Ahead of him, Vavavoom Grupp was in sixth place, less than a second behind Travis Cannon.

Behind Shock, Napoleon was coming up fast, his custom-built machine sailing past Aposcar Kresky in eighth as though he were standing still.

Napoleon and the other surviving Muties had been bombarding Shock with obscenities and threats constantly since the accident in The Crowbar, and Shock's screen showed that public opinion had completely turned against him.

Even if he won the race, he'd be despised. There would be no big-name sponsorship deals.

For a moment, he considered pulling out. There was still time to pretend that he hadn't grasped the extent of the crash. He might just be able to get out of this mess and save face. Might even find a way to persuade everyone that his brake light came on as the result of a malfunction, not a deliberate action.

But now he wanted to win. He wanted that more than the money any sponsorship deals might bring. He wanted to win so that next time he met that smug drokker Napoleon Neapolitan face-to-face, he could brush it off like it was no big thing.

And it wasn't just for him. The Spacers was one of the city's largest biker gangs. A thousand members were rooting for him, desperate to finally shut those damn Muties up once and for all.

A warning message flashed on his screen: "Caution—track compromised! Cut speed and prepare to stop!"

Yeah, right, Shock thought. *Easy enough to hack into a bike's computer and send fake messages. Clever trick, Napoleon, but you're not fooling me.*

He wiped the warning message off the screen and called up the positions. Napoleon was in eighth place now, only a kilometre behind Shock, and maintaining his speed. All of the other racers were slowing down.

Okay, that's *not good*, Shock thought. *If the warning was real, then—*

Directly ahead of him, something large, dark and fast streaked across the track.

Shock swore and slammed on his brakes. The Blenderbike's speed dropped to three hundred, two hundred, one-fifty...

And Napoleon Neapolitan's giant-wheeled monstrosity shot past him.

"Drokker!" Shock screamed. He jerked back on the accelerator again, ramped it up to full speed as he passed a barely-glimpsed gap in the barrier. Napoleon was already a dot in the distance.

DREDD'S LAWMASTER ROARED along Avenue Double-A and he tried not to notice the horrified expressions on the thirty-citizen-deep crowd as he approached the narrow gap the Judges had forced between them.

Three more Judges were heaving frantically at the temporary barrier, trying to shift it aside before Dredd reached them. Dredd knew he could tear it to shreds with his bike's cannons, but that would be disastrous for anyone standing nearby. He eased his fingers toward the Lawmaster's brakes, though he knew that at this speed he'd never be able to stop in time.

With a last shove, the three Judges shifted the barrier just barely wide enough for the Lawmaster: it lost some chrome as it passed through, and then Dredd was darting across the track toward the gap on the other side, aware that any number of fast-moving bikers could be barrelling toward him from the right.

He kept his eyes straight ahead. No point looking—if one of the bikers was going to crash into him, at the speed they were all travelling he'd get a fraction of a second of warning, nowhere near enough time to get clear.

Then he was on the other side, his Lawmaster coming within a centimetre of clipping one of the Judges who was trying to keep the crowd back.

"I'm through," Dredd said to Control.

"I see that," Walton said. "Damn. Should have had money on you, Dredd."

"Gambling's illegal, Walton. What's the situation with Chalk?"

"Still not confirmed that it *is* him. Judge Meacham's got the suspects pinned down in the block's multi-storey parking lot. He reports that the suspects are armed. All interior cams are down. No fault reports logged—must have just happened."

Dredd slowed his bike to ease it around a corner. "Send Meacham's current position to my bike and patch me through to him." He ramped up the speed again. Joanne Vanderbilt Block was directly ahead.

"Meacham here," a voice over the radio said.

"Meacham, this is Dredd. I'm your back-up. Status?"

"Parking lot's full—overflowing, in fact. I'm on level twenty-six. Perps are somewhere above me. All exits are sealed. The only way out is through me."

"Acknowledged. ETA two minutes. Don't let him get past you."

"Wasn't planning on it."

Joanne Vanderbilt Block was a mid-sized building, ninety storeys tall, clad in polished plasteen—designed to be resistant to graffiti and general weathering—and home to over one hundred thousand citizens. Running vertically through the building's core was its parking lot. Although few of the block's citizens actually owned vehicles, they still guarded their parking spots with extreme vigour and took great offence to anyone using them. Except on occasions like the Mega-City 5000, when the residents hung a huge, hand-painted banner from the roof announcing that parking for the day was available at only twenty credits per vehicle, per hour.

The fifty-metre-high banner flapped gently in the breeze, matching those of the surrounding blocks.

Dredd had read the reports of last year's race: in Sector 86, one particularly enterprising block manager had locked access to the parking lot an hour before the race ended, and gone to the movies. Sixteen thousand vehicle owners had been forced to wait an extra three hours before they could retrieve their cars. Three extra hours meant an extra sixty credits per vehicle, netting him a nice bonus of almost a million credits in cash. He'd kept half, divided the rest between the block's residents and everyone was happy, until one of them killed him and took his half too.

As Dredd's bike hit the intake-ramp for Joanne Vanderbilt Block, the ground trembled and almost immediately his radio came to life once more. "Dredd... Meacham. *Damn*, these guys are hard-core. And they're seriously packing. Grenade-launcher and Grud only *knows* what else. Two of us aren't going to be enough." Another explosion rippled through the building, and above Dredd several windows shattered, showering the ramp ahead of him with crystalline shrapnel. "Stomm! A couple more like that and they'll bring the block down!"

Dredd skidded his bike to a stop. "Fall back, Meacham. Let them see a way out—it'll be easier and safer to take them out in the open." He could already hear screams from within the block.

Meacham's voice came back, softer now. "All right... they're going past me... Vehicle's big, armoured, I think. Looks like a Chameleon, ten years old maybe. Dredd, that thing's going to smash through anything you put in front of it. Nothing short of a H-wagon is going to be able to stop it."

"I know the model," Dredd said. "Built for use in the Cursed Earth. Doesn't have a lot of speed."

"I don't know about that... It's moving pretty damn fast right *now*."

Dredd heard the roar of the Chameleon's engine and the screech of its tyres as it rumbled and scraped its way down the parking lot's interior ramps. "Control—you following this?"

"We are," Judge Walton said. After a slight pause, he said, "Dredd, not good news. The Chameleon is registered to Meredith Rousseau. She was senior mechanic on Chalk's scavenging team. She wasn't present at his arrest in Eminence—safe to assume she's one of the few who didn't side against him. A month ago Rousseau bought—"

The entire ramp shook and buckled as something powerful exploded inside the block. Dredd looked up: directly above him, the block's plasteen facade was cracking. He spun his bike about, and roared down to the street, moments before a five-tonne chunk of steel-reinforced plasteen slammed onto the ramp.

High above, through the billowing dust, Dredd saw the Chameleon crashing through the wall. It tumbled as it plummeted, straight down toward the shattered ramp.

And then its descent slowed. The two-tonne, armour-plated vehicle quickly righted itself, and soared over Dredd's head, rapidly gathering speed as it headed toward the crowds gathered to watch the Mega-City 5000.

"Dredd? Dredd, you read me?"

Dredd fired up the Lawmaster and peeled off in pursuit of the massive flying craft. "I read you, Walton."

"Don't know if you caught that last part... A month ago Rousseau bought fourteen reconditioned skysurf anti-grav motors."

"Yeah," Dredd said. "Yeah, I can see that."

SHOCK'S SCREEN TOLD him that Napoleon Neapolitan was thirty-one kilometres ahead, in third place, when the bulky vehicle passed overhead, following the path of the race. For a second, he thought it was a H-wagon—and there was a fleeting moment when he saw himself being arrested for causing the crash in The Crowbar—but it was the wrong colour, the wrong shape.

And it certainly shouldn't have been there.

Muties, he thought. *Has to be*. Though they were genetically normal, the team mostly operated in the Cursed Earth—hence their nickname—where the terrain was rough and the weather appalling. They were good, too, there was no denying that. They knew how to cope with pretty much anything. It was said that Napoleon Neapolitan himself had once travelled on foot from Mega-City Two to Texas City, a journey that few people would have the courage or the tenacity to take behind the wheel of an armoured truck.

But the Spacers were tough too. Many of them, like Shock, had spent years working in the asteroid belt, or on the Lunar colonies. Tooling around on your bike in the Cursed Earth was one thing, driving a skimmer towing a million-tonne iron-ore asteroid from the belt to the moon was quite another.

The flying vehicle—Shock didn't recognise the make or model, but then he rarely saw them from this angle—was fast, approaching supersonic speed, and ahead he saw it veer sharply to the right. *What the hell? He's following the race route!*

Another two vehicles zoomed overhead, followed quickly by a third, then a fourth and fifth close together. Justice Department Hover-Wagons, definitely recognisable from below. And at the speed they were travelling, Shock guessed they were in pursuit of the first craft.

If this *was* a Mutie tactic, Shock couldn't see where it was leading. He called up his race-planner on the comm-link. "Amanda, what the drokk is happening?"

"No idea, Shock. The Jays are all going nuts; there's talk of shutting down the race. Might not be a bad thing right now—you'll be hard pressed to catch Napoleon at this rate."

"I'm *not* letting that Mutie drokker win. Not this time."

"Figured as much. You're faster than he is, but it's not going to be enough unless something slows him down."

"The rest of the team?"

"Endrian's just made it out of The Crowbar. She's riding well. Tiny chance she'll catch up with you. The rest of them are close behind her, but they're not likely to place. You want a Spacer victory, it's up to you to take it. Your machine holding up?"

"Everything's still in the green."

"Then keep on Napoleon until we hear that the race *is* shut down. He's still got Silver and Cannon to pass, and Silver's got a four-second lead on him. Odds are he'll take her before they reach Sector 141. By that stage you want to be no more than eight seconds behind him."

DREDD'S LAWMASTER ROARED back through the gap in the crowd and again clipped the edge of one of the barriers, but it was a glancing blow, barely enough to slow him down. Now he was on the track, following the route, gradually gaining on one of the riders. "Control..."

"Sorry, Dredd," Walton said. "We shut the race down now, we'll be looking at a hundred-million-strong riot."

"What's the status on Chalk?"

"Spy-cams have positively identified him as the driver of the Chameleon. We've got two of the H-Wagons locked on but if they open *fire*—"

"The debris will rain down on the crowd," Dredd said. "Chalk knows that. That's why he's following the route."

"We've got the results of the DNA test on the diner shootings... Two of the grenade victims are on the list Moeller gave you. Squire and Kinsley. That leaves only one... Winston Fierro, resident of the Abbitat Habitat, Sector 115. Dredd, that's on the race's route, the last major turn before the finish-line." A map of the route appeared on Dredd's screen. At Sector 102, four hundred kilometres from Dredd's current position, the route took a turn to the right, heading west until it reached the edge of Sector 141, where it took a meandering south-east path back to Sector 115. Then came the last stretch, a two-hundred-kilometre run down to Sector 124, the southernmost tip of the city.

"Tell me you've already got a squad on the way to pick up Fierro." Dredd activated his bike's sirens as he reached the racer, the celebrity rider Jeremiah Kentson, who stared open-mouth at Dredd as he steadily cruised past him.

"Affirmative," Walton said. "Expecting a report from them any minute. If Chalk is going to stick to the route, you can exit the track at Sector 102 and cut across MegSouth to 115. That'll take close to seven hundred kilometres off your journey. I'll have the Judges at 102 prepare an exit route for you."

"Understood." Dredd wondered why Control was being so cooperative all of a sudden, but this wasn't the time to ask. Stopping Percival Chalk was the only thing he should be focusing on right now.

What's his end-game? Dredd asked himself. *He knows we're after him. There's no way he can escape. Even if he heads out into the Cursed Earth, the H-wagons are more than capable of following him.*

And there was something else niggling at the back of Dredd's mind... the Chameleon was running on AG motors designed for skysurf boards, and the Chameleon was a lot heavier than a board and its rider. Even fourteen AG motors wouldn't be able to power a vehicle of that mass for longer than a couple of hours, and that was only if the Chameleon wasn't carrying anything heavy. Dredd estimated that Chalk still had over nine hundred kilometres to go before the route hit Sector 115. At five hundred KPH, he was going to be cutting it close.

And then what? He's got to know by now that we're anticipating his targets.

IN HER ROOM in the Justice Department Med Centre, Judge Amber Ruiz flipped the TV screen to Channel Epsilon. Her wounds had been sealed and her torso was encased in a rapid-heal unit, and even though she'd been anaesthetised from the chest down, she was sure she could feel the machine's needles and scalpels working away inside her.

There was no longer any pain, and for that she was grateful. In her career as a Judge she'd been shot eighteen times, but this one had been by far the worst.

"Now, Peter," one of Channel Epsilon's unseen commentators said, "no doubt you'll correct me if I'm wrong, and I wouldn't blame you, but isn't this an unusual turn of events?"

"A Judge on the track? Indeed it is, Ted. I don't think we've seen a Judge on the track before."

Ruiz shook her head in dismay. *The man is fearless.* She'd been following the case from the moment she regained consciousness.

The screen cut to a close-up of Dredd, sitting grim-faced on his Lawmaster as it hurtled past the baffled crowds. "I'm wondering..." the first commentator said, "well, he's moving pretty fast there—viewers at home, you can see on your screens that he's close to five hundred kilometres per hour—and I'm wondering, at this late stage in the race, *can* he win?"

"Well, Ted, he's young, he's fresh, and as we all know the Lawmaster is one of the most powerful motorcycles ever built. I'd say he has every chance."

"Y'know, it puts me in mind of the late Rip Venner. He was a Judge before he took up scramble-biking. Played Inferno for the Harlem Hellcats for a while. Or did I dream all that?"

A med-Judge entered the room, and Ruiz beckoned her over. "How much longer do I have to stay here?"

The young woman checked the monitor at the end of Ruiz's bed. "Another day, at least, then maybe six to eight days before you can return to duty."

Ruiz pulled back the thin sheet covering her body. "And suppose I check *myself* out?"

The med-Judge smiled. "Go ahead. If you can walk as far as the door, I'll even drive you back to your quarters."

After a moment, Ruiz said, "I can't move my legs."

"That'll be the anaesthetic. We need to have you immobilised so that the rapid-heal can work." She moved closer and pulled the sheet back into place. "My advice... Take the time to recover. And prepare your case, obviously."

Ruiz raised an eyebrow. "My case?"

"You were in charge of that hot-dog run. You take responsibility for anything your cadets did." The med-Judge regarded Ruiz with an expression of pity. "They say this is the first serious blemish on an otherwise exemplary career. If you're lucky, the SJS will take that into account."

The Judge leaned back against the bed's headrest. "The SJS."

"That's what everyone is saying. They're going to want to talk to you." The med-Judge gave her another pitying look as she left the room.

Ruiz sighed. The Special Judicial Squad were the Judges who judged the Judges, given special dispensation to act in any way they felt was necessary to root out corruption and incompetence. No one came out of a meeting with the SJS unscathed. Ruiz had even heard of Judges taking their own lives when faced with the SJS. *I didn't do anything wrong*, she told herself. *We gave Chalk a fair sentence. We can't be held responsible for his actions after his release.*

She suppressed a shudder. *The SJS. Grud-damn it, that's* it *for me. Pendleton and Collins are dead, and they're going to want to blame someone for that.*

An unexpected, bitter thought jumped into her mind: *And they won't blame Joe Dredd, because he's one of Goodman's little golden boys. They'll pin it all on me.*

She took a deep breath—as deep as the rapid-heal would allow her—and forced herself to relax. *It could be just a rumour. Surely if the SJS wanted me, they'd have shown up by now.*

Then the door was pushed open, and a tall, slender woman stepped in. Her black uniform was graced with silver instead of gold, skulls in place of eagles. The woman removed her helmet and ran a black-gloved hand through her close-cropped hair. "Judge Amber Ruiz. I was told you were awake. Gillen, SJS."

Fifteen

SHOCK CHECKED THE map of the race's route. He was still in fourth position, behind Silver Sylvia, leader of the Fishsickles. Neapolitan was six kilometres ahead of her, in second place. In the lead was Travis Cannon, an independent rider who'd been quickly dismissed by the bookies and pundits as a no-hoper. Cannon had taken the lead early, and stayed there far longer than anyone had anticipated. Now, there was every chance that he'd cross the finish-line in the top three. Possibly even first, if Napoleon Neapolitan couldn't catch him.

For most of the other riders, the race might as well be over.

The route took Shock up onto the Southern Pass Elevated, a long banking highway that swept to the right. Here, Shock could make up some of the lost time. Neapolitan's custom-built machine had done well on the flat, straight roads below, but hadn't proved to be as capable on the curves. Shock opened the throttle all the way, revelling in the tremble in his arms as he held on with all of his strength.

A glance at the speedometer: Four-eighty. Four-ninety. Five-twelve. *Come on, come on! Push it!* He cursed himself for using up his one-shot afterburners coming out of The Crowbar.

The speedometer on his screen touched five-thirty-one, and flashed red. Shock couldn't help grinning. *Oh, man... New record! Eat that, Napoleon! Even if you* do *win, all anyone's gonna remember is that I slowed down to let the Judge cross, and you didn't. They'll be wondering how much faster I could have gone if I hadn't dropped speed.*

Far ahead, as the elevated highway smoothed out, he saw a dot on the track that could only be Silver Sylvia. His screen showed her a kilometre away. He'd overtake her in less than a minute.

And just beyond Silver the H-wagons were still in pursuit of the other vehicle, now bearing down on the sharp right-turn at Sector 102. Already, two of the H-wagons were peeling away from the herd, banking to the right. If the unregistered flyer stuck to the race's route, they'd be able to cut him off.

As Shock came within grabbing distance of Silver's bike, another three H-Wagons also cut the corner.

He's either an idiot or a genius, Shock thought. *If that was* me *flying that thing, I'd follow the route closely until a sharp turn like that, get them to anticipate where I was going to be... And then* not *take the turn.*

Sixty kilometres behind Shock, Dredd had come to the same conclusion. "It's a bluff," he told Walton.

"Has to be. Otherwise what's waiting for him at the finish-line? He knows he'll be shot down once he's no longer a danger to the citizens below."

"Our strategists have considered that," Walton said. "If they're right, he'll pass through Sector one-twelve en route to one-fifteen. We'll force him down when his vehicle is over the Trent river. He... Hold tight, Dredd. The team's closing on Winston Fierro's apartment. They're operating on the assumption that Chalk has anticipated them."

"Good," Dredd said. "If Fierro is there, get him out and clear—and make sure it's *seen* to be done. We want Chalk to be chasing us, not the other way around."

Dredd switched his bike's screen to the feed from the camera slung underneath the lead H-wagon. *If Chalk's going to take the corner and follow the route, he'll have to reduce speed now...*

The screen showed the flying Chameleon rocketing over the track at a height of twenty metres, low enough that the turbulence it generated ripped at the crowd's home-made banners. Directly ahead of the Chameleon, the first-place rider Travis Cannon pulled in to the left in preparation for taking the right-angled turn.

As Dredd watched, something fast and bright erupted from the passenger's side of the Chameleon and an instant later Travis Cannon's bike was a tumbling fireball, crashing, bouncing, shedding white-hot parts as it ploughed into the barrier and cut a charred, blood-spattered path through the crowd.

Drokk... Dredd shut off the screen and concentrated on the road. There was nothing he could do now to help the dead and wounded.

★ ★ ★

SHOCK ALMOST MISSED the accident. He was a hundred metres behind Napoleon, gradually gaining on him, when Channel Epsilon cut to show Travis Cannon's last seconds, then repeated the clip over and over, from different angles.

In slow motion, it was clear that Cannon had been shot by an occupant of the flying craft.

"Son of a...!" Shock put a call through to Napoleon's bike. It was answered immediately. "That's how you're gonna play it, Napoleon? You're gunning down your rivals?"

Napoleon glared back at him. "*What*? Don't try to pin that on *us*, drokker! You *knew* I was going to overtake Cannon on the next stretch!"

"You wanna take this to the next level? Is *that* what you want, Mutie? Then here's the deal. Screw the track. Screw the rules. And screw the damn prize-money. It's just you and me, first one to cross the finish-line alive wins."

Napoleon snarled, and nodded. "You're on."

Shock slammed on the controls to disconnect the call.

He'd always known that sooner or later it would come down to this, the Spacers versus the Muties. The Mega-City 5000 was just a way to vent some steam, but instead of damping the tension between the rival gangs, it had only served to stoke it. Regardless of the race's outcome, there was going to be blood on the streets tonight.

The Judges would come down hard on them for this, that was certain, but Shock didn't care. Once past the finish-line at Sector 124, he'd keep going, out into the Cursed Earth. They might follow him, but they'd never find him.

His comm-link buzzed, and the team's race-planner Amanda Quisling said, "Shock—no. I'm shutting you down! There's no proof that the Muties have anything to do with that!"

"You're fired, Amanda." He flipped the communicator to connect with every other member of the Spacers. "You all hearing this? The Muties are willing to shoot down their rivals, so the rules no longer apply. They've still got five riders in play. You take them out any way you can, or I swear to Jovus you'll answer to me. Anyone got a problem with that?"

For a second, the only response was silence, then Brown Clancy said, "No problems here, Shock. I've been stuck behind Sharry Bean for an hour and the drokker's just weaving back and forth making sure I can't get past. Wouldn't hurt me one little bit if I ram her off the road."

"Do it, Clancy. Same goes for the rest of you. The race is over. Now it's war."

Napoleon was forty metres in front of Shock as he approached the turn's optimal point, the spot at which he should pull to the left before swinging right, to take the turn with as little loss of speed as possible.

The Mutie pulled to the left, but kept going. His giant-wheeled bike streaked toward the flaming remains of the barrier into which Travis Cannon had crashed... and smashed through, punching a ragged, screaming hole through the already-injured crowd.

A Judge in Napoleon's path drew his Lawgiver a second too late: the bike's left wheel struck him head-on, crushing him instantly.

Shock was right behind. He steered his Blenderbike directly at one of the scattered fragments of the barrier. The angle was ideal, his speed perfect. The Blenderbike sailed into the air above the heads of the terrified citizens closest to the track.

He felt the bike's still-spinning rear wheel shudder as it shredded the face of a particularly tall onlooker, then he was crashing down, hard, landing on the shoulders, backs and legs of a dozen citizens trying to scramble clear.

No going back now, Shock thought. Not that he wanted to.

He slammed into a citizen who'd been getting to his feet after diving out of his rival's way, opened the throttle again and rocketed down the almost-empty street in pursuit of Napoleon's bike.

"SHUT DOWN THE race—now!" Goodman roared at his assistant. As Judge Brannigan reached for his communicator, Goodman added, "Jam the TV feeds and arrest every rider on the Mutant and Spacer teams. All their support people, too... Hell, arrest them *all*. Round up everyone connected with the race—easier to sort them out in the cubes."

Goodman dropped back into his seat, staring at the screens in front of him. One screen showed the casualty figures. Fifty-eight dead. As he watched, it was updated. Sixty-five dead. Sixty-seven. He mentally pictured his InstaFeedback approval rating dropping as the body-count rose.

Seventy dead, hundreds injured. And that was just the citizens watching the race: it didn't include Percival Chalk's victims.

"TV feeds jammed, sir, but I think it might be too late. The word's already spreading through the social networks."

"Shut them down, too."

There had been worse days in his tenure as Chief Judge, and he had no doubt that worse days yet were still to come, but this one was personal. *He*'d opened the race. The citizens associated it with him, and by extension the entire Justice Department. The Mega-City 5000 was official. Stamped with the Department's metaphorical seal of approval.

Already, only minutes after the murder of Travis Cannon, there was chaos on the streets. As always, opportunistic low-lifes were rioting and looting, taking out old grievances on other citizens. In Sectors 52 and 180, citizens had torn down the barriers and were on the track, oblivious to the bikers hurtling toward them at two hundred kilometres per hour.

The bikers themselves were side-swiping each other, trying to slam their opponents into the barriers or even into the crowd.

"Riot foam," Goodman said to Brannigan.

"H-wagons already on the way, sir," the assistant said. Then he added, "Sir... there *is* a way to quell the riot before it really gets going."

"Knew I kept you around for some reason. What is it?"

"We declare a winner. Make the citizens think it's all over. We can blame the attack and the subsequent loss of feed on dissidents."

Goodman nodded. "That might work."

"One problem. Before they left the track, the leaders were still a couple of hours away from crossing the finish-line. And that's where the biggest crowds are. If they don't *see* their favourites cross the line, they'll never believe it."

"Then to hell with subterfuge. We're going to defy tradition and tell the citizens the truth for once. They never believe what we say anyway."

Sixteen

As the Justice Department analysts had predicted, Percival Chalk's souped-up Chameleon left the Mega-City 5000 route at Sector 102, but instead of heading straight for Sector 115 and passing over the uninhabitable region surrounding the Trent river, it took a wide curve to the west, sticking to the populated areas.

Dredd's Lawmaster roared down the dead centre of the track, sirens blaring, as thousands of panicked spectators scrambled over the barriers to escape other rioters, or to just cause some mayhem of their own.

Walton's voice said, "Dredd—make a choice. Go after the race leaders or follow Chalk. My team here will support you all the way, whatever you decide, but right now we can only give our full attention to one of them. It's your call."

"Chalk," Dredd said. "Send a H-wagon after the bikers. Tell them to shoot on sight."

"You prefer them wounded or dead?"

"I want them *stopped.*"

"Understood. Dredd, drop your speed—there's a wagon approaching you from behind, ramp down."

Dredd's screen showed the craft hurtling along the track behind him, only four metres above the ground. His radio buzzed again. "Judge Dredd, this is H-Wagon 22. Control instructed us to give you a lift. Prepare to ditch the bike and grab on as we pass."

"Negative," Dredd said. "You're taking me *and* the bike. Get in front of me, match my speed. And watch out for civilians."

The craft passed overhead, the ramp in its undercarriage so close to Dredd he could have reached up and brushed it with his fingertips. The H-wagon dropped down ten metres in front of Dredd, keeping pace with him. He nudged the Lawmaster's accelerator a little, and screeched to a stop on the ramp. The H-wagon's co-pilot and engineer grabbed hold of the bike as the ramp rose back into the craft. The H-wagon was already rapidly gaining altitude.

"You okay?" the engineer asked. "You must have been doing over—"

Dredd climbed off the bike. "Engine's running hot, fuel's low. Give it the works."

He pushed past the co-pilot and dropped into the man's vacant seat. "Chalk?"

The pilot tapped a screen in front of Dredd. "That's him. There's eight wagons on his tail. Nine, counting us. There's no way he'll escape—that monstrosity just can *not* have the range and speed we do."

Dredd activated his helmet radio. "Walton, what's the situation with Chalk's last target?"

"Winston Fierro wasn't home. Neighbour said he was planning to be at the race's finish-line. I've already issued his ID to the spy-cams. We'll find him."

We've been assuming that Chalk is going after Fierro because Moeller gave us his name, Dredd thought. *But it could be a bluff.* "Call off all the H-wagons but the two closest to Chalk. Send one after the bikers. The others are better employed dealing with the crowd."

"Won't be so easy to herd Chalk with just three of you up there."

"Chalk was a weapons dealer, Walton. We don't know what he's carrying. More H-wagons in the air just gives him more targets." Dredd checked the monitors. Far ahead, already over Sector 111, the modified Chameleon was keeping low, never more than a hundred metres above ground level.

Dredd patched the screen into the lead H-wagon's camera feed. It showed the Chameleon zipping back and forth between the sector's blocks and skyscrapers, always too close to them for the H-wagons to risk opening fire.

To the pilot, he said, "We'll never catch him by following his path. We need to meet him at his destination."

"Right. Fierro's block—the Abbitat Habitat in Sector one-fifteen."

"What if that's *not* his destination?" Dredd called up a map of the city's southern sectors, then contacted Walton. "There were four others with him in Eminence. Rose, Morante, Kinsley and Squire. They're all dead."

"This much I know," Walton said. "Point?"

"We've been assuming that Winston Fierro is next on his list because he's on the race's route. But five years ago Fierro had been temporarily assigned to a different team exploring the undercity."

"And we know from Judge Meacham's report that Chalk wasn't alone in Joanne Vanderbilt Block. You think maybe Fierro's the other man? That's possible. If Fierro wasn't in Eminence, he couldn't betray Chalk."

On the screen in front of Dredd, Chalk's vehicle dipped and soared, dodging left and right as it wove a complex path through the tangled junction of two dozen elevated highways, known locally as The Knot. The other H-wagons were having difficulty anticipating its path.

"I think I know what he's planning," Dredd said. "We need to head him off. Take us up," he told the pilot. "High arc, top speed. Head for the finish-line."

SEAMUS "SHOCK" O'SHAUGHNESSY saw nothing but the road ahead and the back of Napoleon Neapolitan's bike.

He was only dimly aware of the pedestrians scattering before them, of the vehicles skidding to a stop as they blazed through junctions, of the Lawmasters' sirens trailing them and the H-wagon dogging their path behind them.

His mind was filled with fury at the Mutants, and Napoleon in particular. Whichever way this ended, Napoleon was going to die.

Shock didn't know this part of the city too well. He'd studied the race's route carefully in the previous months, but now they were off-track, and if he hadn't been following Napoleon, he'd be lost, especially since his Blenderbike's on-line map was no longer functioning. *All* communications were down, and he was certain that Judges had ordered a full block on the networks.

But that didn't matter. All he had to do was stick close to Napoleon until the finish-line was in sight, and then they'd see who was the better rider.

The wheels of his bike rumbled over the inlaid rails of the sector's old-style tram system, slowing him a little, and ahead he saw that Napoleon's larger wheels were not suffering as much. Shock nudged the bike over to the rail-free side of the road, and his speed picked up a little.

He wished he'd brought a gun. He was a good shot: even at top speed on the bike, racing through unfamiliar streets and dodging panicking pedestrians and swerving vehicles, he'd have had no trouble blasting off the top of his opponent's head. And no qualms.

Ahead, at the massive Discount of Monte Cristo outlet store, a full-scale riot was in progress as citizens took advantage of the chaos to swarm through the store and help themselves to last season's fashions. Shock saw Napoleon collide with a woman staggering under the weight of so many rat-fur coats she could neither see nor hear him coming. As the stolen and now blood-spattered merchandise scattered through the air, the Mutie clipped another woman, this one laden with armfuls of shoulder-bags and purses.

Shock's bike, only half the width of Napoleon's, made it through the throng unscathed, and he gained a few metres on his rival.

★ ★ ★

"SET ME DOWN on the plaza," Dredd said.

"In the middle of the *crowd*?" the H-wagon's pilot asked. "Are you nuts? There's got to be twenty thousand citizens still down there, and they're all looking for trouble."

"They're always looking for trouble," Dredd said. "Today it's the race, tomorrow it'll be something else." He turned back toward the engineer. "How's my bike?"

"Refuelled," the engineer said. "Checked the tyres, re-sprung the rear suspension. Not much else I can do for it here. You could call for a replacement."

"No time," Dredd said. He got out of the co-pilot's seat. "Chalk?"

"Still on this vector," the pilot said. "About eleven minutes behind us. The wagons in pursuit still have their weapons locked on."

"And they still can't risk shooting," Dredd said. "That's what Chalk's counting on."

The co-pilot asked, "You reckon he's going to land and try to lose himself in the crowd?"

"That's my guess," Dredd said. "Only one way to find out for sure." He climbed onto the bike. "Take us down fast but steady, pilot. Make sure the citizens below know we're coming—don't want to squash any if we can help it."

The H-wagon shuddered and lurched a little as the pilot adjusted its course, then began to descend.

"Faster. Set down just long enough for me to get clear," Dredd said. "Then take off and vacate the area." To the engineer, he added, "Prep the ramp."

Less than a minute later, Dredd was back on the ground with the shadow of the H-wagon passing over him.

He glanced around the litter-strewn plaza. In front of him, the large podium erected for the winner was being attacked by a gang of juves, and on all sides the rioters were giving him a wide berth, those who had seen him having dropped their wares before running for the relative safety of the surrounding blocks.

An angry voice behind him yelled "Judge! Let's get him!" and Dredd turned to see a man bearing down on him, wielding a hardball bat. The man was huge, a head taller than Dredd, with a face so pitted with acne scars that he looked like he'd have to shave with a potato peeler.

"There's only one of him—there's thousands of *us*!" the man snarled.

The circle around Dredd widened as he climbed off his bike. "Drop the bat, creep."

He continued to advance on Dredd, thumping the bat against the palm of his free hand. "Who's gonna *make* me, Judge? You?"

"Last warning."

The scarred man broke into a run and bellowed with rage as he pulled his arm back, ready to strike.

Dredd side-stepped the swing and slammed his fist into the man's stomach. The hardball bat clattered to the ground and the giant dropped to his knees, gasping. Tears of pain spilled from his eyes and took meandering paths down his craggy face.

Dredd patched his helmet mike into the Lawmaster's loud-hailer, and pushed the volume up to eleven. "Attention, all citizens. Your identities have been logged—we know who you are. Disperse now, quietly and quickly, and you will not be charged. You have two minutes." On the ground beside him, the scarred man was crawling away.

"Walton? You got eyes on the crowd?"

"It's working, Dredd. They're starting to filter out of the plaza."

SHOCK HAD FOLLOWED Napoleon onto the packed pedestrian concourse at Sector 115, where the race's route looped back for the final run south to the finish-line at Sector 124. Once they knew where they were, they both began to pick up the pace.

Now, they were half-way through Sector 122, racing on empty, open streets running parallel to the Mega-City 5000's course.

Can't be more than fifty kilometres to go... I can do *this. I can* beat *the drokker.*

Cross the line and then keep going, right out into the desert where the Jays won't follow me.

Ahead, a cluster of citizens scattered out of Napoleon's way, and Shock followed in his wake. He saw a panic-stricken man throw himself flat on the ground and the oversized wheels of the Mutie's bike pass safely either side of him. The man was not so lucky a few second later, when Shock ran over his foot and crushed his ankle.

Then they were through the throng and Napoleon picked up speed again.

Shock wouldn't entertain the possibility that they weren't going to make it. He knew the Judges were after them, but they hadn't caught them yet, so maybe whoever it was that gunned down Travis Cannon was a higher priority.

Napoleon shot across a busy junction without slowing, expertly weaving his bike through the dense, slow-moving cross-traffic. Shock was right behind him, his own crossing made a little easier because many of the drivers had hit their brakes when they saw Napoleon.

A few more of those, and I'll be close enough to touch him.

They entered The Cobbles, a region of the sector that was popular with tourists, especially at this time of the year when the prevailing winds from the north kept the stench of the Black Atlantic to a minimum.

On a long stretch of road, Napoleon overtook a roadtrain on the wrong side, narrowly avoiding an oncoming Resyk truck. Shock had followed him, but by the time he saw the truck it was too late to pull back. He nudge his bike to the right, mounted the wide pavement and rapidly weaved around the pavement's trash cans, benches, plasteen statues of local celebrities and artificial palm trees.

As they exited The Cobbles, Shock saw Napoleon glance back for a second, and then they were passing into Sector 124, the final sector of the race.

Thirty kilometres to the line.

Seventeen

Despite Dredd's warning, the citizens took more than five minutes to clear the plaza. But save for a few stragglers who were very slowly ambling out of the area and constantly looking back to see what was going on—there was always at least one citizen who didn't grasp that the word "everyone" included them—there was more than enough clear space.

Dredd waited, watching the skyline to the north. With a little over a minute to go, a trio of teenaged girls darted around from the other side of the podium, each of them wearing dozens of freshly-stolen wedding rings and so many chains around their necks that they had to run hunched over. They skidded to a stop when they saw that the plaza was now empty, save for a lone Judge on a Lawmaster, watching them.

"Drop everything you've taken and get out of here," Dredd yelled at them. "Now!"

One of the girls froze in place, eyes and mouth wide as she stared, horrified, at Dredd. The other two grabbed an arm each and hauled her away from the plaza.

Dredd activated his radio. "Walton."

"I'm here. Chalk's still heading toward you, ETA fifty seconds. Dredd, he's *not* going to set down. If he was planning to lose himself among the crowd, that option is now closed. You've scared them away."

"I know. Instruct the H-wagons to keep the pressure on him. We want him to have no choice but come in low and fast."

"I don't get why he's going to the finish-line. Why not anywhere else along the race's route?"

"Because this is the southernmost sector of the city. The Cursed Earth is only five kilometres behind me. He's hoping we won't know whether he's stayed in the city or gone out into the desert." Dredd glanced north; the Chameleon would be approaching over the top of Brian Alexander Robertson Block.

"Dredd, he'll change course the second he sees there's no one in the plaza. He'll head out into the Cursed Earth for sure."

"No," Dredd said. "He won't. Remind me again why we haven't shot him down yet?"

"Because the falling debris would likely kill thousands of..." Walton paused. "Grud. You emptied the plaza. Dredd, you'll be in the line of fire!"

"And if I move, the citizens will come swarming back."

Then there was no more time for conversation. The customised Chameleon roared up and over the roof of the apartment block in an arc that would set it down in the heart of the plaza, coming straight toward Dredd.

He had a moment to lock eyes with Percival Chalk, the first time he'd seen the man in five years. The expression on Chalk's face changed instantly from shock at seeing the empty plaza to resignation when he realised what it meant.

Then the pursuing H-wagons opened fire.

Dredd gunned his Lawmaster's engine, its massive tyres squealing as it darted out of the Chameleon's path.

The H-wagons' cannon-fire tore through the rear and roof of the vehicle, shredding its armour-plating as though it were paper.

The Chameleon crashed nose-first into the plaza's rockcrete slabs, rippling through them with a shockwave that almost knocked Dredd from his bike.

Even before the perforated vehicle had scraped and ground its way to a stop, Dredd was off his bike and running toward it, Lawgiver ready.

The passenger-side door shuddered once, then a second time, then it collapsed out onto the ground, followed by a man Dredd recognised as Winston Fierro, his body-armour pierced a dozen times by the H-wagon's large-calibre bullets. Fierro arched his back once, groaned, then lay still.

Dredd leaped onto the Chameleon's buckled hood, crouched, with his Lawgiver aimed at Chalk. Inside the cab, Chalk was still held firmly in place by slowly-deflating airbags: a safety feature that clearly hadn't been added to the passenger's side of the vehicle.

Weakly, barely able to turn his head among the airbags, Chalk said, "Stop him, Judge! He'll get away!"

"I doubt that," Dredd said. "Not unless he's holding the world record for crawling with broken arms and legs."

"Fierro *kidnapped* me, forced me to—"

"Not this time, Chalk," Dredd said. "You only get to use the fake-hostage trick once."

Chalk narrowed his eyes as he stared at the Judge. "I *know* you... You were the cadet who arrested me back in Eminence! Then this is *your* fault. Everything that happened today is down to you!"

"Yeah, I've been hearing that one a lot. Still don't buy it. Percival Chalk, on the charge of the premeditated murders of your former colleagues, the murders of Judges Pendleton and Collins, the attempted assassination of Judge Amber Ruiz, extensive property damage leading to the loss of countless lives, and piloting an unregistered flying vehicle without a permit, I sentence you to execution."

Chalk's expression collapsed for a moment, then he shrugged—the airbags had almost fully deflated now—and broke into a wide smile. "Almost made it through, right? Well, go *ahead*, Judge. Pull the trigger, like you should have done five years ago."

"That's not how it works, Chalk," Dredd said. "First, there's the interrogation."

There was a dull *whump* from somewhere beneath Dredd's feet, and a small flame erupted from the front of the Chameleon. Keeping his gun aimed at Chalk, Dredd jumped down from the hood and wrenched open the driver's-side door. "Out. Hands on your head, fingers interlaced."

Chalk started to climb out, then jerked to a stop. "My foot's stuck."

Dredd glanced toward the flame. Black smoke was starting to billow out from the vehicle's buckled hood. "Try harder."

"Damn it!" Chalk struggled, grabbing onto the doorframe for leverage. "Help me!"

"Figure you've got a few seconds before anything explodes." From the north, Dredd could hear engines approaching.

"Help me, Grud-damn it, I'm *trapped*!" Chalk reached down and started to pull at his right leg with both hands.

Dredd moved closer to Chalk. He knew that this could be a trap—was *likely* to be a trap—but at the Academy, the cadets were taught a simple solution to this kind of situation. Dredd pulled back his fist and slammed it into Chalk's jaw.

The man toppled to the side, and as he lay groaning and clutching his face, Dredd leaned in past him, peered into the Chameleon's footwell and saw a small handgun taped to the underside of the dashboard.

He grabbed Chalk's arm and hauled him out of the cab, dragged him ten metres across the plaza, away from the burning vehicle.

The roar of engines grew closer, and Dredd looked up to see an odd-looking machine approaching at speed, with a large wheel on each side and its rider suspended between them. Right behind it and gaining ground was a motorbike, its rider hunched over.

Then something cold and hard sliced deep into Dredd's left leg, quickly cutting through the muscle until he felt it scrape across bone. As Dredd collapsed to the ground, he saw Chalk rolling to his feet, holding a large hunting knife, its blade dripping with Dredd's blood.

Dredd's Lawgiver had fallen from his grip. He made a dive for it, snatched it up—

But Chalk was already darting around to the rear of the Chameleon.

Last push, Shock thought. The finish-line was five hundred metres ahead, with nothing in the way but Napoleon Neapolitan.

Ahead, close to the line, a man was running from a downed Judge, but that didn't matter now. Nothing mattered but the line.

The running man pulled open the rear of the crashed vehicle—it was only later that Shock realised it was the same craft that had blasted Travis Cannon—and removed a skysurf board.

Napoleon was three metres in the lead now.

Two metres.

The line was tantalisingly close, but—just like last year—Napoleon was still ahead.

The man clambered onto the skysurf board and hit its thruster just as the Judge fired at him.

Dredd's aim was true. His shot ripped into the back of Percival Chalk's skysurf board. Chalk toppled back as the board shot forward.

Clearly an experienced surfer, Chalk had taken the extra couple of seconds to tether his ankle to the board. It was a safety precaution, lesson one for all skysurfers.

The board streaked across the plaza, dragging Chalk screaming behind it.

★ ★ ★

Shock saw the board coming, and instinctively hit the brakes. Napoleon saw it coming too, but his own instincts told him it was safe: the board would pass directly over him.

He turned back to grin at Shock. "You lose, Spacer. Again."

Ten metres from the line, the skysurf board sailed over Napoleon Neapolitan's bike... but the screaming man it was dragging behind it was a lot closer to the ground.

Dredd saw Percival Chalk strike the oversized wheel of the speeding bike face-first.

The bike flipped, out of control, spinning and tumbling at first, then shedding parts and limbs as it grated across the cracked rockcrete and came to a stop just over the finish-line.

The other biker was only seconds behind it, but there was no doubt which of them had crossed the line first.

Dredd pulled three medi-patches from a belt-pouch and slapped them onto the wound in his left calf, then tried to stand. He limped toward his Lawmaster, pain shooting through his entire body every time he put his left foot down.

Over the radio, Walton said, "Damn it, stay down, Dredd! The H-wagon's coming back to you. You need urgent medical attention."

"Not done yet," Dredd said, his teeth clenched. He climbed onto the Lawmaster, and slowly rode it toward the tangled mess of metal-and-flesh that had once been a customised bike, its rider, and Percival Chalk.

Overhead, three H-wagons were coming in to land.

The other rider was still on his bike, its engine purring softly, looking down at the remains of his opponent. To Dredd, he said, "I won. You saw it, right? Sure, Napoleon crossed the line first, but he had to be dead by then. That was the *agreement*. The winner is the first one to cross the finish-line alive!"

Dredd regarded him for a second. "Yeah. Yeah, you're the winner. And when we examine the spycam footage of the race, we'll be able to determine exactly *what* you've won. Reckon it's safe to assume that a very long stretch in the cubes will be part of the package."

The other rider laughed. "I don't think so. You know who I am? I'm Shock O'Shaughnessy. I'm the winner of the Mega-City 5000! I'm the best biker in the world—and that's *official*! So if you think you can out-ride me on your Lawmaster, I'm up for the challenge." He began to rev the bike's engine.

Dredd drew his gun and shot out its tyres.

Shock jumped back off the bike and stared at it.

"Run, and the next one punctures a lung," Dredd said. "Face down on the ground, creep. Hands behind your head. Your racing days are over."

Eighteen

"You sure you don't want a wheelchair? Or a crutch, at least?" the med-Judge asked Dredd.

"It's barely a scratch," Dredd told her as he started to pull on a fresh uniform.

"A scratch. The perp damn near severed your leg, Dredd. After an injury like that, you shouldn't even be *standing*, let along thinking about returning to duty."

"Don't need to stand if I'm on my bike, Doc." He pulled on his boots, then strapped his kneepads into place. As he was transferring his badge to the new uniform, he asked, "Judge Ruiz... She still here?"

"Upstairs, room 200." The med-Judge gave him a look of severe disapproval—Dredd figured that it probably worked on some of her patients—and again asked him to reconsider her suggestion that he take a few days to recover.

"Not interested." Dredd pulled on his gloves and flexed his fists. "Thanks, Doc. Be seeing you."

She nodded as he turned toward the door. "Yeah, I expect you will."

Dredd tried not to limp as he strode through the corridors of the Justice Department Med Centre. A couple of older Judges nodded at him as he passed. He didn't recognise them, but they seemed to know who he was. He wasn't certain that he liked that. He'd done his job, that was all.

He found Ruiz's room and pushed open the door without knocking. The Judge was sitting up in bed, watching TV. "You seen this?"

Dredd glanced at the screen, which showed shaky footage of him on his Lawmaster racing past some of the participants of the Mega-City 5000. "I saw it. Some people are saying that the Department ought to field its own team next year."

Ruiz said, "TV off," and the screen blanked. "There won't *be* a Mega-City 5000 next year. Or any other year. The Chief Judge is going to announce it in a few months, when everything's calmed down a little. Over a hundred dead, not counting the bikers. Thousands injured. Millions of credits of property damage."

"Most of that wouldn't have happened if not for Chalk," Dredd said. He paused for a moment. "I heard that you were visited by the SJS."

Ruiz nodded.

"Can't have gone too bad," Dredd said, nodding toward Ruiz's helmet and uniform, which were resting on a chair close to the bed. "You're still a Judge."

"Yeah, pending investigation. They're saying that I was negligent back in Eminence."

"You were."

Ruiz sighed and rolled her eyes. "Damn it, Joe! You don't *say* stuff like that! Don't you have *any* social skills?"

"Never saw the need for them."

"You know, your brother's a lot more empathic."

Dredd shrugged. "If it means anything, I think you're a good Judge. I doubt they'll take you off the streets."

The door opened behind Dredd and he turned to see an SJS Judge entering. She gave Dredd a thin-lipped smile, and said, "I was looking for you downstairs. I expected to see you still in recovery. Name's Gillen." She pulled off her helmet and nodded toward a chair. "Sit."

"I'll stand, if that's not an order."

The SJS Judge peered at Dredd for a moment, then slowly walked around him in a tight circle. "Interesting day, Dredd. Something of a crucible for you, I think. Senior Judges hampering your work, openly expressing negative opinions of your judgement."

Judge Gillen stopped in front of him and took a step back. "Five years ago you had the option of shooting Percival Chalk. Given the situation, you would have been well within the law to do so. Yet you chose to use minimal force. A decision that led to today's events."

Ruiz began, "That's—"

Still looking at Dredd, Gillen held up her hand to silence Ruiz. "I'm still speaking. And today, you had that same chance. I've seen the spycam footage. Chalk attacked you, ran for his skyboard, and you drew your weapon and shot the board." Gillen stared at him. "The *board*. Chalk was a much bigger target, much easier to hit. He was a known murderer. And you shot the board." She spread her arms. "Haven't you learned *anything* from today's events?"

"Sir?"

"Damn it, Dredd, it's not a hard concept to grasp! You let the bad guy live, the bad guy gets out and commits more crimes. You kill him in the first place, that won't happen."

"Chalk wouldn't have lived," Dredd said. "I'd sentenced him to execution."

"Right," Gillen said. "And there you were, in the perfect position to carry out that execution, and you chose not to do it. You deliberately went for the harder shot. Yes, Chalk died when he collided with that bike, but that wasn't your intention."

Dredd considered everything she'd said. Then he nodded. "Correct."

"Explain yourself!"

"I'm not an executioner. I'm a Judge. In my judgement letting Chalk live was the correct option."

"Don't tell me that all human life is precious, because if you do, I'll have you dishonourably discharged within the hour."

Dredd regarded Judge Gillen for a moment, then said, "Judges make the law. We uphold the law. We *are* the law. But beyond the law, there's something else. Justice. If you don't understand that, Gillen, then you are not fit to be a Judge."

She stared up at him, eyes wide. After a moment, she reached up and tapped her badge. "You see that? SJS. Special Judicial Squad. Don't you grasp what that *means*?"

"I do. You're the proof that our system is not yet perfect. We shouldn't need you. Judges should be above corruption, above error. But we're not. We're human. The Judges exist to guide and protect the citizens, and SJS exists to ensure that the Judges perform their duties to the best of their abilities."

Gillen didn't reply. She hesitated for a moment, then again walked around Dredd in a slow circle. "You're Fargo's clone. We've been watching you from the moment you left the Academy. Every action you've taken, every judgement you've passed, has been logged and analysed. You're idealistic, Dredd. Stubborn almost to the point of arrogance. You're intelligent, highly skilled, not especially imaginative, almost completely devoid of ego..." She stopped in front of him. "And you're *right*."

"I know."

"I didn't come here to chastise you, or Judge Ruiz. I'm here to offer you a job. Consider it, Dredd. You are *ideal* SJS material. You want to improve the Justice Department, to weed out corruption and increase efficiency? Well here's where you get to do that." She extended her hand.

Dredd ignored it. "Not interested."

"Dredd, I'm offering you the opportunity to—"

"Don't waste your time trying to persuade me," Dredd said. "It's not going to happen. My job is out there, on the streets. That's what I trained for. It's what I believe in."

"No one has *ever* declined a position in the SJS! Dredd, we are the pinnacle of justice in this city. It doesn't *get* higher than us!"

Dredd moved toward the door. "Wrong."

Gillen frowned at him. "*What*?"

"You're wrong. The Judges serve the citizens, Gillen. We don't rule them. Just as the SJS doesn't rule the Judges... Like I said, you're here to keep us in line. We don't work for you: *you* work for *us*."

"No... Wait! Dredd...!"

Dredd opened the door, and paused long enough to nod to his former mentor. "See you on the streets, Ruiz."

He pulled the door closed behind him.

His leg was still aching, and it was a long walk back through the med-centre to his Lawmaster parked outside.

Judge Dredd didn't complain.

About the Author

Irish Author **Michael Carroll** is a former chairperson of the Irish Science Fiction Association and has previously worked as a postman and a computer programmer/systems analyst. A reader of *2000 AD* right from the very beginning, Michael is the creator of the acclaimed *Quantum Prophecy/Super Human* series of superhero novels for the Young Adult market.

His current comic work includes *Judge Dredd* for *2000 AD* and *Judge Dredd Megazine* (Rebellion), and *Jennifer Blood* (Dynamite Entertainment). *Judge Dredd Year One: The Cold Light of Day* is his first book for Abaddon Books.

www.michaelowencarroll.com

WEAR IRON

AL EWING

PART ONE

MEGA-CITY ONE
2080 A.D.

One

Strader raised the gun and fired twice.

The first bullet scored a trench down the security guard's cheek, glanced off the bone of the jaw and then buried itself in the plasteen behind him. The second round made a neat hole just above the man's left eye, pushed its way through his brain and ploughed out of the back of the skull in a shower of blood and fragments. The guard's eyes rolled back and he staggered once, his feet doing a little shuffle like a soft-shoe entertainer in an old-time cabaret club; a macabre two-step. His finger tightened reflexively on his own trigger, sending a bullet wild, a stray lump of lead that careened off the polished chrome of the front counter and into some poor woman's leg.

Then he finally dropped.

The second guard hesitated—Strader could see the desire to be a hero warring in his eyes with the urge to lower his gun, survive, maybe go home to see his wife and kids again—and then Petersen opened up with the stuttergun and took him apart like a jigsaw puzzle.

Petersen wasn't the best aim, but with a stuttergun all you had to do was point it in roughly the right direction and hold on tight. The hardest part was lifting the damn thing. It had stopping power, Strader had to admit that much.

Which didn't change the fact that they should never have brought it along in the first place. It was too much gun for a simple jewellery-store heist like this—the wrong gun for any kind of serious work. It was cheaply made, prone to jams and misfires, and it only had three or four seconds of sustained fire in it before the ammo ran out. After that, changing out the mag and loading fresh ammo was so fiddly and overcomplicated that it could easily get you killed—and it usually did. Stutterguns had a reputation.

And yet somehow this piece of crap, notorious in its day as a wartime boondoggle slapped together by some enterprising defence contractors to line their pockets at President Booth's expense, had become the go-to killing machine for the juve gangs that were on the rise in the blocks. Probably because they *were* juves, because they didn't know any better—after all, the stuttergun was big, it was mean-looking, and it made a mess. What else was there to care about?

So the gangs were using it for drive-bys, assassinations, block rumbles—lots of spraying and praying, firing indiscriminately like a kid with a water pistol. Most often they'd end up taking out two or three cits for every rival gang member, until whatever Judge was first on the scene took them out in turn.

So while no serious professional worth his salt would touch a stuttergun, the thing had grown itself a reputation among the average Joe Cit as a thing to be feared—the weapon of choice for psychos and crazies who didn't give a damn about collateral damage. It was on all the news channels—special bulletins telling you how to recognise one being pointed at you and what to do about it. *Anything you're told to,* was the short version.

And suddenly, otherwise-smart people like Petersen were taking a second look.

There were advantages to being feared, Petersen had argued at the planning sessions—advantages they maybe couldn't ignore. He'd explained at length that he didn't want to bring one of these deathtraps along on a heist to *shoot* the damn thing—hell, no, he wasn't *stupid*. He's just wave it around a little—it was all about the threat, that implicit promise of violence.

"They see these things every day on the vid," he'd said earnestly, with the smile of a man who thought he'd discovered the secret of turning lead into gold, the magical shortcut that was going to make them all millionaires. "They're already trained to respond—psychologically, you know? They take one good look at that baby, they ain't gonna think twice. They'll drop onto their knees and pray we leave enough pieces of them for the Resyk belt! Right? Know what I'm talkin' about?" He'd guffawed like a donkey on a vid-cartoon. "Hell, you guys probably won't even *need* to bring anything else!"

Strader didn't even bother to reply to that one. It wouldn't have mattered if Petersen was talking about a gun that shot lightning, crapped thunder and counted out the shares for you afterwards—only an idiot relied on someone else's piece.

Wear Iron. That was the rule.

Strader hadn't liked Petersen's big idea one little bit. For one thing, he'd patiently explained as if talking to a two-year-old, a gang of three professional stick-up merchants with more than twenty years' experience between them shouldn't need to play psychological games to knock over a small jewellery store in a chintzy block mall.

For another—but that was when McKittrick, the bagman, had chimed in and cut Strader off. McKittrick thought the idea was 'badass,' and thought Strader was wetting his u-fronts over nothing. And with that, Strader was outvoted two to one. The stuttergun was the official fourth member of the gang.

Strader knew he should have walked then and there. Anybody using the word 'badass' in the context of work was not somebody you could trust to make the coffee, never mind to help pull off a job.

But he was short on options, still over a barrel after the stommshow in Texas City, a casino heist that'd gone south and left five dead and two more cubed, with Strader in the wind only by the skin of his teeth. People had invested in that one—serious people with serious money and serious ways of getting it back—and his share of this job would go a long way to digging himself out of that particular hole.

Last time he'd talked to the Cowboy—a big, one-eyed Texan who hadn't given his real name but had given Strader three all-terrain vehicles to make the getaway with, all of which were now smouldering hunks of twisted metal in a judicial impound somewhere—the Cowboy had made it pretty clear that unless Strader came up with the original investment, plus a hefty vig, inside of thirty days, he'd be breathing rockcrete under the new intersection. That had been ten days ago. Time was running out.

Strader didn't have time to be picky, so he'd let his need—or his greed—get the better of him. He'd swallowed his pride and told himself it'd probably all work out.

Probably.

And to give Petersen his credit, it had worked out just fine. When Strader, Petersen and McKittrick had burst into that jewellery store, everything had gone as smooth as butter.

For a whole minute.

Maybe more.

Petersen had screamed like a futsie and waved his brand-new stuttergun around like a gangster on an old-time vid-show, and the other two had played their part in turn, aiming their .45s at anyone who looked like they might not be getting the message. Four horrified customers hit the floor on command, and the kid behind the counter—some girl fresh out of block college—curled up like a foetus, not even thinking about hitting the silent alarm button under the till. Strader kept a weather eye on the two security guards—they had the biggest potential to make trouble, but right then, in that one perfect moment, they were good boys, the best you could want, keeping their hands well away from their holsters and not letting the thought of death for a paycheque cross their tiny minds.

And in that first golden minute, Strader was happy he'd been proved wrong.

But he wasn't wrong.

The big, ragged hole in Petersen's big, ragged idea was this: not all fear is good fear. Three professionals, armed with professional weapons, acting in a professional manner, and very professionally telling Joe Cit just what'd happen if he stepped out of line for even a moment—that created a useful kind of fear. That made Joe Cit afraid of what would happen if he didn't do what he was told. *These are professionals,* that fear whispered. *You might get through this, if you keep your head and do what the nice men want.*

One maniac waving a stuttergun around and screaming his head off, on the other hand, made Joe Cit afraid of what might happen if he *did* do what he was told. That wasn't useful. That kind of fear was bad for business. It whispered: *these people are crazy, and anything could happen. There's no percentage in keeping your head. If I were you, I'd start taking chances, because they might just be the last chances you ever take in your short life.*

It was the kind of fear that prompted action, in other words. The kind of fear that made the first guard—who wasn't being paid nearly enough for gunplay, and would, under ordinary circumstances, have remembered that—go for his piece in a blur of barely-trained motion and send a slug right through McKittrick's throat.

In that one moment, the whole operation had collapsed like a house of cards. As McKittrick staggered back—scrabbling at the bloody wound that used to be his jugular, making noises like fish used to, back when there were fish—Strader raised his gun and fired twice, and the guard fell, and then

Petersen opened up with the stuttergun he'd sworn up and down he wouldn't use.

And now here they all were.

Strader tore his eyes away from the wet chunks of flesh that'd once been guard number two—the swaying remains of the man's legs, still bizarrely standing like that statue of Ozymandias, the blood and cartilage dribbling down a wall that looked like Swiss mock-cheese—and took a look over at McKittrick.

There was no saving him. He was still twitching, but there was nothing left in his eyes. Next to him, the dame who'd taken the ricochet in the leg lay stiff and lifeless as stone, bright red blood gushing from the wound and soaking the carpet in a spreading pool. The bullet had made a neat hole in her pulmonary artery. Petersen's stuttergun had turned a simple heist into a triple murder.

Quadruple. Petersen, eyes glassy, cold sweat pouring down his face, swung his too-much-gun at the college girl behind the counter and opened up with a second burst that turned everything above her shoulders into wet munce. Her finger slipped off the button she'd been pressing—the silent alarm—as what was left of her slumped to the ground, legs twitching and spasming, heels drumming in the familiar rhythm of the freshly dead. Strader felt numb at the sight of it.

Everyone was being stupid now. The remaining three cits were out of control—whatever spell the stuttergun had cast over them in the first moments had reversed itself when Petersen actually fired the thing. One of them, a bald man of about forty, was kneeling down next to the dead woman with the torn artery, trying fruitlessly to wake her back up, tears splashing from his double chin into the pooled blood. The other two—punk-jocks in fake-leather jackets who'd been shopping for new cheek-rings—took their chance and made a run for the door, crying out for someone, anyone, to help. Crying for the Judges.

Petersen barked an order, hoarse and almost unintelligible, and swung the heavy stuttergun around. In that moment, his wild eyes and the set of his jaw suggested he really had gone futsie. When the stuttergun misfired and jammed, he made a strangled noise deep in the back of his throat and shook the weapon helplessly, as if trying to jar some loose part of the mechanism back into place.

In the distance, Strader could hear a siren. Closing in.

That was another of Strader's rules—the Judges were the law, and brother, you had better believe it. The Academy of Law made them faster, better and harder than you could ever be, even if they weren't Atom War veterans with itchy trigger fingers. Facing down the Jays was for first-time juves and mugs with more guts than brains. A true professional never tangled with the Judges. Not ever.

It was time to go.

He'd already given the job—and Petersen—up for lost. Rule three—no such thing as a job you can't walk away from. The moment he heard the siren, mixing with Petersen's muttered curses as he shook the massive gun like a bad father shaking a crying baby, Strader was already stepping calmly over the remains of the counter-girl and through the door that led into the back offices, walking away from the whole sorry mess.

He turned as the door swung shut behind him, risking a last look at what he was leaving. A Judge was already leaping off his bike just outside the door, Lawgiver at the ready. For his part, Petersen had grabbed the bald man by the shirt collar and was holding the useless stuttergun to his head, yelling obscenities, trying to bluff it out. Strader winced—it looked like suicide by Judge as much as anything. Maybe Petersen's mind really had gone. But then, the Judge seemed young, fresh from the Academy—just a kid, really. After the war, they were rushing them through, trying to bolster the numbers. It was just possible Petersen had lucked out and caught one of the dumber ones—but those weren't betting odds.

Just before the door swung shut, Strader caught a glimpse of the kid Judge's badge: *Dredd*.

Strader turned and walked quickly past the empty office in back and the meagre break room, moving as silently as he could to the fire door—it was alarmed, but Strader knew which wire to cut with his pocket las-knife to fix that.

As he pushed the fire door open, he heard the familiar dull flat boom of a standard execution bullet. It was too bad—and it put a timer on things. Even if the Judge didn't know there was a third man on the job, he would as soon as one of the cits started talking.

Strader was just thankful he had his wrist-com working—or rather, the surveillance blocker built into it, a wireless pulse designed to scramble the software of any cameras within a hundred feet or so. A brief victory for his side in the endless war between those who made security systems and those who broke them—they were already working on plugging the hole, but for the moment, Strader had the edge. And a few other tricks besides.

He reversed his jacket quickly, moving the shocking, fluorescent green from the outside to the inside, replaced by a sombre, fashionable grey. The false moustache and eyebrows went into his pocket, before he pulled off his shoes and tossed them down the stairwell, making sure his bloody footprints ended at the fire door on the thirty-eighth floor. He gave the wires there a quick slash to complete the illusion, then carried on running down the fire stairs to ground level barefoot.

He felt safer now. The black dye in his hair might still identify him, but he could take care of that soon enough. Somewhere above him, a cit was describing some schmuck in a day-glo green jacket that had a moustache a hell of a lot like Rudy Conn's in *Fight Thru The Night* at the Bijou—and that wasn't him, not any more.

Still, he allowed himself the luxury of a little self-loathing as he ran—he'd acted desperate, teaming up with a couple of characters he was better than on his worst day, and as a result he was right back in the hole where he'd started. Worse—he had four murders on his rap sheet he didn't have before, and he had a bad feeling they'd come back to haunt him.

He'd only caught a glimpse—but this Dredd kid didn't seem the type to forget.

Two

FOUR HOURS LATER, Strader was a sector away, staring into a mirror at his naked face.

The hair dye was the cheap one-wash stuff, made for the juves and the club-hoppers—it washed out with just a little help from the cold tap in the toilet sink, leaving Strader's hair a close-cropped, silvery grey. The brown disposable contacts had been removed and dropped into the sink to melt with the dye, leaving behind a pair of eyes that were as cool and green as a mint freezy-whip on a hot summer day.

Strader ran his fingertips over the stubble on his chin, wondering if it was worth a shave, if he could change himself any more completely. Razor burn was a red flag for any Jay looking to fill a day's stop-and-search quota, but part of him wanted to risk it. There was something about the five o'clock shadow scraping the pads of his fingers—something unprofessional, something that felt like bad luck. He shook his head, as if to dispel the urge—superstition was an occupational hazard in his line of work, and something to be avoided. He'd seen too many otherwise-good men take one in the back of the head because their minds were on a missing plasteen rabbit-foot charm or a hat left on a bed in a motel somewhere. Not him. Casting a last look at his own reflection, he dried his hands under the air-jets and walked back into the bar.

He'd picked the joint at random—the Tony Hart Working Cit's Club, a no-account hole buried deep in a block he'd never set foot in before. It was a relatively safe place to work through his options, to try and think of a way of squaring things with the Cowboy and getting out from the net he knew had to be closing in on him. He wasn't there for any company but his own.

So when Bud Mooney waddled up out of nowhere, a wide, almost malicious grin creasing his chubby cheeks, Strader told him to go to hell.

Mooney was poison in the circles Strader worked in. Two hundred pounds of gut and sweat, crammed into a pre-war op-art jacket that made him stick out like a sore thumb. He couldn't run or even move that fast—word had it that he took his leaks into a bag on his leg, the legacy of the same run-in with the Jaybirds that'd sent him for a ten-year holiday in the rockcrete hotel and given him his nervous twitch. When he talked, one side of his face jerked spasmodically upwards into a rictus sneer. He kept a hip flask full of bathtub hooch in an inside pocket to calm the jitters, and after a few pulls—common in any long conversation—his speech became even more audibly slurred, and his eyes flickered and rolled nervously back and forth in his head.

Bud Mooney was a wreck, pure and simple. A wreck and a liability.

There was even a rumour doing the rounds that he might be a snitch, or at least half of one—at one point his name still carried some water among the older school of yegg, but over the past few months, those few friends who'd kept in contact had developed a serious blackmail problem. Those who didn't pay a modest fee to an anonymous voice on the vidphone before a job would find themselves pinched by the Judges during—whoever was behind the scam was probably a Judge themselves, or at least had their ear. But the trail went back to Mooney, and now there was nobody left willing to say two words to him.

It hadn't always been that way. Back when the jacket was still in style, before the ten-stretch and the twitch and the urine bag, Bud Mooney had been one to watch, the undisputed king in a world of princes, a master of his chosen art. Stick-up kids still talked about the Bullet Train Heist of '62—they'd made a movie out of it, though it'd gone straight to vid-slug—but if you pointed Bud Mooney out now and told them how that stumbling, alcoholic wad of blubber had been the mastermind for that caper... if you were lucky, they'd only laugh in your face.

And who could blame them? That Bud Mooney had died with a dumdum bullet in his bladder, and now a fat, broken ghost shuffled through the streets in his place, dreaming impossible dreams of jobs that'd never happen, carried out by crews who could never trust him again, in between pulls of a dented metal flask in an eternally twitching hand. A human shipwreck.

The shipwreck made another attempt at a smile.

The twitch turned it into a leer. "Paul? Paul Strader?" He had teeth missing. Strader winced in disgust.

"I said go to hell, Mooney."

But Mooney didn't go anywhere. He shuffled closer, pulling out a chair and carefully cramming his bulk into it, smiling obsequiously in between sips of some cheap soygin that smelled like lighter fluid. "Listen, I got a job for someone like you."

Strader closed his eyes, shaking his head and hoping the other man would vanish away like a daydream. What were the odds of running into Mooney here? He felt a momentary flash of paranoia shoot down his spine—if someone like Mooney could find him here, the Judges or the Cowboy's people probably weren't far behind. He didn't know which of those options was worse.

On the one hand, he'd be safe from the Cowboy in the cubes. But on the other hand, death might be preferable—even that kind. Maybe it was because he'd never been inside, even for the basic thirty-day misdemeanour stretch that every cit seemed to hit sometime or other, but there was something about the idea of those four grey rockcrete walls closing in on him that filled him with a primal terror.

To be cubed, he knew, would be like being buried alive. Even if the Cowboy took things slow with Strader, he'd be dead and out of it eventually. But he was looking at a life stretch for the fiasco in the jewellery store—and medical technology was only getting better. He could live for a hundred years, maybe a hundred and fifty, crammed into a tiny rockcrete box, spending day after lonely day praying for another atom war to finish him off quickly...

Strader wet his lips, shooting a narrow glance at

Mooney. "Why are you even here? How did you find me?" He tried and failed to keep the panic out of his voice.

Mooney heard it, and smiled. "Don't get your u-fronts in a bunch, Paul." He held up a shaky hand, a little conciliatory gesture. "Pure coincidence, I swear. See, I got this hab across the street, over in Daniels Block—nothin' special, just a dump on the twenty-second floor, but it's got a real good view of the pedway into Tony Hart."

He grinned a little wider, and Strader resisted the urge to smash his glass into those rotten teeth. Maybe save Mooney a few creds at the robo-dentist. "Anyway," the fat man babbled on, "I like to sit and watch the people go by. I had to sell the vid—I got bills—and, y'know, you gotta watch somethin'. Anyway, guess who I saw? I mean, you had black hair, so maybe I thought I'd got it wrong, but I'd know that face anywhere and it sure *walked* like you do—"

Strader slumped back in his seat, listening to Mooney describe how he'd followed Strader into the block, then searched the block directory for a likely bar, some dive where people might go not to be found. He felt a wave of depression stealing over him, like a heavy blanket. Mooney's story sounded like it was at least half a lie, but if it was true—was that how easy it was? All his disguise, all his preparation, and it had been seen through by a half-smart rummy in less than a second.

He thought back to the young Judge, the one who he was sure had caught a glimpse of him—Dredd. That kid had infinite cameras at his disposal, most of them well out of wireless range—plus countless audio bugs, chemical tracers, human snitches and snoops, the whole sweep of surveillance available to Justice Department. Every day there were more eyes and ears on the streets. All "for the good of the citizenry," of course—but all the same, all Dredd had to do was be as smart as Bud Mooney and Strader would be warming a cube by nightfall.

Mooney grinned and drained his soygin, then glanced left and right like some animal watching for its natural predator. When he was sure the barman wasn't looking, he tipped a measure of whatever rotgut swilled around his hip-flask into the empty glass. "Screw 'em," he chuckled, obscenely pleased with this small piece of cheapness. "Crappy drinks here anyway."

He leant back and raised his glass of Grud-knew-what in a parody of a toast. "So here we are. Feels like it's fate, you know? Like it's meant. You walkin' past my window like that. Just when I got something lined up that's perfect for a guy like you. A *professional.*" He meant it as flattery, but coming out of his mouth it sounded like trash talk. "Seriously, I got the sweetest score you ever heard of, all but set up—just *waiting*—and I just need maybe three guys, you included. But, y'know, people don't take my calls these days, so..."

Strader shook his head. There it was. The pitch he'd known was coming since he'd spotted Mooney approaching. He sighed, feeling that depression stealing over him again, and idly wondering if Bud Mooney was the type to drop a dime on him to the Jays or the Cowboy if he didn't get his way. Strader realised he barely even cared anymore. The Texas City mess had left him vulnerable, desperate for half a cred to keep the wolves from his door, and his wild thrashing in the face of that—getting in with goons like Petersen and McKittrick, eating their pie-in-the-sky and asking for seconds—had sucked him into a quagmire there was no getting out of. And now Mooney was here, a man who'd died and still didn't know it, showing up with a pipe dream that'd only make things worse.

"I'm not interested," he muttered.

"Come on..." Mooney's face twitched again, his voice growing shrill, wheedling. "You ain't even heard it yet, how can you say—"

"I've got my own problems, Mooney. I don't have time for whatever daydream you've got rattling around that damn flask of yours, so..." Strader tailed off, hearing how unconvincing he sounded. That was the problem—he had nothing but time. He had nothing at all, and he was out of options. So he shook his head, drained his beer, and damned himself. "Hell with it. Tell me."

Mooney laughed, louder than he'd meant to, then did his prey-animal impression again, glancing around the bar to make sure nobody had heard. When he was satisfied that nobody was watching or listening, he leaned in closer, locking eyes with Strader.

"It's the Herc," he said.

Suddenly he had Strader's full attention.

Three

Kool Herc Infernodrome was a white elephant waiting to die.

They'd only built the damned thing three years before—back when everyone figured Inferno was going to be the sport of the future—but already it was on life support, and the so-called wise heads in the sports business were nodding sagely and telling everyone who'd listen how they'd seen the crash coming all along.

Which was a lie—pure, corn-fed bull. At the start of it all, everybody had been right on board.

Back then—and to sports fans it already seemed like a lifetime ago—Inferno was the undisputed king. It was Aeroball with all the safeties taken off, and a whole lot of extra carnage put in to spice it up a little: bikes with spiked wheels, giant clubs for smashing the ball or somebody's head across the arena. A little slice of the Ancient Roman circus to keep the hoi polloi of the Big Meg happy and satisfied with their otherwise-dreary lives. If you could sum the whole thing up in a single word, that word would be *decadence*.

Decadence was in that year—it wasn't so long after the war, and a fair chunk of the city was still running their water through a Geiger counter every morning while they scratched their heads and tried to work out if the weird-looking birds with dog's heads that kept landing on the windowsill were safe to eat. A little honest decadence went a long way, and there was nothing in the world more decadent than Inferno.

So it was only natural that Donald T. Donald should get in on it.

Donald T. Donald was the Investments King of Mega-City One, at least according to *Rich Geek Weekly,* which he happened to own. He was all about decadence—he knew that what the average cit craved right now was a taste of unimaginable luxury, a promise that things were going to get better one day soon. Small luxuries and big promises were two things Donald T. Donald knew how to work with.

Besides, he loved Inferno—loved the glitz and the guignol of it, the audacity, the spectacle. When Donald T. Donald loved something, he had a tendency to buy it, turn it into solid gold—metaphorically and sometimes literally—and then sell it again. So nobody batted an eyelid when he bought the top six teams in the league and announced he was going to build a multi-billion dollar stadium to put them in.

Donald never did anything by halves, and the Herc was no exception to the rule. He spent a year designing and building a monument to excess for the little people to spend their creds in, a huge, gleaming chrome and plasteen palace, his gift to the game that was taking the world by storm.

Everything had to be the best. Unlike most building projects in the Meg, there weren't any half-measures applied or corners cut—Donald paid top dollar for the best architects, the sturdiest plasteen mix, for a building that'd stand the test of time. The insides were just as fancy as the exterior—one hundred thousand capacity seating, with real leather seat covers and holo-projectors that livecast the action to the back rows, all while smiling waitresses brought muncedogs and brewskis direct to your seat at the push of a button. There were gold-effect taps in all the bathrooms, and the bathrooms seated a hundred at a time, so comfortably that you could spend a whole match dropping a deuce and think of it as creds well spent.

It was a palace of the people, and the people loved it. They couldn't get enough of all those small luxuries, even though they had to pay way over the odds to use them—though, since all the biggest games of the season were being played in the Herc, it wasn't like a real Inferno nut had much of a choice in the matter. What were they gonna do, watch it on the vid?

So the Herc was on course to make back its capital in three years, maybe less—and after that it was pure profit all the way, a money bin that would never empty. Inferno was here to stay. It was making big creds in tickets, in concessions, in share prices for the teams—there wasn't a surer thing going in the spring of 2077. Donald T. Donald was so sure of the quality of the Herc as an investment that he'd sunk two billion and change of his own money into it.

When the financial zines asked him about that, he'd said the cash was as safe in his stadium as it would be in a bank.

But then, banks in Mega-City One aren't all that safe.

And what nobody really noticed, at the time, was that the sport of Inferno was already under attack. From the second it came into the world to the second it went out, it was being hit hard from two sides, and that was what would eventually kill it.

On the one hand, you had the Judges, who didn't like the game one little bit, even if it was technically within the law. Under the infamous 'No Foul' statutes of the Booth era, all manner of assault and battery had been made fully legal, just as long as it happened on a pitch during a game. That had been one of the things that won Robert L. Booth the election—that and stealing it. But he was gone now, and the Judges weren't exactly slaves to popularity.

Besides, they didn't call Inferno a 'death-sport' for nothing. Top players were being sent to the cubes on a weekly basis, for everything from performance-enhancing drugs to good old-fashioned manslaughter. When the Judges had to stop play in the last quarter of the Wolves-Steelers game—so they could arrest the Sector Ten Steelers' star player, Tony Lanzarotti, for murder in the first—the writing should've been on the wall for anybody smart enough to read. But that game, arrest and all, had been hailed as the most exciting sporting event of the season, with more than three hundred million cits tuning in live to watch Lanzarotti hauled to the cubes and double that buying it on pay-per-view after—and those numbers were all anybody saw.

Had they been left to their own devices, Justice Department might have swallowed Inferno in the name of keeping the cits content. A thousand people sitting down to watch one crime are a thousand who aren't pulling crimes themselves, and the Judges were never above that kind of mental arithmetic, no matter how much they might protest otherwise.

But from the other direction, you had the syndicates.

Inferno was the biggest new thing in sport for fifty years, and the rougher it got, the crazier everybody went for it—and that included gambling. Suddenly, the kind of fear-the-law types who'd fill their pants if they even had a library book overdue for a day were placing big, illegal bets on their home teams. There were more arrests for illegal betting in the summer of '77 than there were for assault.

So the gambling syndicates were making more money than they'd ever seen, more than they knew what to do with. This was the two-cred end of the business, the nickel-and-dime stuff, and suddenly the low-rent shmoes who'd been put in charge of it were hauling it in hand over fist. With big money came big power—when gambling was suddenly the city's number one racket, the Godfathers and Bosses of Bosses were more than ready to sit back and listen to the experts. And these were people who knew how to reward profitable work.

Inside of a month, the lowest-tier soldiers in the whole operation started cruising the streets in brand new, top of the line gravmobiles, eating hotties with real meat in them, being handed penthouse suites in the best hotels the mob had in their pocket. More than that, they were calling the shots—they were the money men, after all. The Bosses weren't about to say no as long as the creds kept coming.

But maybe they should have. It's a truth universally acknowledged that if you take some schlub who's never had more than ten creds in his pocket, and give him more wealth and power than he can even comprehend, said schlub is going to go more than a little screwy.

And decadence was in that year.

It was the Hellcats Murders in '78 that finally upset the applecart and blew the roof off the good thing the syndicate boys had going. The schlubs and shmoes had been throwing their weight around for months, taking every bit of rope the Bosses gave them and throwing themselves big fat necktie parties with it. The Jays were all over them like a rented tuxedo, trying to get something they could use, but the lawyers the mob provided were just too slick. Except now the legal bills were starting to eat into those giant gambling profits in a big way, and the Bosses were taking a second look at what their shiny new lieutenants were up to.

So naturally, these idiots, these little Caligulas in an empire they didn't build and had no idea how to run—they doubled down on their own stupidity, figuring there was nothing they couldn't do, no way they could ever get caught. And right when these saps-in-wolves'-clothing were looking around for something really dumb to get caught doing, the city's best-loved Inferno team—an old Aeroball squad trying their hand at the new game, a real underdog story making waves on all the vid-shows—decided they wanted to buck the syndicate system.

Very few knew the exact details of what happened

next—but the rumour that did the rounds was that the syndicate goons wired the Hellcats' team captain to a bomb, then made the rest of them fight robots in the Inferno arena until they were all dead.

There's decadence and there's decadence. It takes a lot to shock a Megger, but that story did the trick—it was all the sports shows were talking about for weeks, if not months.

That was when attendance at the Herc—at Inferno stadiums in general—began to fall off. There were a number of reasons—for one, most of the Hellcats fans refused to transfer their allegiance to a new team. Instead, they waited patiently for the Cats to get back on their feet, like the old-time Heroes had after the bus crash that'd killed half their squad.

But that kind of lightning doesn't strike twice. The Hellcats never returned, and their fans never returned to the game. Other sports took over.

For fans of the other teams, there was more than a little guilt in the mix—you don't get a Roman circus without people going to watch the lions, after all. But for the most part, what was cutting attendance at the big games was fear. Too many of the people who'd been going to those games, going to those gold-tap bathrooms, spending that money, were now taking a long hard look at the syndicate problem and asking—*what if next time it's us?*

What if next time they decide to take out the whole stadium and all the fans in it? These are crazy people. They're capable of anything. Let's stay home and watch it on the vid.

Joe Cit had never been known for bravery in the face of danger. Within the month, everyone was watching the game on the vid, from the comfort of their couches, in the relative safety of their habs. Which left the Herc a year shy of paying for itself, and suddenly high and dry.

Donald T. Donald did what he could. He gave vid interviews, cut ticket prices—he even bought the stadium the Hellcats had died in in the neighbouring sector, just to tear it down, like it was carrying some contagion he didn't want spreading to the healthy stock.

But the dominoes were falling now. The Judges cracked down hard—not just on the syndicates, but on the whole game. Pretty soon, if you figured on playing Inferno by the standard rules, you should factor in a half-time break of about three years so the players could do their cube time. Everything had to be dialled down—the game was slower, the plays softer. The teams would pussyfoot around each other, afraid to even try tackling the ball.

Suddenly, the circus was closed. Inferno with the blood and guts taken out was just a bunch of people chasing a ball around, like any other sport. That was the last nail in the coffin—towards the end, the Herc seated six. Six people out of a capacity of a hundred thousand, and five of them didn't even order a beer.

A month later, attendance was at zero, and by now they weren't even tuning in on the vid. Inferno was dead, and the biggest, most luxurious infernodrome in the city was haemorrhaging cash like there was no tomorrow—hundreds of thousands of creds a day, every day for month after month, as the cits and even the players moved on with their lives.

The last person ever to die in the Inferno arena was Donald T. Donald, the one-time Investments King, who blew his own head off with an antique shotgun on the five-yard line. His creditors divided up what little he'd left behind, which included the Herc. By the time 2080 rolled around they were still trying to get some use out of the damned thing—putting on concerts, crude robot fights, even musical theatre. But it was a band-aid on a severed limb. The Herc was dying, and unless some new sport came along to replace Inferno—something just as decadent, something reeking just as strongly of overindulgence and spectacle—it'd be dead in a year.

And then someone had an idea.

Four

"Eating?"

Strader looked at Mooney like one of them had gone crazy.

"*Competitive* eating." Mooney clarified, taking another long gulp of his cleaning fluid and grinning through his brown and missing teeth like a cat with cream.

Strader shook his head, impatient. "I don't get it."

"Here's how it is." Mooney shifted his chair forward, eager to describe the horror of it all in copious detail. "You round up a whole bunch of fatties together. Not carryin' a few extra pounds like I am, I'm talkin' real gutbuckets. Like they gotta walk with special wheels underneath 'em to hold up their bellies or whatever, just so's they can put one foot in front of the other. And you line these hambeasts up in front of... they're kinda like feeding troughs, like conveyors dropping food down from these overhead storage lockers. So you got pies, sausage, cake, ice cream, whatever, all in this constant flow right into their fat mouths—and they sit there and eat as much as they can. Sometimes it's in ten minute bursts, sometimes it's eat 'til you drop, it varies with the rounds. They get judged on capacity, speed, uh, weight gain..." Mooney laughed at the disgusted look on Strader's face..

"Sometimes they weigh the puke after." Mooney laughed again, almost a giggle, as his twitch pulled his face into a manic sneer. "Y'know, so's they can check speed of digestion."

Strader felt a little like he was about to throw up himself. He'd imagined something like a pie-eating contest from an old vid, or maybe one of the sick challenges restaurants used to do back before the war, before the concept of conspicuous consumption had fallen so heavily from grace. If you went to the halls of records, you could find seventy-year-old vid-shows where a guy tried to get a ten-pound burger down in an hour, or eat twenty plates of oysters in a sitting, like that was an achievement. Then again, maybe it was—Strader had never seen an oyster up close, but from the pictures they looked a lot like phlegm in a shell, and he had to imagine they tasted about the same.

This, though... Strader couldn't get his head around it. Inferno was one thing, but what Mooney was describing...

How far was this city going to fall?

He shook his head, as if trying to jar the mental picture loose from his mind. "These..." He swallowed hard. "These contests. How much do they actually get through? How much to they eat?"

Mooney smirked, getting more comfortable as he

poured himself another shot of whatever-it-was. He had Strader on the hook now, and Strader knew he knew it. "Ah, there's usually eight to ten piggies at the troughs, and every trough holds around a ton. Not that anybody's ever eaten that much, though—it's just there to be sure, y'know? Like, just in case anybody can do it. Usually, though? Unless it's a real good game, maybe a third of it gets thrown away. Just dumped on a landfill for the rats." He smiled, a malevolent gleam in his eyes. "They pour bleach on it first. So no vags eat it."

Strader did the arithmetic in his head. Somewhere around three tons—pure waste. "Three tons..." Strader blinked, his face pale and sweaty. He remembered his mother, in the tiny, cramped apartment they'd shared after his father had walked out of their lives, watching him with a smile creasing gaunt cheeks as he devoured a single slice of processed, meatless baloney—their food for the day. That had been when the wage crisis was at its height, when fifty-five per cent of Americans just couldn't afford to eat. Paul Strader's family had been poor even by those standards.

To this day, the thought of wasted food could wake him from a sound sleep. What Mooney was describing was like a nightmare come to life. "Why don't the Jays do anything?"

"What, the Judges?" Mooney snickered, shaking his head. "They love it, brother. Ain't nothin' illegal about eating food—hell, the way they see it, the cits need to be a little tubbier. Less trouble that way. It's the hungry cits that cause the problems."

Strader stared at his empty glass, suddenly craving another drink. He knew all about hungry cits.

Mooney leaned forward, warming to his theme. "You know what your problem is? You still think it's how it was right after the war. Or back when we were kids. Advances have been made, Strader. We got mock-proteins now. We can grow pretty much anything we need to put in our bodies on one of them new food printers—make it up outta munce and synthoil. Maybe a bit of plasteen in there for texture—sure, it's indigestible, but who cares? Point is, things ain't hand to mouth anymore. We can afford to live a little."

Strader winced, hard. Mooney cocked his head, a brief flicker of sympathy crossing his face in between the twitches, and he took another quick look around. If the barman had a problem with people bringing their own booze into the place, he was doing a good job of hiding it—Mooney drew his battered flask out once again and wordlessly poured two fingers of clear fluid into Strader's pint glass.

Strader didn't usually drink on a planning session—if that's what this was—but at this point, he was glad Mooney had made the gesture. He nodded his gratitude, then look a careful sip of the liquid, wincing harder than before as it crawled across his tongue, raw as paint-stripper. A sickly feeling seeped into his gut with the bathtub booze as he realised he was listening attentively to a man who drank this stuff twenty-four hours a day.

"Listen," Mooney hissed, all traces of humour vanished. "I'm not trying to sell you the sport. You think it's sick—well, maybe it is. It ain't healthy, that's for sure. But the point I'm trying to make here is that this thing, these eating contests—none of this is going away. This ain't a passing fad, Paulie, y'know? The cits are spending money like water to go see these lumps fill their bellies, and promoters are starting to take notice. It's all over the vid—which maybe you should start watching occasionally, by the way. I heard on the news that they're talking about making it a new Olympic event, like taxidermy. This is *big*."

With the rotgut burning a pleasant hole in the pit of his stomach, Strader was starting to see the full picture. "Big enough for the Herc?"

Mooney grinned, poking the tip of his tongue through one of the gaps in his teeth, looking particularly pleased with himself. "Got it in one. They finally found something freaky enough to put in there. See if you can picture this without throwing up, Mister Sensitive"—Mooney laughed, making a little vid screen with the fingers and thumbs of both hands—"ten of the biggest, hungriest porkers in the grunt-and-guzzle game, gorging themselves to the finish in an odyssey of supreme piggishness that will—"

Strader narrowed his eyes, holding up one hand. "Skip the colour commentary, will you?"

Mooney shrugged and smirked. "I'm just quoting what they said on the ads, Strader. I can't help it if they get so excited. The Mega-City Munch-Off—ten fatsos, ten rounds, one hundred tons of food. Binge and purge—each round, they sick it all up and start over, otherwise they'd burst like pinatas. Vomit pinatas." He sneered malevolently. Maybe it was just the twitch, but Strader again found himself resisting the urge to punch the big man right in the face—or maybe throw up neatly in his glass. Either would get the message across.

"Mooney—"

"Okay, okay. I get it. Skip the commentary." Mooney chuckled, shaking his head genially. "Here's the point. This is the inaugural eating contest at the Herc. This is whatever suckers got landed with the Herc putting every cred they got on making it work—and these guys know what they're doing, y'know? This ain't like the last days of Inferno—the wheels ain't come off this bus yet. Maybe they never will." He shifted in his seat, taking another furtive look around at the empty bar. "Okay, you ain't a sports guy, you don't watch the vid, you want to throw up just thinking about this—I get it. But you gotta understand that this eat-off is all some of the vid-channels are talking about. There's gonna be a turnout for this thing for you wouldn't believe. That means *creds,* Paulie."

"I dunno," Strader mused, frowning. "Most of that's going to be electronic—straight from one computer to the other. You'd need a hacker to get at it, and guys like that don't generally need guys like us. Different skill sets."

"Not this time. That's the beauty." Mooney was grinning wider now, the twitch making his face jitter like a broken vid. "Like I said, the guys who own the Herc? They know what they're doing. They're smart cookies. See, they know that what Joe Cit wants more than anything is what he thinks he might not get." He giggled again, so pleased with himself Strader could smell it on his breath. "They're not selling these tickets, Paulie. The only way you get into this thing is to come to the Herc on the day and queue. They ain't letting anybody camp out, either. On the day or nothin'."

Strader blinked, amazed at the stupidity of that—

or maybe it was genius. He couldn't tell. "Jovus. There'll be a riot."

"Sure there will. That's probably what they want." Mooney drained his glass, setting it down with a flourish. "They run out of tickets, they start turning folks away, the trouble starts, the Jays roll out—suddenly the Herc's on all the vid-channels, with cits rioting 'cause they can't get in." He laughed, unscrewing his hip flask and taking a swig from that to chase the rest. "Because they can't get into the *Herc!* You imagine telling someone that a week ago? It'll be the best damn commercial that place ever had."

Strader rubbed his chin, brushing his fingertips against the stubble. "How big is the score?"

"Thousand creds a ticket. You do the math."

One hundred million creds. Strader frowned, brow furrowed, looking for the catch. There had to be a catch. "They can't all be paying cash—"

"Cash or nothing, Paulie. No change given, either." Mooney shook his head, as if he couldn't believe it either. "Makes sense. Credit swipe takes three, four times as long to process as a cash payment, especially with exact change. Multiply that by a hundred thousand cits, you got no time for the game. And Joe Cit don't care. He's a simple sorta animal—make something a little harder for him, he'll just want it more. Hell, you know what I'd do if I didn't have this damn bag strapped to my leg?" He wet his lips, looking into the distance. "I'd find an alley on the way—between the Herc and some super-rich block like Pete Andre or Clive Dunn. I'd just stand there with a blackjack and wait. Half the dumbos scurrying by would have crisp thousand-cred bills in their pockets—it'd be like bears fishing for salmon."

"Salmon?" Strader had a vague memory of the word.

"Something my Dad used to talk about. The point is, even accounting for the creeps who bring their change jar along—" Strader nodded at that. Coins, unless they were rare or somehow worth more than face value, were no good as part of a score. Even the new lightweight plastic ones were too much weight for too little value. "Even if we only grab the hundreds and above, that's seventy, eighty mil. Easy." Mooney looked him dead in the eye. "And we can do it with a crew of five."

Strader frowned. "You said three."

"I said I needed three. I'm in, and I got another guy in—the guy who brought it to me—that's five." He chuckled again, as if remembering something funny. "Well, technically there's gonna be six, but one of us ain't coming back, if you know what I mean..."

Strader narrowed his eyes. "We're not stiffing anyone out of their share—not on a score this big. It's just asking for trouble down the line. People have long memories in this game."

Mooney lifted his hands in a little placatory gesture. "That ain't what I meant. And..." He sighed, as if he'd run through this in his head a hundred times and still not thought of a way to put it. "That ain't the part you're going to have a problem with. See... you remember I said there was another guy in already? Besides me? The guy who brought me this thing?" He took a deep breath.

"Well... that guy's a Judge."

Five

Strader walked through the block park in a dour mood, lost in thought.

Above him, the mechanical sky sputtered and fritzed. The beautiful, calming blue overhead, marked with just a wisp of cirrus, was provided by a dome of curved vidscreens, set flush with one another. In the richer blocks, the effect was seamless, but in Tony Hart the borders between the screens were clearly visible, and several weren't working at all. The results gave the place a distinctly eerie air, like being trapped in some old movie about machine intelligences run amok. The grass underfoot was cheap, too—plastic blades of astroturf that shone unhealthily in the artificial light. A lone plastic tree, sticking out of the acre-and-a-half of fake green like an afterthought, completed the lack of illusion.

Not many people came to Tony Hart Block Park. Which was the way Strader liked it—he needed somewhere to be alone and think, after the impromptu meeting with Bud Mooney.

After the revelation about the Judge, Strader had pressed Mooney for more details, but Mooney had clammed up. If Strader was in, he'd said, he was in—no compromises. His Judge friend, he'd hinted darkly, was going to make sure nobody went back on their word.

"I mean, right now, we're just talking, y'know?" He'd said, eyes darting this way and that. "I'm talking about a possible score, you're listening. I ain't named any names. You walk away now? Well, it'd be a shame to lose you, Paulie. You're one of the best, or you were last time I checked. But if I tell you all the details... if I tell you who I'm *with* in this... I can't let you walk, Paulie. I mean, *he* can't." Mooney'd lowered his voice further, looking uncomfortable in a way Strader hadn't seen before. "He's dangerous, y'know? The kind of dangerous that gets you paid, sure, but... you do not want to cross the man."

Strader had finished his rotgut—regretting it even as it hit his throat—and stood, meaning to say he was out. This situation broke two of his rules. For one thing—never, ever have anything to do with the Judges. Even the corrupt ones—they were either double-bluffing you, waiting to reel you in on a sting, or they were genuinely crooked, in which case they were unpredictable and hard to work with. The whole point of Judges was that they weren't part of the real world—they were on the monk trip, celibate, almost completely removed from society. A corrupt one wasn't fully part of their world *or* yours—which made them dangerous. And not the kind of dangerous that gets you paid.

Not to mention that Mooney having a friend on the force was confirmation of all the whispers that had done the rounds, the ones that said he wasn't to be trusted. So there was that.

The other rule—once upon a time he'd had them all written down—was never to say yes to a job before you know all the details. Ideally, you can massage any flaws in the details yourself, but some plans were just unworkable, and you didn't want to be locked in to an unworkable plan. Especially with the kind of people who might decide not to let you out again. Like, for instance, bent Judges who ran protection rackets on operators like him.

He'd stood, looked Mooney in the eye, and...

"I'll think about it."

And now, here he was, in an empty plastic park. Thinking about it. He leaned against the artificial tree and looked up at the fizzing screens. As long as you didn't try to pretend they were a sky, they were pretty soothing.

He *was* locked in, that was the problem. Within days, he was going to be either dead or cubed—unless he had enough money in his pocket, in cash, to pay off his debts and get out of the city before the net closed in. And now this opportunity had fallen into his lap, as if karma was paying him back somehow for the mess in Texas City.

He scowled, looking down at the sickly grass, squashing the superstition before it took root in his mind. In his experience, the day you started using words like *karma* and believe that there was any kind of balance in the universe was the day you booked your trip on the Resyk belt.

Still, a score like this would net him a cool ten

million share at the absolute lowest—enough to set him up for years, maybe even enough to retire on. He could, if he wanted, buy a bar somewhere with no extradition treaties and live comfortably off the proceeds for the rest of his life. This could be his ticket out of the game. Was that something he could afford to say no to? He might not believe in karma, but he believed in the laws of probability, and a payout as big as this wouldn't come his way again.

He looked back up, focussing on the flickering sky above his head, and decided, as a mental exercise, to assume the worst. Everything that could go wrong, would go wrong.

He assumed Mooney's mysterious Judge-buddy was going to blackmail them—or worse, was working undercover to trap and cube them. He assumed that the plan Mooney had in mind was a drunken pipe-dream with more holes in it than a bagel factory. He assumed at least three other teams were working on heists of their own at the same time, looking to swoop in on their score—Mooney couldn't be the only one to have noticed what was under everyone's nose. He assumed that the Jays had closed off every angle, thought through every possible plan of attack, that he was going to the cubes no matter what he did.

Strader scowled a little more at that, the mental image too much to take. He changed it to an assumption that he'd come out of this with a bullet in the head, and felt much better—the daydream of his own brains splattered on a pristine stadium wall seemed infinitely preferable. A measure of fatality gripped him—even assuming the worst, assuming that he'd come out of this warming a cube or, preferably, riding the belt... what would he have lost? Not a thing.

He was headed in the same direction now—a little slower, that was all.

The thought was bizarrely relaxing, like a weight lifting from him. He looked down from his reverie to see that three juves had wandered into the block park through one of the entry-ways—their spiked leather jackets, a well-worn cliché that was enjoying a brief comeback, were covered with dancing brown homunculi in various sizes, amidst the words TONY HART BLOCK MIGHTY MORPHS. One of the new juve gangs.

Strader gave them a quick look-over, checking to see if they had any real weapons. They weren't carrying stutterguns—a bitter smile crossed his face at the thought—but they'd have switchblades on them at the very least. The toughest-looking of the three, a girl of about sixteen with torn-off sleeves, subdermal implants running up her forearms and jet-black eyes—eyeball tattoos, Strader realised, and found himself wincing in sympathetic pain—had the tell-tale bulge of a shoulder holster under one of her lapels. He supposed that made her the leader; the other two, a couple of barely-pubescent boys—one shorter than she was and still covered in a layer of babyfat, the other tall and gangly—seemed like they were just along for the ride, playing entourage.

Suddenly, the girl turned, looking at Strader with a snarl, revealing that her teeth had been filed down to points. "What you wincin' at, geeko?" Strader sighed gently, irritated with himself. He'd been caught staring—never a good thing with juves.

The two boys with her grimaced and postured in

turn, trying to one-up each other. "Sorry." Strader set his face in what he hoped was a smile. "Didn't mean anything by it." His eyes flicked over her shoulder holster, and he found himself wondering just how much practice she'd had with it. She was young, but they started early these days.

"You know that's our tree, geek?" She spat, hitting the toe of his shoe. The file teeth gave her a slight lisp, which on someone else might have seemed comical. She gave him a hard stare with her jet-black eyes, and he quietly stepped to the side.

"Sorry. I'll go somewhere else." He was smiling, keeping his tone pleasant, ingratiating, but he had a feeling he already knew how this would end. The fingers of his gun hand twitched, and he felt the iron hanging, heavy with bullets, in his jacket. Waiting for its turn to speak.

"Who said you could leave?" The girl took a step closer, and the boys, swapping glances, reached into their jacket pockets and pulled out a pair of plasteen-handled flick-knives, cheap mail-order crap from the back of a Citi-Def magazine. Strader felt his mind numb, as it had in the jewellery store when things had gone bad. Rationally, he knew there was still a way to escape the situation without violence, to keep hiding out peacefully in this quiet, near-derelict block while he considered his next move. But at the same time, he felt his hand slide closer to the concealed holster in his jacket.

Once he made the move—once he drew—it would all happen very quickly. He had no doubt he was faster than the girl, although she was close enough that she might be able to leap on top of him before he could aim—at which point those file teeth would probably bite into his neck. He had a feeling she'd done that before. But assuming she didn't think of that, he had enough in the magazine to put two into her and then deal with both of the boys before they could—

"Hey!"

Strader turned towards the sound of the voice—a deep, rough growl, like gravel passing through an industrial hopper—and he felt ice shoot up his spine, freezing him in place.

It was a Judge. More—it was *the* Judge, the one from the jewellery store, the kid.

Dredd.

He'd been scary—scarier than a kid with a badge should have been—when Strader had glimpsed him through the closing doorway in the jeweller's. There, he'd been all lean, violent muscle and black leather, all purpose—but there was something even more terrifying about him now, as he strode across the livid fake grass to meet them, fists swinging almost jauntily at his sides.

Strader didn't know how he knew.

But he knew that face wasn't meant to be smiling.

"Well, well, well," Dredd grinned, and there was a cruel joy in that deep gravel voice that made Strader shudder. Dredd smiled with his teeth, pearly white and incongruous against the black of the uniform. He flashed his grin at Strader, and for a moment Strader wondered why his hand was back at his side, why he hadn't gone for his piece and fired a bullet through that visor already. But there was another part of him that knew with a cold, hard certainty that Dredd could drop to a firing position and put a hole right through his heart without even breaking his stride. Without losing that smile.

"Take a step back, Paul," Dredd said in that deep, dark voice, and Strader felt his blood ice over in his veins.

"What?"

But Dredd wasn't listening—he'd already turned his attention to the three juves. "You know, you three are a long way away from the hundred and sixtieth floor. That's home turf for you Morphs, right? Down here belongs to the Mister Bennett Boys."

The three of them had backed up a little—the boys were shooting nervous glances at their leader, visibly sweating, the hands holding the knives rammed deep in the pockets and out of sight—it was pretty clear they hadn't signed up for this. Up until now, they'd been playing pretend, making believe that they were grown-ups, that they knew what they'd do when things got serious—and now it was real, now they were a heartbeat away from years of cube-time, they'd remembered they were just kids after all.

The girl didn't say a word.

"So I guess this is an initiation. You three go back with a scalp, and you get to keep those jackets. Am I right?" Dredd was still smiling, the deep voice genial, amused. He jerked a thumb in Strader's direction. "Grandpa over there, maybe? Let me see if I understand—you weren't going to hurt him. You were just going to get his tie. Or his wallet. Or maybe his thumb."

"It ain't l-like that—" the taller of the boys stammered, looking helplessly at the girl—she shot him a look back with her jet-black eyes, shutting him up.

Strader could see how Dredd was narrowing his focus in his body language. He was concentrating entirely on the girl now—she was the key to the situation. Strader couldn't work out why Dredd was taking the approach he was, though. He took another step back, away from whatever was about to happen.

"Sure it is," Dredd said, almost crooning, flashing another smile. "Come on, sweetheart. You think I don't see that pistol you've got strapped to your shoulder?" The smile dropped, and Strader held his breath. "Here's how it is," Dredd said, very quietly. "You three are heading to the cubes. Nothing you can do about that. But there's two ways you can do this. Easy or hard."

The girl opened her mouth, ready to spit venom, but something in Dredd's eye shut her up. He let her have the moment, and then carried on speaking. "The easy way, you go away for about six months. No more. That's the lowest end of the weapon possession charge—if you hand over what you've got right now. That's me being nice." He smiled again, and there was something in that smile that made Strader want to run for one of the exits—but he knew he wouldn't make it three feet.

"The hard way... we go high end on the weapon possession, add in a little mugging, intent—you can get real finickity with intent, that's one of the first things you learn at the Academy. We could go right up to attempted murder. Thirty years." He cocked his head, looking her up and down. "With those teeth and that eyeball-ink, I could get away with fifty. You can't even imagine that kind of time, can you?" He smirked. "Half a century without seeing a human face."

One of the boys broke down in tears. The other looked white, ghostly, and like he might vomit at any second. Strader looked at the girl, and saw that her eyes had gone very wide, and her bottom lip was starting to tremble. It was one thing to be defiant in the face of the law when it was implacable and intractable, Strader knew. When you were given the choice, like this—comply or face the consequences—it was the easiest thing in the world to knuckle under. To take the deal.

"Just show me the gun. You too, boys." Dredd's voice was soft—softer than Strader would have believe that cracked-gravel larynx capable of. There was something wrong about all this—about the whole approach—but Strader couldn't quite put his finger on it.

The girl blinked, those big black eyes suddenly seeming very large and vulnerable, not menacing at all. Then, hand shaking, she reached into her jacket, gently sprung the clasp on the holster, and very slowly—making sure not to point it at anyone—she drew the gun out.

Dredd shot her.

He moved so fast Strader didn't realise what he was looking at at first. One minute, the Judge was standing, hands empty, quietly cajoling—the next, he was in a crouch, the gun in his hand, barrel smoking, and the girl was stumbling back a pace, the gun clutched in her hand and a dark red puncture wound right in the middle of her forehead. The back of her head was gone.

As the girl toppled back, the bright red of her blood staining the livid green of the plastic grass, Dredd aimed and fired twice more. The smaller of the two boys had time for a scream, shrill and hideously truncated.

And then Dredd slid the Lawgiver back into its boot holster, straightened up, and turned back to

Strader. "You saw it," he smiled. "Well, you were never here, but you get the point. They drew on me. I had no choice."

"You..." Strader swallowed hard, mouth dry. "You killed them."

"Kill shot's the safe shot, Paulie. That's what they drum into you at the Academy." He smiled, glancing over the cooling corpses. "Pretty good shot placement, don't you think? Dead centre, head or heart—perfect as always, that's what they used to say about me. Maybe I should go back to the Academy shooting range one of these days—don't you think? Give the instructors a thrill."

"I..." Strader's legs felt weak, jelly-like, as though he was in a dream. Some part of him was already starting to put it together, but the rest didn't want to believe it. "You were at the jeweller's. Barry Scott Block. You killed Petersen—"

Dredd cocked his head, giving Strader a hard stare. "No, I don't think I was there," he murmured, "I think you might have me confused with someone else." He smiled again, and Strader had a sudden understanding that he should shut up about that, right now, that he should let this cold, cruel, dangerous maniac in a Judge's uniform tell him when and where they'd met before—not the other way around.

He was still trying to tell himself that he didn't know how this Judge, this Dredd, should know him, or why he was doing the rounds in Tony Hart, just a stone's throw from Mooney's apartment in Jeff Daniels, when Dredd stuck out a hand, forcing Strader to shake. The grip was firm, hard enough to grind Strader's knuckles and make him wince in pain, and Dredd smiled that maddening, psychopathic smile as he did it.

"Paul Strader. I understand you're something of a star turn in the stick-up game. My old friend, Buddy Mooney"—he put a special inflection on the word *friend*, like it was a private joke—"gave me a call and said you were thinking over my little, ah... proposal."

Strader looked back at him, at the eyes hidden behind the visor. "Oh, Jovus..." He shook his head, suddenly wanting very much to be out of this, wanting to be as far away from this man and his plan as he could possibly get. But he knew it was too late for that now.

"Oh, no." The Judge laughed, giving Strader's hand an agonizing squeeze for luck, then letting it go. "Actually, my name's Dredd." He indicated the badge. "*Judge* Dredd, to the world at large. But you, Paulie..."

He smiled wider, showing his perfect teeth.

"...*you* can call me *Rico.*"

PART TWO

Six

RICO WAS THE best.

And Rico knew it.

Mega-city was *his* city—it had been since he'd came out of the tank. When he rode down the street, watching that mixture of love and fear on the faces of the cits, that look he lived for, he felt like one of the kings of old, parading before his conquered subjects. Then he'd see his own face in a mirror—the Father of Justice, young again, strong again—and he'd know that's exactly what he was, a princeling of Mega-City One, playing games in the city he loved and owned. And he'd laugh.

Sometimes, in his quieter moments, he wondered if there was something wrong there—something wrong in his head. When he was a kid, there'd been an accident on a hotdog run, out in the Cursed Earth. He'd cracked his skull, messed himself up pretty bad—taken a lot of rads in the process. It was comforting, every so often, to blame it all on that—all the cynicism he felt, the growing hatred for the system he lived and worked in, all the blind sheep stumbling around in it, never seeing it for what it was. Maybe he was the problem—wouldn't that be nice?

He wasn't, obviously. The system—the Judges, the Mega-Cities, the whole damned circus show—was pure nonsense, straight from the head of some lunatic Grud playing loaded dice with the universe. Justice Department in particular—that was the blackest, filthiest joke Rico could ever imagine, a savage act of dark comedy imposed on a populace who'd never asked for it but didn't know how to ask for anything else. The party line was that the city was crazy, and that if the Judges relaxed their grip for a second, that craziness would spiral out of control—nobody seemed to be willing to admit that it already had, and the Department was the cherry on the top of the whole sick, sad sundae.

So of *course* Rico was corrupt. The *law* was corrupt—an ugly, festering mess that existed only to squeeze every last drop of dignity out of the people and kick the broken husks around a little for good measure.

And Rico Dredd *was* the law.

Better believe it.

He worked alone, for the most part. It was technically against regs, but then so was the lux-apt he kept in Oldtown, and nobody said a word to him about that. They might have, if he hadn't been as good as he was—but he knew how to play the game, how to juke the stats, get the arrests. Sure, his bodycount was a little high—and occasionally he'd lean on people a little harder than he had to during interrogation, especially if they were innocent—but so what? His cleanup rate was high and he made sure his record looked clean—or at least not too dirty to let stand—and at the end of the day, that was all the higher-ups cared about.

Very, very occasionally, when he was bored, he'd ask his straight-laced clone-brother Joe along on a patrol with him. It made for a few sick laughs. Little Joe, the cleanest Judge on the force, who still kept coming around the apartment occasionally to argue or deliver lectures, who'd probably blow his big brother Rico away in a heartbeat if he ever knew the full truth. And hey, wouldn't that be a kick? Maybe if he ever got so bored that he wanted to quit the whole game, that would be the way to go out: at his brother's clean hands. It'd be more fitting than any other exit.

So that same Little Joe, so squeaky clean, would ride right alongside him. He'd be just as violent and brutal and merciless as brother Rico, cracking the same skulls, loosening the same teeth, putting bullets in the same fleeing bodies... but ask Joe after he'd washed off the blood if he thought he'd done wrong—committed a crime—and he'd tell you were joking. Or crazy. Then he'd probably put you on report for unjudicial thinking.

Not that Rico ever did ask Little Joe about things like that—he'd learned that his brother didn't enjoy answering questions that troubled his boxed-in little worldview. No, he'd just return to his high-rent apartment, fire up the hot tub, sit back in it with a little shampagne and maybe a lady friend or two—everybody loved a man in uniform—and he'd laugh and laugh and laugh. Laugh until he was sick.

Of course, the lifestyle he deserved wasn't exactly cheap. Oh, he had his rackets, his payoffs—the Prince must have his tithes—but while all of that kept him comfortable enough, there was still plenty of room for improvement. The landlord who owned Rico's block had a penthouse available—right at the top level, a full view of the city, electron showers, two robo-butlers as standard. Everything Rico deserved. The landlord, a slick old skel from the Greek Wastes who knew how the world worked, had hinted to Rico that he could hold onto the property for a little while, in case the 'anonymous donor' who paid Rico's rent every month as a 'reward' for his 'sterling service in defence of the city' could maybe stump up another half million a month.

Half a million extra was a tall order, but Rico could probably extend his net of bribes and protection rackets a little further if he had to. Still, that'd take time and increase the risk of scrutiny—it'd be better if he could get the cash together in one big lump. Let's say, for the sake of argument, he could get himself a decent share of a major-league score—something in the tens of millions...

Which was about when the Mega-City Munch-Off had entered his life.

To begin with, it was just one more notice in the first shift's morning briefing. "Item!" Deputy Sector Chief Koslowski had bellowed, before taking a second look at the printout and rolling her eyes. "Jovus. Now I've seen it all. You goofballs are gonna love this one." Koslowski ran an informal squad room—Rico liked that about her. It allowed him to get away with more.

"Let's hear it, Koslowski," grinned Muttox, a big, half-smart lump of a man—the kind the Academy didn't want to admit they made any more—around a stick of cheap munce-gum. Rico sat back in his chair, only half-listening. The briefing room bored him—he preferred to be out on the streets, taking calls as they came, with the freedom to do his business in between. And there was a lot of business that needed to be done if he wanted to secure that penthouse.

"The Mega-City Munch-Off Inaugural Eating Championship of 2080," Koslwoski had said, sneering and shaking her head. "Some kind of eating contest in the Herc—set for the second Saturday of next month. They figure they're going to fill it this time."

Someone at the back of the room snickered. "Yeah, I know"—Koslowski sighed—"but this nonsense doesn't seem to be going away. Actually, word from above is maybe it shouldn't—a fatter cit is a more obedient cit, and all that. So we need to work on the assumption that it's going to be filled to—" She paused, reading a little further. "Drokk-a-doodle-doo," she muttered, and Rico leaned forward, paying a little more attention. Could be this was going to be more interesting than he'd thought.

"No tickets will be sold ahead of time," Koslowski read, slowly and carefully—as if to make sure she could believe the evidence of her own eyes. "Thousand creds a ticket, cash only. Only the first hundred thousand will be seated. Jovus on a plate." She shook her head, disgusted, as a murmur went through the room. "You couldn't come up with a better recipe for a riot if you tried."

"Shut it down," Friedricks scowled. She was a no-nonsense type who'd transferred from Sector 47—word had it that she'd done her assessment while the first bombs were dropping in the war. Rico avoided her—she was a stickler if he'd ever seen one. Almost as bad as his brother.

And now—if his math was right—she was trying to get in the way of the kind of payout he'd been hoping for. Rico began to wonder if avoiding her had been the right move—maybe he should have taken a more proactive approach. Maybe he should have killed her.

Like he'd killed Kenner, the invigilator at his assessment, when the old man had started to get wise to what his golden ex-rookie was up to—and what a kick *that* had been! He'd set the old bastard on fire first, then played target practice—shooting to wound, not to kill, denying the craggy old has-been his mercy shot. And all the time, he hadn't stopped laughing.

Good times.

Rico leaned forward, trying not to look to anxious. Surely this had already gone through all the channels...?

"It's gone through all the channels—rubber-stamped from on high. Guess some desk jockey really likes the idea of eating contests." Koslowski sighed, aggravated. Rico nearly sighed along with her. He could *taste* his relief.

"All right. Every single one of you is going to be on crowd control for this thing—probably all of Shift Two as well. I'll draft Shifts Three and Four in to cover you on the streets, which is probably going to mean a double shift for all of you somewhere down the line..." There was a low rumble of dissent at that, and Koslowski shot the room a hard look in response. "Do we have a problem? Because if you don't like being a Judge today, I've got good news—civvy street is just down the hall. Have fun spending your life watching vid-soaps with the rest of the cits."

The murmuring died down.

"Now, it looks like we'll need most of our units on the outside of the Stadium, controlling the queues and dealing with whatever backlash we get when the gates close. I figure if we have enough helmets on the ground, we can keep control of the situation and maybe—*maybe*—shut down any serious trouble before it starts. Friedricks, you'll be heading up that contingent."

"Yes, ma'am," Friedricks said, snapping an unironic salute off.

"Meanwhile, we'll do our usual search and sweep job on the gate and in the crowd. That'll have to be the bare minimum for a crowd that size. I can spare maybe fifty of you, so you'll be working overtime and then some."

Muttox chewed his gum contemplatively—like a cow, Rico thought—and stuck his hand up. "Outside people can help wit' that. Search the queues—pick out any weapons, drugs, search anybody even smells weird. Then we run a scanner over what's left at the gate—you know, to make double sure. That way, we got most of the trouble weeded out, and it's just, uh..." He grinned. "Naturally-occurin' trouble. Like when any two cits get in the same room."

Friedricks looked over at Muttox, impressed despite herself. "Not bad, Hector."

"I ain't just a pretty face," Muttox grinned, and carefully spat the wad of gum into his palm before folding it up in his spare glove pouch.

"You just won yourself command on the inside, Muttox," Koslowski said, then scanned the room.

"We'll come back to this next week, once I've got a clearer idea on what kind of numbers we'll have. In the meantime—any questions?"

Rico waited, hoping nobody in the room would ask the big question. *"Hey, Koslowski, I'm a dumb old street jock without the brains Grud gave a dog vulture, but doesn't this mean there'll be a hundred million creds, mostly in large bills, just lying around the Herc someplace? What are we doing about that?"*

Nobody in the room did. They were all thinking about the riot Koslowski had forecast, planning for the worst—either that, or just anxious to finish up and get back out onto the streets. Rico suppressed a smile, and raised his own hand.

"Koslowski?"

"What is it, Dredd?" She didn't like him, he knew—thought he was a little too full of himself. Luckily, he was too full of himself to care.

"What happens if a riot breaks out inside the Stadium too?"

Koslowski looked him square in the eye.

"Then Grud help us, Rico. So let's try and make that not happen, huh?" She crumpled the printout and tossed it into the waste receptacle behind the podium. "All right, briefing over. I want to see some good arrest figures today, so all of you get out there and do what you do best."

Rico did just that.

Seven

"Close the door, Buddy boy."

Bud Mooney froze in the door, and the grocery bag tumbled from his chubby, sweaty hands. Rico—sat in Mooney's old, battered armchair, which he'd turned to face the hab door—sipped some of the cheap soymash whiskey he'd found in the kitchen cupboard and grinned. It was hard not to take a sadistic pleasure in watching all the cans of off-brand soda and budget mock-choc bars and all the other cheap crap Mooney called a diet spilling out onto the carpet.

Sure, he could have broken into Mooney's hab while the fat slob was home, and maybe that would have been easier... but it wouldn't have been half as fun as seeing the fear in Buddy-boy's eyes. That was a treat worth waiting for.

"Now, c'mon there, Buddy boy. You're not going to give me the simple courtesy of a hello? I already had to pour my own drink." Rico laughed, drained his glass, and tossed it over his shoulder, enjoying the sound of it shattering against the wall.

Mooney was down on his hands and knees, pale as a ghost, scrambling to get it all out of the way so he could do what Rico said and close the door. "H-hello, sir," he stammered, looking at Rico with eyes like saucers, then looking away, as if eye contact might get him killed. Which, Rico reflected, it might at that. Depending on his mood.

"That's more like it. So how have you been, Buddy-of-mine? Nice place you've got here, by the way. I especially like the view." He jerked a thumb behind him at the blacked-out windows—he'd set the controls as soon as he'd made his way in. Whatever happened here, he didn't want any witnesses.

"Aw, jeez," Mooney whined, getting up on his knees, pressing his palms together as if praying. Rico liked that. "Please, Judge Dredd, sir, I know I ain't checked in lately—but it's like I told you, nobody wants to talk to me any more—"

Rico smirked at that. It had been one of his more profitable ideas—leaning on this old rummy to get useful information about his peers. It hadn't taken much—one cracked rib and Mooney had been happy to play the narc, pumping his booze and poker buddies for all the info they had about upcoming scores. Rico let a heist go ahead for ten per cent of the take—a bargain, under the circumstances. Any crew who didn't like the deal, Rico fed through the proper channels—he was allotted a certain amount of narc money a month for his 'informant,' which naturally he pocketed himself, so either way he came out of it ahead.

As for Mooney, he ran out of poker buddies pretty

fast. There might not be honour among thieves, but there is a hell of a lot of gossip, and it tickled Rico to put his ear to the grapevine and listen to Buddy-boy's fall from grace. In the space of maybe three months, Mooney had gone from being a salt-of-the-earth yegg—*everybody's pal, a joe you could trust with your life, sure, he's got a couple of health problems, but you try havin' the luck he's had*—to a lousy, scheming, stinking tub of lard, a twitchy, toothless little rodent who pissed in a bag. *We oughtta make him drink that gruddamned bag*. Rico couldn't help but hope somebody had.

"Some narc you are, Mooney. Why, anybody would think you didn't want to turn in your friends. Oh, wait—you don't have any." Rico laughed, sliding his boot knife out of its sheath on his ankle. Mooney gave a visible start, scrambling back. "Did you just pee yourself there, Buddy-boy? Can you tell when you do that? Does the bag inflate a little, or what?"

"D-d-don't kill me," Mooney pled, tears in his eyes. His twitch was going nineteen to the dozen, making him wink and smirk, as if he was being ironic about it. "Please. Ain't you already done enough?"

Not nearly, Rico thought. There was a lot more fun to be squeezed out of a piece of human flotsam like Bud Mooney. It was almost a shame the wretched little creep still had his uses—Rico had never drowned a man in his own urine bag before, and he had a feeling it'd be a kick.

There was always later.

"Relax, Buddy-boy. I'm not going to hurt you." He grinned, flipping the knife in his hand. "Not unless you do something that makes me mad. You won't do anything that makes me mad, will you, old friend? Old pal?"

"Please," Mooney croaked, eyes ready to pop as they followed the knife. "Anything."

"That's the boy," Rico laughed, slipping the knife back into his boot. He didn't want to give the asshole a heart attack, after all. "See, before you became... this..."—he waved a hand in Mooney's general direction, wincing—"I heard you were pretty hot stuff. When it came to the heist game, I mean."

Mooney blinked, uncomprehending, and Rico leaned forward in the armchair, steepling his gloved hands. "What I'm saying, Buddy-my-buddy, is that I have a job for you. A little planning work." He stood up, walking back in the direction of the kitchen to fetch another whiskey. All this intimidation was thirsty work. "Come on, up off your knees."

"But..." Mooney blinked, rising shakily to his feet, as Rico cracked a few cubes of ice into a fresh glass. "Wait, what are you saying? You want to be the finger on this?" Rico frowned—his turn to look confused—and poured what was left of Mooney's whiskey while he waited for the explanation. "When a guy on the inside of a place brings the job, y'know? Like, maybe there's some shnook working in a bank, and he wants fifty thou to fly down to Cuidad Barranquilla, and he notices how the manager keeps the vault combination in a drawer in his desk so he don't forget it, and—"

"Let's not write a screenplay here, Mooney."

"—right, right. Anyway, a guy works in a place sees a weakness, and brings it to a crew in exchange for a share of the job—that guy we call the finger. Finger usually makes ten per cent."

"Ha ha ha." Rico grinned, taking a sip of the whiskey. "Try again."

"Uh, thirty? Forty?" Mooney mopped his brow with his sleeve. "Look, Judge Dredd—you know I ain't gonna say nothin' about what share you get, but... well, you want much higher than forty, there might not be enough cash left over to make it worthwhile. For the other guys, I mean."

"On this, there will be." Rico smiled, leaning back against Mooney's refrigerator. "Take is one hundred million—cash. Mostly large bills."

Mooney's eyes grew wide again, but this time it wasn't through fear. Rico could almost see the cred signs in them. "Y-you robbin' a casino or what?"

Rico snorted. "Gambling's illegal, Bud. Why, you know of any illicit casinos around here? Maybe you've been holding out on me?" Mooney opened his mouth to protest, and Rico shook his head with a grin. "Relax, Mooney. You're too jumpy, you know that? One day you're going to jump right out of your skin. No, I'm talking about a stadium—the Herc."

Mooney blinked. "The—wait, you mean this speed-eating thing? The Munch-Off?"

Rico drained his glass. "We've got one advantage. I happen to know for a fact that every available Judge in a mile radius of the Herc is going to be stopping two riots that day—one outside the building, one inside. That's to start you off—I want you to work from there and give me a foolproof plan that gets every single cred of that money out of the Herc and into our pockets before the dust settles. You've got three days."

"Three days?" Mooney swallowed hard, looking down at his shoes. Rico was amused to note his bag made a taut bulge against his pants-leg—full to bursting. He supposed he must have made an impression.

"Three days. Work your magic, Buddy-boy." He pushed past Mooney, heading for the door.

"W-what if I can't?" Mooney whined, trembling. "What if I don't have what it takes any more? Or if I—if I can't get hold of the floor plan or something?"

Rico paused at the door, looking back at the fat man with cold contempt. "Come on, Bud," he said, as if talking to a child. "You know the answer to that one."

Eight

"THIS IS ALL highly irregular," murmured Doctor Hoenikker, chief of staff at the Noel Edmonds Institute for the Criminally Insane, as she idly picked the excess varnish from around her fingernails. It wasn't said with any kind of reproach—just as a simple statement of fact, like *it's a nice day,* or *I run an asylum,* or *you're a bent Judge offering me money, and it's not enough.*

Rico sighed, popped open the pouch on his belt and withdrew another thousand-cred bill. "Final offer, Doc," he said, trying to keep the edge of irritation out of his voice. Hoenikker was a pain in the ass, and this was costing him two grand more than he'd figured it would, but this was still the cheapest way to get what he wanted in the time available.

"Oh, I think I could go higher. But it'd be a risk." Hoenikker leaned back in her office chair, looking at him critically, head cocked to one side. "You strike me as rather an unstable young man. I wouldn't want you to harbour feelings of resentment against me or the facility."

"You probably wouldn't at that." Rico grinned, showing teeth, and handed the money over.

Hoenikker calmly folded it into the inside pocket of her white coat before standing and briskly walking to the door. "Come with me, please. I think the sort of person you're looking for will be down on sub-level four—the paranoids."

That sounded about right. Rico smirked and followed along.

One of the very few victories the ACLU had won against the Justice Department was to secure a guarantee from Chief Judge Fargo that those deemed not guilty by reason of insanity would not be placed in the nascent Isolation Cube system. Instead, they were housed in private, non-judicial facilities such as Noel Edmonds.

There was talk, at the Council level, of going back on this pledge—creating a separate stream of 'psycho-cubes' to house Mega-City's growing criminally insane population. Dr Justine Hoenikker, a practical, level-headed woman in her middle fifties who hadn't survived a nuclear war and risen to the top of her field by being anyone's fool, knew that the days of the facility—and her own as its head—were numbered.

Thus, she'd begun using her one significant resource to build up a small but healthy retirement fund. Rico was far from her only customer—she'd offered similar deals in the past to Mega-Mob assassination cartels, off-the-books pharmaceutical laboratories, pimps, organ-leggers and a group called the Mega-City Long Pig Appreciation Society.

Dr Hoenikker's one significant resource was a plentiful supply of human beings.

"Down here," she said, leading Rico past a corridor of plasti-steel doors with small, reinforced windows. He could hear the sound of shrieking coming from one of them—as they passed it, Hoenikker retrieved a small communicator from her pocket, flipped it on and dialled a three-digit number. "Jeremy?" Her voice was cold. "G/134 hasn't taken his medication. I'm assuming he hid the pills under his tongue again. You're supposed to check for that." On the other end, Jeremy—whoever he was—made his excuses. "I don't care, Jeremy. We'll have to inject him now. Handle it, please." She flicked off the comm-unit and put it away, shooting Rico a brief look of exasperation. "Twice this week. It's because he knows more than he should—he thinks that means he can slack off." She sighed. "As soon as a suitable replacement is lined up, I suppose I'll have to have him killed."

Rico found himself impressed. If they did end up shutting down the Edmonds Institute, he'd have to look her up—she'd make a good consigliore.

At the end of the corridor was an elevator. "Those were the workaday patients," Hoenikker said, as she pressed the button marked S4 and the elevator smoothly whirred into life. "The ones we're expected to do something about. In the lower sub-basements, I keep the ones that have fallen outside the system—mostly just forgotten, although a couple I made sure to deliberately lose when I noticed how useful they could be. Those are the serial killers, the torturers, the would-be geniuses. I tend to sell them to foreign interests, although there was one I let go to the

Mega-Mafia..." She thought for a minute. "Jimmy Jigsaw, I think the papers called him."

Rico remembered. Jimmy was a psycho who'd 'escaped' from Noel Edmonds and started cutting people into one-foot cubes and sewing them back together funny. All the people he'd gone after post-escape had—coincidentally—made an enemy of Don Vito Corelli in some way. Not that anything could be proven. "I remember."

"Well, never again. Too many hard questions over that one." Hoenikker gave Rico a stern look. "I'm relying on you to be a little more discreet."

Rico smiled. He wasn't planning on being discreet, exactly, but he was pretty sure she wouldn't be caught in the fallout. And if she was—well, there were ways to make sure she didn't have to answer any of those hard questions.

The elevator doors opened, and Hoenikker led Rico onto another corridor lined with cells—although these ones were fronted with transparent plasteen, with small, barely visible seams where the cells could be opened electronically. For a moment, Rico wondered why the design was different from the cells upstairs, with their steel doors and small windows—then he understood. This floor was designed strictly for window-shopping.

He walked past the cells, taking a look at the inmates. Most of them were in straitjackets or some other means of restraint. Some were male, some were female, some old, some young—there wasn't an order or system to it that he could detect, beyond the fact that all of them were for sale. None of them seemed to be on their meds—Rico stopped for a moment to watch one woman in her twenties screaming in fury at him through the soundless glass. He tried reading her lips, but all he could make out was the word 'many-angled,' over and over again—the rest might as well have been glossolalia for all he knew. He nodded at her. "Something like that. But dialled down a little."

"Don't worry," Hoenikker murmured, giving him a businesslike smile. "I have someone here who should be perfect for your needs." She stopped, indicating a right-hand cell. "Tellerman, Rockford J—found wandering the ruins a year after the war. Nobody's quite sure what happened to him—we thought we knew, but it turned out he was just saying what he thought we wanted to hear. He's pathetically eager to please, under the right circumstances."

"How do you know his name?" Rico was taking a good, hard look at Rockford J Tellerman. He was a little on the scrawny side, but otherwise in decent shape, and his hair and beard would calm down with a little maintenance. Throw some product on there and he could be a newsreader. Physically, he was perfect—or he would have been, if not for the constant, terrified tremble that wracked him from head to toe. He was scared out of his mind by something—something invisible, that he seemed to be constantly checking for.

The question was, could he be used?

"Driver's licence," said Hoenikker, matter-of-factly, before taking a few steps towards a small intercom unit on the wall next to the glass window and flipping a switch. "We can hear him now, and vice versa. Rockford? This is Judge Dredd. He's come to visit you."

Tellerman just stared for a moment, as if the information was some kind of trap, ready to spring closed around him. When he spoke, it was in a terrified whisper that Rico had to strain to hear.

"Uh, has he been *checked?* Doc? Has he been checked for the *death signals?* We can't take chances, Doc. He could be a *carrier.* We need to know he's..." He tried to drop his voice even lower. "One of *us.*"

Rico looked at Hoenikker, then at Tellerman, then Hoenikker again. "I don't know if he's worth six thousand creds..."

Hoenikker gave him an icy look and flipped the switch, making sure Tellerman couldn't hear. "His kidneys are worth that alone—although his lungs are damaged. Ex-smoker, I'm afraid—well, we think."

Rico didn't bother hiding the irritation this time. "I'm not going to cut him up, *Doctor* Hoenikker—"

Hoenikker cut him off with a raised hand. "No, you're going to blow him up. You want someone suggestible enough to do exactly what you tell them to—to the *letter*, I assume—who won't stand out in a crowd. The price is six thousand—take it or leave it."

Rico shrugged and nodded, and after a pause Hoenikker flipped the switch back. Rico could hear Tellerman's quick, nervous breathing.

"Rockford, Judge Dredd is *one of us.* He actually came here to talk to you about the death signals, as a matter of fact. There are some things he wants you to do to help fight them." Her voice dripped with honeyed sincerity. Once again, he was impressed with the woman.

"That's right, Rockford," said Rico, giving the man in the straitjacket one of his brightest, toothiest smiles. "Only you can save us all. You just need to do as you're told for a while. Can you do that?"

Tellerman swallowed hard, then nodded, eyes

flicking left to right wildly as if something beyond the periphery of his vision was coming to eat him. "You're one of us, Judge," he whispered, gnawing at a fingernail. "Doc says. You tell me what to do and I'll do it. We gotta fight them, Judge. Gotta f-fight the death signals. Any minute, one of them death signals could come outta the sky and—"

Rico nodded to the switch, and Hoenikker flipped it. Tellerman continued to rant behind the glass, unheard. "So, does he come with sedatives?" Rico asked. "Because I take your point about suggestibility, but there's a... jittery quality there that I'm not exactly in love with. He's going to draw attention if he has to stand in a queue for hours—even assuming he doesn't freak out, someone's going to ask him what the matter is."

"Well..." Hoenikker considered it for a moment. "Right now he's been without medication for some time. I can start him on a few things to remove the *jitteriness,* as you call it—obviously, we want to calm him down without curing the basic delusions." Hoenikker gave Rico a quick, almost apologetic smile. "But then, if I could cure those—on our budget, I mean—well, I wouldn't be selling him in the first place, would I? I'm not a complete monster."

"Of course not, Doc. None of us are." Rico grinned, amused despite himself, then reached past her and flicked the switch again. "So, Rocky—can I call you that?" He grinned again, even wider than before. "How would you like to never have to be afraid of the death signals again?"

Tellerman looked at Rico for a long moment, and then started to cry.

Rico almost felt bad for the guy.

Nine

"SO WHAT THE hell's this wacko gotta stay with me for?" Mooney's voice was shrill and a little slurred. Tellerman, shaved clean now and dressed in a suit and shirt, watched him nervously from the armchair in the main room, his hands fidgeting in his lap. He didn't say much unless he was prompted to—the pills Hoenikker had left with Rico seemed to have mitigated some of the terror that gripped him, so much so that he'd pass for normal unless you had a conversation with him. Rico figured he'd probably have to be coached a little, but they had time.

"Rocky here had to be signed out in somebody's name, Buddy-boy. I figured I'd use yours." Rico shot Mooney an amused glance, then directed his attention back to the plans on the kitchen table. "Don't worry. He got lost in the system years ago—I doubt anybody outside of you, me and Hoenikker even remembers he exists."

"But he's gonna—" Mooney started, before casting

a fearful glance at Tellerman. He walked quickly over to the kitchen door and slammed it shut, then turned back to Rico, whispering at a volume a little louder than his natural shouting voice. "He's gonna blow himself up! They're gonna know he exists *then*, ain't they? They're gonna know and they're gonna trace him right back to *me*—"

Rico rolled his eyes. He was starting to wish he hadn't told Mooney about that part. He'd got it stuck in his head. "He's not blowing himself up, Buddy." He watched Buddy-boy exhale for a moment. "*I'll* be the one sending the detonation signal. And if you've got a better way to start a riot indoors, I'd like to hear it." He grinned, enjoying the way Mooney had tensed up again. "Here, take a look, I'll show you how it's going to work."

Carefully, he placed the liquid explosive—disguised as a bottle of soda gum—on the kitchen table, along with a detonator small enough to swallow. "Eat, drink. This is my body, this is my blood. Rocky ingests these before he starts queueing. Friedricks and her squad won't have the tech to scan for it—the Judges on the gate will, but I'll be the one who scans Rocky, so that won't be a problem. Rocky blows on my signal, and that's when the panic hits. Suddenly we, by which I mean the good men and women of Justice Department, are all looking after the crowds and not looking after the take sitting in the money room. Any questions?"

"Why does it gotta be a human bomb? We could just plant one—"

"They'll scan for that before the contest. Use your noodle, Mooney."

"Oh, okay." Mooney slumped in his chair, visibly

sulking—the suicide-bomber aspect seemed to be rubbing him the wrong way, but he'd been up for three days straight and didn't have an alternative. He unscrewed his hip-flask and took a swallow, grimacing a little at the cleaning-fluid taste of the booze. He couldn't seem to take his eyes off the bottle on the table. "Where the hell did you get that stuff, anyway?"

A couple of hours before he'd kept his appointment at the Edmonds Institute, Rico had stopped in with another of his ever-growing list of contacts. Vassily Grochenko, late of Moscow-St-Petersburg—or East-Meg, as they'd called it since the war ended—was an old man with a reedy voice and a permanently sour expression, who'd kept a connection open to the thriving arms trade in what was left of the Euro-cities. He was the man to see about explosives.

"Is so difficult for me here, Rico," the old man had sighed, nursing the same cup of cold tea that he always seemed to have in his hand whenever Rico dropped into the frozen hole he kept over in Dan Duryea. "I am missing home. The children, when they are buying the guns from me, they are *so* rude." He'd shaken his head, taking a sip of the tea. "You want your money, yes? Is always money with you. You are Judge—what you spend the money *on*, eh?"

"Oh, this and that. I always need money." Rico had smiled. "But I don't necessarily need yours. If you play ball, you won't need to worry about paying me off ever again." The old man's eyes had lit up, and Rico'd known then that he'd be walking out of there with everything he needed.

Vassily had come through, all right, and Rico had been true to his word. Vassily had no worries now. It was a shame to cut off such a neat source of revenue so messily, but Vassily could be a little too chatty for his own good sometimes—besides, old men fell and broke their necks all the time. It probably would have happened anyway. At least that was Rico's way of thinking.

"None of your beeswax," he smiled at Mooney, leaning back on the kitchen chair. "Come on, Buddy-boy, I'm due on the streets in ten minutes—I really don't want to go back out there with your blood on my knuckles. You know how we're pulling off the riots, and you know when. Let me hear what you've got."

"Okay," Mooney rubbed a knuckle in his eye socket, scowling. "I managed to scare up the plans for the Herc, no thanks to you. Had to pay a few people a few bribes—creds I don't exactly have, y'know? If this job don't work out the way we think it will, I'll be out on the street."

Rico nodded sympathetically. There was no danger of Mooney being left on the street, though—the only place he was going was the Resyk belt. But he didn't need to know that.

"Now, creds are paid in the ticket booths here—they'll all be automatic. Exact change only. So the cash is all gonna get funnelled through to this room over here"—he tapped another part of the map, a storage room close to the ticket machines—"and once it's in there, it goes right into money sacks for collection. So there'll be a couple of schmoes in there working. Plus guards—maybe four or five? Nothing special, mind—just your average rentacops. Not good enough for the Academy, y'know?"

Rico nodded. "Oh, I know."

Mooney narrowed his eyes, giving him a hard stare. "Are there gonna be any Judges back there, you think? Could mess up the plan if one of the guys has to take on any real opposition."

Rico considered the question for a moment. "If there are—Muttox is pretty dumb, but I wouldn't put it past him to think of it—they'll be needed, either when the panic hits in the stands or when the bodies start piling up outside. They won't be backstage long." He sat back, rubbing his ample chin, and for a moment the frown on his face made him seem like a different person entirely. "Way I see it, we've got two problems. If I'm reading these plans right, the money room has some kind of in-built security on the door..."

Mooney nodded. "Right. Not exactly a bank vault, but there's a lot of alarms there. It'd take a good half hour's work to get through without setting them off—and once we do, the folks inside will have had time to call the Jays."

"Problem two is moving the cash. That many creds—we're looking at maybe six hundred pounds of weight." Rico checked the time on the chronometer on his glove, then quietly drew the Lawgiver from his boot holster.

"W-what's that for?" Mooney blinked, the colour draining from his face.

"Like I mentioned, Buddy-boy. I'm back on duty in eight minutes. If it gets to seven minutes and you've not given me something I can use..." Rico shrugged. "You're not going to like the last sixty seconds all that much."

"You don't gotta threaten me, Rico," Mooney muttered, reaching in his pocket for something. "I've got answers. Hold on a sec, I gotta find this—it's mixed up with my prescriptions—"

"That's my Buddy-boy," Rico smiled. He sat back, waiting patiently for Mooney to produce whatever he was going to from his pocket. Eventually, the fat man smoothed a clipping from a trashzine out onto the table—some kind of advert. Rico cocked his head, looking at the image of a blow-up rubber doll staring back at him. "Buddy, Buddy, Buddy... if this is a suicide method, it's kind of roundabout."

"It ain't a blow up doll!" Mooney snapped, then flinched, as if expecting the bullet. "Sorry. But I know what it looks like. Listen, what these are—they're woman suits. Like, rubber woman suits for perverts to wear—over their clothes, even. Like a gimp suit, but flesh-coloured, and... y'know." He reached up, miming a pair of breasts in the air with his sausage fingers. "Y'know, like that. They even got hair."

Rico raised an eyebrow behind his visor. "The world is a strange place, Bud. Thanks for reminding me. You've got five more minutes." He tilted his gun, flicking idly at the dial that selected which bullet it fired. "Ricochet's fun. You ever fired a ricochet in between someone's ribs? If you angle it right it'll bounce about like a pinball—major agony, but the perp won't actually die for—"

"All right, already!" Mooney was getting angry now. Lack of sleep, Rico figured. "Listen, the guys who make these super-perv suits—they do custom jobs. I ordered a guy—big fat guy. Like the contestants, y'know? Zips up in the front." He stared at Rico, as if expecting him to get the gist immediately. "Jeez! It's like a bag, okay? A big bag that looks like it's a guy!"

"A guy who weighs six hundred pounds." Rico nodded, satisfied. "Not bad, Mooney."

"We steal an ambulance from someplace—it'll have to be a civilian one, I ain't stealing one from the Judges. But it's not out of the question one of these big-time eating champions is gonna have private cover, y'know? Anyway, we steal one of those, modify it for a quick getaway if we need one, beef up the suspension a little too. Two of our guys pretend to be paramedics—we'll need a third guy in the money room, loading the skin-bag up, but after he's done that our fake medics can lift it up onto a hoverstretcher and carry it out with a sheet over it. Figure in the confusion, anybody looking will think it's a dead contestant." Mooney exhaled hard, slumping back in his chair.

"Not just a pretty face, are you? What about that half-hour on the door?" Rico grinned, aiming the Lawgiver right between Mooney's eyes. He had to admit, he was getting a real kick out of this—he'd have to plan heists a little more often. "Tick-tock, Buddy-mine. Two minutes."

Mooney shook his head, looking disgusted. "Ain't no way to run a damn railroad, Rico." He scowled, taking a long gulp from his flask. "We go in the night before. We time it right—the night watchmen'll give us a half-hour easy if we don't get caught on any cameras—and then we leave a guy in there overnight. When the money-counting shmucks come in to fill the bags, he steps out from behind the door and takes care of 'em. Tells 'em to be good little boys, ties 'em up—"

Rico rolled his eyes. "Shoot them."

"Nobody wants a murder rap—"

"We're starting a riot—maybe two, if we have to. If we get caught, everyone involved in this is doing life." Rico smirked, humourlessly. "Well, everyone except for me. I'll be getting worse." He checked his chronometer. "Thirty seconds spare. So." Rico slid the Lawgiver back in his boot holster, then got up from the table. "I count three extra guys—your two paramedics, and whoever we put in the money room."

"I could—" Mooney started, and stopped, letting his head hang.

"No, you really couldn't." Rico paused, his hand on the door control. "So who are our three? Anyone I know?"

"That's just it." Mooney swallowed hard, unable to meet Rico's eye. "It's what you had me doing, y'know? Snitching on people. Nobody's gonna come in with me anymore. Nobody's even takin' my calls. I—I was hoping you knew somebody—"

"That's a shame, Buddy-boy," Rico said, and showed Mooney a big, toothy grin, the one he knew Mooney didn't like. "A real shame. I guess I'll see you when I see you." He opened the kitchen door, giving Tellerman a curt nod on the way out. Tellerman cringed, shrinking into the armchair. "Look at Rocky there, Bud. He knows how to be a team player. He knows what I like."

Mooney stumbled to his feet, following Rico to the front door like a lost puppy. "Rico—c'mon, Rico, please. You ain't bein' fair here—" He was trying to keep the whine out of his voice—and probably hating himself for not being able to manage it, too. Which was a kick, as far as it went, but it wasn't exactly solving the problem at hand.

"I've been more than fair, Buddy-boy. You've been taking advantage of me, that's the trouble. Taking advantage of all my kindness." Rico paused before he left the hab, giving Mooney a long, hard stare. "But listen, if you do manage to come up with somebody—just one guy will do—you've got Justice Department's number, so you can arrange a meet with me. Just act like you're a narc." He grinned, enjoying Mooney's sullen expression. "If I were you, Bud, I'd make sure you got in touch with me before I reached out and got in touch with you. Just a word to the wise."

Mooney tried to protest, but Rico closed the door in his face. It'd give him something to think about, at least.

Still, while fear was a pretty good motivator—certainly the best one Rico had come across—it couldn't work miracles. If Mooney was as used-up as he said he was, Rico was going to have to start looking elsewhere for talent—and they'd need real talent if they wanted to break into that money room without getting caught.

Rico turned it over in his mind as he climbed onto his bike—still sitting where he left it in the watch-bay just outside Jeff Daniels—and started the engine. Maybe he'd get some inspiration on patrol—hell, he could even see if Little Joe was available to break a few heads open. That always cheered him up—

As he logged back in on the onboard computer, his own voice filled his helmet speakers. Speak of the wind and in it blows, he thought. Little Joe—probably passing through Rico's sector on the way to some assignment or other. He had a habit of jumping whenever the Council snapped their fingers.

"This is Dredd to all units," he heard his brother say. "We have an ARV"—armed robbery with violence—"Barry Scott Block Mall. One suspect down, one fleeing—Caucasian, black hair, day-glo green overjacket, Rudy Conn moustache. Suspect may be a professional thief—cameras were hacked wirelessly. Now believed headed west on Trudeau—"

Trudeau Street—that would take the perp onto the pedway, if he was smart, right past Jeff Daniels. ARVs were a dime a dozen, but this one had a couple of interesting factors. That Rudy Conn 'tache had to be a fake, for a start, and Little Joe wouldn't have mentioned the 'professional thief' angle unless he was sure.

And if he was a pro heister, maybe Mooney could be useful after all.

"This is Rico Dredd responding—on my way, Little Joe." Rico grinned into the radio. "I've got Trudeau locked down, don't you worry. If your man comes by here, I'll take him out for you. Save you a job." He was careful to pack in just the right degree of arrogance—although he preferred to think of it as natural charm. Any more humility than they were used to out of him and they might just smell a rat.

Once he'd clicked off, he set the bike radio to dial Mooney's apartment.

The fat slob picked up on the second ring. Rico had him well trained. "Buddy-boy? Well, who else would it be? No, no, I know what I said—look, just shut up and listen, Mooney. You go to your window and watch the pedway, see if you spot any familiar faces. The hair might be a dye-job, but keep your eyes skinned and tell me if you see anybody you know. And if you do see someone from the old days—some *talent,* I mean—don't let them get away."

He flicked the radio back to the main band. "Rico Dredd to all points—no sign of your man on Trudeau Street. Over." That should be enough to throw them off and give his heister a head start.

Rico was playing a hunch here and he knew it, but his hunches had served him well in the past—and besides, if he was wrong and this was just a no-account punk who wasn't part of Mooney's criminal fraternity, it wasn't like anything was lost. Easy come, easy go. He sat back in the seat of his Lawmaster, smiling up at the sun, and waited for Mooney to report in.

A few seconds later, the call came through. "Rico!" Mooney's excitement crackled through the static. "I know the guy! He's gone into Tony Hart—I figure he's gonna lay low there for a while. Listen, I'm gonna go talk to him—I'll call you back—"

Rico smiled. Once they had the first of their three-man team on board, he could bring in others—whoever this one remaining friend of Buddy-boy's was, he'd know people, just like Mooney had before Rico had drained him dry. It all clicked into place.

Everything clicked into place for Rico Dredd.

He knew he had a certain overconfidence problem—the tutors at the Academy had commented on it more than once, and Joe occasionally worked it into one of his endless lectures—but with his boots up on the handlebars, the sun shining into his visor and everything just falling into his lap, it really did seem like there was nothing he couldn't accomplish. Even stealing an ambulance didn't seem like a major issue at this point—just one more thing to check off the list. One more kick.

He couldn't wait for the big day.

PART THREE

Ten

THE CLOCK TICKED past midnight.

The big day was here.

Strader—crouched on the fire escape across the street—trained his binox on the Herc, watching the guards patrolling. There were three of them, as far as he could see—one taking the weight off on the front steps with a synthi-caf and a trashzine, keeping half an eye on the front, the other two slowly walking circuits around the circular building, stopping every now and then to rest. Every hour or so, they'd swap positions—every six, they'd be replaced by a new shift. He'd spent all of last night watching them, and by now he had their routine down to a science.

These three were mainly worried about stopping people camping out overnight—they'd be relatively easy to slip past. There were a set of fire doors at the side of the building that he could get to without being seen, the same double doors they'd be using to carry the 'body' out during the heist itself. Once he was inside, though, he'd have at least four or five other guards to worry about—guards whose patterns he didn't know, whose readiness he couldn't fathom. Would they be bored old men nursing hot drinks and old paperbacks, like the boys out front? Or would they be young and keen, eager to prevent any attacks on the Herc on the eve of its return to greatness?

He didn't even know the people he was working with. He still couldn't trust Mooney—not after he'd found out how deep in Rico's power the fat man was—and the getaway crew, Prowse and Ramirez, weren't that well known to him either. He'd worked with Gina Prowse once—which was how he'd managed to convince her to come on board—but that was in Mega-City Two, and while Prowse was a great driver, he found himself worrying that she might be more used to the wide, empty freeways of the west coast than the choked, traffic-heavy loops and whorls of the Big Meg. Ramirez, meanwhile, was an unknown quantity—a thin, sour-faced man with a pencil moustache and a six-cube-a-day sugar habit.

Usually Strader preferred not to work with sugar addicts—it was often the sign of a deeper problem. If only they'd had more time to get a crew together, they might have found some better people—just like they might have worked out a way to properly case the joint, or maybe get some cameras in there. As it was, Strader was going in blind. *Another rule broken,* he thought, bitterly—he'd started this off as a man bound strictly by rules, a man who pretended to have a professional code. One bad year, one bad month, one bad day—the bad second when the firing had started in the jewellery store and sent him down this road—that had been all it took to strip that from him.

If Strader could, he'd walk away, start again—take it on the lam to somewhere he'd never been, like Paris or Vegas or Antarctic City, and hole up there while he found an easier score at his leisure. But that was the whole problem in a nutshell—he couldn't. He was trapped between a rock and a hard place—between the Cowboy, inexorably counting down the time until he could make Strader dead for his debts, and that grinning maniac Dredd. He felt almost like he was being ground between two millstones, the hard shell of rules he'd once considered so unbreakable being slowly worn away until there was only one left.

He reached down to his hip, feeling the outline of the quick-release holster, drawing reassurance from it.

Wear iron. That was the rule.

He checked his wrist-com—a quarter past. The three men were out front, dickering over whose turn it was to sit and read the trashzine. Strader wasn't going to get a better chance than that. He pulled the old-style black watch-cap he was wearing down over his face to make a balaclava. That, with the all-black clothing he was wearing, would make him harder to spot in the darkness—like an old-time cat burglar. The downside was that if any passing Judge—or security guard—caught a decent look at him, he wouldn't be able to explain the outfit away... and he doubted Rico Dredd would let him live to be interrogated.

Another man might have frozen up, faced with the risk. Strader actually found himself breathing easier than he had in a while. Everything was reduced to this one moment—either he'd succeed, or he'd be dead. No in-betweens. It was liberating, in a way.

He took a single deep breath.

Then he was down the fire escape and across the street, the soft pads on his boots keeping him silent as he ran for the fire doors ahead of him. The pack on his back—black, like the rest of his outfit—was weighing him down a little, but it had a change of clothes, the zip-ties and duct tape he'd insisted on bringing along over Rico's objections, Mooney's weird blow-up-doll money bag—and most importantly, the tools to get through the door to the counting room. He figured he had maybe a minute before one of the guards rounded the corner and spotted him, but that would be all he'd need.

As he ran, he reached behind him, ripped the bulky las-cutter free of its snap-fastenings and brought it to bear on the white plasteel to the right of the door—where the alarm wires would be. He turned the cutter up to maximum, made a quick horizontal slash—not too elegant, but it did the job—and forced the doors open. He had just enough time to slip a little of the white tape over the burn mark—not something that'd stand up to expert scrutiny, but it was the same shade as the wall and it'd fool the guards—and then he was inside.

Now the game was different. He didn't know where the guards were or what pattern they were taking—he'd have to case the joint as he went along. Haste was the enemy. His best bet was to hide in dark alcoves, in the spaces between vending machines, in the ostentatious toilet stalls—slowly make his way through to where he needed to be, then find somewhere he could hide and watch—

somewhere he could wait for two, three hours, or even longer, counting the guards, memorising their patterns, learning the timetable enough to sneak out and work on the alarms to the money room door. The hardest part—assuming the system was the one on the plans, and it hadn't been updated—was getting the casing on the keypad unlocked and open. After that, he'd be able to work for a few minutes at a time on the innards, cutting and splicing the wires in the order he'd memorised, replacing the casing and returning to whatever hiding spot he'd picked when he knew the guards were coming by again.

It was going to be a very long, very tense, very dangerous night, but there was one consolation.

The day after would be worse.

Eleven

MORNING BRIEFING AT the Sector House.

"All right, we all know why we're here." Koslowski looked tired—eager to get it all over with. The room was crowded today, with Shifts One and Two crammed together in the same space. As Koslowski ran through the details of who'd be with Muttox on the inside of the stadium and who'd be helping Friedricks deal with the potential riot outside—details she'd gone through ten times or more already—Rico found himself looking around the room, examining each of the new faces in turn. Something was bothering him—a sensation in the back of his mind, a feeling that he was in two places at once. He'd had flashes of that occasionally all his life, from the clone tank on, but this time it was particularly acute, as if he'd defocussed his eyes and was seeing the same room from different angles. Come to think of it, the last time he'd felt anything like that was on a patrol with—

"Dredd!"

Rico looked up suddenly, assuming Koslowski was chiding him for being distracted—but she was looking across the room. "You're with Friedricks," she said, curtly, "and glad to have you with us. Hope you don't find you've bitten off more than you can chew." Rico blinked. What in Grud's name was she talking about? He was with Muttox on the inside, working the gates and the spectators. The whole plan depended on—

Then the cred dropped.

Rico let his eyes follow Koslowski's... and he saw himself standing there—or rather a ramrod-straight version of himself, not even sitting down but standing stiffly to attention, arms at his sides, chin raised imperiously at a forty-five degree angle. He'd maintain that pose through the whole briefing, Rico knew—all day, if his precious concept of the law demanded it. That was just how Little Joe was.

He was a stickler.

"Other Dredd..." There was laughter from Shift One at that, as Koslowski turned her attention on him. Rico felt his face redden a little at the jibe. "You're still with Muttox. But I expect you to co-ordinate with your clone here—I figure Ike and Mike should maybe think alike for once." More laughter. Rico smiled curtly, pretending to appreciate the joke at his expense, but inside his blood was boiling. *Co-ordinate* with Little Joe—the word stuck in his throat like a fishbone.

Rico spent the rest of the briefing holding back the mounting fury building inside him, but the second Koslowski dismissed the two shifts—giving them a good ten minutes to check ammo and belt pouches and synchronise their chronometers before they all rode down to the Herc and the action began—he'd marched up to Joe, fuming, and demanded an explanation. "What the hell are you doing here? This is *my* sector, Joe—all you're doing here is getting in my way, the way you've been doing ever since the Academy. Nobody's going to help you pick up your scores this time, *little* brother. You can forget about riding on my shoulder pads."

A couple of the street jocks around them grinned, watching the new kid with the attitude problem having an argument with himself, and that just made Rico angrier. It was humiliating, that's what it was—not to mention it could be the spanner in the works that wrecked the whole scheme. Was that what Joe was planning? How much did he know?

It was no use looking in the man's face. The sour, tight-lipped frown that had always struck Rico as equal parts contempt and self-righteousness was plastered all over his big chin—*their* chin, Fargo's chin. Rico occasionally had nightmares that one day his own face would be permanently fixed in an expression like that.

After a moment's pause, Joe spoke, with a trace of sardonic humour. "Figured you could use a hand, Rico. I put in a transfer to your sector for a month or so—just to make sure you're okay. You let that jewellery store thief slip past you, after all. The one you said wasn't on Trudeau Street." He locked eyes with his brother, unblinking. "I worry about things like that."

"You stay with your team, I'll stay with mine," Rico hissed. "We'll get on famously." He turned on his heel and stormed away, not wanting to prolong the situation any further—he'd already been made a laughing stock in the briefing room. It was Joe who was the joke, dammit—Little Joe, the stick-up-the-ass, ever-saluting, never-smiling lawbook on legs—not *him*. Never *him*.

A thought occurred. He didn't like his brother. In fact, he kind of hated him. He pretty much never brought Little Joe up in company. Did any of his team actually know, he wondered?

Did any of them know there was another him?

He grabbed the radio from his belt and tried to dial Mooney's number.

Twelve

Corey Cleveland was looking forward to his work for the first time in months.

It was a selfish thing to admit, even to himself—unemployment was at a record high, and there was all kinds of scaremongering talk going around that the new advances in robotics would take away what few jobs there were left.

But to be a money-counter with no money to count—to come to the Herc on a weekend and sit there while the sorting machine gave a few desultory belches, crapping out a ten-cred note here, two fives there... and then to spend the rest of the shift watching on the monitors as they panned around the empty seats, to have to watch the rot set deeper and deeper into this wonderful place... it was more than a soul could bear. And for what? Wages had been slashed—they were paid five creds a week less than welfare.

It was love of the Herc that kept Corey coming back. Love of the days when he'd been part of a team who'd made people happy, before that awful business with Mr Donald, before the Herc had fallen ill and started to die.

Well, maybe now those days were coming back.

Corey couldn't say he was a fan of the new competitive eating craze—it was kind of disgusting in a lot of ways, especially since the competitors weren't known for eating with their mouths closed. But he hadn't been a huge fan of Inferno either, when it came down to it—he hadn't watched the games on the monitors, while the cash trickled in from the beer and mechandise sales, he'd watched the crowds, the audience, the joy and excitement on their faces. That was always what he'd come into work for—and those times were about to come again.

"Morning, Phil," he grinned, waving to the other money-counter, Phil Hartsdale. Phil was a dour man in his middle fifties with a heart condition, a broken marriage and a daughter he never saw—none of which made the job any less depressing. Phil nodded, barely raising his head, and shuffled through the front door as if today was no different from any other. Corey made a private resolution, then and there, that he wouldn't be letting Phil get to him today—today was going to be a special day for the Herc, and for the money room. Of that he was sure.

Corey stopped briefly in the men's room, checking his fade—they were back in style, and he'd had his cut specially for the occasion—and making sure his tie was straight. Sure, they were going to be locked in a windowless room for the duration, until the bank truck came to take the money away to the vaults at six-thirty, but that wasn't an excuse not to look your best. When he caught up to Phil, at the door to the money room, the older man was stabbing fruitlessly at the keypad with his finger.

"Damn thing's busted," he muttered, voice deep and heavy as lead. "Tried putting the code in—nothing. Won't read my card, ether." He shrugged. "Maybe I should get somebody."

"Aw, crem," Corey sighed. He was anxious to get in there, to fire up the machines and run the checks, to get started on the best working day of his life, and the darn alarm was on the fritz again. Always the way. "Have you tried the handle at least, Phil?"

Phil took hold of the handle and gave it a desultory quarter turn. The door hissed smoothly open.

"Well, there you go," Corey said, relieved. "Guess your code worked after all, huh?" He tapped his ID card against the sensor on the keypad, hearing no familiar beep but pushing the door open and striding in anyway. "I figure probably it's just the thing that beeps that went wrong. Like the acknowledgement signal that lets you know you put your code in right or—" He froze in mid-sentence, his eyes widening.

There was a man with a gun in the money room.

He was dressed all in black, with silver hair and bright green eyes that didn't seem to blink. Corey didn't recognise the make of pistol—he didn't know much about pistols, he'd never run with that kind of crowd—but it was semi-automatic, it had a silencer and the barrel seemed very big as Corey stared down it.

"Come in. Nice and quiet, both of you." The man with the gun spoke softly, gently, as if talking so a skittish bird that might take off at any moment. "I don't want to use this. But if I have to, I will. Do you want that?"

Corey opening his mouth to answer, and the man

made a little beckoning gesture with the gun. Corey shuffled forward obediently, his hands automatically rising to shoulder level. Phil followed behind, his hands doing the same.

"Close the door."

Corey heard the click as the heavy metal door locked into place, and he felt his stomach sink. Unless someone took a good look at the busted keypad—noticed the lights weren't flashing—he didn't think anyone was going to figure out what was happening in here now. Nobody would come to help—nobody would even know. His eyes moved over to the wall by the sorting machines, the alarm button that was there for emergencies—the man was standing between it and him, but if he darted forward suddenly, maybe caught him a good sock on the jaw, he could probably—

"What's your name?"

Corey blinked. The man was smiling at him now—all sympathy. "Corey," he said, slowly. "Corey Cleveland." *Dope!* A voice in his head screamed. *Give a false name!* But it was too late for that.

"Phil Hartsdale," muttered Phil, in a stoic, defeated voice, as though all this was as preordained as the sun rising. The man with the gun nodded, and reached behind him with his free hand, tugging something from the pack on his back. Two wide loops of plastic.

"Corey and Phil," he said, smiling reassuringly. "You can call me John. And now we all know each other's names, we're less likely to do something stupid, aren't we? Because I'd hate to have to use this thing." He moved the gun from Corey to Phil, from Phil back to Corey. "If I have to use this thing, it won't spoil my plans at all, Corey. I want you to understand that. I'll feel bad, but that feeling will pass. It makes no difference to the plan if you're alive or dead." He shot Phil a quick, appraising glance—then focussed completely on Corey, singling him out. "Do you understand that, Corey?"

Corey swallowed hard, and nodded. He understood. The man with the gun had seen him thinking, had read his intentions on his face, and now he was the main threat. And suddenly, it came to him very clearly that if the man with the gun pulled the trigger right now—if he sent a wad of lead through Corey's skull and made his wife a widow and his children orphans—Phil would simply accept it. Phil would not fight back, or try to avenge him, or resist in any way. If Corey died now, he'd die for nothing.

"I need you to say it, Corey."

Corey shot Phil an angry, judgemental look. "I understand," he muttered.

The man with the gun tossed one of the plastic ties to Phil, still keeping the gun on Corey. "Hands behind your back, Corey." Corey sullenly obeyed, feeling Phil slide the plastic loop up over his wrists before even being asked. "Now, Phil, I'm going to be checking your work. I want you to know that. Don't make it too tight if you can help it—you'll cut off circulation, there'll be nerve damage—but if you make it too loose, and when I check your work I think there's a chance he can get loose, you know what I'm going to do?" Phil opened his mouth, then hesitated. "I'm going to shoot you, Phil. And then I'm going to shoot him."

Phil was already tightening the tie, forcing Corey's wrists together, palm to palm. Corey let out a yelp of pain, and the man with the gun walked over, held the gun on Phil while he zip-tied his arms the same way—but a little less tight—then checked Phil's work. "Little tight, Phil. That's going to pinch. Apart from that, good work."

"Thanks," Phil said, quietly. Then he shuffled over into the corner of the room and sat down.

Corey had never hated him more.

Thirteen

THE BIG DAY was here, and Mooney was hating every second of it.

To start with, he'd woken up that morning from dreams of choking to find Rico standing in his apartment, leaning over his bed. If he could have pissed himself without detaching his catheter first, he would have—no doubt.

He sat in his diner opposite the Herc, drinking hot synthi-caf to try and soothe the sore throat he'd woken up with and watching the Judges forcing the mob into a queue. He kept half an eye out for Tellerman, the way he'd been told to, and tried to remember a time when he hadn't been afraid of Rico Dredd.

I mean, the guy was a baby Judge, fresh outta the Academy—he couldn't be more than nineteen years old. But there was just... something about the guy. He had a kind of raw presence to him—the guy filled any room he walked into. He could even be Chief Judge one day, Mooney figured.

Y'know, if his head wasn't so full of crazy it leaked.

Mooney shuddered, unscrewing his hip flask and taking a long swig. He brewed the hooch in a still he kept in the bathroom, next to the toilet—it was pretty much fermented garbage—so he'd learned not to expect too much from it. But it tasted really off today—tainted, almost. Still, he couldn't afford soymash every day, or even every month, and a little nip from his own supply every so often kept him mostly regular.

Mooney turned his mind back to Rico. How crazy was he, anyway? That was the thing about that guy: you could never really tell if he *was* crazy, or just faking it—to scare you, or get you to underestimate him. He sure seemed to like tormenting Mooney; but then again, at this point Mooney wasn't exactly liked by anybody he knew, so it seemed almost natural. It wasn't like Strader thought much of him either, or the two he'd brought in to handle the ambulance. In fact, the only guy in the gang who had any time for Mooney was Tellerman, and as long as he took his meds and nobody mentioned Martian death signals, Tellerman liked pretty much everybody.

And anyway, Tellerman was gonna be dead soon, so he didn't exactly count.

Mooney stared out of the diner window. Tellerman was somewhere in that queue—the queue that was already snaking back and forth through the paved area in front of the Herc, between the decorative fountains. If he craned his neck, he could see where it snaked around the corner and down the street, to wind between the blocks and through the alleys. He figured at least a hundred thousand people were in that line already—probably more. He could see the Judges moving back and forth, doing random searches—strip searches, sometimes, the perverts—generally making their presence felt. But the Jays were kidding themselves if they thought there wasn't going to be a riot happening the second the last ticket got sold.

Hell, Mooney thought glumly, he was there to make sure it happened—that was his job in this, according to Rico. He'd explained it all, leaning over Mooney's bed and grinning like something out of a nightmare: if things looked like they were kicking off a little too slowly, Mooney's role was to head out there and stir it up. Yell stuff. Throw things. *Incitement,* they called it.

Mooney didn't see a way he could manage it without getting himself cubed up for a couple of years minimum—except if that happened, he had a nasty feeling Rico would get to him somehow, most likely before he reached the interrogation cube. Mooney knew that folks with dirt on Rico had died in custody before—always before they told the other Jays what they knew. Mostly, he knew because Rico had told him.

So where did that leave him now? What was his move?

Mooney took another swallow from his hip flask, ignoring the strange, rotten taste of the liquid—so much worse than usual—and the cold stare of the waitress. He stared out of the window, watching the Judges moving up and down the long queue. The hell with Rico anyway, he thought—he didn't have to be a part of this if he didn't want to be. He could walk away now, head for a new sector, change his name—he wasn't like Strader, stuck with his bad debts and the warrant on his head. The Jays didn't have a damn thing on him. So how would Rico even know if Mooney decided to—

—and suddenly, Mooney was looking right at Rico.

Somehow, he was right there, outside the window, strip-searching some poor dummy who'd brought a rod along—not to mention a little primo brain chowder, by the look of it. Only wasn't Rico supposed to be inside? How was he going to let Tellerman in to do his thing if he was out here instead of working the gates? What the hell was going on here?

Mooney stared, wondering if maybe he had it wrong somehow—like maybe this was just coincidence, some other jaybird with a similar build, some schnook who'd look nothing like Rico Dredd at all, if Mooney could only get a clear look at him. Yeah, that had to be it. In just a second the Jay would turn around and there'd be a different name on the badge, a different face—

—and then the Judge outside the window noticed him staring and stared right back.

It was Rico, all right.

But it wasn't.

The name on the badge was *DREDD*—Rico's name. The face was Rico's, too—but somehow it was meaner, if that was possible. Mooney never imagined a situation where he might miss Rico's unnerving smile, and now here it was, literally staring him in the face.

"Something the matter, creep?" the Judge outside the window snarled, lip curling. He sounded just like Rico, too, but where Rico's gravel-pit voice constantly sounded amused, like he was always laughing at a private joke, Mooney couldn't imagine this version ever finding anything funny.

"I—I—" Mooney stammered, eyes like dinner plates. *I don't understand what's going on, Rico,* he wanted to say, but somehow he couldn't make his mouth work.

Rico—Rico-but-not-Rico—leaned closer, his upper lip pulling up into a vicious sneer of irritation. He barked like a drill instructor, making Mooney flinch in his seat. "I said spit it out, meatball! If you've got something to say to me, say it!"

"I—I—I'm sorry, sir! I was—I was just looking—" Mooney turned his eyes away from the strange, scowling, barking man with Rico's face and kept them firmly on his cup of synthi-caf, hoping maybe the vision would go away if he didn't look at it. "I'm sorry, sir. I-It won't huh-happen again." He could feel a drop of sweat working its way slowly down over the folds at the back of his neck. His armpits were drenched.

"Damn right. On your feet, punk. I want to get a closer look at—" The Judge turned, hearing he sound of gunshots coming from down the street, and suddenly Mooney was forgotten—a lower priority, put to one side. When he looked up from his synthi-caf, the man with Rico's face was gone.

"Jovus," muttered Mooney, taking another long pull on his tainted hooch. He wondered if he'd finally had too much of it—crossed some threshold into seeing things. Or worse—what if that *had* been Rico? What if he'd been transferred to working the queue with the rest of the Jays on duty, and the whole plan was kaput? Maybe the whole strange exchange had been some coded message, some attempt to warn Mooney off before the riot started.

Mooney craned his neck, hoping to catch another glimpse of Rico—he was sure now that was who it had been—but there was no sign. He fumbled with the frayed cuff of his sleeve, feeling around for his wrist-com—he could at least put a call through to Strader—but he realised suddenly that he'd been so spooked after the way Rico had woken him that he'd left it on his bedside table, doing double duty as an alarm clock. With a sinking feeling, he realised he was incommunicado for the duration.

"Aw, man," he muttered, slumping in his seat. "Rico's going to kill me."

Fourteen

Rico was going to kill Bud Mooney.

As soon as Hoenikker at the Edmonds Institute had mentioned the unfortunate need for a working paper trail for Rockford Tellerman—the need for a patsy, in other words, just in case—that whole section of the plan had fallen neatly into place in Rico's mind. The hard part, as it turned out, had been getting the second detonator into Mooney's stomach—Tellerman had swallowed his on command, along with half the bottle of liquid explosive, but all Rico had needed to do there was present it as a working vaccine for the death signals that were even now being beamed into human brains by... well, Rico had never worked that out. He suspected Tellerman hadn't either.

Anyway, that kind of strategy just wouldn't have worked with Mooney—he was a terrified bowl of easily-manipulated jelly, but there were limits.

Instead, Rico had broken into Mooney's hab one more time, tranquilised Buddy-boy with a mild sedative to keep him in dreamland, and then simply—and a little roughly—forced the thing down his gullet. Mooney had woken up—the sedative couldn't be that strong or he'd be useless today—but he hadn't suspected. And assuming he was drinking the usual amount from that hip flask of his, he was getting enough to the explosive into his system to make a decent-sized bang. Mooney wouldn't be a problem.

Tellerman, on the other hand... right now, he was the biggest issue. Over the past five hours, tickets sales had passed the ninety thousand mark, and Rico still hadn't seen hide not hair of him. Rico had spent a couple of days, in between patrols, coaching Rocky on how important it was to choose a particular entry point to go in through—with the number of tickets that were being sold for the event, there were no fewer than thirty Judges performing the weapon scans, running their wands over the human cattle as they filed into their gaudy pen. If Tellerman had gotten confused—gone to the wrong place, been scanned by the wrong Judge...

...wait. There he was.

Rico had been right—with his hair cut and a decent suit, Tellerman could pass for an unassuming newsreader. Looking at him now, after a triple dose of his meds, you wouldn't know about his problems at all—he was smiling, happy, just another productive member of society, or as close as Mega-City could manage. You could put him to work in a bank, Rico thought—sure, he'd natter about death signals over the water cooler, but by this city's standards that was almost normal. Watching Tellerman follow his orders—the way he obediently separated himself into the correct queue when it subdivided, the way he let a young couple with a kid go first so Judge Trelawney would scan them instead of him, the way he approached Rico as quietly and gently as a lamb—Rico had to wonder how Hoenikker dealt with her conscience. Maybe Tellerman couldn't be cured, but it was obvious he could be managed.

Then again, she probably didn't have a conscience. Rico certainly didn't.

His scanner-wand flashed red when it passed quckly over Tellerman's belly—Rico kept his thumb over the light, making sure nobody else saw, then clapped Rocky on the shoulder, ushering him through, making no sign they'd ever met. "Good to go," he muttered.

Tellerman smiled, and leaned close for a moment. "Thank you so much for everything. I haven't felt this good in years. It's going to be so great not to have to worry about the death signals—"

Rico clapped him on the shoulder again, a little harder, checking to see if anyone had heard. "Good to go. *Sir.*"

Tellerman walked into the Stadium, smiling beatifically. A saint among men.

Meanwhile, the remote for the detonators sat in Rico's belt pouch, small and malevolent.

Waiting.

Fifteen

In the money room, Strader was starting to feel the adrenaline—like an old friend. Events were moving faster now, but still running to plan. He'd bound Cleveland and Hartsdale with the zip-ties, wrists and ankles, then gagged them with the tape. Cleveland had thrashed around plenty at first, but when Strader had shown him the gun for the second time—making it clear, in his low voice, that he wouldn't hesitate to keep Cleveland quiet the hard way—the kid had settled down. Meanwhile, Hartsdale was being as good as gold.

On the monitors, Strader could see ten men—there must be a separate women's event—being led out onto the pitch. He tried not to look for too long—the sight of that blubber, undulating its way forward, the sweat on those pink and brown rolls of flab glistening horrifically in the sunlight, it all made him want to be sick. But the arrival of the competitors onto the field of play meant that all the spectators—the lucky 100,000—were now in the stands, which meant things were probably getting ugly outside. He could expect Prowse and Ramirez pretty soon.

Strader turned back to the sorting machine, watching it count up the last of the thousands and hundreds—a few fifties—as they came in, sorting them neatly into bricks of cold cash for the convenience of the bank they'd never arrive at. The skin-suit, which he'd laid out on the floor, was packed tightly with the various denominations, the fleshy latex or neoprene or whatever the hell it was straining a little at the joints and seams. True to Mooney's word, it weighed about six hundred pounds—it'd take all three of them to lift it, once the other two got here.

All notes, of course. Strader had been a little worried about the amount of coinage that was coming through at first—the one, two and five cred tokens, cast in heavy plasteel, that were clattering down a side chute on the machine and into separate bins. Since they couldn't take it with them, every coin that tumbled down into those bins might mean less profit once the score was divided up, and with Rico unlikely to want less than his already mammoth share, that meant less to pay off the Cowboy at the end of all this. Then again, the queue snaked past several vending machines, all connected in the same way the ticket booths were, and there were the automatic bars and snack machines inside the Herc to think of as well—people mostly used coins for those, so maybe it worked out. They'd find out when they got back to Mooney's hab, their temporary safe house—always assuming they made it out alive and with the cash in hand.

There was still everything to play for.

Strader froze, cocking his head, listening—and then pointed his gun back at Cleveland. The kid's eyes went wide, and he almost cried out into the gag—until Strader put a finger to his lips. He'd heard the sound of footsteps in the corridor outside—not the squeak of the security guards' plastic soles, but something much heavier. The tramp of a Judge boot.

His eyes flicked to the side, checking on Phil Hartsdale, making sure he was going to be good too—then narrowed. Phil—good old Phil, the smart one, who'd followed orders like a pro—wasn't moving. And he hadn't moved for a few minutes now. He took a step forward and leant down, putting two fingers against Phil's thick neck, feeling for a pulse.

Nothing.

Phil was dead. Could be anything from a heart attack to a brain embolism, but he'd had it without making a sound. Even in death, he hadn't made any trouble. Well, almost no trouble—Strader sniffed the air, detecting the faint but unmistakable odour of human feces.

And now Strader had a problem, because Corey Cleveland had been watching all this. And he'd worked it out.

Suddenly, he was thrashing again, banging his heels against the floor, the back of his head against the wall, making what sound he could through his nose—anything to try and get the attention of the heavy footsteps passing the door. Strader cursed under his breath and gave Cleverland a hard backhand—no dice. It just made him flail around more.

The footsteps were right outside now—and if the Judge on the other side of the door tried the handle, or noticed the dead keypad, it was all up. Cleveland's eyes were bulging with the effort—he was doing his best the scream his lungs out into the gag. Now that Hartsdale was dead, there'd be no calming him.

Strader hesitated for a moment, weighing the risks—then put a single bullet through Cleveland's left eye and into his brain. The silencer helped, but there was no such thing as a silent gun—if you were close enough to the sound, you'd know exactly what it was you'd heard.

The heavy footsteps stopped.

Strader held the gun on the door, trying not to look at Cleveland leaking onto the carpet.

The handle of the door began to move.

The moment stretched. Strader's eyes flicked up at the monitor, a flash of movement—

—and he saw that the camera was panning over the crowds, that they were panicking, running, stampeding. Rising out of one of the stands was a plume of smoke.

There was a crackle of static outside the door—the shrill sound of an order barked—and the heavy footsteps took off down the corridor at a run.

Strader slumped against the wall and let go a long, ragged breath.

Sixteen

Through the diner window, Mooney watched the news spread through the queues—there were no more tickets, the last lucky sucker had been let in, they'd spent hours standing in line like geeks for nothing at all—and he wondered if the riot would kick itself off without him.

Then he exploded.

The diner window blew out, sending spinning chunks of glass shrapnel out into the street, to slice through faces, bodies, throats and arteries. A vast swathe of people pushed forward, terrified and screaming—and the rest of the crowd pushed angrily back against them.

The riot was on.

Seventeen

It took a lot of effort for Rico not to laugh. The timing had been absolutely beautiful—he'd seen Tellerman, smiling his saintly smile up in the back seats, and Muttox pushing his way through the same row, daystick at the ready, yelling at a couple of young juves fighting over a mock-ice. And he'd realised there would never, ever be a better moment than this.

All it took was pressing a fingertip into the right pouch on his belt. Rocky had gone up in Muttox's face, spraying him like a water balloon across the stands, along with a nice clutch of bystanders. Now that whole section of the crowd was a big, beautiful, gory mess, and chaos reigned—it wasn't like Muttox would have been particularly effective at controlling things, but with him splattered all over the ad hoardings, it really was headless chicken time.

With a mighty effort, Rico somehow kept his face straight as he watched two of the contestants barge their way off the stage and try to force themselves through the screaming crowd, trampling and smothering them with their bellies. What a way to go. And meanwhile, on stage, the largest of the contenders—Dale 'The Whale' Tucky, known in Texas City as the man with the biggest heart in competitive eating—had died of a massive coronary, brought on by the stress. *So much for that theory,* Rico thought. A couple more of the fatties had taken advantage of the confusion to start in on their first round of food—when the referee tried to stop them, the larger of the two punched him in the eye.

It really was Christmas.

Now it was all up to Strader and his people. If they didn't screw this up, Rico would be fifty million creds richer by sundown—assuming he let them live to enjoy their share.

He wondered if now was a good time to check in on his investment.

Eighteen

STRADER OPENED THE money room door to the sound of the secret knock. *Shave and a haircut, two creds*—an oldie but a goodie.

"Prowse is back at the ambulance. We're parked near the fire door—holy Jovus, what the hell happened here?" Ramirez stared at the bodies as he pushed the hover-stretcher into the room. Without taking his eyes off them, he handed Strader the paramedic's uniform they'd stolen for him when they'd heisted the getaway vehicle. It didn't quite fit, but beggars couldn't be choosers. "Didn't they know to keep quiet?"

Strader shrugged, pulling off his black shirt. "One of them died, the other didn't like it. It doesn't matter. Come on, grab the bag—"

"Wait." Ramirez was looking down at the skin-bag, the dead fat man Strader had painstakingly built out of rubber and money. The belly was still unzipped, thick wads of green poking out through it.

Idly, Ramirez popped a cube of sugar onto his tongue, crunching down on it. "There's room for more."

Strader shook his head curtly as he shrugged the bulky paramedic jacket on, irritated that the lean-faced man had even brought the subject up. Technically, he was right—there was space left for more money, if there'd been any more money—but that was neither here nor there. "Doesn't matter. There is no more. I packed up every bit of paper that came through here—even the *tens,* for Grud's sake. Now, can we get moving before—"

"What about that?" Ramirez cocked his head, pointing a thin finger at the coin bins. Without another word, he started grabbing handfuls of coins from the five-cred bin, shovelling them into the empty spaces in the skin-bag.

"What the hell are you—" Strader couldn't believe what he was seeing. He grabbed hold of Ramirez's shoulder, trying to pull him away, and Ramirez shrugged him off. The thin man had and aggrieved look on his dour little face.

"Watch where you're puttin' them hands, man. Don't come here to be pawed by you."

Strader just stared, dumbfounded. "Ramirez—those are *five-cred coins*—"

"So? There's room." He honestly didn't seem to understand what Strader was talking about. Dear Grud, where had he come from? Was this his first ever job? "More the merrier, right?"

"Listen to me. The weight—"

"Hover-stretcher can take it. And we can take our time—the Jays are gonna be busy for a while, right? I mean, it's crazy out there. Like, all-out war." He shot Strader a look of total contempt and carried on ladling great handfuls of heavy, clattering metal into the bag. "Don't help me or nothin'. Cheez."

Slowly, the skin-bag grew fatter, the seams bulging until it seemed barely human even by the grotesque standards of the contestants. When Ramirez finally decided he'd packed enough in—somewhere in the region of five thousand creds, Strader figured; chickenfeed—they could barely get the thing onto the stretcher, which dipped dangerously at one corner. "There, see?" Ramirez said, looking angrily at Strader. "Now we got a bonus. No thanks to you."

Strader considered punching him in the face. Or shooting him in the head. Or walking out the door and never coming back—if he stripped the paramedic outfit back off, he could slip into whatever madness was happening outside and be lost forever, or at least for a little while. But he knew these weren't real options. He wasn't a professional anymore—maybe he hadn't been since Texas City, or even before that. He was just another gun-happy idiot who thought he was a thief.

The hell with it. At least he had the chance to be a rich idiot. "Come on, let's get this back to the ambo."

Nineteen

But the ambo wasn't there.

It was flipped over on its side a little way up the street, on fire. Prowse was hanging out of the side window, badly burned, with her brains blown out.

Standing nearby, Lawgiver smoking—a lone figure amidst the chaos on the streets—was Rico Dredd. He turned to look Strader in the eye.

He wasn't smiling.

"Cheez—" Ramirez gasped, letting go of the stretcher. Without both of them to keep it under control, the overloaded stretcher tipped over, spilling the rubber corpse out onto the street. Weakened by the mass of the coins, a seam in one armpit split, tearing a fissure up the side of the thing, spilling a great torrent of creds out into the gutter. "It's a double-cross—"

Strader didn't think so. That had always been on the cards, but not like this, not out in the open. But Ramirez was already reaching into the paramedic's jacket for the squat, black snubnose he kept there—and then he was dead, toppling back onto the mountain of spilled notes, a red geyser bursting from the centre of his forehead.

"I know you from somewhere, creep," Rico said, his face twisted into an unfamiliar scowl. He really didn't seem to know who Strader was. Like they'd never met. Strader had never seen Rico's face look quite like that before—set like stone into a grim, unyielding frown that didn't seem to move. "Raise 'em."

Strader didn't move. He couldn't. It was impossible, it couldn't be, but—but he *had* seen that look before. At the jeweller's. The jeweller's where Rico said he didn't think they'd met. That Strader must be thinking of someone else.

Oh, Grud, Strader thought.

Oh, Grud, there are two *of them.*

PART FOUR

Twenty

DREDD HAD KNOWN something was off from the start.

The ambulance had arrived almost the moment the riot began—about thirty seconds after the bomb went off in the diner. A private ambulance at that; while it was conceivable, even probable, that some eldster in the middle of the violence had hit an aid-call button, the response time was way too fast. Civilian ambulances didn't have access to the special Department-Only lanes, so they could take up to half an hour longer than a judicial med-team.

So there was that. Then you had the one paramedic staying and keeping the engine running while the other went in through the fire doors. Not exactly standard procedure.

"Something wrong over there," he'd mentioned to Friedricks.

"You think?" Friedricks was busy. The whole paved area in front of the Kool Herc Infernodrome was a mass of bodies—running, screaming, fighting, doing anything they felt they could get away with. Always the same story—scratch a cit and underneath you'd find a perp. Give them an inch and they'd take whatever wasn't nailed down. Friedricks hauled a woman off her husband—she'd been trying to drown him in one of the decorative fountains—and cracked her upside the head with a daystick. "I swear to Grud, whoever owns the Herc is doing time for this. I don't give a damn who rubber-stamped this nonsense—as far as I'm concerned, they should go down too."

Dredd nodded. "Maybe." He lashed out with his own daystick, snapping the wrist of a creep with a broken bottle. He had one eye on the ambulance, in the distance. It was still idling, and the driver—a tough-looking woman with a distinctive tattoo on her lower arm—was leaning out of her window, watching the fire doors intently.

Dredd snapped his helmet mic into place. "Control—I need records of paramedics and drivers working for Well-Wish Incorporated—the private medical firm. List any with dragon tattoos on the left arm. And run the plate—" He squinted, focussing, and read the number off, before driving his fist into the face of an old man who'd drawn a sword from his cane. "I'll wait."

Morley—a heavyset Judge in his thirties who fancied himself next in line for Koslowski's job—rolled his eyes. He was trying to get the cuffs on a juve without breaking the kid's arm, and it didn't look like he was going to manage it. "You don't got enough to do, junior? Crem, kid, settle down—"

"Crime doesn't stop just because we're busy, Morley." Dredd brought the end of the daystick down hard on the juve's right temple—he went out like a light.

Control was back in his ear. "No records of any dragon tats, Dredd. Plate number comes up as stolen—missing since two days ago."

Dredd nodded to himself. Friedricks and Morley were trying to stop a young girl being slashed in the face by what looked like her twin sister—their hands were full. A quick glance confirmed the other Judges on the scene were engaged and unavailable for backup.

Which was fine by him.

"You in the stolen ambulance!" he bellowed. "Out and on the ground! Now!" The woman with the tattoo stared at him—white as a ghost—then gunned the engine into gear and tried to peel out, wheels spinning on the roadway, kicking up smoke.

Dredd drew his Lawgiver, aiming to knock out the back tyre and force the vehicle into a controlled skid—but the driver was panicking and the ambulance flipped over instead. Dredd noticed modifications on the underside as it turned—a jury-rigged nitrous-pyrothene booster. Which meant this had to be a getaway vehicle.

Of course, the trouble with those home-made boosters was volatility. They didn't react well to heavy impacts—like, say, an ambulance turning over.

The vehicle went up like a Roman candle—the fire died down quickly after the initial flash, but not quickly enough for the driver. Her flesh was already charred black when Dredd finished her with a mercy shot to the head.

"I need someone to watch these fire doors—" Dredd called out to Friedricks, but she was barking orders to Morley and a couple of others, locking down a juve gang who'd breezed in from Graham Greene to have a little fun in the middle of the chaos. He was still on his own.

There was a clattering noise as the doors opened—the perp who'd run in earlier and a buddy, pushing a hover-stretcher loaded down with what looked at first like a dead fattie, until Dredd noticed the hand peeping out from under the sheet was made of some kind of latex. One of the perps went for his gun, screaming that it was a double-cross—*why a double-cross?* Dredd wondered, but filed that away for later—and without his hand steadying the overloaded stretcher, it tipped its contents onto the street.

As Dredd returned fire, blowing the gunman away before he could squeeze off his first shot, the fake body burst at the seams, ripping open and disgorging what looked like tens of millions of creds onto the slabwalk. Dredd couldn't help but wonder where they'd got a bag like that—mostly because whoever made it was guilty of aiding and abetting under the current law. You don't make a giant hollow fat man without asking what it's for—not in this city.

The last of the thieves was familiar. The hair and eyes were a different colour—and he was missing a moustache—but the bone structure, and the grey-white stubble on the man's chin, brought back memories. He'd only seen that face for a second, through a closing door, but... "I know you from somewhere, creep." That jewellery store robbery in Barry Scott—the morons with the stuttergun. This was moron number three. "Raise 'em."

Moron Three was frozen in place, eyes wide and glassy, mouth working like a fish. "You," he mumbled, hands jerking spasmodically up towards his chest. "There are—"

Then a standard execution bullet slammed right through his head.

Dredd turned. Rico was standing there, his own Lawgiver smoking. "Helped you out again, Little Joe," he grinned. Dredd had never much liked that grin. It seemed flippant.

"He was about to tell me something." Dredd holstered his weapon, looking around at the rest of the riot. Things were mostly dying down, now—Friedricks showing her natural talent for controlling uncontrollable situations. A shame things hadn't been in hand a little earlier—it might have turned out differently if he'd had some backup.

"He was about to shoot you in the face, Joe." Rico prodded the corpse with the toe of his boot, and the jacket fell open, revealing the quick-draw holster Moron Three was wearing up near his chest. "*Wear iron.* That's the rule with these people. If I hadn't come along, who knows what he would have done?"

"Or said." Dredd gave Rico a long, hard look. "You're meant to be helping with the spectators, Rico. I could have handled this alone."

"Can I help it if I care about my only brother? Come on, Little Joe, I just saved your life." Rico slapped Dredd on the back and smirked. "Lighten up a little."

"Request denied. I'll be filling out an adverse report when I return to the Sector House." Dredd looked down at the pile of creds at their feet. The wind was picking up—if they didn't do something with it soon, it'd blow down the street and the riot would start all over again. "I'll have some recommendations for the security team here, too. These punks nearly got away with a hundred-million creds—at least."

Rico nodded. For a moment he almost looked wistful.

"Oh well," he said, "Easy come, easy go."

And he laughed.

About the Author

Al Ewing has been a Judge Dredd aficionado since the age of nine, and is best known in the UK for his work on Dredd in *2000 AD*, where he also co-created *Zombo* and *Damnation Station*. In addition, Ewing has written various novels for Solaris and Abaddon Books, including *The Fictional Man*, *Pax Omega* and *Gods of Manhattan*, and is currently writing *Mighty Avengers* and *Loki: Agent of Asgard* for Marvel Comics.